DANZIG

A NOVEL OF
POLITICAL INTRIGUE

WILLIAM N. WALKER

ISBN-13: 978-1533073921
ISBN-10: 1533073929

.

DEDICATION

For
My wife
Janet Smith Walker
with deep thanks for her love and support
and for my children,
Gilbert, Helen and Joanna,
who mean the world to me.

CAST OF CHARACTERS

Joseph Avenol. *Secretary-General of the League of Nations 1933–1940.*

Stanley Baldwin, *Powerful British Conservative Party politician in 1930's. Leader of the opposition 1931-1935; Prime Minister 1937 -1937.*

Josef Beck. *Polish Foreign Minister and President of the League of Nations Council*

Gladys Bigelow. *Active member of the League of Nations Union and co-host of the Berkshire Abbey weekend in July 1933.*

Robert Bigelow. *Muller's university friend and fellow chorister; co-host of the Berkshire Abbey weekend in 1933.*

Victor Boettcher. *A Senate assistant to President of the Danzig Senate who was assigned the title Foreign Secretary.*

Ernst Brost. *Editor of the Danzig Volksstimme, the Social Democratic Party newspaper, and an opposition activist in Danzig.*

Lord Robert Cecil. *Prominent British politician and founder and Chairman of the League of Nations Union.*

Jaczck Demchuk. *Head of League of Nations Minorities Sub-Section.*

Anthony Eden. *A leading British statesman of the time. Rapporteur for the Danzig file before the League Council and an architect of British appeasement policy toward Nazi Germany.*

Duncan Elliott. *Participant in the Berkshire Abbey weekend, a Foreign Office official critical of Nazi Germany.*

Albert Forster. *Hardline Nazi, Gaulieter of the NSDAP in Danzig.*

Joseph Goebbels. *Germany's Reichminister for Propaganda.*

Hermann Goering, *Germany's Reichminister and head of the Gestapo.*

Gustaf Grundgen. *President of the Danzig Central Bank.*

Eirene Jones. *Participant in the Berkshire Abbey weekend, a leader of the League of Nations Union, later a member of Parliament.*

i

CAST OF CHARACTERS - CONTINUED

Thomas Jones. *Eirene's father, the influential "TJ," who served as Cabinet Secretary for successive prime ministers. Member of the Cliveden Set that promoted British appeasement policy.*

Stephan Kreutzer. *Journalist and Social Democratic Party activist.*

Frederic Krabbe. *Chief of the League of Nations Danzig Sub-Section.*

Elsie Lester. *Wife of Sean Lester.*

Sean Lester. *High Commissioner of the League of Nations in Danzig.*

Tom and Phoebe Low. *Participants in the Berkshire Abbey weekend.*

Ramsay MacDonald. *Leader of the British Labor Party. Twice Prime Minister, including 1931–1935.*

Kasimir Papee. *Polish Consul General in Danzig, related by marriage to Polish Foreign Minister, Josef Beck.*

Otto von Radowitz. *Consul General for the German Reich in Danzig.*

Milhan Rostig. *League of Nations official who served as acting High Commissioner in Danzig, preceding Sean Lester.*

Hjalamar Schacht. *President of the German Central Bank, the Reichsbank.*

Rudi Schmitz. *Butler in the High Commissioner's residence.*

Sir John Simon. *British Foreign Minister in 1933-1934, and Rapporteur for the Danzig file before the League Council; succeeded by Anthony Eden.*

RCS Stevenson. *British Foreign Office official responsible for advising British leadership at the League of Nations.*

Guste and Pyotr Starbusch. Guste was a member of the Danzig Police Chorus, her husband was employed at the Polish Post office. They had two children.

Franz Schiller. *Detective in the Danzig National Police Force and member of the Police Chorus.*

Ernst Stieberitz. *Concertmaster of the Danzig Police Orchestra and Chorus.*

CAST OF CHARACTERS – CONTINUED

Viktor Truczinski. *Manager of a Danzig sawmill. He and Muller lived in the same boarding house and became friends.*

Richard von Beckmann. *Senior SA official assigned in nearby Stettin, Germany.*

General Walter von Brauchitsch. *Commander of German forces in East Prussia; later a leading German General during World War II.*

Konstantin von Neurath. *Foreign Minister of the German Reich.*

Elizabeth Wiskemann. *Journalist/author; foreign correspondent of The Statesman, a London-based newspaper*

.

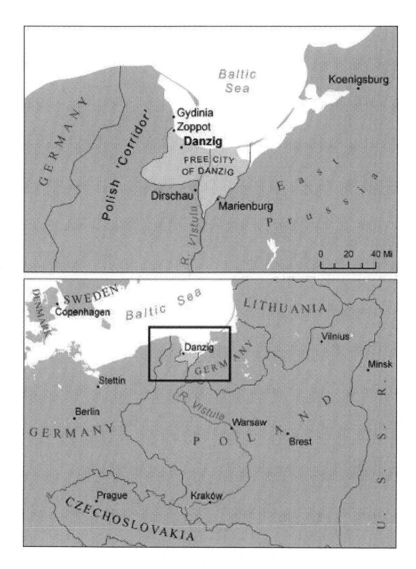

THE FREE CITY OF DANZIG
AND THE POLISH CORRIDOR

WILLIAM N. WALKER

TABLE OF CONTENTS

INTRODUCTION

August, 1939

The Free City of Danzig was basking in the warmth of a late August sun.

As afternoon shadows lengthened, Max-Halbe Platz became a beehive of activity as crowded trams from the beaches at Zoppot and Brosen glided into the square, warning bells clanging, and disgorged sunburned passengers returning to the city. Children in terrycloth robes clutching tin beach pails and toy sailboats ran and jumped, squealing and shouting, as mothers in beach skirts tried to corral them. The men–fathers, uncles, brothers–most in sandals and shorts and carrying canvas sacks filled with wet towels and bathing suits, clapped one another on the back and guffawed at each other's jokes. A group of teenage boys began kicking a colorful beach ball around at one end of the plaza. Lines formed in front of the ice cream stand with its bright blue umbrella and a fez-topped organ-grinder added his tinkling notes to the general happy hubbub.

Pyotr and Guste Starbusch gathered their things, waving goodbye to her sister and brother-in-law who were remaining on the tram for two more stops. Firmly taking the hand of 3-year-old Marguerite and her 5-year-old brother Constantin, Guste alighted from the tram and waded into the noisy throng, steering her way to the left toward the Ringstrasse. Pyotr was in her wake, but stopped to shake hands and share a laugh with two of his fellow postal workers. When Pyotr spied them at the edge of the crowd, Guste was having a serious conversation with Constantin, who seemed on the verge of tears.

"He left his new beach towel on the tram," said Guste, looking up as Pyotr joined them.

"Well, maybe Uncle Herbert will see it after we left the tram," said Pyotr brightly. "Anyway, this is our last beach day for this year. Summer's over and this warm sunny day is a special gift for us to enjoy, so let's not worry about a lost towel. Besides, when next summer arrives, you'll be nearly a whole year older, a really big boy, and big boys are better at keeping track of beach towels."

He laughed, hoisting Marguerite on his shoulders, took Constantin's other hand and he and Guste swung the giggling boy between them as they crossed the Ringstrasse, heading to their apartment in the Polish settlement.

The apartment was small but cozy, with a tiny second bedroom for the children. Guste began preparing dinner, chopping salad and peeling potatoes. Pyotr hauled the washtub out from under the small sink and began filling it with water, putting some water in a kettle to heat on the stove which he would pour into the tub for extra warmth. "Time to sponge off all that Baltic salt water and sand from the beach."

"But Papa, we took that cold shower at the beach house before we changed to come home," said Constantin, looking dejectedly at the wash tub.

"That was a good start," said Pyotr, "but this is the finishing touch."

"Papa, I like the idea of another bath," said Marguerite, sticking out her tongue at her older brother.

"Then you shall be first," said Pyotr, lifting her into the tub.

After the children were bathed and as they put on pajamas, Pyotr soaked the four bathing suits in the tub and kneaded them over a washboard to get the ocean salt out of the thin wool fabric. It never seemed to work very well. The suits always felt stiff and scratchy the next time you wore them. But, he thought, this is the last time we'll use them this year. Maybe when next summer arrives I'll get a raise—or even a new job—and we can afford to buy new bathing suits. He rinsed them out and laid them on a clean towel to dry overnight.

By now the sun had set, so Guste served dinner at the small table with four red candles for light. "Let's make it a little romantic," she said, winking at Pyotr. "Winter will be here soon enough and we'll need our electricity then. For now, let's continue our last day of summer by candlelight.

"And," she added, smiling at the children, "by finishing the very last of Grandma's special summer sausage that you like so much."

Constantin and Marguerite clapped their hands, squealing in delight.

After dinner, Pyotr rinsed the dishes and glasses, carefully drying them and stacking them in the cupboard. Guste took the children to bed and began reading one of the Mother Goose stories. She came out and shut the door even before he was done.

"They were so tired," she said, smiling. "I didn't get more than three paragraphs into Little Red Riding Hood before they were both sound asleep."

She kissed him lightly on the cheek and helped him dry the last glass. Standing by the open window, looking down on the darkened courtyard below, they each took a gold-tipped Regatta from Pyotr's rumpled pack and lit up, drawing deeply on the sweet tobacco flavor.

"A wonderful day," Pyotr said, taking Guste's hand. "One of the things I was thinking about on the beach and especially in the crowd at Max-Halbe-Platz was that despite all the Nazi banners and flags, all the swastikas everywhere, nobody cared today. This was just a day to savor, a day for everyone to enjoy—without any politics."

"It was special," she replied, "and you're right; a propaganda day off. It's nice not to be called a 'Polish swine' for at least a day."

"You prefer 'subhuman slav'?" Pyotr said teasingly.

Guste elbowed him in the ribs.

"I know, I know," he said, wincing. "It's very irritating. They really do seem to hate us. But at least my job is safe. The Post Office is Polish territory, guaranteed by the League of Nations mandate—not that that's good for much these days. But they can't throw us out—even if they'd like to."

"Anyway, I've got the 2 AM shift this morning," he added. "Let's go to bed so I can get at least a little sleep. I'm setting the clock for 1AM to be sure I'm on time."

Guste shrugged out of her nightgown as she slipped into bed and ran her hand up his left leg, feeling him harden. He clasped her tightly and they moaned together as they rolled against one another. She mounted him and they coupled as he caressed her breasts with hands and tongue. Her breathing became heavy and she ground her hips, making short cries that grew in passion and intensity as they reached a heaving climax, both crying out, then giggling as they subsided, shushing one another not to awaken the children.

Afterward, they shared a last Regatta together. Then they fell into deep sleep, entangled in one another's arms.

***

Pyotr did not oversleep. He awoke with the alarm, washed at the sink, put on his official dark blue post office uniform, checked to make sure he had his wallet and post office pass, and quietly let himself out of the apartment. He strode back to the deserted Ringstrasse and walked down Altstadischer Graben toward Heveliusplatz, a large plaza, named for the famous Danzig astronomer Johannes Hevelius, who had published a catalog of 1,564 stars in the mid-17th century. Crossing the plaza, Pyotr showed his papers to the guards at the iron gates of the massive red brick Post office and entered the building through a heavy wooden doorway, directly beneath four tall, narrow windows that faced the plaza.

At precisely 4:47 AM Pyotr Starbusch was obliterated in an explosion caused by a direct hit from a 530 lb. base-fused high-explosive shell with ballistic cap (*Sprenggranate L/4. 3 m. Bdz. (mit Haube)*) fired at a muzzle velocity of 2,700 ft. /sec by the 13,000 ton German battleship *Schleswig Holstein*. The vessel had arrived in Danzig several weeks earlier, ostensibly on a 'courtesy visit', among other things to honor sailors lost on the German cruiser *Magdeburg*, sunk in 1914, some of whom were buried in Danzig. It was anchored in Danzig harbor at the mouth of the Vistula River. At 4:30 AM on September 1, 1939, the ship moved slowly down the Port Canal, took up a position directly opposite the Polish Post Office and at 4:47 am, opened fire at point blank range. It was the opening salvo of a new War.

***

At 11:00 AM the same morning, Albert Forester, Gauleiter of Danzig, mounted the podium in the vast legislative chamber of the Volkstag, situated in the Center of Danzig, to thunderous applause from members of the legislature and the executive offices, most of whom were uniformed SA brown shirts or SS black shirts, all be-decked with red Nazi armbands. Because of the continuing summer heat, the tall windows of the hall were open; smoke drifted in from the smoldering wreckage of the Polish Post office and the pop of small arms fire could be clearly heard as fighting continued between German soldiers and Polish fighters.

Forster, his face grim, ignored the ovation. Head of the NSDAP, the Danzig Nazi Party, since 1930, long before it seized power, he was well-known to party members for his fierce adherence to Nazi ideology and personal loyalty to Adolf Hitler. On the podium, he drew himself to attention, his black uniform with its red and white piping dazzling in the bright sunlight that filtered into the room. Raising his right arm in the Nazi salute, he shouted "Heil Hitler"

The party returned his salute and bellowed, "Heil Hitler" in return.

Forster spoke with a thick Bavarian accent that always seemed too loud. Today he made no effort at modulating his tone. Triumphantly he shouted, "Home to the Reich!" And the party members again responded in kind.

"Today," he said, "our Fuehrer and the Fatherland have embarked on a great mission to re-assert our rights as Germans. We have finally broken the shackles of the hated Versailles Treaty. Today we are attacking the traitors, the socialists, the communists and their Jew allies. We are attacking the Polish swine; we will destroy them all!" His audience roared its approval.

"I bring you joyous news of two trophies we have already won," he cried. "First, by order of the Reichschancellor, our Fuehrer, the Free City of Danzig, as of this moment, no longer exists. Danzig is now formally and legally part of the German Reich. We are now in fact, as we have been for so long in spirit, Home in the Reich. That so-called Free City Mandate forced upon us by the League of Nations is now annulled. Done! Destroyed! Crushed under our boots! THE HATED MANDATE NO LONGER EXISTS." Forster snarled the words.

After pausing to let the crowd roar again, he continued, "And second, earlier this morning, I paid a visit to the current High Commissioner–that latest of the strutting League representatives who have for so many years sought to thwart us and to lecture us–who tried to stand between us and the German people. Well, today, I had had the honor and personal privilege of telling this lowlife High Commissioner that his office no longer exists, his property now belongs to the Reich, and that he had three hours to remove himself from our territory. Get out, I told him, NOW."

Forster grinned from ear to ear, shouting, "So they're gone, the whole lousy lot of them. The League, its mandate, the so-called High Commissioner, all of them. GONE. Good riddance. Our party is victorious! Heil Hitler." He made his way down from the podium to be greeted rapturously by his party supporters. They linked arms and, in unison, bawled their marching song:

> *Und heute gewhort uns Deutschland, und morgen die ganze Welt*
> *'And today we rule Germany, and tomorrow the whole World.'*

***

Excerpt from an article dated September 2, 1939 from the Statesman newspaper, datelined London, written by Elizabeth Wiskemann and entitled simply "WAR!"

"The German invasion of Poland yesterday is a monstrous act of aggression, launching the world into a terrible new conflict with consequences we cannot yet even begin to fathom. If news reports are accurate, that the first shots were fired in Danzig at around 5:00 AM on September 1, 1939, then by my calculation it is only 20 years, 9 months, 19 days and 18 hours since the last shot of The Great War was fired–and we have scarcely had time to recover from that awful conflict.

But how striking–and symbolic–that the first shots in what is already being called World War II were fired in Danzig. Danzig! The Free City of Danzig, created at Versailles as a mandate of the League of Nations that would be administered under democratic laws and protected by the collective security of freedom-loving nations assembled in Geneva.

Danzig: A Free City no more. I mourn its demise.

Regular readers of this column will recall my reporting from that beleaguered enclave in the mid-1930s. A seismograph for European politics at large, I called it, where democratic values directly confronted totalitarian intolerance. I described how the then-High Commissioner steadfastly tried to defend the rights of Danzig citizens against repeated assaults by the local Nazi party–helped by not a few bigwig Nazis from the German Reich itself.

From the date in late May 1933 when the local Danzig Nazi party took control of the government–by the slimmest of margins, winning precisely 50.03 percent of the vote–the party leadership tried to seize total control in Danzig like Hitler did in Germany. But they were repeatedly thwarted by the firm, diplomatic hand of Sean Lester, the League's High Commissioner, who overturned Nazi seizure of opposition newspapers, secured the release of arrested opposition leaders and held up Nazi misconduct–for all the world to see–in his low key, but wholly convincing reports to the League Council in Geneva.

Nazi leaders were furious at Lester's interference–and not just local leaders in Danzig. Berlin took a very direct hand in stymying Lester and the League in Danzig and tried to stifle news reports about what they were doing. Readers will recall my story in July 1936, reporting that

Gestapo officials had snatched me off a train in Berlin returning from Danzig after writing a column for this publication pointing the finger at the Nazi leadership and praising Lester's commitment to democracy. They whisked me off to their fearsome headquarters on the Prinz Albrechtstrasse and subjected me to a frightening interrogation, mercifully cut short only upon direct intervention by the British Legation.

As we now know only too well, Lester's efforts ultimately came to naught. League of Nations Council members repeatedly delayed, backed down and declined to take steps to support the leader they had sent to defend the democratic mandate the League had assumed. Collective security became collective passivity; the buck was ultimately passed into the void.

As I reflect on all this in light of yesterday's attack, I am struck by the missed opportunities. When we look back at history, we tend to assume that whatever finally happened was inevitable; that the outcome we see today was somehow pre-ordained.

But that decidedly was not the case with the Free City of Danzig.

There were moments in the mid-thirties when it seemed likely that the League would intervene; that it would order new elections to be held in Danzig that would turn the local Nazis out of power. They had bungled the economy, devalued the currency and made themselves deeply unpopular with their thuggish behavior. Rejection of Nazi rule by a solidly German electorate in Danzig would have resonated across the continent. A Nazi defeat would have deeply embarrassed Hitler, offered new hope to Germans opposed to his leadership, and conceivably forced him to modify his behavior. It could have revitalized democratic leadership in Austria and Czechoslovakia and sidetracked local Nazi efforts to destabilize those nations. The outcome we see today might have turned out very differently.

There was, then, a crucial window of opportunity for the League of Nations; a moment when, had it asserted itself, it might have made a decisive difference. The contest for Danzig was a conflict in the heart of Europe after all, not in far off Abyssinia or Manchuria, where the League failed. This was an opportunity of manageable size involving a European city state of only 400,000 people. And most of all, it was a case where the League was being asked to protect an entity that the League itself had created, and endowed with a Constitution embodying fundamental democratic values. That the League failed is a story of missed opportunities, mistaken judgments and failure of will. But it is an important story for all of that.

***

What follows is that story, the story of the struggle for Danzig. It begins in 1933 in Britain.

CHAPTER 1

July, 1933

Paul Muller alighted from the train at Datchet. It had been a short trip; Cambridge to London, then a good connection to the local train. The Datchet leg had offered glimpses of the sun-dappled Thames from time to time, revealing quick images of punts and small sailboats and the occasional lone sculler.

As Muller stood on the small station platform, he saw, parked off to the side, the shiny Bentley town car that Robert Bigelow had promised would meet him. A liveried driver hurried toward him, elderly and bent, but energetic and wearing a genial smile. "It'll be Mr. Muller, I assume sir?"

Muller said, yes, it was he, and the driver nodded, "Welcome to Old Windsor, sir. Everyone at Berkshire Abbey is waiting to greet you. Now, let's collect that trunk of yours.

"Ah, is that the one the porter is unloading from the baggage compartment? Let's stow it straightaway." Muller handed the porter a coin and followed the driver to the Bentley where he opened the door for Muller to enter the passenger compartment. "I'll just strap the trunk on the back and off we'll go," said the driver. "Name's Stanley. It's only about five kilometers to the Abbey, so won't take long."

Muller smiled to himself; a large trunk for a short weekend. But Bigelow had said that they dressed for dinner, and he should certainly bring his tennis gear and, of course his riding breeches and boots. So a trunk it had been; at least he'd be properly attired. But he wondered if he would be as well-prepared for what Bigelow had predicted would be a free-wheeling weekend of debate about the current state of European politics.

"I'm assembling a group of guests who are all intensely interested in the subject and have strong feelings about British policy and the role of the League of Nations," he'd said. "I've told them that you're going off to Geneva to join the League Secretariat and everyone wants to tell you what ought to be done—not that any of them agree." He'd smiled. "You can expect to be bombarded from all sides; it should be lively."

And probably a little intimidating, Muller had thought to himself. He had no idea what his role would be at the League, and he was very conscious that he would face a steep learning curve. It was one thing to study political science at Cambridge; actually becoming a practicing diplomat was something very different, particularly at the League of Nations, an organization that embodied the aspirations of so many citizens around the globe. It was a daunting prospect.

As his local train had puffed its way south along the Thames, he'd decided to play the role of the Cheshire cat. The other guests would doubtless press him on matters he didn't yet know much about; in response, he'd simply smile and let his questioners see what they wanted. He hoped the strategy would work.

Stanley mounted the open air driving compartment, brought the big-throated Bentley engine to life, engaged the gears and off they went, trailing a fog of sandy dust behind them. Elms and chestnut trees overarched the road, offering shade from the noonday sun. Only a few minutes later, the Bentley turned into a long curving driveway leading across a well-kept green meadow and, over a rise, Muller could see a large Tudor-style structure begin to emerge from the trees that he assumed must be Berkshire Abbey.

Stanley guided the Bentley into the circular entry and pulled up before a high, white portico with two tall doors, wide open to the summer breeze. A butler accompanied by a servant hurried down the front steps and opened his compartment door with a flourish. The butler then stepped back, drew himself to full attention and, smiling broadly, boomed out "Welcome to Berkshire Abbey, Mr. Muller." Muller thought to himself, he's probably been doing that same routine since visitors were arriving by coach and four. But he stepped out of the car and smiled back gamely, saying, "Thank you. I'm very pleased to be here."

"Paul!" Muller looked up to see Robert Bigelow bounding down the steps toward him. "I thought I heard the car arriving."

They shook hands warmly, clapped one another on the back and then stepping back, on cue and in unison, sang "Je-ru-sa-lem." They both bent over, laughing heartily, and clapped one another on the back again.

"So good of you to come."

"My pleasure," Muller responded, with a grin.

"We're all gathered on the terrace in back enjoying a little gin before lunch," said Bigelow. "Martin, here, will show you to your room and Stanley will deliver your trunk. Wash up, change into something light and join us straight away." Bigelow led the way into the large hallway, where Muller caught a glimpse of a shady terrace where several young men and women were gathered.

Martin preceded him up the wide curved staircase, turned right along a carpeted walkway, and opened a doorway about half way along, standing aside for Muller to enter. It was a bright, sunlit room with two tall, full length windows wide open, white taffeta drapes dancing in the breeze. There was a large bed with chrome head and foot boards and a small sitting area where two upholstered chairs flanked a round table. Muller glanced out the window and saw the terrace down to his right, a tennis court across the lawn, and beyond that, half hidden behind a copse of trees, what surely had to be the Thames.

Muller unlocked the trunk that Stanley had delivered and Martin began unpacking his things, hanging them in an armoire on one wall and stacking shirts and underwear on adjoining shelves. On the other side of the room stood a washstand with a large stoneware pitcher and basin and hand towels. "Lavatory is the first door just around the next corner, sir," said Martin. "I've brought some cool water in the pitcher so you can sponge off the soot from the train." He gestured to a button next to the doorway, "I hope you're comfortable, sir, but just buzz me if you need anything else."

"Thank you, Martin," said Muller, "I'm all set."

After washing and changing into white linen slacks with a light blue open-necked shirt, Muller descended the stairs and walked through the open doorway to the terrace, where he could hear the buzz of conversation.

"Everyone," said Bigelow as Muller joined the group, "this is Paul Muller, my friend and fellow-chorister in the Cambridge Choral Society." He looked mischievously at Muller. "Shall we do it again?"

"Sure," said Muller.

So he and Bigelow repeated their musical greeting to one another. "Je-ru-sa-lem." They laughed again, and Bigelow explained. "It's from the Fauré Requiem, one of our favorite works; we performed it last fall, when Paul first joined the Choral Society. Paul as a bass and I as a tenor were standing next to one another in the chorus and loved singing the piece–and especially that little harmonic interlude. So we adopted it as our secret greeting, which we've now generously shared with all of you."

"Wait," said a slender brunette coming over to stand next to them, wine glass in one hand and cigarette in the other. "Do it again."

So they did, and the brunette joined in right on key, singing the soprano line. "Je-ru-sa-lem." Everyone applauded and laughed.

"So," she said, "it's no longer just *your* little secret. And by the way it *is* a perfect harmonic resolution." She stuck out her hand to shake Muller's. "Eirene Jones. I sang the Fauré at school."

Muller smiled back at her. "Welcome to our secret fraternity–well, no longer a fraternity; our secret–fellowship, let's call it."

"So," said Bigelow, "come get a gin or some wine, and I'll introduce you around."

They were five in addition to Eirene and Bigelow. Bigelow's older sister Gladys; his girlfriend Margaret, an accomplished violinist; a dark-haired, intense-looking man named Duncan Elliott from the Foreign Office; and a married couple, Phoebe and Tom Law, he was a banker at Barclay's and she worked at a prominent London gallery. Everyone was clad in light summer wear, Phoebe Law sporting a fashionable white bonnet and Tom a straw boater.

The staff had laid a round table in the shade of a large elm tree just to the left of the Terrace. Muller exchanged pleasantries, had a gin and smoked one of his French Gitane cigarettes. The butler–still formidable in his demeanor and whose name Muller gathered was James–signaled that it was time, and Bigelow shooed everyone to the table.

Two women in starched white, high-necked blouses served plates of smoked trout with dill sauce and quickly filled waiting wine glasses with a chilled white Bordeaux that had evidently come from a cool wine cellar located somewhere in the bowels of the large home.

"A toast," said Bigelow, raising his glass. "To all of our guests, thank you for joining Gladys and me on what certainly seems to be a lovely summer weekend. Our parents are off in the Lake Country, so we have Berkshire Abbey to ourselves. We toast you all, but especially I toast my

Swiss friend, Paul Muller. We've been studying together at Cambridge during the last year; we share a passion for choral music and we've become good friends. But Paul is leaving Cambridge to assume a position in the Secretariat of the League of Nations in Geneva. A formidable opportunity indeed! I persuaded him to spend this weekend with us before taking up his new position. So, to Paul: congratulations." Glasses clinked around the table.

"I should think you'll need a lot of luck for the League to be able to accomplish much now," said Duncan Elliott, a little sourly. "The Nazis are at full throttle in Germany and they're determined to change the map of Europe to suit themselves. It's going to require a lot more spine from the League and its member governments—including our own government—to keep them in line."

A chorus of voices erupted around the table, all vying to speak at once.

Well, Muller thought to himself. That didn't take long.

Eirene Jones, seated to Muller's left, smacked her hand on the table, pointing her fork directly at Elliott and exclaimed, "Duncan, What a monstrous accusation. Germany was terribly mistreated at Versailles and has a litany of genuine grievances. And now the Germans have a new government which has both the self-confidence and the popular support to insist that these wrongs be righted. It's time for the League to respond positively."

Bigelow interrupted. "For those who don't know, Eirene's father is Thomas Jones, Deputy Secretary to the Cabinet under four separate Prime Ministers; the formidable 'TJ', as he's known. She's a fount of information."

"And strong opinions," added Eirene. "If nobody in power seems willing to make the changes Germany wants, then of course they're going to react badly, sound shrill and behave crudely; you would too if the world had mistreated you for fifteen years and lent a deaf ear to your complaints. So the job is to accommodate Germany."

She nudged Muller with her elbow. "Maybe that should be your role at the League, Paul, settling Germany's claims."

"Eirene's right," said Tom Law. "Why continue picking on Germany? Communism is the real enemy, not the Germans. At Barclay's, we're doing quite a lot of business with German business concerns and banks; we find the new German government very helpful," he added.

"You're probably financing Germany's re-armament program," Elliott interrupted. "It's an open secret that they've been re-arming since at least 1930, notwithstanding the Versailles prohibition."

"Well, in the current state of the economy, any business is welcome, and we'll take it," Law retorted sharply.

"The Soviet Union is the one calling for world revolution," he went on, "all this talk about the dictatorship of the proletariat. They're the real threat and England and Germany are the only nations able to confront them. Look at France, riven by Socialists–and even Communists; they haven't the stomach to tackle the Soviet Union. So by all means, let's close ranks with the Germans to oppose the Soviets."

Bigelow spread his arms wide for emphasis. "Why are we talking about new alliances?" he asked. Why aren't we talking about disarmament?"

"Exactly," echoed Gladys, "that's got to be the goal."

Everyone around the table began speaking at once, gesturing and turning in their seats for emphasis. Muller found himself amused; this really *was* an intense group, as Bigelow had promised. He smiled, as planned.

"Our most important ally is still France," Elliott said loudly, recapturing the floor, "and they continue to view Germany as a threat. I'm sure no one here has any more sympathy for the Soviets and their revolutionary pretensions than you do Tom. But they don't pose an immediate threat; they don't even seem to be able to feed themselves. By contrast, the Germans have installed a dictator who has announced his determination to undo the whole fabric of the Versailles Peace Treaty. Why aren't we taking him seriously?" he asked, looking around the table. "The French certainly are and right now they're negotiating a bilateral non-aggression treaty with the Soviets for the express purpose of strengthening their hand against the Germans.

Muller's resolve to remain silent melted.

"That's precisely the kind of old-fashioned diplomacy, conducted outside the League, that needs to stop," Muller said. "The League was established precisely to abolish bilateral treaties and secret deals like that. The whole objective was to promote diplomacy based on open dialogue backed by League members. That's the system that we need to be encouraging, not the old secret deal-making that failed so catastrophically. Think about it," he continued, pausing to glance around the table, "here we are at the end of July in 1933, almost exactly nineteen years since Europe went to war. We should have learned our lesson."

Muller felt himself reddening; he had resolved not to stick his neck out like this. But he added gamely, "I feel pretty strongly about this. It's why I decided to leave Cambridge and go to work at the League and why I'm so excited about getting started."

"Great power habits are hard to break, Muller," Elliott responded. "We're still an imperial empire, after all, and the French Army remains the biggest in Europe. We're accustomed to acting in our own best interests—though at the moment I think we don't even have a clear understanding of what our best interests really are."

"But Paul's absolutely right," Gladys said loudly. "We've got to stop playing the old Empire game and use our power to support of the League. Duncan, even you must recognize that."

"Gladys, I'd be delighted if this bloody government of ours would show some resolve somewhere–anywhere," Elliott spread his arms in exasperation. "The League would be an excellent place to start. But I'm afraid this government has lost its way; it's weak and it's floundering."

"Then all the more reason to push them in the direction of disarmament," said Gladys triumphantly.

"Bravo," said Bigelow, pushing back his chair. "Everyone can agree on that. Now, there's time for a snooze or a walk along the river. Let's meet at 4:00 at the tennis court. Tennis whites only!"

As they stood up, Duncan Elliott approached Muller. "What about a stroll? There's a path along the Thames we can use. I've been here before and it's a nice place to walk."

"I'd like that," Muller replied.

They strode together across the meadow toward the tree-lined riverbank. "How do you and Bigelow know one another?" Muller asked.

"My father was a banker and Bigelow's was a valued client. They became good friends and we used to be invited here as a family when I was growing up. Bigelow's mother is a Jardine, owners of the big Hong Kong trading company; she's fabulously wealthy and Berkshire Abbey was in her family. My father's bank failed after the crash and he had to sue Bigelow's father over some rather large loans. It got messy and then my parents' marriage broke up, so the family ties we once had are finished. But Bigelow and I remained friendly, though we haven't seen much of one another for a couple of years. I used to love coming here; but I was posted overseas until very recently, so when he invited me to come down this weekend, I accepted eagerly."

"Where were you posted?' inquired Muller.

Elliott turned and smiled at him. "That's why I wanted to have this stroll and a chance to chat with you. I'm just back from two years at our embassy in Berlin."

"Really? Why that's extraordinary; I'd no idea. So you must really know what's going on there."

"I wish I did," Elliott replied with a rueful smile. "But I thought we might have a quiet chat together. I didn't want to get into it with everyone at lunch and start a major row, but what I witnessed during those two years is very unsettling, especially during the last six months since Hitler came to power.

Elliott ran his fingers through his hair nervously and hunched his shoulders as they walked. "Muller, I have to say I've concluded that the Nazi movement is a reign of terror. That's a serious accusation to make and I'm mindful that most people don't agree with me, including the friends who are with us this weekend, and, I'm afraid, more importantly, my superiors in the Foreign Office. I see the whole Nazi system as built on violence. The Party rank and file specializes in terrorizing political opponents. The Gestapo is everywhere and those brown-shirted SA storm troopers strut around breaking heads and singing lusty songs. They've destroyed the judicial system and crushed the trade unions; even churches are under siege. As of just two weeks ago, all opposition political parties were abolished. I think it's a nightmare," Elliott said, "but British public opinion seems indifferent."

"But Elliott," Muller interrupted, "Britain has a few problems closer to home that it's trying to deal with, things like the depression, unemployment, the collapse of the pound; Germany's hardly at the forefront of British concerns at the moment."

"I understand that," Elliott replied, kneeling to retie a shoe, then straightening up and turning to face Muller directly. "But Britain needs a

Europe that's stable, and right now Europe is splintering. Italy is a Fascist state under Mussolini; Germany seems to be under Hitler's Nazi thumb; France is careening from government to government. Your League of Nations seems to be the only thing they all have in common. So Britain should be taking the lead in trying to use the League as a much more robust instrument in restoring order. But we won't do it; we're too timid and we just seem to ignore what's really happening."

They came to a bench along the riverbank and sat, each extracting a cigarette from their cases. Elliott proffered his lighter and, after lighting their cigarettes, showed Muller the Nazi death head symbol affixed to it. "A souvenir to remind me of what we're up against."

"Let me tell you a story," Elliott said, pocketing the lighter and leaning back. "Last month, just before I left Berlin to return home, I went to visit my tailor, who was a Jew—but a very good tailor and very affordable. When I got to his store, I saw half a dozen Nazi brown-shirts standing over him in the street, kicking him, screaming taunts, one of them even urinating on him. They'd broken his shop window, smashed his sewing machines, trashed the clothing—including my new suit, I might add—then they threw him down on the curb and forced him to eat a pile of shit that one of them had deposited for the occasion. The police stood around laughing and goading them along.

"Muller, I could hardly believe what I was seeing. All this in broad daylight—and in the middle of Berlin, for God's sake.

"I started to protest, yelling that they were destroying my stuff. One of them, a very nasty looking bruiser, grabbed my shirtfront, stuck a brass-knuckled fist in my face and told me that I was another swine if I traded with this stinking Jew.

"What about my suit?" I said, unwilling to back down.

"'Oh, a foreigner are you?' he said, hearing my accent. 'Well take a good look at this and tell all your friends at home that this is what we do with stinking Jewish swine. And if you know what's good for you, you'll get the Hell out of here now or I'll beat you to a pulp'. He flung me against the wall and went back to kicking my tailor. I decided that I had better leave or they really *would* turn on me next.

"It was terrible," Elliott said, shaking his head. "I felt like such a coward afterwards. How could I have just stood there while they just beat the shit out of that little guy? Of course I was outnumbered, not to mention out-muscled," he smiled thinly," but I came away feeling really ashamed. In fact, I still feel that way, though I know there wasn't anything I could have actually done to break up the attack."

"And it's not just that these Nazi toughs are assaulting their Jews," Elliott went on. "Every week, for the past few months, we've had to deal with a half a dozen or more cases where British citizens have been roughed up. The usual reason is that they didn't salute some Nazi banner as it was being paraded around. But sometimes there wasn't any reason; just a random Nazi bully playing tough guy. This is a nasty regime and it means trouble for the rest of Europe, make no mistake about it."

"So what do you think we should be doing?" Muller asked. "Are you advocating taking military action to depose Hitler?"

Elliott shook his head. "No, that's not in the cards. But I'm impatient with people like Eirene—and many diplomats in the Foreign Office—who see a solution in simply accommodating them. These are bad guys. There are good reasons to keep the Treaty constraints in place; Germany's still big enough to threaten the rest of Europe. The French understand this only too well; the rest of Europe seems to want to wish it away."

They ground out their cigarettes and resumed their stroll along the riverbank.

"Frankly I'm in despair about British policy at the moment," Elliott continued. "Stanley Baldwin and Ramsay Macdonald are hopeless leaders. Our military is in terrible shape. There doesn't seem to be anyone paying attention to this menace and I'm viewed as a disruptive influence when I try to press the subject in the Foreign Office. So I'll probably resign from the service. I'm thinking about standing for parliament, though I hope that you'll keep that to yourself.

"Given what you said at lunch, Muller, and the League of Nations job you have ahead of you, I thought I would take the liberty of sharing my thoughts. It's a perspective you're probably not going to hear very often. Think of it as my contribution to your preparation for joining the League."

They came to a sharp curve in the path and turned back toward the Abbey.

"Well, thank you for that," responded Muller. "I've certainly read newspaper stories about occasional Nazi violence, but it's all a little abstract. Listening to your descriptions makes it seem more personal. What do you think ought to be done?"

"I meant what I said at lunch, about governments having to show more spine at the League than they have," Elliott responded.

"Look what just happened with Japan. They invaded China last year and set up a puppet state in Manchuria. China complained to the League; the League appointed a committee to investigate which came back with a report condemning the invasion as a clear violation of the League's covenant. In February, the League unanimously adopted the report and demanded that Japan remove its troops."

"I remember that," said Muller. "The Lytton Report, right?"

"Yes," said Elliott. "And do you remember what happened afterward?" He paused and snorted. "Nothing. Absolutely nothing! The Japanese Government simply rejected the report and said it had no intention of leaving Manchuria; then a month later–just this past March–they withdrew from the League. And that was the end of it. No sanctions, no military retaliation, not even diplomatic censure. Nothing; the Japanese simply walked away."

Elliott threw up his hands to punctuate his annoyance, then he turned to face Muller, pausing to emphasize his point.

"The League's reputation took a very big hit with its failure to act," said Elliott. "The member nations were simply paralyzed by indecision. Paralysis is not a good prescription for peace-keeping."

Elliott turned back and they continued walking. "Now, I'll grant you, that was a hard case. Manchuria's a long way off, America's a vital player in the Far East and offered no help, and China is nobody's idea of a nation deserving much support. So there were some extenuating circumstances. But it makes my point; collective security requires some backbone if it's going to be effective."

"Point taken," said Muller, pausing as he scooped up some gravel and began tossing stones into the river. Elliott followed suit.

"What's your impression of Hitler, since you've been so much closer than the rest of us?" Muller asked.

"Complicated," Elliott replied, skipping a stone on the smooth surface of the river. "My ambassador met with him regularly and found him difficult and generally rude. But he's also very clever and not to be underestimated; charming when he wants to be, but absolutely unyielding. Remember, he's only been in power for six months, so there's a lot we don't know about him. For instance, nobody quite knows what to make of *Mein Kampf,* that book of his that rants about the subhuman Jews and Slavs and lays out claims to a Greater German empire to the East."

"It all seems pretty delusional" Elliott added, "but then, so does a lot of the Nazi doctrine he's already managed to impose. It's scary, but we're not paying attention."

"The BBC doesn't broadcast Hitler's speeches here," said Muller, "and it's hard to pick up German wireless stations, so I haven't actually heard him speak. But newspaper stories report that he often seems to go a little mad,"

"He does," Elliott nodded. "He delivers long speeches–harangues, really–screeching imprecations, boasting of Nazi power, ranting about Jews, Communists, trade unionists; he sometimes works himself into such a frenzy that he's literally spitting his words into the microphone. Then suddenly he'll turn off the histrionics and sound rational–even accommodating." He shook his head. "He's a hard man to understand."

Then he smiled. "The only amusing thing about Hitler's long speeches is a Nazi rule that forbids bartenders from serving beer while he's speaking. So both the Nazis and their opponents have to sit in their bars listening on the radio–with empty beer mugs–sometimes for hours, as he goes on and on. There's always a huge rush to the bars when he finally finishes."

By this time they had turned back into the meadow leading toward Berkshire Abbey. "I'm glad we had this opportunity to chat," Elliott said. "I've decided to make my excuses and go back up to London tonight. I got here early enough to have a good visit with Bigelow and I don't want my black mood to interfere with the party–which it surely would do if I were to stay. I love Eirene dearly, but we'd quarrel and I'd certainly quarrel with Tom Low's ideas about the need to fight the Communists. I've already worn out my welcome at the Foreign Office; I don't want to do the same thing here at Berkshire Abbey too. Besides, I have a very nice friend who will welcome my early return to London. Good luck at the League. We all have a lot riding on that institution; I hope you can make it work."

They shook hands and Elliott went to gather his things while Muller changed for tennis.

***

After a lively dinner, merriment continued as the party gathered around the piano. Bigelow played show tunes and familiar melodies and everyone sang along. Margaret accompanied on her violin, with a few solo riffs of her own. They concluded with a flourish and a rousing chorus of 'Rule Britannia'. Everyone applauded.

Eirene came over to Muller and suggested one last brandy on the terrace.

They seated themselves in adjoining lounge chairs and she accepted one of his Gitanes, drawing deeply. "Paul, I didn't want to say anything tonight at dinner because I didn't want to begin another round of political discussion, but I wanted to take you aside to tell you how splendid I found your remarks at lunch about the League of Nations." She waved aside his rejoinder. "I know, I know," she said, "you feel strongly; I understand. The reason I understand–and the reason I wanted to have a quiet chat with you– is that I am deeply involved with the League of Nations Union, a strong backer of the League here in Britain. Daddy has been friends for decades with Lord Cecil, who's been Chairman of the organization since it was formed right after the League was established. He's actually Uncle Robert to me," she added.

"We're very active in generating support for the League. We have hundreds of local chapters throughout the Kingdom and close to a million individual members. I'm busy raising money and generating publicity and I also have a hand in developing policies supporting the League which we urge the British government to adopt. Anyway, I wanted to tell you about it; I'm excited about my involvement, as you can tell," she said. "You're actually going to be at the League, in the front lines in Geneva, so to speak. Maybe we can work together on some of this."

Muller sensed Eirene was about to launch into another policy discussion, but instead she looked around; all the others had left for bed. "That's enough," she said a little sheepishly, "it's late; let's continue tomorrow. I've got lots more to tell you. I'm getting up early to ride with Robert and Gladys, are you joining us?"

"I am," he said smiling. "I'll look forward to talking more about all this tomorrow." They finished the last of their brandies and he offered his arm as they entered the Abbey.

***

The next morning, Muller awoke with a pounding headache and regretted the brandies. But he pulled his riding costume together, slid into his high leather boots and made his way to the front portico where a groom had assembled four horses, saddled and ready. Bigelow and Gladys were stroking their mounts, chatting together and James, the butler, presided over a small table where he had assembled four plates, each holding what appeared to be a biscuit with jam, and four tea cups. "A little something before setting off, sir?" said James.

"Delighted," said Muller eagerly consuming the biscuit and taking a large gulp of tea.

From somewhere in his butler's regalia James extracted a small silver cup which he filled with brandy and handed to Muller. "And this will help too, sir," he said.

Muller hesitated.

"Better do it, Paul," said Bigelow, "part of the ritual." He wiped a biscuit crumb from his mouth and exchanged his empty teacup for his own silver cup, coiffing down the brandy with a smacking of lips. "Ah," he said, smiling.

As Muller followed suit, Eirene hurried down the steps and stood upright in front of Muller and Bigelow. "Ready?" she asked. Then, raising her hands like a conductor, she led them together, "Je-ru-sa-lem."

They all laughed and, wolfing down her biscuit and a cup of tea—and declining the brandy, she said, "I'm as ready as I'll be, so let's go."

They all mounted.

"It's just the four of us," said Bigelow. "Margaret and the Laws don't ride. So, tally-ho," and he set off at a brisk trot.

They followed the bank of the Thames, along the same path where Muller and Duncan Elliott had taken their stroll the day before. Turning right, they soon entered Great Windsor Park where Bigelow pulled up his mount and they all stopped together.

"Muller, this is a very large forest preserve—nearly twenty square kilometers. It was formerly the hunting preserve of the Windsor kings, dating from the 14th century. Windsor Castle itself is just a few miles off," he gestured to his left, "but we'll ride out a few miles this way," he pointed to his right, "so you can catch a glimpse of the Royal Lodge. Two years ago, King George gave it to the Duke and Duchess of York as a country retreat; a modest little place with only 30 rooms," he smiled. "We've been there a few times and it's quite nice. The Royal family is off in Scotland now for the summer, so we'll have no issues with Royal security. It's splendid riding country, so let's enjoy it."

"And Paul," added Gladys, "Be sure to keep up. There are tales of stragglers in these woods being snatched away by Herne the Hunter, with his stag antlers, riding a massive black stallion at the head of a pack of hounds." She laughed, wheeled her horse, and they cantered off across the deer meadows and the undulating parkland, through small woods and coverts, passing ancient oaks, long dead but standing, limbs akimbo, like weary sentinels.

When they returned to the Abbey, a proper English breakfast was awaiting them along with Margaret and Tom and Phoebe Law. "We're starved," said Phoebe. "Come join us straightaway."

Over fried eggs and English bacon Bigelow regaled them with the splendors of the Park. "There's an interesting tidbit about Windsor Castle," he added. "Most castles are named for the king or noble that owns them. But the opposite is the case here. When Queen Victoria married Prince Albert back in 1840, he was German; consequently, the British Royal family became known as Saxe-Coburg-Gotha. During the War, King George decided a German name was decidedly unpatriotic, so he discarded it and adopted the name Windsor, after the castle. And, voila; overnight the House of Saxe-Coburg-Gotha became the House of Windsor Our easiest victory over the Germans," he chuckled.

"Speaking of victory," said Eirene, "last evening I told Paul a little bit about the work of the League of Nations Union and our agenda."

"Did you also tell him that it's an organization that actually allows women to participate?" asked Gladys. "Oh, all the bigwigs are men, of course, but Eirene and I are the ones really running the place and we've become very influential. We're pushing our proposal for restoring Germany to equal status after all these years of unfair treatment under the Versailles Treaty, for instance, and we've persuaded Lord Cecil–your Uncle Robert, Eirene–to press the government on disarmament."

Warming to her subject, Gladys put down her fork and began gesturing. "Under the Treaty, there are categories of offensive weapons that Germany is forbidden to produce; big cannons and other things. But no one else is operating under the same constraints. So what we're saying is, let's get an agreement where everyone is forbidden to make those awful weapons. That way everyone is on the same footing. Germany would no longer feel that it is being held to some inferior status, and everyone could be confident that the weaponry needed to start some new war would no longer exist anywhere. I mean it's absolutely logical, isn't it?"

Eirene chimed in, "Gladys and I are also pushing a Union proposal to have the League of Nations establish its own air force. The idea is for nations to abolish their national air forces, and create a League of Nations monopoly on military aircraft. Part of the plan would be to make sure that only the League could acquire the most powerful aircraft engines and use them in its air force; other airplanes, including commercial airlines, would have to use slower engines.

"We persuaded Uncle Robert to present it to the government and they put the plan forward at the League's disarmament conference in Geneva this spring. Once the conference reconvenes from its current adjournment, the aircraft issue will be near the top of the agenda."

"Churchill and his crowd keep dismissing us as 'silly women'," Gladys added, glancing around the table, her voice louder, "but we're having a real influence on government policy."

Then she paused, with a broad smile, "And about time, too."

Muller observed Gladys and Eirene. Both were intelligent and obviously very involved with the issues, but how different in appearance. Gladys was plain and large; not fat, but a big frame. Good natured, but bad hair and a little horsey, thought Muller; not very feminine. Eirene, by contrast, was small and trim with dark, curly hair, bright blue eyes, a nice figure and a vivacious manner. Very feminine, Muller decided.

Bigelow offered his lighter around the table as people lit up. "You all remember Stanley Baldwin's speech in the House making the point that there's absolutely no defense to aerial bombardment?

"The bomber always gets through!" whooped Tom Low, spreading his arms, mimicking the wingspan of a bomber. "Boom," he said loudly; "Boom, BOOM."

Bigelow smiled. "Exactly; can you imagine how terrible it would be if someone bombed London? Unthinkable. So yes, by all means, let's get rid of national air forces and place the awful power of an air force in the hands of the League, where it can be safeguarded."

"Hat's off to the women of the Union for a really good idea," he added, bowing in his seat toward Eirene and Gladys.

"You all know that I'm in the art business, not politics or diplomacy," Phoebe Law interjected, "and the gallery I work for competes with the bigger galleries in France. Since I'm a fluent French speaker, part of my job is to read the daily French press and learn what our French competitors are up to.

"So I'm looking for stuff on the arts. But inevitably, I find myself scanning the news articles too. And I must say, I'm struck by the contrast with the coverage here. We're all about disarmament, as Gladys and Eirene were saying; but they're all about *re*-armament. They remain scared to death of the Germans, especially since Hitler came to power. I can't imagine a conversation like the one we're having now occurring in Paris. So, Eirene," Phoebe wagged her finger, "a word of caution."

"But that's all the more reason to keep up the pressure," Bigelow interjected. "If we can find common ground with Hitler, then he'll calm down and the French won't have anything to fear. The point is to keep working toward disarmament."

Eirene broke in. "That's precisely why Gladys and I are getting the Union to begin work on a big project we're calling 'the Peace Ballot' which we think can inject new energy into the disarmament movement. We're drawing up a series of questions which we intend to put on actual ballots that we'll distribute around the whole of Britain, asking people to actually vote on whether they support disarmament and the League. We're planning to use all of our chapters to organize this, galvanizing local leaders like ministers, mayors, trade union leaders, and so on."

"We can generate huge publicity around the campaign," she added. "With the advent of radio—and the newsreels we all see at the movies—people feel much more connected to world events than was true even ten years ago, let alone during the War. So what appeals to us about the Peace Ballot is the opportunity it offers individual citizens to participate, in a very personal way, actually casting a vote and depositing it in a ballot box—to promote a safer world. That's a goal that everyone seems to agree upon."

The staff had cleared the breakfast and the last of the tea had been consumed, so they began pushing back their chairs. "On your own till lunch," said Robert. "Let's gather here around noontime. Our cousin, RCS Stevenson, is coming down from London to join us and he'll be here by then. You'll enjoy meeting him."

Muller went up to his room and sat in one of the upholstered chairs overlooking the meadow and the river in the distance. He'd intended to read the morning newspaper that had come down from London and been delivered during breakfast. But his mind kept returning to the conversation over breakfast. The support manifested for the League and its agenda was certainly reassuring, and the Peace Ballot idea sounded especially intriguing. But he wondered what Duncan Elliott would have said if he had stayed instead of returning to London. His alarm about Germany under the Nazis certainly conflicted with what everyone else was saying. He probably *would* have provoked a quarrel, Muller thought with a smile.

He was glad he'd accepted Bigelow's invitation. It was an interesting cast of characters and he certainly was learning about British political priorities. And he was glad that it was not as intimidating as he had feared.

What, he wondered, would this Stevenson cousin with the strange name add to the mix?

***

"So, Muller, as a Swiss, you'll be too reserved to ask me the question I'm sure is uppermost in your mind," said Stevenson as they strolled to the tennis court for the match they had set up at lunch.

"What question?" asked Muller.

"How I came to be called RCS of course." Stevenson said, smiling. "So I'll tell you anyway. My real name is Ralph Chester Stewart Stevenson. My father was also Ralph. He had three sisters; two proceeded to marry men named Ralph. They each had children named Ralph and I found myself surrounded by Ralphs. There even was a horse named Ralph, and someone's dog was a Ralph. I decided, enough Ralphs. But I didn't want to choose between Chester and Stewart for fear of offending the name I didn't select. So I decided on RCS. So that's what I'm called now. And that's the story."

"If I win both sets I'm going to call you Ralph," Muller said, smiling broadly.

"Then there's no way you'll win both sets," Stevenson replied.

They began warming up, hitting easy ground strokes to one another over the net. Bigelow had said they should be evenly matched, and that's the way it looked, thought Muller.

After a few practice serves they started. Muller discovered that Stevenson had a strong backhand and was not afraid to charge the net. Back and forth they went for more than an hour, Muller finally winning the second set at 6-4 after having lost 6-8. They agreed that was enough and walked up to the terrace where James brought them each a cool beer and a towel to wipe off the perspiration.

"We'll have to do this again in Geneva," said Stevenson. "I'm assistant director for League of Nations Affairs in the Foreign Office, so I visit Geneva a lot. I'm the guy who drafts the remarks for our delegation when they're addressing the League. That's why Eirene was trying to extract information from me at lunch today, which I tried politely to duck. She and Gladys are involved and well-connected so I can't just snub them, but a lot of my work is confidential so I'm obliged to be discreet—much to their annoyance, I'm afraid.

"But since I'm there so frequently, I've joined the Tennis Club de Genève which has a couple of good courts and I'm sure we can find a way to play after the League Council meetings are out of the way in September and before it gets cold in November."

"I'm scheduled to report to the secretariat on September 1," said Muller. "I don't know where I'll be assigned, but I'm pretty eager to begin."

"A good going-in attitude, Muller," Stevenson smiled. "There's time and ample opportunity ahead to get frustrated and disillusioned.

"Incidentally, Bigelow told me that Duncan Elliott was here but left early."

Muller nodded. "We chatted a bit on Friday."

Stevenson shook his head. "Elliott's become a nuisance about the Nazis. All he can do is prattle on about their violent behavior and how the Foreign Office isn't taking Hitler seriously enough. Frankly, I think he left early because Bigelow told him I was coming down and he didn't want to face me again; we've had some pretty sharp disagreements since he returned from Berlin.

"He spoke to me about the street violence," Muller said.

"He's always harping on that," said Stevenson. "Yes, it's true the Germans have their brown shirt storm troopers and yes they can be pretty violent, but they're hardly unique. Mussolini's Fascists have their black shirt *squadristi* and while the French don't have a favorite shirt color, both the right and the left have street gangs they periodically unleash; the same is true in Spain, even Portugal. And he keeps complaining about Nazi mistreatment of the Jews. Hell, there's nothing new about that either. Jews are a problem for everyone–including us, for goodness sakes; they control so much money and exercise so much behind the scenes influence that no one trusts them." Stevenson pursed his lips and shook his head.

He continued. "But Elliott persists in making dark pronouncements and criticizes us for being weak. I'm afraid that two years in Berlin must have overwhelmed him. Certainly no one in Whitehall has much use for him anymore; I think he knows that."

Yes he does, Muller thought, but he simply smiled, deciding nothing was to be gained by weighing into what was clearly a serious personal quarrel.

They finished the last of the beer and went upstairs to change.

***

Dinner that evening was less boisterous. Another English meal–why do they always overcook the fish, Muller wondered–accompanied by fresh vegetables and fortified by ample quantities of chilled white Bordeaux and a good claret. Eirene was again seated on Muller's left and she returned to the subject of the League of Nations Union and its disarmament agenda. She made several attempts to draw Stevenson into the conversation, but Muller could see that Stevenson was keeping his distance, apparently determined to avoid engaging her.

Eirene rolled her eyes. "He's got all this authority at the League," she whispered to Muller, "and he always seems to have secrets he won't share." Then brightening, she turned to Muller with a smile, "You and I can have our own secrets that we don't have to share with him."

The two of them launched into animated discussion of the League and its agenda that Muller found engrossing and much more entertaining than the talk of royalty and fashion that ensued among the other guests.

After the meal, Bigelow gamely accompanied Margaret in two Mozart sonatas for piano and violin; they all agreed that Bigelow had made a fine effort and that Margaret played beautifully. Muller saw that Stevenson had nodded off in a wing chair off to one side.

There was a bright flash of lightning and a loud clap of thunder. Everyone–including Stevenson–jumped, startled by the violent onset of the summer storm. A rush of wind blew the white curtains in the open doors and windows. A downpour pounded the terrace, soaking the cushions in the lounge chairs that had been left out. They stood by the doorways watching as lightning illuminated the distant tree line and tennis court, cringing at the nearby claps of thunder.

"Not quite like the trenches I guess," joked Bigelow, "but close enough. Fortunately, no one has to go outside to get to bed, so we can retire on this high note."

Watching the retreating storm next to Muller, Eirene slipped her hand into his. She put her cheek close to his face, "Don't lock you door tonight," she whispered. Then she followed Gladys up the wide staircase.

A few minutes after Muller got into bed he heard his bedroom door open and close and felt Eirene's warm body slide next to him.

"Now, Jerusalem," she said kissing him hungrily. "I need to inspect your League of Nations member," she whispered and then proceeded to do so thoroughly and enthusiastically.

As he rolled over on her, Muller murmured something about needing to cast his Peace Ballot in her ballot box. Later, entangled together, they lay dozing until she began moving on him, whispering, "I need you to cast another ballot." And not long thereafter, he did just that.

***

They assembled the next morning for breakfast, Eirene skipping down the stairs smiling broadly and leading the now familiar Je-ru-sa-lem greeting, which they explained to an amused Stevenson. The previous night's storm had left a chilly, rainy mist in its wake, suitable neither for tennis nor riding. Stevenson said that he would take an earlier train back to London and Muller decided to join him, saying that he was trying to get away to Grindelwald. "It's likely to be my last vacation for quite a while with the new job."

Muller had Martin pack his things and a short time later Stanley brought up the big Bentley to drive Muller and Stevenson to Datchet station. Farewells were said; Muller warmly embraced Eirene, kissing her on both cheeks. She pressed a piece of paper in his hand. "My mailing address and telephone number," she whispered. "I want very much to remain in touch."

He whispered back, "lovely weekend."

CHAPTER 2

August 1933

Arriving back in Cambridge, Muller packed up his belongings and shipped them to Zurich. He paid his landlady, said farewell to the handful of students and faculty remaining in the summer term and departed for Grindelwald.

Chalet Muller was situated just above the village, perched on a ridge at the foot of the Jungfrau, with a striking view of the South face of the Eiger. It was a large structure featuring a prominent single gable with bright red and white geraniums that tumbled out of boxes mounted beneath tall windows framed by wide green shutters. In front, pointing toward the Eiger, was a broad gallery bordered by a railing that capped vertical boards, closely spaced and decorated with traditional Swiss carvings. This gallery was where the family gathered on warm evenings to enjoy an aperitif and watch the sunset play out on the craggy face of the Eiger. His mother caught sight of him as he mounted the incline and she stepped down from the gallery to greet him, hugging him tightly. He kissed her cheek and stood back gazing fondly at her slender build and bright complexion, always fashionably dressed, even informally as now, with a fitted blue linen skirt and white short-sleeved blouse.

"You look about half your age Mum," he said grinning broadly, "Father is a lucky man. We all are."

Mounting the gallery he turned to catch his younger sister Mathilda, who bounded out of the doorway straight into his arms. They began pushing one another affectionately around the gallery and burst out laughing together. "Finally," she exclaimed, "back from England and where you belong. We've been waiting."

"So have I," said Muller. "Let me drop my valise in my room and get out of these traveling clothes. Then we can begin my visit properly—with an aperitif here on the gallery."

Muller came back downstairs to see the staff setting out a tray of drinks on the sideboard along with a plate of viande des grison, wrapped around fresh cornichons. "Ah, this is a treat," he sighed as he savored one and greeted the elderly couple whom he had known since childhood.

"I brought Oskar and Greta down with me on the train," his mother said. "Your father and Thomas will have to fend for themselves back in Zurich. Anyway, your father will be here next week for about ten days, so they'll survive."

Relaxing on the gallery and watching the shadows creep over the face of the Eiger, Mathilde enthused about her first year at university in Zurich. "I've gotten over being angry at Father about refusing to let me take courses in economics and accounting. He's just so dead set against my playing any role in the bank. It's silly. I'm much better with numbers than you—let alone Thomas. And you know that I've played around with stock-swapping formulas for years, just for fun. But Father won't hear of it. Private banking is all about trust, he says, and I'm afraid our clients are not ready to trust their wealth to my daughter. He says it very nicely, of course. Mum tried to persuade him that at least some of his wealthy widow clients would like the idea. But he won't budge, and I was pretty peeved about it."

"But then I got to university," she continued, "and was introduced to quantum physics. Well, that certainly changed things. It's a lot more challenging—really daunting to be fair, but absorbing. Now Albert Einstein is my new heart throb," Matilda laughed.

"Will you go down to Geneva for university for a couple of years as I did?" inquired Muller.

"Maybe," she answered. "I've actually looked into going to Tubingen University, in southern Germany near Baden Baden. They have a very highly-rated physics program and that's what I'm really looking for. But I've been put off by all this Nazi stuff since Hitler came to power in January. The strutting around, goose-stepping and saluting, the swastika-draped rallies, it's all rather alarming.

"One of my friends is thinking about going to America instead and enrolling in the physics program at the University of Chicago. That sounds exciting," she said. "Maybe I'll do that; if so, I can probably date a gangster!" She giggled.

The staff had laid out a cool poached salmon and fresh salad on the sideboard, so they each took a plate, refreshed their wine and dined in the gathering darkness as Oskar lit candles along the railing.

After dinner, Muller and his mother sat in the candlelight with light sweaters, enjoying their Gitanes. "Paul," she said, suddenly animated, "what about that declaration adopted at Oxford this spring refusing to fight for King or country under any circumstances. *Under any circumstances*? That certainly doesn't sound like the England I grew up in. You were there—at Cambridge, not Oxford, of course—but what did you make of it?"

Muller took a drag on his Gitane. "I thought it was daft, Mum," he said, "some kind of stunt. What else could it be? But they were serious. It happened at a debate organized by the Oxford Union and the resolution not to fight was adopted by a vote of something like 275 to 153. The newspapers picked it up calling it the Oxford Pledge and it was later adopted at the University of Manchester and the University of Glasgow too. It caused an awful row. Actually, Cambridge threatened to pull out of the annual sculls race in protest.

"So my country is now pacifist?" said his mother skeptically.

Muller shook his head. "I don't think that the resolution represents the view of most Englishmen. But there's no doubt that a pacifist streak has taken hold in Britain. I sense that the growing stridency of the Nazis in Germany and the desperation at home caused by the depression have led people to despair about the future. Pacifism seems to offer respite to some of them."

"And you, Paul?" his mother asked.

"My reaction was a lot different," he replied. "I decided I wanted to get more involved, not less. That's why I asked Father to use his influence and find me a job in the League of Nations secretariat. I think the League is the best way to deal with our problems, not retreating into some kind of cocoon. Actually, I was at a country house weekend party near Windsor just before coming home and I met some influential League supporters. It's an absolutely vital institution in my view; I just hope I'm up to the task of playing some role in its work.

Muller's mother laid her hand on his arm and smiled. "I'm glad you made that choice," she said, "and I'm sure you'll succeed.

"We'll speak more of all this, especially once your father gets here. But now it's time for bed."

***

Karl Muller was a mountain of a man. In fact, as a reliable second row man on the Oxford rugby side he had been referred to as "the Swiss Alp." Now, 35 years later, he retained his size and still looked remarkably fit. He greeted his son warmly. "Let's hike up the Eiger trail after lunch," he said. "I need to get my mountain legs under me."

After a brisk climb, they arrived at a ridge line. They followed it for a few hundred meters to a small chalet that served in ski season as a hot chocolate stop on the trail down to the village, but now offered a comfortable wooden gallery to sit and catch their breath, wiping perspiration from their brows in the warm sunshine.

Karl began rubbing his knees. "I've decided I pushed too many scums all those years ago," he said ruefully. My knees get stiff now, and I've got a balky ankle. "You were smart to stick with tennis; your mother's physique and her brains too."

"Thanks again for your intervention on my behalf with the League, Father," said Muller. "I begin in about two weeks, and I'm excited."

"Well, Switzerland is playing host to the League and senior Swiss officials have long had dealings with the bank; it wasn't so difficult to arrange," said his father, smiling. "Some other things are a lot harder." His manner grew serious.

"I can't tell you how nice it is to get away from the bank and escape to our chalet. It has been a very stressful few months.

"Returns on our investments are at historic lows, and we're not making money for our clients—or for ourselves either, for that matter. Everyone else is in the same boat, so we're not alone, by any means. Still, it's very troubling. The American tariff choked off international trade, so there are almost no commercial transactions to finance. But the worst of it is that capital flows have collapsed. No one is willing to make loans against assets that aren't backed by gold, but most of the world's gold reserves are now sitting in vaults in the Banque de France or the US Federal Reserve. So there's almost no lending; the system has just seized up. I've never seen anything like it."

The elder Muller stood to stretch out his legs and he shook his sore ankle. When he sat back down, his face grew even more serious and he dropped his voice, even though no one else was in sight.

"Then there's this whole Jewish issue. The bank has never catered to Jews over the years. Not that we've refused to deal with them; we've had a few Jewish clients. But most Jews preferred to deal with Jewish bankers—Warburg or Rothschild, or someone like Kuhn Loeb in New York. Now, all of a sudden, we have Jews coming to us *because* we're not Jews. Hitler's only been in power for six months, but already we've seen scores of German Jews—including some Germans who didn't even know they were Jews, families with a Jewish ancestor or two, for example, trying to protect assets by getting them out of Germany and into our safety deposit vaults. And it's a very dangerous business; the Nazis have imposed strict prohibitions against exporting valuables. If you get caught, you're liable to wind up in one of those new concentration camps."

Karl Muller looked down at his hiking boots, kicking some pebbles. "Paul, I actually had an elderly German Jew come into the bank last month who had removed valuable paintings from their frames and taped the canvases to his torso and legs to smuggle them out. I had to go into the safety deposit vault with him to help him disrobe and remove the canvases. Others come with jewelry sewn into hats and other bits of clothing, or with stock certificates hidden in false bottom briefcases. They're all looking for safekeeping."

He paused, kicking more pebbles. "I'm not sure if we're going to be allowed to continue this business much longer. Swiss authorities are nervous about offending the Nazis. Also, I have to ask myself, how vulnerable is Muller & Co. to potential German retaliation if I accept these people as clients? At this point, I don't know the answer, and it makes me very uneasy."

Karl got up and stretched his legs. "Let's start back down," he said. "It's easier to talk going downhill."

They walked together companionably down the grassy slope toward the village.

"What I said a moment ago about so much of the world's gold sitting in vaults at the Federal Reserve and the Banque de France is not entirely true," he said smiling, as they scrambled around a rocky outcropping. "Most of the world's bullion is physically stored in London at the Bank of England. It's so heavy–and so expensive to move–that everyone's agreed to leave it there, but to 'earmark' who owns it. So every day, a group of men descends into the vault in London. They load some bars of bullion, stacked by one wall onto a wooden cart and roll the cart thirty feet across the room to another wall, where they offload the bars and carefully attach white name tags indicating that the gold now belongs to the French or the Americans.

He chuckled. "It's a bizarre fact that we're experiencing the worst credit squeeze we've ever known because there's too much gold stacked against one wall and not enough against the other."

***

Dinner that evening was served indoors as a chilly breeze descended from the summit of the Jungfrau. It was a low key affair as they talked of plans for Karl and Ann Muller's 35th wedding anniversary in February and related familiar stories about how they had met at a raucous party following an Oxford rugby match.

"My friend Gwen's boyfriend was the fly half, and she persuaded me to come," smiled Ann. "There was this big, good looking guy standing separate from the crowd. Your father was still a bit of a standoffish Swiss at that time. But we had an instant connection, and we still do today," she said mischievously, smiling at her husband and grasping his hand.

"Your grandfather thought an Oxford education would be a good way for me to become a fluent English-speaker," added Karl. "It would also offer an opportunity to troll for new English clients for the bank. And it was successful on all counts. What he didn't expect was that I would bring back an English bride." They both laughed in fond recollection.

"But he—and your grandmother—could not have been more welcoming," said Ann. "They were my primary source for learning to speak Switzerdeutsch, that impenetrable dialect spoken in Zurich—especially by the bankers. I still find it challenging."

"That's the whole purpose, of course," chuckled Karl; "it's our secret code."

Mathilde announced she was going to the village to meet friends, so they got up from the table to allow Oskar and Greta to clear and Paul and his parents moved to couches in the living area before the fireplace.

"Ann, I shared with Paul some of the troubles we've been experiencing at the bank," said his father. "I thought he should know. We're certainly financially secure; I'm not worried about that. But the banking industry is facing uncertain times and that could affect Muller & Co. in ways I can't yet foresee," and he paused, before continuing, glancing around to make certain Oskar and Greta were not within earshot.

"I need to share with both of you an especially difficult encounter just before I came to Grindelwald. A young man about Paul's age made an urgent appointment to see me. He was very distraught and nervous. It seems that he was a Jew who is trying to get his family out of Germany. He said that the family had been beaten up by the Gestapo and his father was imprisoned somewhere; they wouldn't even tell him where. He was desperate to get the money in his father's account so he could return to Frankfurt and pay the bribes to get the family out. But he said that my staff had refused him access to the account because he didn't have the proper identification. He pleaded with me to intervene, shoving his passport at me, insisting he was the son of our client and was acting at his direction.

"Well, you both know the rules under which we operate. If you can't provide the proper identification, we are required to deny access to the account. That's how the system works. So I had to tell him no. He looked at me, wild-eyed, and literally collapsed in sobs. 'You're going to get us all killed,' he hissed, again and again softer and softer. Finally, he straightened himself up and managed to stagger out of my office. 'You're going to get us all killed,' he said again, louder this time, 'because you have our money and you won't let us take it when we need it most'. And he left," finished Karl. "I could see him through the window, lurching into traffic, scarcely heeding the oncoming cars. Finally he boarded a tram and I lost sight of him."

Karl paused and lit his pipe. "I have never had an encounter like that," he said quietly. "The father is indeed a client of the bank as the young man had told us; I'd even met him once. He was a very successful banker in Frankfurt, but wanted to safeguard some funds with us in Switzerland. The account had a very precise identification procedure; not complicated, but precise. And the young man didn't have it. So I had to say no. But I keep asking myself, did I save the account from being raided by an imposter, or, as the young man accused me, have I condemned a family to death at the hands of the Nazis? Swiss law didn't give me any choice in the matter. But that doesn't offer much solace." He shook his head.

They sat silently, for several moments.

Then Paul related his conversation with Duncan Elliott at Berkshire Abbey in July. "He described a number of violent incidents that are apparently commonplace, like beating up Jews and anyone else they decide isn't sufficiently Nazi. He thinks Hitler's regime is evil and aims to re-make Europe. At a minimum, he says they mean to overturn the Versailles rules that are stacked against them. There was also a group of strong supporters of the League at the same weekend party. They're trying to persuade the British and French governments to accommodate German demands. Their idea is to get agreement by everyone to disarm to the same limits as the Treaty imposes on Germany; they're persuaded that if this result can be achieved, Hitler will modify his behavior, cooler heads in Germany will prevail and tensions will ease off."

"And you, Paul? What do you think?" His father asked.

Muller smiled at his parents. "You know I'm no expert and I'm frankly a little anxious about going from studying political science to actually practicing diplomacy at the League. I've got a lot to learn and I'm not really sure how to judge all the competing agendas being kicked around. So I guess my answer to your question is to reserve judgment on what the right policies are and concentrate on seeing how I can help the League work effectively."

"They pay bankers to be cynical and cautious," Karl Muller said. "And I'm not very optimistic that things will turn out the way your friends envision. Still, I can at least be hopeful; it's one of the reasons I'm happy that you'll be at the League."

CHAPTER 3

Autumn 1933

The League of Nations secretariat was located in the Palais Wilson, a large and imposing structure with a five-story brick and stone façade dominated by tall marble columns. It was situated alongside Lac Léman in Geneva, facing east toward the Salève, the steep mountain abruptly rising above the lake, and on the occasional clear day it offered views of the Swiss Alps and a gleaming Mont Blanc summit in the far distance.

Muller reported to the Personnel Section and spent most of his first two days being processed and attending to a myriad of administrative details. During an especially long wait for one of the clerks, Muller struck up a conversation with a secretary who smilingly sympathized with his visible frustration about the process.

"Mr. Muller, as a fellow Swiss, I'm sure you share my admiration over the way the League has adapted itself to our penchant for thorough paperwork."

"Has it always been this bureaucratic?" Muller asked.

She nodded. "Of course, it's bigger now, so everything's even slower. And the building's gotten so crowded. I hope you aren't expecting your own office."

"You know, this was once a fancy hotel, built before the war and catering to a luxury clientele that came here to visit their bankers," she continued. Seeing Muller's face register surprise, she went on. "It was called the National. In 1920, when the League was established, the Swiss government requisitioned the entire building and converted it into the League's headquarters. I wasn't here then, of course, but I'm told it was really pretty comfortable at the start. But all those big suites have now been subdivided many times over and converted into offices that seem to keep shrinking. They're now trying to pigeonhole even more people into the same cramped space. We may be the League of Nations," she said with a toss of her head, "but we're not the lap of luxury."

"Still, with any luck, you'll at least get your own desk." She winked at him and passed him off to the next office.

Eventually, Muller found himself assigned to the Minorities Section of the Secretariat, one of the larger organizations within the League structure. It had been established in the earliest days of the League to implement the League's responsibilities for protecting the rights of minorities in the new countries established under the Versailles Treaty.

The Minorities Section was divided into four sub-sections, Muller learned: 2A for the continuing Turkish-Greek and Greek-Bulgarian population exchanges, 2B for the Free City of Danzig mandate, 2C for the Occupied Saar Basin mandate and 2D for "Minorities"—a resting place for All Others. That was where Muller was assigned.

His sub-section chief was a heavyset, balding man in his early 50s named Jaczck Demchuk. Muller later learned that he was Austrian, having begun life as an ethnic Ukrainian in a region of the Austrian-Hungarian Empire that had now become part of Poland. Muller introduced himself and Demchuk smiled faintly, saying the sub-section had a lot of work, so he was glad for a new hand.

The offices of the Minority Section were on the third floor of the Palais. Demchuk's subsection comprised a dozen small offices facing one another across a narrow corridor. Each office contained several desks crowded together amid file cabinets and stacks of papers. Demchuk introduced Muller absently to four or five men none of whose names he caught and waved at an office converted to a typing section, where a half dozen female typists sat together looking, Muller thought upon first inspection, very much like typists. Demchuk pointed Muller to a desk in an office with a dirty sticker above the doorway identifying it as # 38H. Well, Muller said to himself, I did get my own desk in a very crowded space, just as the secretary had predicted.

The office was evidently a main filing destination and his desktop was nearly covered with stacks of paper. He sat in the desk chair and found himself surrounded with petitions and complaints involving most of the minority treaty countries. He picked up several of the file folders at random. One labeled 'Poland' had dossiers dealing with Germans, Lithuanians, Ukrainians, Russian Orthodox and something labeled General and Miscellaneous. Yugoslavia's dossiers included Albanians, Hungarians, Germans, Bulgarians and, again, General and Miscellaneous. There were even dossiers regarding Assyrian rights in Iraq and Syria–and strangest of all, it seemed to Muller–in British Guinea. The documents were all neatly bundled in brown file folders and had been placed in numbered cartons that apparently responded to some organized numerical sequence, the key to which did not appear evident to Muller.

Finding it all a little overwhelming, Muller decided to start by removing the files from his desk, stacking them neatly on the floor. Then he pulled out his handkerchief, dusting the desktop, and he removed rubbish from the desk drawers. Demchuk appeared and deposited four large dossiers on his clean desktop. "Upper Silesia," he said. "It's an active file. You'll see a number of petitions we need to address. There are some background documents you'll want to read first to get oriented. But get started on this." Demchuk then disappeared down the corridor.

Well, Muller thought, I guess this is where that learning curve begins.

***

Muller counted himself fortunate that he was familiar with Geneva, having attended two years of university there. He decided to rent a comfortable apartment in the Old City, between the Theatre and the Parc des Bastions. It was close to restaurants and only a short walk down the hill to the Quai Gustave-Ador, where he could catch a tram to the Palais Wilson.

Over the next few weeks, Muller immersed himself in the files, as Demchuk had directed. Upper Silesia was a heavily industrialized region north of the Oder River that had been divided between Germany and Poland by the Treaty of Versailles in a manner satisfying neither of them. Eventually, most of the region was awarded to Poland, leaving in its wake a large population of disgruntled Germans living uneasily under Polish rule. In the ensuing years, numerous petitions had been filed with the League seeking redress of a wide range of alleged grievances. These were all a part of the dossiers Muller was handed.

Among the active petitions was a dispute between Germany and Poland over a hospital situated in territory awarded to Poland. The Germans claimed the building was owned by the Knights of Malta under an agreement giving Germany rights to the facility. Two more involved a German claiming he was unlawfully expelled from Polish Silesia and another who claimed to have been fired from his job on discriminatory grounds. There were several very new petitions from Jews in German Silesia complaining about Nazi racial laws.

All of this was interesting and certainly the petitions seemed worthy of attention by the League, thought Muller. But it was pretty small-bore stuff compared to the more glamorous work like the Disarmament Conference. So Muller was feeling a little sorry for himself when, to his surprise, RCS Stevenson stuck his head into Office #38H.

"I'm in town for the first two weeks of October and the League Council meetings," he said. "I've booked a court for us at the Club tomorrow at 6 PM. We'll play, then have dinner unless you have a better offer."

"I'd love to," responded Muller, smiling and gripping Stevenson's outstretched hand.

"Meet me at the entrance to the Palais at 5:30 with your kit, then," said Stevenson. "I'll organize a car."

The next afternoon, they drove out along the Route Suisse past Bellevue, then turned left into Collex-Bossey and the entrance to the Tennis Club de Genève, where a red clay court awaited them. Changing quickly, they were able to play two vigorous sets before the twilight faded. After showering and dressing, Stevenson suggested a beer and dinner at the small lakeside restaurant in nearby Genthod. They were led to a table on a terrace facing the lake. The lights of Evian twinkled across the way and brightly-lit lake steamers could be seen paddling toward Versoix and Lausanne, further up the lake.

Gazing out over the lake, Stevenson leaned back contentedly. "Well, it's pretty wretched for a lot of people in other places, but it's awfully nice here."

Muller smiled. "Someone in the cafeteria yesterday called it 'a happy city in a shattered world.' It's also become the most expensive city in the world."

"And the League Secretariat is pressing member states to increase salaries and pensions for League employees still more," Stevenson said, smiling. "They say higher pay is necessary because the city is so expensive. But of course, they don't say that it's expensive *because* the League's here."

They ordered filets des perche with frites and a nice bottle of Aigle Les Murailles from the Valais.

"So Muller," said Stevenson when they were served and the waiter had left them, "I wanted to see you about more than just beating you on the tennis court. I've been asking around and I gather you're learning all about Upper Silesia. Not exactly what you'd hoped for I'll bet, right?"

Muller nodded.

"I may have something more interesting for you," continued Stevenson. "It involves Danzig. But let me begin with a primer on how the League works. You probably know some of this, but you'll understand in a moment why I'm telling you.

"The League Assembly is composed of all the nations that are members of the League and it meets annually, in early September; this year's session was just three weeks or so ago."

Muller replied that he had been aware of the meeting but had been trying to get himself situated and hadn't paid much attention.

"Not much real work gets done at the Assembly," said Stevenson. "A lot of Foreign Ministers come to make speeches—delivered here, but really aimed at an audience back home. There are a lot of meetings, a couple of excellent cocktail parties and there are always attractive wives, mistresses and other hangers on that enliven the event." Stevenson smiled knowingly.

"The League Council is where the work gets done. The Treaty writers set it up so Britain, France, Italy and Japan had permanent seats on the Council. Germany was awarded a permanent seat in 1926 and the Japs have now resigned. Then there are ten other nations that are elected to non-permanent seats for a couple of years. The Council meets much more frequently, often several times a month.

"Big countries have delegations resident here more or less full time, since the workload is rather heavy, as you've already experienced from a Secretariat perspective. For example, Britain–including our Dominions–has several hundred people here. We took over the Hotel d'Angleterre, just down the street from the Palais, when the League moved here in 1920, and we're still there. In fact, I'll take you back for a drink tonight on our way home.

"Anyway, to continue," he said, "the Council appoints a one member nation representative to take the lead in organizing each individual agenda issue. Sir John Simon, Britain's Foreign Secretary was appointed, 'Rapporteur'–that's the term that's used–for the League mandate over the Free City of Danzig.

"As you know, the Secretariat has a Danzig Sub-Section too."

"Right," said Muller, "it's located just down the corridor from my office." He felt he had to say something to show he was getting used to League procedures. In fact, he still found the whole process opaque, and he had to admit he was finding Stevenson's comments helpful.

"We also have our own delegation staff working on the Danzig issue," Stevenson continued. "I'm the guy that has charge of that and I report to Anthony Eden, who's an MP and Lord Privy Seal, and to Sir John, who's the Rapporteur, as I said. But he's also Rapporteur for fifteen other issues pending before the Council, so we're pretty damned busy, I can tell you."

Stevenson paused to refill their wine glasses.

"Danzig is a big deal. The League has a mandate to protect Danzig's constitution and it appoints a High Commissioner to oversee its role there. Lately it's become a flashpoint because of conflict with an ascendant local Nazi party.

45

Stevenson took a long sip of wine and smiled at Muller, clearly relishing the tale he was spinning out. "The reason it's pertinent to talk about Danzig tonight is that we're trying to find a new League High Commission there. The last one died, suddenly and inconveniently, almost a year ago. The League appointed an official there on a temporary assignment, a man named Rostig. But he was just a minor official in the Secretariat, a glorified clerk, and not at all what we need. Also, he's just been appointed Director of your Minorities Section here in Geneva when his Danzig term ends.

"Sir John has taken personal charge of the process for appointing a new High Commissioner. Over the past nine months, he's proposed no fewer than 28 potential candidates but each one has been vetoed by Josef Beck, the Polish Foreign Minister. Just yesterday, Sir John proposed two Norwegian lawyers and an even an American. No luck; Beck rejected all three candidates; Norwegians too inexperienced and the American, well—too American.

"Sir John is at the end of his rope and he's decided to bring matters to a head once and for all. He selected his final nominee. The plan is to inform Beck tomorrow afternoon and to tell Beck that, if he won't agree, Sir John will resign as Danzig Rapporteur and publicly blame Beck for the impasse.

Stevenson paused conspiratorially. "This is all confidential, of course, Muller, but you'll understand in a moment why I'm telling you.

"The man Sir John has decided to nominate is Sean Lester, the Permanent Representative to the League from the Irish Free State. Lester became the Irish representative in 1929, so he's been at the League for four years now and he's earned a good reputation as being fair-minded and industrious. He worked on the Manchurian issue, he successfully arbitrated some boundary disputes in Latin America and in March, after Japan left the League, he was appointed Rapporteur for Upper Silesia, taking over the

Japanese responsibility for that file. Sir John has concluded that he would be the right man for what is shaping up as a difficult assignment in Danzig. He approached Lester yesterday and Lester seems willing to take on the job.

"Have you met Lester? The Upper Silesia file is your bailiwick."

"I recognize his name," replied Paul, "but no, I've not met him."

"No matter," said Stevenson. "But here's the thing."

"Lester does not speak a word of German, let alone Polish, and even though he's been here at the League for four years, his French is barely passable. That's a problem. The population of Danzig—even though it's located in the Polish Corridor—is roughly 95 percent German. So, German is the *lingua franca* there. The Polish diplomats and senior officials there all speak French and that's the language they prefer. In fact, when the last High Commissioner tried to address the Polish Consul General in Polish, he was curtly informed that they would either communicate in French or not at all.

"So we have a problem. Sir John is determined to nominate Lester and force Beck to accept him. But Lester can't speak any German at all and speaks French badly. So what's the solution? I have suggested to Sir John that you, Paul Muller, should be appointed Sean Lester's secretary and accompany him to Danzig. You speak fluent German, French and English, so you can be Lester's official translator.

"An elegant solution, it seems to me," concluded Stevenson, with a broad grin on his face. "The League gets a new High Commissioner in Danzig, armed with a well-qualified, tri-lingual secretary to help him communicate, and you get to play a new role and pass the Upper Silesia file along to some other unlucky stiff." He signaled the waiter for a second bottle of Aigle Les Muraille.

Muller was looking intently at Stevenson. Then he stabbed his fork at the last unfinished filet, put it in his mouth and began chewing slowly, his gaze shifting to follow a lake steamer passing toward Geneva. The waiter opened the wine and cleared the table; Stevenson asked for a coupe Danemark dessert "with two spoons."

"What does Lester say to all this?" asked Muller, his mind spinning.

"One of the concerns he expressed in his discussion with Sir John and Eden was about the language barriers. Your assignment solves that issue, so, we're confident he'll agree," said Stevenson. The waiter brought the dessert and retreated.

Muller took a long sip of the new wine and stared down at the bottom of his glass. This seems to be a done deal, he thought to himself. No doubt it's an opportunity for me on a much bigger stage. But it's a trade; I get to be a player and Stevenson gets himself an informer next to Lester. There was probably no way around it, but he decided to test Stevenson's reaction.

"And what do you expect from me, Stevenson?" he asked, raising his eyes and looking directly at Stevenson, unsmiling.

Stevenson locked eyes with him. "To do the job I've described," he said evenly. "As the translator, you're going to grasp nuances in language that Lester can't understand. This may offer insights that you'll need to share with Lester but that we may ask you to share with us too. You'll be employed as a League of Nations diplomat. This is not an assignment involving personal loyalty to Lester; you'll owe your allegiance to the League."

A fair statement as far as it went, thought Muller, and a confirmation that indeed more would be expected.

"This needs to be a two way street," said Muller, continuing to engage Stevenson.

"To the extent possible," replied Stevenson. "You're going to have to trust me."

He would indeed have to trust Stevenson, Muller concluded. This would be a work in progress. But he decided that their brief exchange had laid about as good a foundation as could be expected at this stage.

Muller relaxed, poured them both some more wine, leaned forward smiling, and they clinked glasses. "I can't imagine what you might have planned for me if I'd won both sets," he said. They chuckled together and the tension dissipated.

"Here's the plan over the next couple of days," said Stevenson. "Sir John and Eden will talk with other delegations and the Foreign Office will put the word out to our embassies in the Council countries to garner support for Lester's appointment. The idea is to isolate Beck if he doesn't go along. Our working deadline is October 14, one week from now, since that's the date the appointment of the current acting High Commissioner officially expires. It's also the date that his appointment as Director of the League Minorities Section is scheduled to begin.

"I'll get Sir John to have a word with Lester and suggest that he set up a meeting between the two of you to get acquainted. You'll have to continue with your current job for the time being as this needs to be very hush-hush until the appointment is actually approved. But at least the two of you ought to meet." The wine was finished, so Stevenson asked for the bill.

As they drove back to town, Stevenson put Danzig aside and began speaking about the difficulties being encountered by the leaders of the Disarmament Conference talks that were also going on.

"That's not part of my responsibility, I'm happy to say. But Sir John and Eden have been consumed by the negotiations; it's a tough slog and it's one of the reasons Sir John is so annoyed about the difficulties with the Danzig appointment. There's scarcely time to do everything.

"The PM and the Cabinet have been actively debating the disarmament issues and Sir John has to be in London to negotiate with them; he and Eden were in Berlin in late September to meet with von Neurath, the German Foreign Minister, and then they went to Paris to meet with Daladier and his crowd. I gather the French are being very bloody-minded, though there's nothing new in that. I'm not close enough to the negotiations to be able to predict what's going to happen, but from all the activity, I'd say we're close to either a breakthrough or a breakdown. I just don't know which."

Stevenson pulled up to the entrance to the Hotel d'Angleterre and handed the keys and a few francs to the doorman. "Thanks, Henri," he said. "My friend will need a taxi later, so take good care of him and guard his tennis kit while we have a drink."

They walked inside and Muller reacted with a start. The lobby of the hotel had been decorated to look like it was in Trafalgar Square rather than alongside Lac Léman. All the signage was in English, the front desk looked as if it belonged in an upper class London club, the large dining room had all the trappings of a London restaurant, and across the way was an unmistakably British pub, replete with dartboards, Guiness draft beer levers and ranks of bottles behind the bar bearing British whiskey labels. It was smoky and noisy and crowded with men, and not a few women, all speaking English, loudly.

Stevenson seemed well-known to the crowd. He led Muller to a small table off to one side and was greeted by numerous well-wishers. "Johnny Walker neat?" he inquired. Muller nodded and Stevenson signaled a waiter. "This is where everyone gathers to let off steam," he said. "There's another bar on the other side of the dining room if you need to have a quiet chat, but by this time of night, people want to have some fun. And Geneva can be a lot of fun!" he laughed.

Their drinks came and they began making small talk when a striking brunette came up to the table and breathlessly embraced Stevenson from behind, pressing his shoulders almost to the table.

"Darling," she said a little too loudly. "I've been waiting hours for you; I thought you'd never come. You haven't forgotten about your Carole have you?" she said teasingly.

Stevenson stood and kissed her on both cheeks.

"This is my friend Paul Muller. Muller, this is Carole."

"Carole with an *e*," she said, "*e* for *elegant* and *extravagant*."

"Not to mention *expensive*, added Stevenson, wincing and laughing as Carole elbowed him in the ribs with a dirty look.

It seemed that Carole worked in the Delegation's travel section and it was apparent that she was a regular part of the evening pub scene. And are she and Stevenson lovers, wondered Muller? Probably, he decided. Well, good for him.

The three of them bantered their way through another neat Johnny Walker, but Muller declined a third and bid them good night. Recovering his tennis kit from the doorman, he agreed that a taxi ride back to his apartment was a good idea.

The next morning, Muller decided he should make an inquiry to find out more about his potential new boss. He went down to the first floor of the Palais where the Press Section was located and inquired if there were a biography available of the Permanent Representative of the Irish Free State, a Mr. Sean Lester. He found a helpful clerk who fished a short document out of a filing cabinet and handed it to him with a smile.

The document was not particularly informative. Muller learned that Lester was 45 years of age, having been born in Belfast in 1888. Though a Protestant, he became an Irish nationalist and after a brief stint working for a railway company, he became a journalist, first in the North then later in the South, working for Irish nationalist publications. He had not participated in the Easter Rising in 1915, but he spent the next few years of the ensuing Civil War and the Black and Tan conflict as a member of Sinn Fein and the Irish Republican Brotherhood. After the founding of the Irish Free State in 1922, he had held various positions in the Department of External Affairs and in April 1929, he was appointed as Ireland's representative to the League. The official biography then proceeded to list Lester's League Council assignments, much as Stevenson had described them the night before, including his most recent appointment in March, 1933 as Rapporteur for Upper Silesia.

Not very detailed, but at least it's something, thought Muller to himself. He found it interesting that a Belfast Protestant would embrace an Irish nationalist cause dominated by Catholics. The fact that he did so successfully and was appointed to a senior diplomatic position suggested that Lester was a deft operator. We'll see, he thought, as he went back to his German Knights of Malta hospital petition.

That evening, when he boarded the tram to return to his apartment, he found a special edition of the Journal de Genève on the adjoining seat and picked it up. 'New British Plan' read the headline, followed by a news story reporting that Sir John Simon had delivered a major address that afternoon in the Disarmament Conference. According to the newspaper account, Simon had outlined a comprehensive disarmament plan proposing major force and armament reductions by Britain, France and Germany. Treaty prohibitions on certain German armaments would be lifted, but with strict limitations, including what Simon had referred to as 'a four year trial period' to test German compliance, after which France would undertake the arms reductions outlined in his proposal.

Muller wondered to himself if this were the British initiative that Stevenson had hinted at last night. He supposed that it must be. But was it realistic to expect that Germany would accept a disarmament regime that obliged them to pass a four-year test of good faith compliance before the French would even begin to disarm? Muller thought that seemed unlikely. He decided this must be the opening gambit of a negotiating strategy aimed at staking out a strong position before moving to narrow the differences; it was hard to think it could be anything else.

***

Muller had a rehearsal at the Cathedral St. Pierre that evening. He had joined the Geneva Choral Society soon after coming to town. He knew the director from his university days and had been welcomed into the group. They practiced weekly in a basement room at the Cathedral, which was located very near Muller's apartment. He stopped at a boulangerie and selected some sliced meats and cheese for dinner. At his kitchen table he consumed the meats and cheese with bread and some red wine while looking over the score of the Beethoven C Major Mass, the work they were rehearsing. It was gorgeous, powerful music; but he was finding it challenging as the tempos kept changing. Clearly enough marked in the score, but sometimes counter-intuitive to sing. More practice, he vowed. He just needed to practice more.

***

Two days later, on October 12, when Muller got to his office, he found a note inviting him to a meeting with Sean Lester at 11:00 AM.

Lester's office was on the top floor of the Palais, alongside offices for the other Council member representatives. It faced Geneva's Old Town, topped by the spire of the Cathedral. A lone secretary in the outer office gestured to Muller to enter Lester's open office doorway. Muller was greeted by a slender, very bald man of medium height with a large oval head and prominent ears. Lester had a wide mouth below straight eyebrows. His appearance conveyed a sense of confident poise and welcome.

"Mr. Muller," Lester said as they shook hands, "my new multi-lingual voice," he smiled. "It's very nice to meet you and thank you for coming to see me." He waved Muller to one end of a couch and took the other end himself.

"I'm honored to meet you, sir," said Muller.

"Sir John Simon told me a bit about you," said Lester. "I gather that you speak at least three languages fluently—fortunately, in my case, including English. I'm sure that you can hear my Irish accent. There are not a few who say it interferes with my English, though I've overcome that enough, I think. But I've never been able to master any other tongues. So I'm excited to meet a man who will enable me to express myself in German—and in much better French than I can muster myself. How did you come to be fluent in so many languages?"

"I grew up in Zurich, Mr. Lester," said Muller. "That's the German-speaking region of Switzerland. But my mother's English and we spoke English at home. So that's two of them. Then I learned French in school and even spent a couple of years at university here in Geneva, where, as you know, the language is French. So it came pretty naturally. Actually, I have a little Spanish and Italian too, but don't use them much."

"You make it sound so easy," said Lester with a wistful smile. "I struggle. But what else do you do besides speak three languages?"

"Well, I grew up hiking and skiing in the mountains," Muller replied. "I took up tennis early and I sing."

"Sing? Lester replied, "As in a chorus or choir?"

"Right. I've sung most of the great choral works—the Requiems by Mozart and Brahms, Fauré and others. Actually, I've joined the Geneva Choral Society and right now we're rehearsing for a performance of the

Beethoven C Major Mass, which is a beautiful piece of music, but a little challenging to perform, so I have to put in some extra practice time after work."

"I have to confess to being quite tone-deaf," said Lester with a grin. "But I'm sure it will sound splendidly in the end. As for tennis, I'm afraid there wasn't much of that played in Ireland, when I was young—at least not among the Irish."

As they talked, Muller learned that Lester was married and had three young daughters.

"Elsie and I have learned to ski here in Switzerland. The girls are beginners and very enthusiastic. I expect the flat plains of Northern Germany won't offer much in the way of downhill opportunities."

"But I'm mainly a fisherman," he said. "Fly-fishing is a passion and I gather the environs of Danzig offer a lot of fishing options, so I'm looking forward to that."

Lester went on, more serious now. "I assume that you are no more expert than I in the issues involved in the League mandate for Danzig. If this appointment goes through, we'll both need to put in some serious study. I gather it's a very complicated story. Lately, it seems to have become the focus of conflict between a local Nazi party, heavily influenced by the Nazi Party in Germany, and the League's mandate to protect the rights of Danzig citizens which are guaranteed under the Danzig Constitution. One colleague told me that Danzig is headed toward becoming the powder keg of Europe. I hope that's not an accurate prediction, but it does seem that these are fraught times there. If this appointment comes to pass, I'll get the Secretariat to prepare detailed briefing documents for us both to study.

"But agreement on my appointment has still not been reached." Lester added. "So this is no sure thing. As I understand it from Sir John, a private Council meeting has been convened for the afternoon of the 14th, two days from now. At that point, Sir John will put my name forward formally. The British have apparently been busy rounding up support among all the other Council members except the Poles, where Beck has continued to balk at any solution. Sir John intends to force the issue and believes that he can ultimately win Polish acceptance.

"So we'll have to see," said Lester. "I've told Sir John that if his plan doesn't succeed I will withdraw my name. I don't want to be put in a position of appearing to plead for the job. Either the whole Council will forthrightly agree to the appointment or I don't want any part of it."

"Is there anything you would like me to do?" asked Muller.

"No," replied Lester. "For now, sit tight. But let's remain in touch. Thank you for coming by. I rather hope that we get the chance to go to Danzig together. I've always wanted to be able to speak in fluent German and French." He smiled as they shook hands.

This is an impressive man, Muller thought to himself as he returned to his office. He seems very comfortable with himself and doesn't seem to be bossy. A Danzig appointment began to appear even more attractive.

CHAPTER 4

Autumn 1933

October 14 was grey and rainy, the lake the color of slate. Muller was late to work and proceeded to go through the motions, his mind on the upcoming Council meeting. He was sitting in the cafeteria at lunch engaged in desultory conversation with a group of his colleagues when suddenly there was a commotion by the entrance doorway; loud voices, hurried departures, a sudden scurrying.

"The Germans have withdrawn," someone spoke over the din. People reacted as if struck by a shockwave, looking at one another in disbelief. "What? What?" General pandemonium ensued.

Muller wolfed down the last bite of his sandwich and followed most of the crowd toward the first floor Press Section to find out what was going on. People milled around the corridor for about 30 minutes. Finally, a Press Section attaché hauled a chair into the corridor and stood on the seat, asking people to quiet down.

"Here's what we know," he said. "At noon today, the German representative to the League, Hermann von Keller, handed a note to League Secretary General Avenol stating that Germany was withdrawing from the League of Nations effective immediately. No reasons were given in the note. Mr. von Keller advised the Secretary General that Chancellor Hitler would be making a speech in Berlin announcing Germany's decision to the world.

"We don't yet have a transcript of Chancellor Hitler's remarks or the text of any written statement. We have only a German news wire report; here's what it says." He put on his glasses and began reading.

'Today, Germany withdrew from the League of Nations and its so-called Disarmament Conference because of the offensive proposals offered recently at the Conference aimed at imposing a new and humiliating four year "trial period" upon Germany. The peace-loving people of Germany have repeatedly called upon world leaders to repeal the arbitrary and fundamentally unfair burdens imposed upon our nation by the Versailles Treaty. Instead of reciprocating German good faith, these leaders have proposed a new layer of insult. They have said that Germans are not to be trusted, so Germany must disarm further today and then–four years later, provided they are satisfied with our behavior during those four years–they will begin to disarm.

'Germany rejects being put on probation.

'Germany is a great and proud nation. We stand ready to contribute our fair share to achieving a safer and more peaceful world. But Germans expect to be treated as an equal in that quest. Germans strive for peace but we also demand justice. The League of Nations is a residue of the Treaty of Versailles and its unfair burdens. The League seeks to perpetuate–and now even to expand–its unjust treatment of Germany. Today Germany has responded. Germany continues to embrace the search for enduring peace and the goals of disarmament. So we say to other nations, come to us with constructive proposals for peace. But come to us as equals. And do not come to us in the guise of the League of Nations.'"

As the Press Attaché concluded, journalists began shouting questions.

"Will the Secretary General hold a press conference?"

"What's the response of the League?"

"Is the Disarmament Conference being dissolved?"

He waved them away and stepped down from his chair. "That's all I have for now."

Suddenly everyone in the crowded corridor began speaking all at once:

"How's that for a kick in the balls?"

"How can they just walk out?"

"I suppose they'll cancel the January Health Conference in Munich now. Shit, I was going to sneak off and ski."

"We're going to look silly in the eyes of the world."

Muller wandered up the stairs back to his office and slumped into his chair. Questions raced through his mind.

Would this announcement change Sir John Simon's Danzig plan? Did they even hold the afternoon meeting, or was it postponed after they learned about Germany's withdrawal? The British had so many balls in the air here aimed at engaging the Germans, they won't want to pile on now in the wake of the withdrawal notice; so will Sir John have second thoughts about threatening to resign over Danzig? On the other hand, wouldn't solving Danzig allow the League to proceed with a show of business as usual despite Germany's withdrawal? Muller shook his head. The only way to answer the questions was to find Stevenson, so he decided to look for him at the Hotel d'Angleterre. But first he paid a visit to Sean Lester's office, telling Lester's secretary to call the Hotel's switchboard and have him paged if Mr. Lester needed to find him.

The secretary smiled. "Mr. Lester has gone over there too."

The Lobby of the Hotel d'Angleterre was crowded, with people standing in knots, talking excitedly. The elevators were in constant motion, the operators looking harried in their red uniforms; dressed almost like beefeaters, thought Muller, absently. He inquired at the desk if Stevenson were in the hotel and was told that he was out. Muller decided to wait. He bought a beer and took a seat in the pub where he could see the entrance and the lobby.

Less than an hour later he saw Stevenson push through the front entrance carrying a large briefcase and trailed by two younger men who appeared to be clerks. Muller moved to intercept him at the elevator. Stevenson turned and grinned broadly.

"Muller! Exciting day, eh? Look, I've got to get a couple of cables off to London. Give me an hour and I'll come down and fill you in; a lot going on." He disappeared into one of the elevators followed by his clerks.

Muller retreated to his seat in the pub and nursed his beer. An hour later he saw Sean Lester emerge from an elevator headed for the door. He resisted the urge to go after Lester. Not yet, he thought.

It was another thirty minutes before Stevenson reappeared. He motioned for Muller to join him in the other bar beyond the dining room. "A bit more private here." They sat in two upholstered chairs set close to one another with a small table in front. He ordered two Johnny Walkers neat.

"Well, Herr Hitler certainly has a flair for the dramatic; I'll give him that," said Stevenson. "We had no inking this was coming. They didn't even bother to inform any of the Ambassadors in Berlin until after the fact. And what a typical Hitler message; menace wrapped in cheesecloth.

"Whitehall is all in a tizzy, of course. A lot of urgent cable traffic back and forth. I think the line we've adopted is to downplay the whole thing and treat it just as a ploy that Germany will try to use as leverage in continuing negotiations. And maybe that's what it really is," he added. "The four year 'trial period' was a French demand that we thought was pretty over the top anyway. So maybe this is a way to move that off the table and get to something more palatable to everyone. But even if we downplay it, those negotiations are at a standstill. Glad it's not my brief." He smiled.

"Anyway, it didn't derail the Danzig business. Sir John put Lester's name forward. Beck objected. As per the plan, other delegates spoke favorably of Lester's qualifications. De Madiaraga, Spain's Foreign Minister, was particularly forceful. France and Italy then questioned Beck on why he was opposed, noting that it could hardly be on personal grounds and Lester's professional qualifications were unquestioned. Sir John then displayed some temper, not very feigned either, observing that he had been thwarted for nearly a year by Beck's opposition to 28—now 29—candidates. He would not consent to yet another adjournment. Failure to agree would compel him to resign as Rapporteur and publicly assign blame to Poland, where it frankly belonged. The Australian, I forget his name, spoke about how weak and ineffectual the Council appeared to the public with these repeated delays. Especially today, after the German walkout, he argued that the last thing the League needed was a public squabble on this important issue.

"Beck was now on the defensive, so he asked for a recess and approached Sir John privately. As I understand it, he said that he would agree to the Lester appointment, but only on October 26, two weeks hence. It seems that Poland assumes the Chair of the Council on October 24. So, he said, if Sir John announced the appointment on October 26, two days later, and included language to the effect that the views of the Polish Chair had been taken into account in the appointment process, he would endorse the package.

"So, we seem to have a deal," concluded Stevenson. "Beck gets some political capital and Danzig gets a new High Commissioner. Eden briefed Lester this afternoon, and he's apparently satisfied too.

"So it looks like you're going to have a new job. I guess we'll have to resume our tennis competition in Danzig."

***

The next morning, Muller attended a meeting convened called by Jaczck Demchuk to sort out the consequences of the German withdrawal on the Minorities Sub-Section's workload. He observed that since the League no longer had jurisdiction within the boundaries of Germany, files relating to German Silesia were to be closed. He concluded by saying that Milhan Rostig had been appointed Director of the Minorities Section. But, he said, Rostig was still serving as acting High Commissioner for the League in Danzig and would not assume his new responsibilities here until after his successor had been appointed and taken up his post in Danzig. Demchuk didn't know when that would be. Muller observed no reaction whatever to the announcement among his colleagues.

When he arrived back at his desk, he had a note asking him to visit Sean Lester at 2:00 that afternoon.

"Well, Mr. Muller, it looks like we'll be going to Danzig together," said Lester as they exchanged handshakes. "I assume someone has briefed you."

Muller nodded. "I gather the announcement is to be made on October 26."

"That's right," Lester replied. "I gave Anthony Eden a letter last night withdrawing my name as I said I would do in the event of an adjournment. But I told him that I would accept the appointment if it is in fact offered to me, and he seemed to think that was fine.

"Incidentally, do you know Eden?"

Muller smiled and shook his head. "Mr. Lester, I'm a pretty junior Secretariat clerk. I don't travel in those circles, I'm afraid."

Lester chuckled. "I know what you mean. It wasn't very long ago that I was a young Irish revolutionary trying to stay one jump ahead of the Black and Tans. Then when the Irish Free State was established, I was a pretty junior guy myself in the External Relations Department and being appointed Permanent Representative here came as a surprise. It was a big step up—for both Elsie and me; we'd never even traveled outside of Ireland at the time. So I understand your comment.

"In fact I think about that occasionally when dealing with Eden. He's everything an Irish revolutionary used to hate about Englishmen: Eton, Oxford, moneyed, privileged, war hero, elected to the House when he was only 26, a bit aloof." Lester paused and smiled at the image he'd drawn of Eden. "But he's damned intelligent and Westminster holds him in high regard. I dealt extensively with him earlier this year when I became Rapporteur for Upper Silesia. One of my files involved a petition by a German Jew who complained about the Nazi racial laws that deprived him of his livelihood as a notary. It caused quite a stir in the Council because of the odious nature of the Nazi laws. The French and the Czechs and some other members of the Council wanted to pounce on the petition and use it as a stick to attack Hitler and the Nazis. I thought that went well beyond the Council's jurisdiction in the matter. Eden agreed and we worked quite closely to tamp things down."

Lester turned to Muller with a broad smile, pulling out a pack of cigarettes, offering one to Muller and lighting them both with a gold Dunhill lighter.

"I found, rather to my surprise, that I enjoyed Eden's company. He's a decade younger than I—only about ten years your senior, in fact—but he has a lot of experience and good judgment. And even a sense of humor sometimes."

"I mention this because it turns out that Sir John's term as Rapporteur for Danzig is expiring and Eden will take over his role next week. So we will be working together on this business and I expect you will meet him in due course–even though I won't need your translation services in communicating with him.

"I'll look forward to that, Mr. Lester," replied Muller. "I expect there will be a lot of new people and places to become acquainted with."

"Precisely," said Lester," and that leads me to the subject of the role I think you should play going forward. I've been thinking about that during the past few days." Lester shifted forward in his chair.

"Obviously you will be my translator in meetings where German and French are being spoken. But I've concluded I'm likely to need some assistance beyond mere translation. I will have no other staff out there beyond you–and a couple of typists, that I don't expect will offer any substantive help. Geneva will not be readily accessible for guidance or discussion. I assume the phones are not secure and the mail is slow at best. So most of the time, I'm going to have to rely on my own judgment. But I believe that judgment will occasionally need some polishing. And I'm hoping that you can fill that role.

"I'm thinking that you should assume the role of–well, I'm not sure of what the right title is, Staff Assistant? Special Advisor? We'll figure out a title. Probably Secretary, now that I think of it. Anyway, someone in whom I can confide and who can help me puzzle through the issues I'm going to face."

Muller listened intently as he stubbed out his cigarette.

"These are early days," Lester continued. "We don't know one another well. Neither of us knows much about the issues we'll face, though I think we can both assume they'll be challenging. But I'd like to start off by assuming that the role I've described will work for both of us. So I want us both to get briefed about Danzig together. I don't plan on having any secret agenda when I assume the new post. I just want to be well-informed—and I want you to be well-informed too, then we'll have to see how we can work together in our respective roles once we get to Danzig.

"What do you think?" Lester asked.

Muller took a moment to reflect; Lester was offering him the chance to play a substantive role in dealing with the Danzig conflict, one of Europe's most important hotspots. This was even better than he had hoped.

"I'm flattered, sir," Muller replied. "I'd like to think that I'm qualified to play the role you envision. You know that my family is in banking. But somehow that profession never attracted me. I've always been more interested in government policy issues. Political science is a bit of a misnomer I think, but that's the course of study I've followed. I decided to cut short my studies at Cambridge and get a job at the League secretariat because I wanted to get involved. You're offering me an opportunity to do exactly what I've wanted to do. So, yes; I'm happy to agree.

"In fact, I'm actually quite delighted to accept your offer," Muller added, smiling broadly."

"Good," said Lester. "Let's try to make it work for both of us.

"I've asked Eden to have his delegation pull together some briefing materials for us. We can't approach the Danzig staff here in the Secretariat yet. I suspect the caliber of the British Whitehall staff is higher anyway and that we'll get a better work product from them. Eden said he would aim to have something ready in two to three weeks, shortly after the appointment is scheduled to be announced."

Lester rose and they shook hands. "After the appointment, I'll have another desk moved to the outer office for you. But for now, I'm afraid you have to go back to Upper Silesia."

***

A week later, Muller returned to his apartment to find a telegram slipped under his door. He slit the envelope.

ARRIVING GENEVA OCT 27 COME COCKTAILS 19:00 STE 501 D"ANGLETERRE LOVE JERUSALEM

He jotted a reply and stopped by the telegraph office on his way out to dinner.

YES JOIN ME ANNECY OCT 28 LOVE JERUSALEM

At the same time, he wired the Imperial Palace Hotel in Annecy for a lake-view suite and a booking for two in the grand Salon dining room for the night of October 28. By that time I should have something to celebrate, Muller said to himself. Eirene will love it. He was sure he would too.

The Council meeting on October 26 formally appointing Lester was anti-climactic. Nations were represented by junior delegates, as the arrangements had been agreed in advance. Lester's name was put forward by the chair and a unanimous vote of approval followed. Rostig was directed to remain in Danzig until January, when Lester would assume his responsibilities. The League issued a press release announcing the appointment. No mention was made of Muller's appointment as Lester's Secretary, but Muller took several copies and mailed them, with a handwritten explanation, to his father in Zurich and to Robert Bigelow in London. He kept a copy for himself and another to hand to Eirene.

The next evening, Muller arrived at Suite 501 of the Hotel d'Angleterre at 7 PM. The door opened and Eirene invited him in, offering her cheek.

"Change of plan," she said. "Leave your coat here, and we're going down the corridor to Anthony Eden's big suite. I invited him to join us but he's too busy and instead asked me to come around for a quick 30 minute drink and I want you to come with me. I've asked the others to delay until 7:30, so let's go now." She took his arm.

Muller smiled to himself. *Of course* Eirene knew Eden; that's how Britain worked.

The door to Eden's suite was opened by a butler who directed them into the main sitting room. Anthony Eden was sitting with a group of other men, who scooped up loose papers and hastily exited, Eden telling them to return in 30 minutes.

"Eirene," he said rising and greeting her with an embrace and kisses on both cheeks. "Your father told me you'd be coming to town; I'm glad we can spend at least a few minutes together."

"Anthony, you're too kind," replied Eirene smiling broadly at him. "Let me introduce Paul Muller, who is a good friend and newly appointed to the Secretariat."

"Ah, Mr. Muller," said Eden, smiling and offering his hand. "I've been hearing a lot about you during the Danzig business. It seems that you've solved one of our main sticking points with the new appointment. Stevenson speaks highly of you and I gather Lester has taken to you too. So I'm very pleased to meet you."

Eirene looked confused.

"You haven't heard?" said Eden. "The League has just appointed a new High Commissioner for Danzig, an important post that we've been trying for months to fill. The new man is Sean Lester, Ireland's representative to the League. He's highly qualified but speaks no German and not very good French. So our Mr. Muller here is to become Lester's Secretary, serving as his translator in both languages, and I gather from Lester, as a shadow advisor as well."

Eirene looked at Muller. "Well," she said. "I didn't know. Congratulations."

"The final arrangements were not completed until just yesterday," said Eden, "so no one's been holding out on you Eirene." He smiled and motioned them to be seated, as waiters delivered flutes of champagne.

As Eden and Eirene began chatting about family and mutual friends, Muller took the opportunity to observe Eden. He was tall, slender, and extraordinarily handsome, sporting a bushy reddish mustache beneath combed-back hair of the same color. What struck Muller was how graceful he appeared. His carriage projected poise and confidence—almost a sense of entitlement. He was a formidable presence.

"So Anthony," Eirene was saying, "You probably know from Daddy that I'm here to generate support for the League of Nations Union. Among other things, I hope to raise a little money. I need to sound very well-informed if I am to be persuasive, so I need you to give me the insider's view on what's happening with the disarmament negotiations."

"Eirene, you need no help from me to be persuasive." Eden smiled.

"Anthony," said Eirene archly. "Don't start being evasive."

Eden took his flute of champagne and raised it to both of them, taking a small sip before replying.

"Well, it's certainly no secret that the Disarmament Conference is in difficulty. It was pretty much a stand-off even before the Germans walked out. We were already exasperated with Germany's escalating demands and this latest step offers further evidence that Hitler seems determined on rearmament. The question is how far and how fast.

"You're aware of the published rumors that Hitler has already begun at least some production of prohibited weapons. I'll say only that we're actively monitoring that subject. But German rearmament is not entirely irresponsible. From their perspective, being held to the punitive levels demanded by the Treaty shows the French and ourselves to be hypocritical; we expound on the virtues of disarmament, but we've been unwilling to reduce our own forces to their levels. So they feel entitled to rearm to some degree, notwithstanding the Treaty restrictions which were imposed a decade and a half ago and hardly seem suited to the current state of affairs.

"So what the Cabinet has agreed upon is to seek a broad settlement of outstanding issues with the Germans, including an agreement that would limit any German rearmament program to levels that can't threaten its neighbors." Eden paused to sip his champagne. "The idea is to establish some kind of new equilibrium that will remove some of the Treaty's territorial and military restrictions so the Germans no longer feel themselves treated as second class citizens, and then find a means for managing that equilibrium."

This certainly sounds familiar, Muller said to himself; it seemed pretty clear that Eden was pursuing precisely the approach that everyone at Berkshire Abbey—everyone except Duncan Elliott, that is—had advocated.

Eden paused and sipped more champagne, then he continued. "Frankly, we don't yet see eye to eye on this approach with the French. They're dead set against permitting any German rearmament and they're quite firmly entrenched on this four year trial period that triggered the walkout. So we have some serious work to do with them too if our plan is to have any chance at success. And they keep changing governments so often that their negotiators always seem to be new people. It's a rather difficult problem, actually."

"But Anthony, surely you aren't going to abandon the League's Disarmament Conference," said Eirene. "That's such an important project."

"Well, there doesn't seem to be any point I trying to restart the Conference if Germany isn't going to be participating," Eden said patiently. "I think the best you can expect is an indefinite adjournment while we try to pursue our plan for a broader settlement."

"But what about our plan to disband all national air forces and create a League Air Force monopoly?"

"Time will tell, Eirene; time will tell. And that," he said smiling, "is about as far as I'm willing to go."

He took the last sip of champagne, looked at his watch and stood up.

"It's time I got back to work and you must go greet your guests." He steered them to the door, once more kissing Eirene on both cheeks, and turning to Muller said, "Mr. Muller, it's likely we'll see one another again before you depart for Danzig. It was nice to meet you."

***

The weekend in Annecy with Eirene was a success. She had never been there before and was charmed by the hilly scenery on the short train ride south from Geneva and by the understated elegance of the small resort town. The Imperial Palace Hotel was as grand as its name implied, a large, elegant structure on neatly trimmed grounds alongside Lac d'Annecy, facing East, with a breathtaking view across the sparkling lake to the high Alps.

After a late lunch they strolled along the lakefront, admiring the nearby castle and the row of neat storefronts with their colorful awnings. Returning to the suite, they fell into one another's arms and made passionate love, then napped. Awakening after dark, they dressed, enjoyed a gin at the bar and dined on fresh fish in the Grand Salon dining room which, at that time of year, boasted only a few other diners. After a brandy, they returned to the suite, made love again, and slept soundly until awakened by bright morning sunlight streaming in through the tall windows. After making love again—this time in the spacious bathroom shower stall—they had a light breakfast and took a boat across the lake to Talloires, gazing up at the towering mountains and admiring the picturesque little village. They lunched sumptuously on the sunny terrace of the Auberge Per Bise, and dozed on the train ride back to Geneva.

Eirene accepted Muller's invitation to spend Sunday night in his apartment, so they walked around Geneva's Old City, with its narrow, cobblestoned alleys, then went for dinner to the nearby restaurant Palais de Justice, one of Muller's favorites.

They returned to the remarks Eden had made to them Friday evening and which they had discussed off and on during the weekend at Annecy. "Some journalists are starting to call British policy toward Germany 'appeasement'," said Eirene. "It's a term Anthony used in the House and it seems to capture the goal of making the right kinds of concessions to avoid future conflict. I think it has a very good ring to it, don't you?"

"Anyway," she continued, not waiting for his response, "I keep thinking of what good news Anthony's remarks were for my League of Nations Union. Our influence with the government seems to be growing."

Their filet de perche and frites arrived along with a bottle of cool Fendant from the Valais. As they ate, Eirene gaily recounted her exploits on behalf of the Union. Muller listened with amusement to her enthusiastic tales.

Then, after they finished their meal and lit cigarettes, she said, "I'm probably not supposed to tell you this, but over the past several months, Daddy's been spending occasional weekends at Cliveden, in Buckinghamshire. It's the country home of Lord and Lady Astor. There's a group of rather prominent and politically influential individuals who are like-minded about trying to repair relations with Germany. They meet informally at Cliveden to discuss how to advance what we're now calling appeasement. Lord Lothian, who used to be Philip Kerr, the author and politician, is a regular, along with Geoffrey Dawes, Editor of the *Times*, Arnold Toynbee, the historian, and a number of others, including Daddy.

Nancy Astor is a superb hostess, so it's apparently a good opportunity for combining weekend socializing with serious political discussion.

"Anyway, Daddy told me that Toynbee had visited Hitler earlier this fall and came back raving about the meeting. He found Hitler to be charming and intelligent and quite reasonable, though very annoyed about punishment still being inflicted upon Germany by the Treaty prohibitions all these years after the war and after all the suffering Germany endured to pay off the huge reparations bill they were handed."

She giggled. "Actually, Toynbee and Dawes got so carried away with the success of his visit that they wrote up a summary of the trip and invited themselves to Downing Street to deliver it in person to the Prime Minister. MacDonald's in failing health and he waved them off to Baldwin, who's increasingly the power behind the throne. So, Dawes and Toynbee went straightaway to visit Baldwin with their report in hand, pressing him to make a visit to Berlin and settle everything with Hitler. Well, it's no secret that Stanley Baldwin is a very unworldly man; he's never traveled outside England—well, maybe as far as Wales—and he has little interest in foreign affairs. According to Daddy, Baldwin replied that he couldn't envision traveling anywhere, let alone to Berlin. He hates boats and is terrified of even the thought of flying, so it was quite out of the question. He left them with the distinct impression that they were wasting his time.

"It's an amusing anecdote and also a little sad," she said wistfully. "But Daddy persuaded Toynbee to put in a word with the Germans that Daddy would be pleased to accept an invitation from Hitler, and he's been led to believe that he'll receive one soon. He's very excited."

Muller smiled. "If your father gets his coveted invitation, then *he* can be the one to make a deal with Hitler to save the world."

Eirene elbowed him in the ribs. "This isn't funny business," she said. "It's serious."

They finished their wine, Muller paid the check and they walked hand-in-hand down the hill to his apartment, where they scampered toward the bedroom, shedding articles of clothing.

The next morning, Muller arose early, put the tea on to boil and went around the corner to pick up croissants.

"I'm not quite sure how a weekend like this is supposed to end," he said to Eirene as she wolfed down the pastry.

"Well, I suppose we could go back to bed," said Eirene laughing. "Actually, don't say a word. It's been fun. Let's see where it goes. I've always wanted to visit Danzig."

Eirene stepped off the tram in front of the Hotel d'Angleterre, two stops before it reached the Palais. She waved back at Muller and blew him a kiss before going inside to gather up her things and depart for Paris.

Yes, thought Muller, let's see where this goes.

Later that morning Sean Lester installed Muller at a desk in his outer office. "Eden is having the Whitehall Danzig brief delivered by noon," he said. "In the meantime, I'm arranging clearances for both of us to get access to the Secretariat's Danzig dossiers that I'm told are quite extensive. It's time for us to go to work on this business."

CHAPTER 5

November and December, 1933

CONFIDENTIAL

November 1, 1933

To the High Commissioner for the Free City of Danzig:
Mr. Sean Lester

From His Majesty's Foreign Office: Mr. Anthony Eden MP

In Re: The League of Nations: The Free City of Danzig Mandate

Historic Antecedents

The nation of Poland ceased to exist in 1795, its territory having been divided between Prussia and Russia. It was simply wiped off the map. The cause of Polish nationalism persisted, however, and achieved success in the upheavals accompanying the end of the World War. The Treaty of Versailles stripped defeated Germany of vast territories in the East by creating the new nation of Czechoslovakia and re-establishing the nation of Poland.

What became the Free City of Danzig was a major source of contention in the Treaty negotiations that led to this result.

On January 21, 1918, US President Woodrow Wilson announced his famous Fourteen Points for Peace. In November 1918, Germany requested an armistice based on 'the stipulation that the peace to follow would be in accordance with Wilson's Fourteen Points'.

Beginning in January 1919, the Supreme Council of the Great Powers, US President Woodrow Wilson, British Prime Minister David Lloyd George, French President Georges Clemenceau and Italian Prime Minister Vittorio Orlando, met to draft the terms of the peace. Neither Germany (as it was not invited) nor Poland (as it did not yet exist) were parties to the treaty negotiations.

The starting point for the negotiations relating to Poland was the text of Point number thirteen in Wilson's January 1918 document which read as follows:

> *"An independent Polish state should be erected which should include territories inhabited by indisputably Polish populations, which should be assured a free and secure access to the sea, and whose political and economic independence and territorial integrity should be guaranteed by international covenant."*

The Supreme Council appointed a Commission on Polish Affairs on February 12, 1919 and charged it with recommending terms of reference for a new Polish state along the lines of Wilson's formulation. The Commission issued its report in Mid-March 1919, drawing generous boundaries for Poland. It proposed what it called 'the Polish Corridor', a narrow strip of land assigned to Poland that extended from the Polish interior due north to the Baltic Sea. The effect was to divide Germany, splitting off East Prussia on one side of the Corridor, separated from the rest of the country on the other side. The Corridor followed the path of the Vistula River and included the port City of Danzig, situated at the mouth of the Vistula where it empties into the Baltic Sea.

The geographic significance of Danzig was lost on no one. Frederick the Great had said over a century earlier, 'Whoever possesses the Mouth of the Vistula and the City of Danzig will be more master of Poland than any King who rules there.' So Danzig was to be the centerpiece of the new Polish Corridor, implementing Wilson's pledge to assure Poland 'free and secure access to the sea'. But Danzig had been part of Prussia for over a hundred years. Of the roughly 350,000 citizens living in Danzig in 1919, all but a handful were German and spoke only German. When word of the proposed settlement leaked out, outraged opposition sparked massive street demonstrations in Danzig.

Clemenceau, wanting the strongest possible Poland as a counterweight to Germany, supported the Commission's Report. Lloyd George, mindful of German resentment at handing Danzig over to Poland, did not. In a moment of high drama during the Supreme Council meeting on March 19, Lloyd George declared, "Gentlemen, if we give Danzig to the Poles, the Germans will not sign the treaty, and if they do not sign, our work here is a failure."

In fevered discussions after adjournment, it was acknowledged that while the Commission's report was faithful to the terms of Wilson's pledge to assure Poland access to the sea, it was in conflict with another of Wilson's negotiating principles: the right of self-determination by the people affected by the negotiations—in this case, the Germans in Danzig—and in Germany—who opposed the plan.

Ultimately a compromise was reached. Danzig was carved out of the Polish Corridor and was designated a Free City, under the protection of the League of Nations. This new Free City of Danzig was neither Polish nor German; instead it became a League of Nations mandate. As someone observed at the time, Danzig would provide Polish access to the sea as Wilson had promised, but it would not be part of Poland.

This negotiated settlement was enshrined in its own separate Section IX of the Treaty of Versailles.

The Treaty went on to provide that the residents of Danzig would vote to establish their own Constitution which 'would be placed under the guarantee of the League of Nations', and it provided for appointment by the League of a High Commissioner residing in Danzig to oversee this guarantee.

The Treaty of Versailles came into force on January 20, 1920. Three weeks later, on February 13, 1920, British troops entered Danzig one hour after the last German soldiers had departed. A Constitutional Assembly was promptly elected by Danzig's citizens and it voted to adopt a Constitution modeled on that of the Weimar Republic, enshrining basic democratic freedoms. This Danzig Constitution was accepted by the League of Nations and the Free City came into being on November 15, 1920.

This result satisfied none of the affected parties. To the Germans, it was a hateful part of a peace dictated by the Great Powers that casually dispensed with the right of self-determination among affected Germans, split off East Prussia from the rest of the country, forcibly consigned millions of Germans to live under Polish rule and arbitrarily removed Danzig from German control. For Poland, creation of the Free City seriously devalued the Treaty's cession of the Polish Corridor by removing the port city that was the whole point of offering access to the Baltic. Danzigers were obliged to choose between renouncing German citizenship and becoming citizens of the Free City (whatever that meant!) or retaining German citizenship and physically re-locating to Germany within a year.

It will come as no surprise that, in the dozen or so years that have passed since the Free City came into being, national resentments have continued to fester.

Governance of Danzig

In addition to enshrining principals of democratic rule, the Danzig Constitution established a familiar parliamentary system of government.

1. An elected assembly (Volkstag) to enact laws;

2. An executive branch (Senate) to administer laws, with officials selected by the Volkstag;

3. An independent judicial system to adjudicate laws;

Political party organizations compete for support in the electorate.

The League's High Commissioner acquired no executive authority under the Treaty and plays no role in actual governance of the Free City. The High Commissioner, as the representative of the League of Nations, is arbiter of conflicts between Danzig and Poland and guarantor of Danzig's Constitution.

Between 1920 and 1933, this structure functioned effectively and the role of the High Commissioner was confined almost entirely to managing conflicts between Danzig and Poland, of which there were many, but which are not relevant this briefing paper.

The situation changed fundamentally after an election on May 28, 1933 when the Danzig Nazi party, the National Socialist German Workers Party (NSDAP, as it is known locally) won control of the Volkstag and appointed a Senate composed entirely of NSDAP members. Although the margin of victory was paper-thin (NSDAP candidates won 50.03 percent of the vote), Party leaders sought to install a Nazi regime modeled on what Hitler was doing at the same time in Germany.

This has created a very different set of challenges in Danzig for the League of Nations and its new High Commissioner as he assumes office.

Political Victory of the NSDAP

Despite having been physically separated from Germany and having become a League of Nations mandate, Danzig continues to be a predominantly German enclave. German is the *lingua franca* and Danzigers are immersed in German culture, German commerce and German politics.

The rise of the NSDAP as a political force in Danzig has paralleled quite closely that of the Nazi Party in Germany and the Nazi Party has a decisive influence over NSDAP leaders and their policies. Hitler sent his deputy, Hermann Goering, to Danzig in 1927 to lay the foundation for the NSDAP and appointed Albert Forster as Gauleiter (Party leader) for Danzig in 1930. Forster, a Bavarian, has been part of Hitler's inner-circle since the early days of Hitler's rise to power. He is a self-appointed "beloved disciple" of Julius Streicher, publisher of the notoriously anti-semitic 'Die Sturm' and, according to our sources, hates Jews, Poles, Socialists, Bolsheviks, Conservatives, Liberals and Catholics. While uneducated, he is an accomplished rabble-rousing speaker and ranks as the most powerful NSDAP leader in Danzig today.

The NSDAP managed to win 16 percent of the vote in 1930 (roughly comparable to the Nazi's 18.3 percent showing in Germany in the same year). During the next three years Forster and his deputy Albert Greiser, another uncompromising Party leader, mounted an energetic campaign to gain power, heavily financed by the German Nazi Party. The NSDAP established its own newspaper '*Verpost*' ('Outpost') prominently featuring its motto 'Back to the Reich'. Hitler Youth and League of Hitler Maidens organizations flourished. Most important, the Party organized a large cadre of SA Brown Shirt storm troopers, mainly composed of street toughs, which it used to disrupt and terrorize opposition rallies.

While the Danzig NSDAP was growing in strength, it by no means had the stage to itself. The German National People's Party (DNVP), a Conservative German nationalist grouping, controlled the Volkstag, and the Catholic Centre Party, the trade union-backed Social Democratic

Party and even a small Communist Party were actively jostling for power. All of these political organizations were largely local branches of their parent organizations in Germany.

The NSDAP was energized by Hitler's appointment as German Chancellor on January 31, 1933. But during the run up to the May 1933 election in Danzig, all of the parties felt constrained by the legal framework of the Danzig Constitution and none of them wanted to risk falling afoul of the League's guarantee or facing criticism from the High Commissioner. Two weeks before the election Forster and Greiser paid a visit to Rostig, the Acting High Commissioner, promising that the NSDAP would not disrupt free elections and that, if it took power, it would uphold the Constitution.

The NSDAP pulled out all the stops during the campaign, draping buildings with swastika flags and banners and holding raucous political rallies featuring fiery speeches by leading Nazis from Germany, including Goering, Himmler and Goebbels. The night before the election Hitler himself addressed a speech to his Danzig supporters. He delivered it in Munich but the NSDAP arranged to have it broadcast in Danzig by radio, setting up loudspeakers on street corners to transmit his message. Invoking the 'common blood' of Danzigers and Germans, Hitler concluded with a call to 'unity under the swastika."

The May 28 polling took place by secret ballot and occurred without serious incident. The outcome was very close: NSDAP 107,331, Opposition 106,797, a victory for the NSDAP by a margin of .03 percent.

The victory of a Nazi Party in a free election attracted international notoriety. While hailed in Germany, the event generated critical press attention in France, Britain and the USA.

Danzig: The Current Situation

Upon securing its victory, the NSDAP invited the Catholic Centre Party into coalition. While this is a conciliatory step, we view it as a largely symbolic and short term arrangement, as no members of the Centre Party were appointed to positions in the Senate, which is the City's governing body.

Hermann Rauschning was appointed President of the Senate. Though a member of the German Nazi Party since the late 1920's when he lived in Germany, he is seen by many observers as a 'moderate' in the NSDAP. Well-educated and worldly, he moved to Danzig in 1930 and took up farming, becoming President of a local agricultural organization which supported the NSDAP. Before being sworn into office, Rauschning paid a visit to Hitler in Berlin, accompanied by Forster. Our sources report that the Fuehrer instructed the two leaders to avoid conflict with the League, telling them that the Danzig question would be dealt with by the Reich.

Upon his return from Berlin and after assuming office, Rauschning spoke to representatives of the local press and reaffirmed the Senate's commitment to the Constitution and the Treaties. Contemporaneous statements by Forster were more bellicose, emphasizing that Danzig is 'linked to the Motherland' and that the NSDAP would strive to make Danzig a 'standard bearer of the National Socialist state'. Still, we believe that the two leaders were following Hitler's instructions not to rock the boat.

This state of affairs has continued into the autumn of 1933. It was also accompanied by a decided thaw in what had been very frosty relations between Danzig authorities and the Government of Poland. Rauschning apparently initiated this change and, in an unprecedented step, he was invited to Warsaw for negotiations that included a meeting with Marshal Pilsudksi, Poland's leader, at Belvedere Castle. Two agreements were signed settling lingering commercial disputes and removing restrictions imposed upon the Polish minority in Danzig. This was followed by agreement by the two entities to adjourn all thirty five bilateral disputes between them then pending before the League Council. At the September 1933 meeting of the League Council in Geneva, congratulations were exchanged all around for settling these disagreements. Rauschning even spoke glowingly about the "Spirit of the League," which we observe is not language usually associated with Nazi views about the League.

In this briefing document we are unable to provide much insight into the new apparent rapport between Danzig and Poland as we don't fully understand it ourselves. The League's mandate confers authority upon it and its High Commissioner to act as arbiter of conflicts between Danzig and Poland. Since 1920, there have been several thousand incidents involving such conflicts brought to the Council. Virtually every Council meeting has had to address multiple bilateral disputes in a seemingly endless stream; then suddenly they were all settled. Something has evidently changed and Hitler and Pilsudski have concluded that a new policy of détente is in their interests. (Danzig and Rauschning would never have proceeded without Hitler's approval.) This is a stunning turnabout.

In February 1933, only days after assuming power, Hitler delivered a strident speech criticizing Poland and threatening to seize Danzig by force. We know from our French allies that Pilsudski reacted with alarm and approached them, proposing a joint pre-emptive attack on Germany to unseat Hitler or, at a minimum, teach him a lesson. Poland's army of 300,000 soldiers in the East, coupled with France's forces in the West could quickly overwhelm the 100,000 man, lightly-armed German security forces permitted by the Treaty. But the French backed away from armed confrontation with Germany and the Polish initiative died. We can speculate that Hitler became aware of Poland's aggressive reaction and decided that he should soften his line toward Poland in light of Germany's weakness. But we don't know for certain. Nor do we know where this policy shift is leading. We simply bring this information to the High Commissioner's attention.

Only two weeks ago, at the end of October, a serious conflict between Danzig and the League arose when the Vice President of the Senate, Arthur Greiser, announced a policy of requiring all Danzig police officials to be members of the NSDAP. All non-Party members were to be deemed enemies of the state and removed from their positions in the civil service. He announced that he was taking a firm grip on the police force in order to make it 'an instrument of the National Socialist State'.

As might be expected, this announcement sparked outrage among the opposition. Newspapers supporting the Centre Party and the Social Democrats published editorials strongly criticizing the new policy. Danzig authorities responded by shutting down both publications as being 'calculated to imperil law and order'. The editors and publishers complained to the Acting High Commissioner and immediately filed petitions with the League Council in Geneva, citing conflicts with the Danzig Constitution. Danzig authorities retaliated by taking all of the petitioners into 'protective custody' for a minimum of three weeks as their petitions 'endanger the State'. As of this writing, the petitioners are being held in the old fortress of Weichselmunde.

The issue is current and awaits attention.

While we intend this briefing document as an unbiased report, the recent aggressive steps taken by the Danzig government are a source of concern to HMG, both directly and in our role as Rapporteur for the League. Given the apparent submissiveness of the NSDAP to the Nazi Government in Germany, we are apprehensive that we may witness a replay in Danzig of the rapid suppression of freedom that occurred in Germany after Hitler took power where, in a matter of less than 60 days, the Constitution of the Weimar Republic was supplanted by a totalitarian Nazi regime.

During the nearly six months that have elapsed since May 28 elections which brought the NSDAP to power, conflict has been manageable. But in the current tense environment, HMG advises the

High Commissioner to assume his position with a high degree of vigilance.

Appendix 1 Administrative Matters

As High Commissioner, Mr. Lester is assigned a large residence situated in the center of Danzig, with a household staff and a car and driver. He will be paid an annual salary of 72,000 Gold Swiss francs together with an allowance for official expenses. These costs are assessed by the League in equal amounts to Germany and the Danzig government.

Mr. Lester is permitted to engage an Assistant/Secretary from the League Secretariat whose salary, living expenses and travel costs are borne by the Secretariat.

Appendix 2 Brief History

Danzig's long history can be briefly summarized: Its origins reach back to the late 10th century and for several centuries it was controlled by the Teutonic Knights, who constructed the vast fortress at Marienburg (that still stands). Beginning in the 16th century, Danzig was a leading participant in the Hanseatic League, a confederation of city states and merchant guilds that controlled trade routes along the coast of Northern Europe, from the Baltic to the North Sea. The Vistula River, which empties into the Baltic at Danzig was (and remains) a vital commercial waterway. Rising in the distant mountains to the south, the Vistula wends its way north toward the Baltic through Warsaw, Krakow and Thorn and was the outlet for Polish amber, furs, timber and a host of other products that fed Danzig's merchants. Danzig was occupied by Napoleon's army in 1812 on its way to Moscow and then by Russia a year later on the heels of the defeated French Army. At the Congress of Vienna in 1820, Danzig was awarded to Prussia and for the next hundred years, it served as the capitol of West Prussia.

Appendix 3 Geography

The territory of the Free City is much larger than the City of Danzig itself, comprising roughly 1900 square kilometers (700 sq. miles). It is bisected by the Vistula River from its Southern border at Pieckel at the confluence of the Vistula and the Nogat River. The Nogat flows North East to the Baltic and forms the border between the Free City and East Prussia. Only one bridge crosses the Nogat, at Marienburg (site of the large Teutonic Fortress). This bridge provides the only direct access between the Free City and Germany. On the West, the Free City borders the Polish Corridor. Tczew (Dirschau, in German) is an important railway junction where the only bridge over the Vistula serves direct rail lines linking Berlin and the East Prussian Capitol of Koenigsberg and Danzig to Warsaw in the South. As Danzig City is situated 30 km North of Dirschau, travelers to Danzig must change trains in Dirschau and take the local train to the city. Alternatively, direct rail connections run West from Danzig's Central Station to Stettin and Berlin.

Aside from Danzig itself, the only other town of any size in the Free City is Zoppot, an upscale resort community on the Baltic Sea, featuring sandy beaches, hotels, movie theaters, a casino, restaurants and a famed open air summer festival featuring performances of Wagnerian opera. Zoppot is situated less than 30 minutes by tram from the center of Danzig and is a popular recreation destination, even in winter.

ADDENDUM

Danzig is very cold in wintertime and the Commissioner is advised to be prepared accordingly.

***

In late November, the Commissioner called Muller into his office. They had agreed that Muller would address Lester as 'Commissioner' and Muller would be 'Muller,' or 'Mr. Muller' in professional settings. By this time, both of them had studied the British Foreign Office briefing document and had examined the confidential Danzig files of the Secretariat which contained, among other things, the petitions filed with the Council by the Danzig opposition newspaper publishers who were arrested in late October.

"I find the petitions filed over the police matter damned persuasive," began Lester. "It's pretty clear that simply shutting down newspapers that carry stories you don't like conflicts with constitutional rights to a free press. And imprisoning citizens for petitioning the League over complaints of this kind is especially offensive. So my first instinct is to throw the book at them; have the League Council adopt resolutions branding the actions as being illegal and ordering them to be rescinded. I can make the case that a strong League reprimand like that would strengthen my hand when I arrive in Danzig in January to assume my post."

Lester glanced again at the petitions, then put them aside, looking outside at the gathering twilight and continued in a thoughtful tone.

"But the more I think about it, the less comfortable I get with that solution. I don't know any of the players, and not yet being physically there, I don't have a feel for the context. The NSDAP is a revolutionary movement. I know about that kind of business; as I've told you, I was an Irish revolutionary myself not so long ago. They've got an agenda; I can understand that. But so do the opposition newspaper publishers—and it's a different agenda. Serious political games are being played here by everyone, but I don't have a very good feel for what's really going on."

Lester pulled one of the files from the pile on his desk. "Then I read the responses from the Danzig government. Rauschning, the Senate President, says there was no intent to violate the Constitution and he pledges to govern in a manner that is consistent with the Constitution. He's the head of the Danzig government, so that commitment carries a lot of weight. And both the British briefing paper and information I'm getting from the Secretariat describe him as being a bright guy who's a so-called 'moderate'–whatever that means. The guy who made the speech that stirred everything up is Arthur Greiser, who is both Deputy President of the Senate under Rauschning and Deputy Gauleiter for Danzig under Albert Forster, whom we're told is a hardline German Nazi. Was Greiser floating some kind of trial balloon in his speech–for himself or for Forster? Maybe. Rauschning complains in his response that the petitions were filed without any real effort at trying to negotiate some kind of local solution with the government. His response certainly hints at being open to some kind of deal to settle the issue."

Lester looked at Muller with a faint smile. "Though I'm a little unclear about how the publishers could go about cutting some kind of deal with the government if they're sitting in jail.

"Still, I can make the case that having the Council come down hard on the Senate is exactly the *wrong* decision. In the eyes of the NSDAP that would make the League appear to be acting arbitrarily and we–the League and I–would both lose credibility. Moreover, the opposition might decide that we can be manipulated and stampeded into acting on their complaints. That could encourage them to become even more aggressive in resisting government actions and put us right in the middle of this local conflict–a place I don't want to be.

"The reality is that this government was in fact elected in a basically fair election only six months ago. So they're entitled to govern. And, in my mind, they ought to be given the benefit of the doubt, at least at this point."

Lester looked at Muller. "So I can come out either way on the issue. Do you have any reactions?"

"Commissioner," replied Muller, "after reading the petitions, I went back to look at the report you filed as Rapporteur for Upper Silesia on the petition by the Jewish notary who complained about the German racial laws; the one you and Mr. Eden cooperated in resolving. I think there may be some parallels."

"Ah" said Lester leaning forward, his elbows on the desk. "Remind me."

"The petition alleged that the new German laws had outlawed Jews in German Upper Silesia from practicing as lawyers, notaries and the like. It argued that these laws were in direct conflict with the German obligations under the League covenant, especially the provisions of Article 147 calling for the protection of minorities.

"In your report you noted Germany's statement that any local laws implemented in conflict with international obligations were a mistake and would be corrected. You said that statement implied that the Jews removed from their professional positions would be reinstated without delay and you directed the Germans to advise the Council on steps taken to implement this result."

"Right. I remember that's how we resolved it," said Lester.

"Here we have a case of Rauschning stating that there was no intent on the part of the government to contradict the Danzig Constitution and that he intends to govern in a Constitutional manner. His statement implies that the newspapers will be permitted to reopen and the imprisoned opposition members will released. It's a similar situation. It seems to me that if Mr. Eden were to follow this approach in his report, the Council would probably agree."

Lester smiled. "That's rather good, Muller.

"I want to include language in the report that publicly reaffirms fundamental rights of citizens to petition the League. We can't be seen as limiting that basic proposition. But I'm confident that Eden will agree to propose report along these lines and that the Council will go along. That way I'll get to Danzig in January with a clean slate and we can begin to find out what's really going on. I think that's a rather elegant solution."

CHAPTER 6

January 1934

Muller had left instructions with the porter to awaken him an hour before arrival in Danzig. He went to the dining car and took a cup of hot tea and a plate of biscuits back to his compartment as the first light of a late winter dawn began to appear.

It had been an uneventful trip. He had boarded the express to Berlin at the Zurich Central Station and bid last minute goodbyes to his family. His newly-minted League of Nations passport had attracted only minimal interest from Swiss and German immigration officials and he settled back in the warm comfort of his first class compartment for the day-long trip, armed with a biography of Beethoven that he had been looking forward to reading. But his attention kept being drawn to the passing countryside outside his window. Everything was snow-covered and the forests were picturesque even with a wintry grey sky overhead. But what struck him was the profusion of Nazi banners on display in every town they passed. Large red flags with the white-encircled black swastika flew from every flag pole, Nazi pennants hung from balconies and doorways in towns and cities and from the roofs of farmhouses. Stations were festooned with Nazi paraphernalia and people standing on platforms, as the train sped past, all seemed to be wearing Nazi armbands. There was a profusion of uniforms too, men with military headgear bundled up in heavy winter greatcoats. Several times he even caught sight of uniformed troops apparently drilling and practicing their marching skills.

It was the same story all the way to Berlin; a little vulgar, he thought to himself, but it was also a little intimidating. The sheer scope of the displays conveyed a palpable sense of energy and determination. It was, Muller had to admit to himself, impressive.

Night had fallen by the time his train arrived in Berlin. His overnight connection on to Stettin and Danzig would not depart for two hours, so he had ample time to complete his transfer to the Freiderichstrasse Banhof, a thronging hub of travelers. It too was hung with Nazi banners and filled with men, and not a few women, in uniform or wearing Nazi armbands. But Muller also noticed large numbers of travelers with no signs of party affiliation, many of them evidently working class–trade unionists perhaps, thought Muller, and also a number of well-dressed, more affluent, businessmen, some with families.

The First Class dining room was largely empty and looked shabby, so Muller found a table along the wall of the restaurant in the main concourse. A middle aged couple took the adjoining table and they struck up a conversation. After ordering–Muller had decided on wiener schnitzel and a beer–he offered them his Gitanes; they readily accepted and lit up. They were laughing together about the waiter's strange accent when a tall man in a black SS uniform strode directly to their table and snatched the cigarette from the lips of the woman, threw it to the floor and ground it under the heel of his hobnailed boot.

"Our Fuehrer does not approve of women smoking," he snarled. "You must obey our Fuehrer." He drew himself up, threw out his right arm and barked, "Heil Hitler."

Their section of the restaurant fell silent. Muller went to rise, but the woman's husband put his hand on Muller arm, motioning him to remain seated. He looked evenly at the SS officer.

"Thank you for your instruction, Major. Heil Hitler."

The SS officer glared at them, then turned on his heel and stalked away.

Muller glanced at the woman, who was flustered and near tears. Her husband gently covered her hand with his. "It's all right," he said quietly. Then whispered it again, taking both of her hands in his and leaning his head toward her.

Other nearby diners averted their eyes and began resuming their conversations, seemingly a little louder now, as if to blot out the incident.

The husband stubbed the remainder of his cigarette in the ashtray. Continuing to comfort his wife with one hand covering hers, he turned to Muller. "My apologies for this incident," he said. "Sometimes these fellows become a little too aggressive." His wife, looking overcome, mumbled "we need to leave." They took their coats and walked quickly to the front reception desk, presumably to cancel their order. As they walked away, the man looked back at Muller waving farewell and shook his head with a look of resigned frustration.

Muller was hungry, so he ate the meal when it arrived moments later, but did not linger. The nearby diners studiously ignored him, but as he picked up his coat and valise and began to leave, a blonde, matronly woman clad in deep red and apparently dining alone, looked up, smiling as he passed and said. "They really are swine, you know."

***

The train arrived in Danzig Central Station on time at 8:37 AM. It was hard to see much of the City as the train approached from the West and curved South toward the City Center. There was dirty snow alongside the tracks and the sky was a gloomy dark grey.

Muller felt a tug of excitement as they approached the city. Here he was, a full-fledged diplomat now, no longer a student, on the threshold of assuming some share of responsibility for preserving democracy in the Free City, all in accordance with a mandate from the League of Nations, as specified in the Treaty of Versailles itself. This was no trivial exercise, he reminded himself; this was very serious business. He gazed out the window as the train slowed, wondering to himself what lay ahead. He'd felt pretty well-prepared meeting with Lester and others at the League in Geneva. But he had to confess to himself that he was nervous now, about to step on stage. He took a deep breath and squared his shoulders, willing himself to put aside his misgivings. He was here, he had a job to do; he would do it.

The train pulled to a stop in the station wreathed in steam. Muller picked up his valise and opened his compartment door, stepping down to the platform. It was cold and he bundled up in his coat. Immigration officials were seated at two desks at the station end of the platform; Danzig citizens with their brown clad identity papers lined up to the left, all others were on the right. Muller was whisked through without more than a glance at his League of Nations documents and he followed the signs to the taxi queue. The Commissioner's office had offered to send the Daimler and driver to pick him up, but he had declined. It was not the way he wanted to make his entry.

He gave the driver the address of his apartment. His predecessor had rented an apartment in a boarding house in the Central District, close to trams and nearby cafes and restaurants and, on nice days, a pleasant walk to the High Commissioner's Residence which also housed the delegation's offices. He had decided to renew the lease and had sent his trunk on ahead.

The taxi deposited Muller at his boarding house and he was ushered into the entryway by his landlady, a tall, pencil-thin, middle aged lady with her hair done up in a bun and a pair of small glasses perched on her bird-like nose. Flashing a friendly smile, she introduced herself as Frau Scheffler and said she had been looking forward to meeting her new tenant.

Muller's trunk was awaiting him in his airy second floor apartment, and he spent the next hour organizing his belongings. He was pleased that the central heating system seemed to work well, especially in the nearby bathroom that featured a large bathtub that was served by plenty of hot water. After bathing and shaving, he dressed, then descended to the front sitting room to study a tourist map of the City that he had picked up at the railroad station. Since I'm finally here, he thought, I'd better get the lay of the land.

Bright sunshine had now replaced the low clouds, so after orienting himself on the map, Muller put on his hat and coat and began to explore his new environs. He turned left, heading East along Langergasse, a main thoroughfare served by the #5 tram. St. Mary's cathedral, an improbably tall red brick structure with soaring towers, dominated the skyline to his left. After a few blocks he reached the market area where open air stalls were busy selling local food products. He saw eggs and butter jars, cod lying on beds of seaweed, kale and other green goods evidently grown in nearby greenhouses, and pocket crabs beneath a sign telling customers they were fresh from Lake Ottominer. Stepping into one of the dingy shops, he saw bags of rolled oats, tins of kerosene, a cask with live herring, bags with currents and raisins, bottles of vinegar and boxes of baking powder. As he stepped back outside he was struck by the sweet aroma of spices mixed with the ranker odors of seafood and butchered meat. Most of the stalls were attended by elderly women bundled in coats with scarves wrapped around them for warmth. He noticed an old man passing by the stalls pushing a small cart with hot bricks wrapped in paper. The man stopped next to each of the women, placing a warm brick under her canvas chair and drawing out a cold brick to be re-heated. He would make a mark on his slate and move to the next stall.

At the bridge over the Mottlau, a tributary flowing into the Vistula, Muller turned North along the embankment, admiring the three and four story homes on either side of the narrow river with their distinctive Hanseatic facades and crow-stepped gables topped by pointed arches. His vantage point offered a sweeping view, and everywhere he saw Nazi banners fluttering in the chill breeze; it was eerily similar to what he had seen from his train window traveling through Germany. But this was supposedly the Free City of Danzig.

Turning West on Breitgasse back toward the City center, Muller saw even grander homes with decorative marble panels added to their ornate facades, many of them guarded by Dutch stoops, with elaborate iron rails on either side of three and four step entryways anchored by short stone columns. The appearance bespoke stolid prosperity, though Muller could see the unmistakable ravages of neglect in chipped paint and pieces in disrepair. Still, the City's beauty was apparent, a bit like an elegant lady whose money is running low and who's beginning to show her age, thought Muller to himself; but still very formidable.

And still the flags. Even in what gave every appearance of being a prosperous residential quarter, nearly every building had a long banner or smaller red flag bearing the familiar white circle around the black swastika. Muller found the displays unnerving and somehow inconsistent with the serious impression conveyed by the solid architecture.

As he crossed Holtz Plaza, Muller could see ahead of him the Commissioner's residence, with its red brick set off by white stone decorative arches and trim beneath the dark slate roof. What a splendid structure, he thought, pausing to admire the large three-story façade which had a carved stone entryway centered beneath three tall, tapered windows, their panes laced by gothic stone inlays and set between two high, pointed gables. Muller had read in the files that the structure had been built between 1898 and 1901 as the General Command Headquarters of the Prussian Garrison stationed in the City. It sat on 1.8 hectares of parkland and included an elaborate walled garden in the rear. According to the file, in 1920 the new Volkstag had wanted to take control of the building but the first League of Nations High Commissioner commandeered it for himself.

Gazing at it, he was glad to see that the flag fluttering from the staff atop the residence was the red banner of the Free City, with its gold crown atop two white crosses.

Muller walked a few paces further, to the corner of a short street with a street sign identifying it as Elizabethwall leading off to his right. He pulled out his map. Next to Elizabethwall, a broad boulevard called Silberhutte would take him directly in front of the entrance to the Commissioner's residence, then beyond it and across the broad Central Square, he could see the railroad station, featuring a tall, ornate clock tower that he hadn't noticed that morning when he'd arrived. Then, looking left, he could see in the distance the Senate building and the Volkstag, facing one another across a broad avenue called Neugarten on his map. Both buildings were even larger than the Commissioner's residence with elaborate gothic brickwork and facades.

He stood gazing at the panorama that unfolded before him. His first thought was to marvel at the structures themselves, which radiated strength and seriousness of purpose. They conveyed an impression of solemn gravitas which seemed to underscore the importance of his mission. There could be no doubt, observing these imposing edifices, that this was serious business. His second thought was, how remarkable; there they were, all three structures, situated less than a mile from one another. If there were to be a confrontation, it would certainly be at close quarters, and right in the center of the city.

Shaking his head and ending his reverie, Muller crossed over to Silberhutte, walked to the entrance of the Commissioner's residence and rang the bell. A buzzer signaled him to open the outer door and he mounted the dozen steps to the entry where a staff member opened an elaborately carved wooden door. Upon being shown Muller's credentials, he introduced himself as Rudi Schmitz, the butler, and took Muller's coat and hat, asking him to wait. Muller looked around at the imposing and very formal entry hall. He found himself standing in a corridor lined with round stone columns rising fifteen feet to anchor still higher graceful archways, each with its single golden lighting fixture descending from the topmost canopy. Facing him was a broad stairway with a decorative stone balustrade that climbed to a landing where it turned sharply left up to a second floor with a matching colonnade. The floor was black and white patterned tiles polished to a high sheen.

Moments later Elsie Lester skipped down the stairs to greet him with a hug and two-cheek kiss. "Welcome, Paul," she said with a big smile. Elsie Lester was slender and energetic, hair still mainly red, with a few wisps of grey, and a band of freckles across her small nose. Muller found her a lively counterpart to Lester's diplomatic demeanor. Elsie laughed easily; she was opinionated and made no effort to disguise her emotions. Muller liked her and was glad to see her.

"It's good to have you here as we begin this new adventure, Paul; we're certainly finding ourselves in surroundings that are a lot grander than we're accustomed to," she laughed, spreading her hands. "Wait till you see everything.

"As you can tell, this is the ground floor. There's a reception area just here," she gestured toward the corner as they walked down the colonnaded corridor. "There's the typists' room and the file room next to it and this nice small corner office is for you."

Muller stepped into a high-ceilinged room with two windows looking onto the Central Square and down toward the railroad station. It was about four times the size of his office at the Palais in Geneva and had a decorative mahogany desk—clean, Muller noted—and a large leather desk chair.

He smiled at Elsie. "Do they know about this in Geneva?"

They mounted the stairway and Muller craned to look up at elaborate decorations in the vaulted ceiling. Turning left, Elsie steered him into a very large, well-appointed reception room, decorated in a warm and welcoming cream-colored décor offset by panels with subtle, olive-hued highlights, and the three tall windows Muller had seen above the entrance. "I can entertain a small army here." Elsie said delightedly. It was true, Muller could see; a reception for fifty or sixty people would hardly tax the lavish space.

Then Elsie led them across the corridor to a large dining room, dominated by a long, highly-polished table, with sideboards on either wall. The walls were lined with dark Mahogany wainscoting surmounted by the same warm cream décor as the reception area, but this time offset by elaborate dark red and gold decorative designs that Elsie told him were intended to evoke Danzig's Hanseatic League heritage.

"They tell me we can seat 28 for dinner," Elsie said with a laugh. "That's a little more than I'm accustomed to."

The Commissioner's large and ornate office occupied the corner. Its windows commanded a view across the Central Square and it was lined with book shelves below brightly decorated ceiling scallops. An imposing desk occupied the corner with a large conference table off to one side. "I think

Sean will find himself able to accommodate these surroundings," said Elsie, still smiling.

"Our living quarters are on the third floor with bedrooms for the girls and a playroom. Everything's currently a mess there, so please give me a few days before offering you a tour," Elsie went on. "You know this was built to be a military commander's headquarters and residence; it's decidedly masculine and a little impractical. I'm planning on some redecoration to brighten things up.

"Oh, and the whole place is centrally-heated, which I'm sure is wonderful when it really gets cold. But I plan on ordering some kind of gas-fired contraption we used to use in Ireland; at least it'll convey the idea of a real fireplace."

Elsie invited him to dine with her and the girls that evening and he accepted, then excused himself to begin arranging his office. He could see a lot of file cabinets; it looked like there was a lot to be read.

***

Lester remained in Geneva through the January League of Nations Council meetings that dealt with the pending Danzig petitions. As he predicted, the Council approved a report prepared by Eden as Rapporteur accepting Rauschning's assurances that governance of Danzig would be carried out in accordance with the Danzig Constitution and reaffirming both the League's authority as protector of the Constitution and the rights of Danzigers to petition the League. Lester had not participated in the proceedings, but he told Muller that Opposition leaders had complained bitterly that the harm they suffered had simply been swept under the rug. Similarly, Rauschning had demanded that any citizen petitions should be submitted to the Senate for resolution before going to the Council. According to Lester, Eden had allowed the two sides to vent their complaints and then had no difficulty in persuading the Council to adopt his report.

By the time of the Council decision, the newspaper suspensions had ended and the prisoners had been released, so the intensity of the controversy had dissipated. Still, Lester's planned arrival in Danzig on January 24, 1934 stirred anticipation.

Muller was asked to assist in planning Lester's arrival ceremony at the Central Station. Members of a Welcoming Committee were selected, including representatives of the Senate and the Volkstag, and the Polish Consul General was appointed to represent the diplomatic corps. The Danzig Police Band, which had a well-deserved regional reputation, was enlisted to participate, but there then ensued negotiations over what music they should play. There was no Danzig national anthem and Muller insisted that it would not be appropriate to use any of the familiar German marches that were the band's standbys. Finally they agreed on the Brahms Academic Overture followed by a chorus of "When Irish Eyes Are Smiling." At least no one will be offended, Muller decided.

Lester's train arrived on time that morning. Elsie and Muller were in the delegation waiting at the station when it pulled in. As Lester stepped down from his compartment, Elsie ran up to him and they wrapped one another in a warm embrace. The Polish Consul General, Casimir Papee, representing the diplomatic corps, stepped forward, extending his hand.

"Welcome to the Free City of Danzig, Commissioner," he said. "We've been awaiting your arrival."

He then escorted Lester and his wife through the waiting room and outside where a podium had been erected in front of the station entrance. It had gotten very cold, so Lester chose to be exceptionally brief when he mounted the podium.

"I come to Danzig on a mission to preserve this Free City as a free and prosperous home to the 400,000 citizens who reside here. Thank you for coming to greet me; I believe I will defer additional comments to a warmer venue."

Lester then doffed his hat as photographers snapped pictures, their flashbulbs giving off puffs of steam as they exploded in the bitter cold. The Police Band decided to skip the Brahms Academic Overture and played 'When Irish Eyes Are Smiling', but only once, and then quickly packed their instruments away and scurried off to get warm.

Muller shook hands with Lester as he descended the podium steps.

"Welcome, Commissioner."

"I'm glad to finally get here, Muller," Lester replied. "God, is it always this cold?"

Muller guided Lester and his wife to the waiting Daimler that he had arranged to be parked nearby for the occasion.

"It's too cold to linger," he said rubbing his gloved hands together. "The car will take you to the residence. It's not far; you can actually see it over there," he pointed. "I'll see to your luggage and meet you in a few minutes."

***

That evening, the Senate hosted a welcoming party for Lester in its imposing building just down Neugartengasse from the High Commissioner's residence. Muller translated Lester's impromptu remarks expressing his hope for harmonious relations and health and prosperity for Danzig and its citizens. He said that he and Elsie looked forward to three of their happiest years during his appointment as High Commissioner.

Hermann Rauschning, as President of the Senate, responded with similar cordial generalities, though Muller noted that, in his welcoming remarks and again during casual conversation with Lester, Rauschning repeatedly referred to the improvement in relations between Danzig and Poland and his confidence in further improvements still to come. Curious, thought Muller, since one of the League's mandates was to resolve disagreements between Poland and Danzig; these issues had dominated Council consideration of Danzig matters since 1920. But he was busy interpreting for Lester and put the thought aside. Afterward, as they gathered at the Residence for dessert and schnapps, Lester and Muller agreed that the event had gone smoothly and that they seemed to have gotten off on the right foot.

A day later, on January 26, 1934, Muller was assisting Lester in organizing his spacious office in the Residence. Precisely at noon, Rudi Schmitz, the butler, ushered two messengers into the office. They were from the German and the Polish Consuls General. Both men handed sealed envelopes to Lester.

"Sir, we have instructions to deliver these messages to you."

Lester took the envelopes and instructed Schmitz to escort the messengers to the waiting room downstairs to await any response.

He then walked to his desk, took his letter opener and slit open the two envelopes. Each was a short statement, one bearing the formal embossed seal of the German Government, in German, the other bearing the seal of the Polish Government, in French.

Lester handed them to Muller with a quizzical look.

Muller translated the German document.

'The German Reich is pleased to announce that effective this date, it has entered into a formal Treaty of Non-Aggression with the Republic of Poland with a duration of ten years. Announcements of this Agreement are being distributed to diplomatic delegations at this same hour in Berlin and Warsaw.'

He then looked at the Polish document. "It's identical," he said, handing them back to Lester.

Lester took the documents, laid them on his desk, and stood, looking down at them.

Finally, he straightened up.

"Muller, kindly go down to the waiting room and advise the two messengers that I am requesting each of the Consul Generals to call upon me at their earliest convenience."

Muller did as he was instructed then returned to Lester's office to find the Commissioner standing at his windows looking out over the Central Square.

"This is an absolutely stunning announcement," he said, turning to face Muller. "Springing this Agreement on the world this way with no prior warning has to have been designed to increase its shock value as well as confuse people and obfuscate its meaning."

Taking his seat and leaning back in the large leather chair, Lester gazed again out the windows at the Central Square, steepleing his hands in thought. "We won't hear anything about this from Geneva for days, and they're not likely to have much to say anyway. So let's see what we can figure out for ourselves."

Muller sat in the chair across the desk from Lester. "Well, at a minimum, Commissioner, this explains why Rauschning kept referring last evening to improving relations with Poland."

Lester nodded, smiling thinly. "It certainly is a rather dramatic way to welcome me to Danzig. And, frankly, I don't find it especially welcoming."

"Clearly one aim of the agreement is to weaken the League and my office," he said, straightening in his chair and pulling a copy of the Treaty of Versailles from his desk drawer. "Here in Article 103 it says the High Commissioner is 'entrusted with the duty of dealing with all differences arising between Poland and the Free City of Danzig'. I think we can assume that provision is a now a dead letter in light of this new agreement. They've taken the minor agreements they entered into last fall at the League Council meeting and moved them to an infinitely higher plane."

Lester paused and looked at Muller. "Remember Eden's briefing paper commenting that Whitehall didn't know what to expect from improving relations between Danzig and Poland? Well, now we have the answer. The pretty clear message to me, as High Commissioner, is 'we can deal with any bilateral disagreements ourselves, thank you very much.'

"For the Germans, it's another swipe at the League," he continued. "They've already dropped out, and this is another convenient way to demonstrate to themselves and the rest of the world that they don't need the League."

Lester smiled. "The Poles probably think this gives them bragging rights because they've never felt they're treated as a 'Great Power' by the other big boys. Beck's saying to himself, 'this'll show the bloody French and Brits'."

Rudi Schmitz came in to say that the Polish Consul General had called and offered to meet at 4 PM. Lester told him to accept. "Let's see how they decide to present this fait accompli," Lester said to Muller.

Kasimir Papee was an experienced Polish diplomat who had been appointed Consul General in Danzig a year earlier. He was said to be related to Foreign Minister Beck by marriage and it was rumored that he and Beck didn't always get along. He entered Lester's office rubbing his hands together for warmth. "Sorry, Commissioner," he said. "I stupidly left my gloves on the heater in my office to warm up. So I came without them and my hands are cold. But this is not a deliberately cold handshake." He smiled as Muller translated.

"You've met Mr. Muller, I believe," said Lester.

Papee offered his hand to Muller. It *was* cold.

"Of course; frankly, I hadn't expected to have a formal meeting with you both so soon after welcoming you to Danzig a day or so ago, Commissioner. I had intended to invite you to a get-acquainted lunch first. But I guess that will have to wait," Papee said.

"It would be a pleasure," said Lester. "But while you warm yourself, I would be grateful for any further explanation you can offer concerning the note that you kindly delivered to my office earlier today concerning the Non-Aggression Treaty with Germany."

Papee spoke very clear French, so Lester was able to grasp what he was saying without needing full translation from Muller. It quickly became obvious that Papee had been provided a briefing message that he had memorized and was now reciting, using the opaque language of diplomacy that conveyed no information, but did so very politely.

When he was finished, Lester smiled and said, "Thank you Consul General." Then he added, "Now, let's pretend for a moment that we're at that luncheon you promised. We've just finished a nice bottle of Gevrey Chambertin burgundy, and you've decided that you wanted to speak more frankly about this matter. What would you say then?"

Papee smiled back at him. "Commissioner, I look forward to having detailed discussions together with you as we get better acquainted, and Gevrey Chambertin would be a very good choice in wine. But I think the only thing that I would add for the moment is that I have requested my government to issue a formal invitation for you and your wife, and of course Mr. Muller, to be our guests in Warsaw next month. I expect to be back to you with proposed dates for the visit in a day or two."

As Papee departed, he turned to Muller. "Mr. Muller, I am a member of the indoor tennis club at the Sportshalle and I see that you have signed up to play. Would you be interested in a match on Monday the 29th at 6

PM? Assuming your boss will allow you the time off, that is." He glanced at Lester, who nodded. Muller accepted. This was Friday. Two days to perhaps glean some additional information.

CHAPTER 7

January – March 1934

Papee and Muller were late arriving at the Sportshalle Monday evening and only had time for a single match before their time expired. Papee handily won a 6-2 set, hitting crisp backhands and forehands that chased Muller from one sideline to the other, then coming to the net for generally easy put-aways. After showering, as they toweled off, Papee admitted that he had been club champion while in school and had even qualified for two French Open tournaments, though he hadn't been able to actually compete.

"Refreshment facilities here at the Sportshalle are pretty limited," he said. "I'll drop you off and we can meet at the Continental Hotel for dinner at 8:30. It's right across from the Central Station. It's the only Polish Hotel in town and you can't miss it because it doesn't display any Nazi banners." He smiled.

After dinner, they moved to the bar and Papee had ordered a bottle of Stobbes Marchendel Double Null, a popular local gin. He was clearly agitated. Watching him, Muller was reminded of photos of Lenin; Papee had the same wide bulging forehead tapering to a narrow chin, but unlike Lenin, he had a neat mustache and no beard.

He filled their glasses, downing his in two gulps, then refilled it.

Finally he said, "Muller, you get to be the hydrant I lift my leg on. My government won't listen to me, I can't say this to Lester, and I'm tired of talking to myself. So you're it." He paused, looking around, then continued, apparently satisfied that no one was within earshot.

"The Polish Government has just aligned itself with Germany against the Allied Powers," he said. "It's fucking madness. And my idiot relative, our Foreign Minister, Josef Beck, is the mastermind behind it." Papee's shoulders slumped, and he took another large gulp from his glass, wiping his mouth with the back of his hand.

Well, Muller said to himself, that's quite a way to begin a conversation. He willed himself to appear composed.

"A little history lesson for you Muller," Papee continued. "When Poland was established after Versailles in 1920, we proceeded to start six different wars. Six! Quite a launch, we had," he grimaced.

"Anyway, one of the wars was against the Bolsheviks, which turned out to be a very bad idea. By that time they had established the Soviet Union and that's who we found ourselves fighting. The Red Army pushed us all the way back to Warsaw and they were just about to overwhelm us when our hero, General Pilsudski, pulled off what has come down to us as 'the Miracle on the Vistula', a surprise flanking attack that broke the back of the Soviet Army and preserved an independent Poland. Three cheers!" Papee refilled their glasses again and took another large gulp.

He took out his pen and started drawing on one of the cocktail napkins. "Look at the map, Muller. Here's Poland." He drew a small box in the middle. "Here's the Soviet Union." He drew a large semicircle covering the whole of the right side of the napkin. "Now, here's Germany." He made another large semicircle covering the left side of the napkin.

"We're situated right between two elephants," he said. "If Central Europe goes up in flames, *this* is where the war will be fought." He drew heavy circles around the small Polish box. "We're a continental power. Maybe not a Great Power, but we're situated right here," he stabbed the box with his pen, "right in the middle of the continent. And who else is there?

"Not the British; they're safely across the Channel. They can afford to sit offshore, rely on their big navy and wait to see what happens. The Americans have disappeared entirely. The Dutch and the Belgians are too small to matter.

"There's only France," he said quietly. "Only France is situated on the continent like we are. Only France understands our fear of a resurgent Germany. That's why we've been so closely allied with France since 1920.

"In 1926, Pilsudski–by then he was a Marshal–mounted a coup d'etat and took over the Polish government. He did so in part to ensure that Polish politicians didn't fritter away the crucial alliance with France.

"Now, the French haven't exactly been easy to deal with through all this. They made a deal with the Germans at Locarno in 1925 to settle Germany's Western border issues. But for us, that only served to raise questions about Germany's *Eastern* borders–that is to say, Germany's borders with Poland. Germany hates the Polish Corridor and the Danzig mandate. Hell, the whole idea of an independent Poland is anathema to most Germans. So the French wobble on this issue was–and, frankly *remains*–a concern to us.

"Then in 1929 the British and French decided to cut German reparations by three-quarters and the French agreed to withdraw their troops from the Rhineland. By the way, Muller, did you know that for a decade the French had stationed black colonial troops from Senegal in the Rhineland to run things for them? Black soldiers ordering Germans around! Not popular in Germany. But so long as the French occupied the Rhineland, they held a trump card. If the Germans defied Versailles or misbehaved in some other way, the French could simply annex and fortify the Rhineland. The fact that they left and surrendered this leverage was very disturbing to us.

"Still, our alliance with France has been the cornerstone of our foreign policy. You've doubtless heard that only two weeks after assuming power, Hitler delivered a bloodthirsty speech calling the Polish Corridor 'a hideous injustice to Germany' demanding that 'it must be restored to us at once'." Papee mimicked Hitler's voice in a mocking way. "Well," he continued, "Pilsudski reacted furiously by calling on the French to join us in mounting an attack on Germany to send Hitler a message—or even topple him from power. The French declined. But at least we were still on the same page—a shared mistrust of Germany.

"Now, with this new ten year German non-aggression pact, we have suddenly changed camps. We're no longer aligned with the French. We're now aligned with Germany; we're relying on Germany to protect us from...*Germany!!!* It is just too absurd," Papee paused to drink another glass of gin, filling Muller's again too and lit gold-tipped Regattas for both of them with a shiny lighter.

"And who's the genius behind this policy somersault? Beck, who's married to my cousin. He's been part of Pilsudski's inner circle for years and he finally persuaded Pilsudski to name him foreign minister in 1932. He proceeded to negotiate a non-aggression pact with the Soviets, but I figured that was acceptable; the Soviets are so consumed by domestic upheaval that they aren't a likely threat any time soon, and Pilsudski, whose judgment I trust, was still in control.

"But now Pilsudski is just a figurehead. I don't know if it was a stroke or just old age, but something happened and he's no longer competent, mentally or physically. When you and Lester come to Warsaw, you'll be invited to the Palace, but you won't see Pilsudski. No one does anymore."

"It doesn't sound like that's going to be a very useful trip for the Commissioner to take," said Muller.

"I'm afraid that's right," Papee replied. "With Pilsudski out of the picture, there's no longer anyone around to control Beck. He's wrapped himself in Pilsudski's cloak and has taken personal charge of Polish foreign policy. And the first thing he does is go to Berlin and make this deal with Hitler. He's patting himself on the back saying, now we have non-aggression pacts with *both* of our big neighbors. I think he's delusional! It may suit Hitler to put his hatred for Poland on hold while he consolidates power and starts re-arming Germany—as he surely intends to do. But if and when he does turn his attention to Poland, the new Non-Aggression Treaty will last about this long." He picked up the cocktail napkin and crushed in his fist.

"Beck didn't even bother to inform the French before he made the deal. They're furious. So he's probably ended our ability to leverage French power as a check on German policy toward Poland.

"Delusional!" Papee repeated and he punched his knee with the fist holding the crushed cocktail napkin.

Papee paused, shaking his head.

Muller, his mind working furiously, decided to remain silent. Papee obviously had things he wanted to get off his chest; let him talk and see what he reveals He waited for Papee to continue and was not disappointed.

"Now, directly relevant to you and Commissioner Lester," Papee continued stabbing a finger at Muller. "Beck's also aiming to undermine the League's role in Danzig. I've been arguing with Warsaw—and with Beck directly—that a strong role for the League in Danzig acts as a constraint on the NSDAP and by extension on Hitler—and that this is in Poland's best interests, so we should be *supporting* the Commissioner's authority. But my instructions are to be obstructionist." Papee sighed and lit another Regatta.

"Warsaw's been hostile to the League's role in Danzig right from the start, and it's no better now. The prevailing mindset of the Polish Foreign Office is that the League mandate in Danzig was established for the benefit of the Germans–to keep Danzig German and keep Poland out. I've told them that the rise of Hitler and the NSDAP means that the League can provide us leverage *against* German interests by protecting Danzig's non-Nazi opposition which includes the local Polish population. No one is listening.

"Poland holds the Presidency of the Council. Beck intends to use that authority to advance his own agenda, and that includes blocking the League in Danzig. He was pushed into a corner by the British on the Commissioner's appointment, so he had to agree to it. And Eden's report in the January Council meetings lacked any backbone, so he let it sail through. But make no mistake. He's just biding his time." Papee filled their glasses with the last of the bottle.

"But that's enough about our side," he said. "Now let's talk about my friends the Danzig Germans. Actually, I find the dynamics on the German side at least as interesting as the cock-ups on our side."

Muller signaled for another bottle of Marchendel. He wasn't going to say a word and concentrated on listening closely.

Papee glanced around the room again and, satisfied that no one was in a position to eavesdrop, took another swallow of gin and continued.

"They've got three very different characters playing leading roles in this drama, each with different constituencies and what look like competing agendas. It could get very interesting, Muller. Rauschning and von Radowitz, their Consul General, who's actually a decent fellow, Muller; I think you'll like him, are both Prussians–not nobility, but with educated Prussian backgrounds and histories. Both joined the Nazi Party around 1930, early enough to be respectable, but not back at the start, like Forster.

He was one of Hitler's original brawlers in Bavaria even before the putsch, when Hitler was jailed. We're told he still has direct access to Hitler whenever he needs it. Forester is the Gauleiter–the Nazi Party leader in Danzig. He's been here for three years and gets credit for building the NSDAP majority. He's crude and accustomed to throwing his weight around. He sees himself as Hitler's representative here and he treats the Senate and the Volkstag as his minions.

"By contrast, Radowitz is a career foreign service officer and protégé of Baron von Neurath, Hitler's Foreign Minister, who's an educated Prussian and whose whole career has been with the Wilhelmstrasse. Von Neurath put his very considerable experience at Hitler's disposal when Hitler seized power and was retained as Foreign Minister. The Wilhelmstrasse is a strong power base and von Neurath is a formidable operator. He negotiated the Non-Aggression Treaty with Beck–obviously with Hitler's approval–and doubtless took delight in humiliating the League in the process. Von Radowitz is a Wilhelmstrasse man. He's among those who consider Forster a loudmouthed fool.

"Rauschning has the weakest of the power bases; no ties to Hitler or the Nazi leadership, but as President of the Senate, he is the reasonable face of the NSDAP to the business community here and to the opposition. If Forster's the bad cop, then Rauschning is the good cop. My reading of him is that he believes in good government for Danzig. He is also acutely aware of Danzig's precarious financial condition and sees no advantage for either the NSDAP or for Berlin in rocking the boat. So he's probably the least hostile to your mission here; at least for now.

"And of course I shouldn't forget Arthur Greiser," said Papee grinning. "He can actually be charming and funny when he's drunk–which is very often the case. But the rest of the time, he's not very smart or interesting. He's the only native Danziger in the leadership; he used to have

115

a business in the summertime running a little motorboat from the long wooden mole at Zoppot out to the passenger steamers in the Baltic. Forster got him a job with the NSDAP, then, once they came to power, had him named Vice-President of the Senate. He and Rauschning don't get along; he's Forster's guy waiting in the wings if Rauschning get pushed out someday—which we see as only a matter of time.

"Everybody's jockeying for power there, Muller," Papee said. "You've only been here for a few short weeks. I suggest that you and Commissioner Lester quickly start climbing the learning curve. These guys are going to be a challenge."

Papee finished the last gin in his glass and stood, only slightly unsteady. "If I order another bottle, neither of us will feel very good tomorrow, so good night Muller. I've unburdened myself enough to feel better."

A freezing mist was blowing in off the Baltic. Muller tightened his coat and pulled his hat lower, walking cautiously across the Central Square trying to avoid the patchy ice, then entering the railroad station café, still open to late travelers. He ordered a large coffee and a chocolate torte, hoping the combination of caffeine and sugar might give him a boost of energy to help to clear his head. His mind was spinning.

What had prompted Papee's dramatic and unexpected revelations? Was he trying to set some kind of trap? Invite an intelligence contact to perform espionage? Clearly he thought the Polish decision to sign the non-aggression pact was a catastrophic error and his contempt for Beck and his Foreign Office superiors was on full display. Did he hope by revealing it somehow to overturn the damage? It was rash behavior. He had to know that Muller would report the conversation to Lester; the risk that his role would be exposed was obvious. He hadn't even asked Muller to keep the information confidential.

Muller felt decidedly uncomfortable.

Gulping down the last of his coffee, he left the café and made his way back to his boarding house, squinting through the freezing mist. Running cold water in the sink, he soaked his face and neck, then toweled off. He had decided what to do.

He spent the next three hours painstakingly writing duplicate copies of a detailed account of what he had been told. He did not identify Papee by name or affiliation. He placed both documents in separate pockets of his briefcase and locked it. He would see what Lester's reaction was the next day. But his plan was to send the second copy to RCS Stevenson in London. He decided to sleep on what he would say in his covering note to Stevenson. He took a long swallow from a stoppered bottle of red wine to calm his nerves and promptly fell asleep.

He took the tram to the office in the morning with a splitting headache. The mist had turned to snow overnight and he had to step over snow piles before mounting the steps to the entrance. He asked Rudi Schmitz to bring him a strong black tea, hoping that would revive him. Unlocking his briefcase, he re-read his reports, made a handful of edits, then locked one copy in his safe. The other he took upstairs to Lester's big office.

"Muller," said Lester, looking up from the papers on his desk. "That must have been a tough tennis game last night. You look more like you're recovering from a rugby match."

Muller smiled sheepishly. "He's a good tennis player, Commissioner," he replied, "and a prodigious drinker too. There's a local gin here, Stobbes Marchendel, I think it's called. We sampled it a little too enthusiastically, I'm afraid."

He made sure the doors to the Commissioner's office were closed. Then he pulled up a chair and quietly told Lester what had transpired.

"I don't know what prompted him to tell me what he did. But once he started talking, he didn't stop until the gin ran out. I didn't say a word, but when I got home I stayed up writing this report while everything was fresh in my mind." He handed the document to Lester. "I've written it without attribution to Papee; I think we need to protect him. Have a look; it's your decision on what to do."

An hour later, Lester called Muller back into his office.

"This is very explosive stuff, Muller," he began. "You did good work in getting it down on paper so quickly. But it's very puzzling." Lester looked out the large windows, his mind working. "Revealing this kind of sensitive information is highly abnormal; it's never done. And why did he choose you as the messenger?"

Lester paused and his gaze returned to Muller. "My best guess is that that he's decided to disobey his instructions and offer us information that might strengthen our hand in dealing with the Germans. He sees the League and my office as a check on Nazi ambitions; he also believes that restraints of this kind are in Poland's interest. He made both points to you a couple of times. So, I may be wrong, but I think he's decided to show us his hand. A peculiar way to do so, I grant you. But I think that's his motive. And you were a convenient conduit.

"The next question is what to do with the information. I didn't see any disclosures that require immediate action now. His warning that Beck is likely to use the Presidency of the Council to our detriment is probably the most important piece of information that he revealed. But there's no Council meeting on Danzig scheduled until June, and we don't know at the moment if we'll even have anything to include on the Council's agenda. So, vital as this information is, it doesn't compel us to act right now. His information on Polish foreign policy is certainly helpful background for us, but doesn't necessitate action on our part. Similarly, his observations on the political infighting among the Germans are really helpful and useful, but it's also background.

"So, I'm inclined not to do anything with the material at the moment," Lester concluded. "Let's just keep it locked up in the safe for now."

"I also think you should carry on your relationship with Papee without any change; business as usual. He knows you received the message he was trying to send. And I'm sure he's confident that you've passed it to me. That's sufficient for the time being. My recommendation is simply to send him a short note thanking him for the tennis and for hosting a nice dinner and expressing the hope to get together again soon for another match and dinner, this time on you."

"I'll do that, said Muller.

He went back to the office and penned a note to Papee. Then he pulled out clean sheets of paper and prepared a new report on what Papee had told him; the same information but a different document. When he was done, he wrote a short covering note:

"Stevenson: At dinner in Geneva, you told me I had to trust you. This information is from an impeccable source. You have the only copy. Please do not circulate it. Lester has the same information. No one else."

He didn't sign it. He folded the document, attached the note and put them both in a sealed envelope. He printed Stevenson's name and title on the front of the envelope and wrote in large letters 'CONFIDENTIAL'. He then placed that envelope in a larger sealed envelope addressed simply to 'Eirene'. Then he boarded the #5 tram, changed to the #3, and entered Sternfeld's Department Store, which was situated just off Langgarten Strasse on the other side of town. He asked directions to the glassware department and found two attractive fluted wine glasses. He told the saleslady that he was sending them to London as a gift and that he preferred to ship the package via ocean freight rather than use the German railroad express option.

"You know, with all the station changes to the Channel ports, they'd probably drop the package a dozen times and everything would break," he said smiling.

She smiled back at him. "Many of our discriminating customers prefer that route. I'll put these in a nice box with lots of protection. Do you want to enclose a gift card?"

He scratched off a short note to Eirene asking her to think of him when she and Stevenson next got together for a drink, which he hoped would be soon, and confidential of course. He placed the gift card and the larger envelope with her name on it in the box alongside the glasses and watched as the saleslady firmly sealed the box inside a corrugated shipping carton. He filled out the shipping label with Eirene's London address and in the return address space entered the name 'Jerusalem' and a phony address he had plucked at random out of the Danzig phone book.

After firmly affixing the label and taping the package shut, the saleslady pulled out a roll of twine and expertly tied it tightly.

"That should do nicely," she said. "I'll see to it that this is delivered to our ocean shipping department right away.

Muller thanked her, and asked where he might find men's furnishings. He needed a warmer coat and better gloves, he'd decided. And warmer boots too. Danzig was a lot colder than Geneva.

***

During the few next months, the High Commissioner's office was called to intervene in a seemingly endless series of disputes between the NSDAP-ruled Danzig government and other Danzig organizations. The opposition complained about rules requiring the Nazi flag to be flown from municipal buildings. Danzig has a perfectly good flag; it should be the banner under which the city's business is conducted, they argued. Uniformed SA Troopers carried large ceremonial daggers at their belt. Opponents complained that they were being used as instruments of intimidation and wanted them banned. But the Brown Shirts responded that Polish Boy Scouts were permitted to carry daggers, so why shouldn't they have the same rights? Brown-shirted SA storm troopers regularly paraded through the streets of Danzig bearing Nazi flags and banners, often singing Nazi songs. They insisted that pedestrians return the Hitler salute as they passed by, and several times a month, Danzig civilians lodged complaints that they had been beaten up for not saluting. Muller himself narrowly escaped a confrontation with a group of evidently drunken parading Brown Shirts by ducking quickly enough into a nearby shop. He thought about his conversation with Duncan Elliott at Berkshire Abbey back in July when Elliott had described similar incidents during his assignment in Berlin.

Some of the issues were more serious. A group of lawyers complained that the Senate was stacking the courts with Nazi judges imported from Germany. Replying to the complaint a Senate lawyer was unapologetic:

"Although National Socialism has attained power, our legal goals are not fully achieved. Our struggle is to replace Roman Law with Teutonic Law. The issue is whether judges are to be independent—whether objectivity is to remain the supreme legal norm. In parliamentary government, legal objectivity is acceptable. But in the totalitarian National Socialist State, the subjective law of the State must replace legal objectivity. The National Socialist State must have National Socialist Law."

In early April 1934, the Senate published a decree declaring it unlawful to wear a uniform in a public place without government approval. As expected, the SA Brown Shirts, Hitler Youth and other NSDAP-affiliate organizations were authorized to wear their uniforms and most Polish organizations that applied were also approved. But the Catholic Youth Organization, which bore the title Christus Jugend ('Christian Youth') by contrast with Hitler Jugend ('Hitler Youth'), was declared ineligible and its members were forbidden to wear their uniforms. A Senate spokesman dismissed Catholic charges of discrimination and defended application of the decree as necessary to preserve law and order.

"Those Danzig associations that have received permission to wear a uniform have the support of an overwhelming majority of the population. The wearing of a uniform by these organizations cannot pose a danger to public order and security. The same is not the case for the youth societies of the Catholic Church. These organizations manifest a hostile attitude toward the National Socialist State and the wearing of uniforms by these bodies constitutes a provocation against the National Socialist State. "

This exchange kicked off a protracted dispute between the NSDAP and the Catholic Church which was to become increasingly rancorous.

Religion was part of the curriculum in Danzig schools. In June 1934, the Senate's Education Director delivered a speech declaring that Catholic priests serving as teachers were 'intolerable to the people and the State'. He went on, "The Old Testament must as far as possible disappear from the curriculum. As National Socialist teachers, we have no time for it. Anyone who knows the obscenity of the Old Testament will have had enough of it without teaching it. We want clean textbooks."

With Muller's assistance, Lester addressed these and numerous other disputes, nearly always dealing with Rauschning, not Forster.

Lester had organized a meeting with Albert Forster soon after his arrival in Danzig. Muller had found Forster's thick Bavarian accent off-putting and hard to translate, but the meeting was civil; each man assured the other of his desire to work in harmony and avoid disagreements. As they parted with smiles and expressions of hope for continuing good relations, Forster paused and, turning narrow-set eyes closely on Lester, apparently decided to add a defiant message. "Commissioner," he said, "your role was established when Germany was weak. For now, I'm still obliged to acknowledge your authority. But Germany's strength is growing under our Fuehrer; at some point soon, we will dispose of your office and you will no longer interfere with our National Socialist program." With that, he turned on his heel and departed. Lester and Muller exchanged glances, shaking their heads, and as the complaints piled up and NSDAP rhetoric became more heated, neither of them harbored any doubt that Forster was behind the increasingly confrontational NSDAP tactics.

The Senate was the Danzig government and that was the proper entity for the Commissioner's office to deal with. Forster was a powerful figure; as head of the NSDAP Party he was arguably stronger than Rauschning, as President of the Senate. But constitutional norms dictated that Lester's principal point of contact should be the Senate leadership and meetings were frequent.

If Greiser was present, Rauschning was more formal and took a more legalistic attitude, usually resisting the changes that Lester was demanding and often dragging his feet–though carefully avoiding confrontation. Greiser was generally clumsy and tended to cling to the party line. When Greiser was absent, Rauschning was often sympathetic to Lester's points and the two of them were generally able to find ways to defuse their disagreements.

Early in the relationship they had discovered that Rauschning spoke English. Muller continued to play a role in their meetings because the documents they dealt with were written in German and his translating skills were still required. But a common language permitted Rauschning and Lester to develop a personal rapport. They also began to see one another socially. Rauschning invited Lester and his wife to his country estate in the hills outside the City, toward the Western border with the Polish Corridor. Lester and his wife hosted lively parties for the Rauschnings in the Commissioner's spacious residence, and the four of them made sightseeing trips together–to Oliwa and Zoppot, one bright cold Saturday, and later to the huge Teutonic Castle at Marienburg.

Muller continued to see Papee periodically. They would play tennis (Papee continuing to dominate, much to Muller's annoyance) and then dine together, either at the Continental Hotel or at one of the restaurants Muller had begun frequenting, Speishaus, with its pool table near the bar and spacious booths along the right wall, or Franz Malthesius' famed Restaurant Zur Ostbahn, with its decorative ironwork above the outside porch, serving the best Koenigberg dumplings in Danzig.

They made no reference to Papee's monologue in their earlier dinner together. But Papee seemed comfortable dropping intriguing pieces of inside gossip. He noted for example, that the NSDAP officials were having great difficulty swallowing the new policy of accommodation with Poland in the wake of the non-aggression pact.

"Forster was spitting mad," said Papee. "He's feasted on hating Poland most of his life. He was told by von Radowitz to make a speech rallying the Party in support of the policy, and he couldn't bring himself to do it. He uttered a few words about Germany's far-seeing policies toward its neighbors, but then couldn't resist taunting 'the sub-human Slavs'. They finally had to get Goering to order him to get in line. But he's still smoldering about it." Papee smiled at Forster's discomfiture.

At their next dinner Papee said offhandedly, "I hope you noticed that I've continued my policy of obstructionism against your office."

Muller looked at him quizzically.

"Yes, I've been telling Warsaw that I'm been sending Polish citizens that have been beaten up by the Brown Shirts over to you to seek compensation. That way, I'm telling them, it's the Commissioner who has to pester the Senate for payment, not the Polish Government. So Warsaw now thinks I have you doing its dirty work. Of course, it's nothing new; that's the way it's always worked. Nonetheless, they're very happy that I'm being 'obstructionist'. They're also more than a little puzzled over how you can somehow get the Senate to pay larger sums in compensation to the guys that were beaten up than we could get when I was pressing the cases." Papee flashed a conspiratorial grin.

Muller regularly briefed Lester about Papee's revelations and Lester encouraged him to continue the relationship. "It's always interesting to hear tales about what the other guys are thinking."

One Sunday in late March the weather turned unexpectedly bright and sunny with temperatures well above freezing, a welcome hint of spring. Danzingers took to the streets and savored the break from winter. Muller sat in the sun at an outside table at Café Weitzke, close to Elizabethwall, sipping mocha and nibbling at a sticky pastry. Muller had become a regular patron and chatted with Heinz, the waiter.

Heinz pointed at a crowd of uniformed men and women pushing their way on the #5 Tram. "Going down to see the NSDAP put on their Sunday show?" he asked.

"What's that?" inquired Muller.

"Ah, of course, you're new here," replied Heinz. "After the weather breaks in early May, every Sunday the NSDAP holds a rally on the parade grounds next to the Sportshalle. There's a big grandstand there and they pack it with bigwigs and put on a show for the faithful. It looks like they've decided to take advantage of the nice weather today to get an early start."

"It's a spectacle," he said. "You ought to take a look."

"Good idea," said Muller. "Thanks, Heinz."

He paid the bill then began walking in the direction of the Sportshalle. The trams were full, but a lot of people were going on foot, enjoying the nice afternoon. It was a festive crowd, everyone seemingly dressed in their Sunday best, with Nazi armbands prominently displayed. Many of the men were in their Brown Shirt uniforms and matronly women wore their Nazi Women's Association attire. As they neared the parade ground, Muller could hear band music and he could see that the grandstand was decked with Nazi flags and standards. Black-shirted SS storm troopers in shiny helmets with sturdy chin straps seemed to be directing traffic. SA Brown Shirts were arrayed in the top rows, then members of the Nazi Women's Association just below them and several rows of party and political leaders just above the podium. At the base, the uniformed Police Band and the Hitler Youth Drum and Bugle Corps were performing. A throng of Danzig citizens had assembled on the parade ground to watch, facing the grandstand.

The band struck up the Horst Wessel Song, the anthem of the Nazi Party, and the crowd bellowed the lyrics:

> *The flag on high! The ranks tightly closed!*
> *The SA march with quiet, steady step.*
> *Comrades shot by the Red Front and reactionaries*
> *March in spirit within our ranks.*
> *Clear the streets for the brown battalions,*
> *Clear the streets for the storm division!*
> *Millions are looking upon the swastika full of hope,*
> *The day of freedom and of bread dawns!*

Albert Forster strode to the podium, to roars of applause.

"Seig Heil," he roared.

"Seig Heil," came the throaty response.

"German blood will prevail," shouted Forster. We will crush our enemies. We will defend our Teutonic heritage, our birthright, our *destiny*! No Slav, no Jew, no stinking Bolshevik or slimy Communist can defy us. We are rising, against the tyranny of the Treaties and against those who would deny our fundamental rights as Germans. Here in Danzig we say to the world, 'Back to the Reich'."

Relating the experience that evening to Lester and Elsie, Muller kept shaking his head.

"It was pure raw meat, Forster and other speakers who followed him; all of them just ranting. The crowd cheered and hollered. There was a lot of 'Heil Hitler-ing'. The band played some more martial music and a contingent of maybe 100 storm troopers in uniform marched onto the parade ground from Hindenburg Allee, all goose-stepping together, rifles on their shoulders, shiny helmets glinting in the sunlight. I felt like I was watching one of those Nazi newsreels from Berlin that we've all seen at the movies. But it was right here.

"I began feeling more and more uncomfortable," said Muller, "so I edged away and then walked back toward my boarding house, staying ahead of the crowd. But as I think about it now, for all of that energy and noise they generated, I'll bet there weren't even 500 people at the event. Everyone there seemed to be fervent—well, except me—but they were shouting only at each other; I wonder where everyone else was."

Lester poured them after dinner drinks. "I find myself increasingly torn about the situation here," he said. "As an Irishman, I have deep sympathy for a revolutionary government that is trying to break old shackles and build a new kind of order. That's what we were doing after our civil war when we finally got the chance to be rid of British rule. And I understand the simmering resentments too; we had to negotiate with David Lloyd George, just like the Germans did, and for many Irishmen, that experience has left deep scars. So, I'm not entirely put off by all the muscle-flexing we see from the NSDAP. New governments feel threatened and tend to over-react to protect the gains they've made. So I'm comfortable with that phenomenon, at least in principle.

"But increasingly, the NSDAP seems to draw their circle tighter and tighter, calling anyone outside the circle an enemy—or even a traitor. It's one thing to separate supporters from opponents; fair enough. I'm always inclined to give an elected government the benefit of the doubt, but the Party's belligerence taxes my patience.

"I've spoken about this with Rauschning when we're alone," Lester continued. "Frankly, he shares some of my misgivings. He's in a tight spot here, with Forster lording over him and Greiser nipping at his heels. He told me he joined the Nazi Party in Northern Germany when it was headed by Gregor Strasser, whom he describes as more pragmatic and less ideological than Hitler. Rauschning gives Strasser more credit than Hitler for building the Party's national strength and he says there are a lot of Nazis, like him, who are apprehensive about Hitler's agenda. According to Rauschning, Strasser and Hitler quarreled and Strasser resigned from the Party, so when Hitler took power last year, Strasser was excluded. Rauschning left me with the impression that he is among those Nazis who would not be unhappy to see Strasser return to power, if not replacing Hitler, at least acting as a check on his ambitions."

"That sounds a lot like the hopes British appeasement policy is trying to generate, betting that cooler heads in Germany would lead Hitler to moderate his radical approach and reach some reasonable accommodation," said Muller.

Lester nodded. "I have the same reaction. It would certainly calm things down if they could find a way to agree. It's something we should keep a sharp eye out to try and promote."

"On a separate note altogether," Muller said, getting ready to depart, "I hope you both will attend my concert with the Danzig Police Orchestra and Chorus on April 15. We're doing the Brahms German Requiem, one of my favorite choral works. Commissioner, I know music is not your favorite pastime, but I hope you'll come."

"We'll be delighted," Elsie responded for both of them.

CHAPTER 8

April – July 1934

The Police Orchestra was well known in Danzig and abroad. The Music Director was Major Ernst Stieberitz, who was also a respected composer. When Muller was arranging for a police band to perform at Lester's Danzig arrival ceremony in January, he had met Stieberitz and found him friendly and helpful. It was Stieberitz who had suggested the Brahms Academic Overture as the compromise for the band to perform. "It's a suitably dignified work for the ceremony," he said, adding that he would be conducting the Brahms Requiem in April, "so performing another Brahms at the ceremony would be fine."

Muller had immediately inquired if he might join the chorus for the Requiem and had proceeded to sing a chorus from the second movement,

> *"Behold all flesh is as the grass,*
> *And all the goodliness of man,*
> *is as the flower of grass..."*

Stieberitz had laughed and clapped Muller on the back. "Well, I should think so," he said grinning.

Weekly rehearsals were held in one of the chapels at St. Mary's Church, a vast, brick and Gothic edifice dominated by a massive tower ending in a rooftop clad in red ceramic tile high above the City. Originally a Catholic cathedral, it had become Lutheran in the sixteenth century and in 1934 it was the largest and most important Protestant church in Danzig. It was also located very close to Muller's boarding house.

One night, following rehearsal, Stieberitz invited him for a drink at the nearby Nue Deutsche Hotel bar. Muller inquired about the origin of the Police Orchestra and Stieberitz told him that it had been established in 1920 when the Free City came into being. Originally intended to serve mainly as a morale-booster for the Police Department, it had attracted non-police musicians and soon acquired a strong reputation, becoming a particular point of pride for police force members.

"The Chief is trying to maintain the Department's professionalism, despite the political changes we're experiencing, and the Police Orchestra has become something of a symbol for him and for the rank and file," said Stieberitz.

"I know your office was involved in the dispute last year over the plan to require all policemen to be NSDAP party members," he continued, glancing nearby to be sure they could not be overheard.

A by-now familiar instinct, Muller thought. He nodded.

"Arthur Greiser gave a speech announcing the policy," Stieberitz said, "and I can tell you the Chief was furious about it. He's known Greiser for years and despises him. He refers to him as 'Little Arthur Motorboat," because he used to have that tiny boat business at the Zoppot Mole. Then he joined the NSDAP, Forster made him Vice President of the Senate and now he's trying to throw his weight around. The Chief doesn't like it one bit. The Police Department has a strong footprint in the City; we don't like being ordered around by a clown."

"The Chief is pretty clever politically," Stieberitz continued. "He's had to accommodate the NSDAP on some issues. For example, we're being forced to downgrade the National Police Force and the Civil Guard, where most of the men are assigned, and beef up the Schutzpoliezei, the Safety Police, which is more closely aligned with the Party. They're going to be issued rifles and helmets and drilled as if they were a military unit. We don't like it, but the Chief's attitude is to go along for the time being. There no assurance the NSDAP will keep its majority; they've annoyed a lot of people, including a lot of policemen. So things can change for the better sometime down the road. The Chief's approach is to go along, for now, where he has to. But he drew the line at responding to Little Arthur Motorboat.

"That's an amusing image," Muller said, smiling. "Do others refer to him the same way?"

"Most members of the Police Force and Civil Guard," Stieberitz replied.

"It drives Greiser crazy and it's one of the reasons he gave that stupid speech last year."

Stieberitz winked at Muller conspiratorially. "Here's the interesting thing about our program to sing the Requiem, Forster's picked a fight with the Catholic Church. Everyone knows that his real target is any organization that's not affiliated with the Party and he's using the Catholics as a proxy to attack all the denominations. Well, the Lutherans are still a powerful force in this City, and of course St. Mary's is their base. So, we're using them as our shield against his and Greiser's interference. Greiser wanted to forbid us from singing the Requiem because it's not a patriotic anthem. But Greiser's uneducated and knows nothing about the piece. We were able to show his minions that even though it's called a 'Requiem', the Brahms is not Catholic or liturgical and it's not a traditional requiem mass.

It doesn't preach Christian dogma and it's written in German, not in Latin. It's *German* sacred music. So he backed off and we're cleared to perform.

"And I can tell you that the Chief—and the rest of us too—are looking forward to reaffirming the reputation of the Danzig Police Orchestra and Chorus when we put on our performance in ten days."

***

April 15 was snowy and cold, but it was a Saturday night and a festive crowd was already gathering as Muller entered St. Mary's and made his way to the large room just behind the soaring high sanctuary where the chorus and members of the orchestra milled around conversing and preparing for their entry on the stage erected just behind the pulpit. The men were in dark suits with white shirts and matching blue neckties bearing the Danzig Police insignia; the women wore white blouses with dark skits.

The orchestra players took their seats in the Sanctuary and began tuning their instruments. At Stieberitz' signal, the members of the chorus lined up and started to file onto the risers erected to accommodate them. The bass section, in the rear, was the first to enter, holding their black notebooks with the score, and turning to face the audience. Muller was among the last basses on their riser. On his right was Franz Schiller, a burly police detective with a rich, deep voice with whom Muller had become friendly during rehearsals. Suddenly, he felt Schiller stiffen.

"Something's wrong," he hissed.

Muller glanced at him. "What?" His eyes followed Schiller's gaze.

A large block of seats on the front left aisle had been set aside for the NSDAP leadership. It was completely empty.

"Shit," said Schiller.

He moved quickly back along the riser and disappeared into the room off stage. The soprano section was beginning their entrance on the lowest riser in front, but they suddenly stopped, looking back into the room.

Moments later, Stiebritz, in his black tuxedo, moved to the podium and raised his arms for attention. "We ask your indulgence for a brief delay," he said. "Please keep your seats."

The audience stirred and there was a buzz of conversation as people turned to one another quizzically. Members of the chorus and the orchestra looked around uncertainly. Muller and the other basses wondered if they should retire offstage too. Minutes went by and the audience became restive.

Muller saw Schiller enter the sanctuary from a side doorway. He strode to the front right aisle and Muller saw him bend over to speak quietly to the Chief of the Police Department, who was seated in the first row, in full uniform, his blonde wife on his right. After a moment, Schiller nodded and straightened up, smiled thinly, and walked back to the doorway. Moments later he re-traced his steps onto the riser and took his place next to Muller. The soprano section resumed their entrance.

"Got the bastards," Schiller said in a low voice. "They were going to cut the power cable. But we caught them."

"Who?" whispered Muller.

"Some of the Party bully boys," said Schiller. "We had a security detail in the building as a precaution. They nabbed them with their wire cutters. We've got another detail outside. I don't think we're going to have any more trouble tonight.

"Forster and Greiser will dearly pay for this. No one fucks with the Danzig Police." He smiled at Muller. "So, now let's sing!"

***

By late May in 1934, the short Baltic spring had finally pushed winter aside. Occasional chill winds swept in off the sea, but tree buds finally began bursting and spring blossoms appeared in the City's neat gardens. Otto von Radowitz the German Consul General invited Lester to a dinner and asked that Muller attend as translator, since several additional German-speaking guests would be present. The appointed evening, June 1st, turned rainy and cold. When Lester and Muller arrived, von Radowitz said that instead of cocktails in the garden as he had planned, he'd instead had to ask the staff to bring in big logs and start the fireplaces. Rauschning would be along directly, said von Radowitz, and he turned to introduce the two other guests.

"This is General Walter von Brauchitsch, commander of German forces in East Prussia. At my request, he is not in uniform this evening so as to avoid any potential embarrassment in seating the High Commissioner of the League of Nations on the right of a senior officer in the German Army." He smiled.

"And this is Richard von Beckmann, who is a senior SA official, stationed in nearby Stettin, just outside the Polish Corridor, where he can keep an eye on Danzig." They all shook hands then turned to greet Rauschning, as he arrived.

Shaking Lester's hand, the General said, "Commissioner, in different circumstances I, not you, would be occupying your splendid residence which, as you doubtless know, was originally built to house the General Command for the Prussian Garrison. I'm quite jealous," he added with only the hint of a smile.

"Spoils of war," Lester replied with similar restraint.

The group engaged in small talk as drinks were served, then von Radowitz closed the drawing room doors and clinked his glass, nodding at Muller to translate for Lester.

"Gentlemen, before we go in for dinner, I would like to have a quiet word with you all." He glanced at the doors as if to ensure they remained shut. "Commissioner, I'm pleased that you could join us this evening," he began. "The four of us remain in rather close contact with one another and we thought that it would be constructive for you to become acquainted with our group.

"We are all Prussian Germans and share certain outlooks. We are also all members of the Nazi Party and share certain outlooks on that subject as well. We have concluded that neither the interests of Germany nor those of the Nazi Party are being properly advanced by the current leadership of the NSDAP in Danzig. You are aware of the disagreements that Mr. Rauschning, as President of the Danzig Senate, is experiencing with Messrs. Forster and Greiser. Those disagreements have intensified in recent weeks. We have therefore decided to take steps aimed at seeking the re-assignment of Forster and the removal of Greiser. I have communicated with Foreign Office at the Wilhelmstrasse to this effect. General von Brauchitsch has advised the General Staff of the German Army and Mr. von Beckmann has communicated with senior echelons of the SA."

Turning to Lester to translate, Muller watched Lester's face stiffen and his eyes narrow.

"Now, we all recognize the delicate position you occupy as High Commissioner here, Mr. Lester. We're not seeking any response from you. That would be diplomatically inappropriate. We are simply advising you.

"We must also advise you that reports have reached us that certain elements within the German Nazi Party and the local NSDAP are seeking the ouster of Mr. Rauschning as President of the Senate. So, much hinges on the outcome of discussions currently underway.

"I request that we not discuss this subject during our dinner tonight, as wait staff will be present. After dinner, we can repair back here, where I have cigars and some very special Danzig Gold Water Liqueur."

When they were seated at dinner, General von Brauchitsch turned to Lester.

"Commissioner, have visited East Prussia since you've been here?"

"Actually, no," Lester replied.

"That's no surprise, Commissioner," said von Brauchitsch, "It's damnably hard to do. Before the Corridor was established, there were bridges and ferries connecting East and West Prussia; no longer. There was a rail link directly East to Koenigsberg from the Danzig Central Station; discontinued. The bridge was dismantled. If you visit the site—which is now largely abandoned—you'd see a signpost telling you that a permit to cross the river can be obtained 50 kilometers South in Dirschau. So you'd better not be in a hurry to get across." He smiled ruefully. "The only land bridge remaining is 30 kilometers South of the Baltic Coast. In fact, that's how I had to come: I took the express train west from Koenigsberg as far as Dirschau, and then I had to board a local train taking me north the last 30 kilometers to get to Danzig's Central Station. These inconvenient travel constraints remain a very real irritant to any Prussian, I can tell you.

"Now, he continued, "if I had wanted to continue traveling East to Berlin instead of coming up to Danzig, I would still have been required to stop at Dirschau—or Tczew as the Poles call it—and I would need to get my passport stamped and pass through Polish customs. Just to get from my country to my capital, I have to ask permission from a foreign government." He shook his head. "It continues to rankle.

"None of us blames you, Commissioner," he said. "But we do blame the Treaty. We see it as a living symbol of the rage and vindictiveness of the victors sitting at the peace table. There must come a time when Germany's rightful parts will be restored to her." Von Brauchitsch spoke calmly and without anger, but he was serious.

Translating for Lester, Muller found himself struck by the fervor of the General's remarks, but also the dignified way he conveyed them. This was a man of substance, Muller thought to himself, not a political agitator.

After dinner, when they retired to the drawing room, they smoked cigars and commented on the potency of the clear Danzig Gold Water liquor. Muller got the impression von Radowitz wanted to say more about what the four of them were planning, but he detected glances from von Brauchitsch that dissuaded him. For his part, Lester did not volunteer any response and directed the conversation toward less sensitive subjects.

When the Daimler returned them to the residence, Lester invited Muller to his study for a nightcap. "Something a little less damaging than that Danzig Gold Water," he said smiling and pouring them schnapps.

"It's a dangerous game they're playing," he said. "Frankly, I was annoyed at being made privy to their scheme. Forster's got a direct pipeline to Hitler. He will certainly resist being ousted and I don't want to be accused of conspiring with the others to get him removed."

"I agree with you Commissioner," replied Muller. "But I have a hunch there may be something more to this. Here are four Prussians teaming up together. Hitler and Forster are Bavarians, not Prussians. I didn't hear a lot of cheerleading for Hitler tonight—for Germany, yes; but not for Hitler. Is there a message there?"

Lester nodded. "And why bring in the Commanding General of East Prussia? What's the military's interest in Danzig? Von Beckmann's involvement is even more curious. He's evidently a regional SA commander of some sort. If you believe their propaganda, the SA has nearly 3 million members. That dwarfs the 100,000 man Army permitted by the Treaty. So, we have to assume he's a powerful player. And we know von Radowitz is a protégé of the Foreign Minister, von Neurath–also a Prussian, by the way.

"So, we're told they've involved the Wilhelmstrasse, the Army and the SA in their scheme. But we didn't hear anything about Hitler's inner circle. Was this meeting intended as a message to expect political changes in Germany?"

"We need to tread carefully," he said softly.

***

The first news of the murders in Germany filtered into Danzig around noon on June 30th, 1934. Fragmentary information reported that in the very early hours of that morning, the head of the SA in Munich had been stripped of office and summarily shot on Hitler's orders. Then reports began circulating that, at first light, Hitler, accompanied by a contingent of Gestapo officers, had stormed a hotel in nearby Bad Weissee where Ernst Rohm and other high-ranking SA members were sleeping. Rohm was said to have been arrested and the other leaders shot. Later that morning, Hitler had delivered a furious harangue to a crowd in Munich denouncing 'treachery in the ranks' and boasting that 'traitors would be annihilated'.

Muller walked from the Commissioner's residence to the Central Station trying to get more information. He arrived to find a crush of people congregating around the news stalls and the radio transmitter in the station waiting room, all of them seeking news. Fear and bewilderment were in the air. News that members of the Gestapo had attacked the Vice-Chancellery in Berlin stunned the crowd. There were reports that von Papen had been arrested, dragged into a Black Maria and driven away at high speed. At least three of his close aides were reported to have been killed. It was rumored that one had been murdered with a pickaxe.

Danzigers stood in clusters, looking furtively about, whispering to one another and shaking their heads.

The next morning, newspapers reported that the violence had spread to East Prussia. Former Chancellor Kurt von Schleicher and his wife were said to have been murdered at their home and Gregor Strasser, Hitler's rival, had been shot, along with other Prussian Nazi leaders. A radio bulletin reported that Rohm had been executed in jail for treason.

Muller bought several German newspapers that purported to publish lists of the victims, but they contradicted one another and the Polish Press reported that the Gestapo was seizing the special editions that were being printed. Later that day Propaganda Minister Joseph Goebbels gave a speech in Berlin praising the 'fast and courageous' actions taken by Hitler to protect the Reich from attack by 'traitorous elements inside the Party and the Government'. Goebbels promised that 'more blood will be spilled' in defense of the Reich.

Muller paid a visit to his Chorus friend Franz Schiller at Police Headquarters. Schiller was on edge and obviously had not slept much during the crisis. Phones were ringing and uniformed policemen and clerks were scurrying around in the corridors.

"So far as we know, there have been no attacks or murders in Danzig," he told Muller, "at least not so far. But my God, what a bloodbath they've unleashed in Germany. At least fifty dead by our count and we all assume there are a lot more that we don't know about." He shook his head, then was called away to the Chief's office. He told Muller he would let him know if there were any local killings, then waved and headed for the stairway.

Hoping to get explanations, Lester went to meet Rauschning at his residence and directed Muller to call on von Radowitz.

The Consul General invited Muller to meet him at the Consulate. Von Radowitz was ashen, with dark circles of fatigue beneath both eyes; he looked uncharacteristically disheveled, his necktie askew and his hair uncombed. Muller was shocked at his appearance.

"I think I am supposed to offer you reassurance that only the quick and firm action of our Fuehrer has preserved the German Reich," he said. "If anyone asks, please tell them that's what I said.

"Please don't tell them that I also told you that I am profoundly shocked by what's happening and that I am frankly scared about my own safety." He offered Muller a Regatta and Muller noticed that his hand shook slightly, holding the lighter.

"Here's what I think I know," he said, straightening up in his chair and visibly trying to compose himself. "The leadership of the SA has been decapitated. Rohm was the SA Commander for a decade or more and was constantly at Hitler's side. Everyone assumed he was unassailable, but Hitler had him shot along with most of the rest of the SA leadership. Von Beckmann called me last evening from Stettin and told me he has been ordered back to Berlin. He didn't know if he would be executed or not." Von Radowitz paused and looked Muller directly in the eye as if to punctuate the threat.

"He is, or was for all I know, a close colleague, Muller," he said. "We overlapped at school and we joined the Party at about the same time. And he's summoned back to Berlin, maybe to be shot?" He shook his head in disbelief.

Muller didn't say anything. What was there to say, he thought? It really *was* hard to believe.

Von Radowitz glanced away and continued. "The crucial point is that Hitler has crushed any potential opponents. Von Schleicher and Strasser had followers in the party, particularly among Prussians, since they were

themselves Prussian and had been the leaders of the Prussian Nazi Party."
Von Radowitz paused. Muller expected him to add that he–and probably
Rauschning as well–were among the adherents that he was describing. But
he apparently decided not to finish the thought. "So Hitler had them
murdered."

"We've been told that Hitler ordered von Papen released from jail.
He's apparently back in the Vice-Chancellery. But I think we can safely
assume that he'll be preoccupied with cleaning up the bloodstains and
removing the body parts of his staff who were murdered. If he makes even
a peep, Hitler will doubtless have him killed too. So it looks like a political
clean sweep. Any expectations that Hitler will be constrained by other Nazi
leaders can be laid to rest. He's in total control."

"I've talked to my contacts in the Danzig Police," said Muller. "There
don't appear to have been any murders here."

"At least not yet," von Radowitz replied. Then he added with a
sardonic smile, "I suppose that qualifies as good news in this kind of
environment."

Muller shrugged. The bar for what qualified as "good news" was set
pretty low in Danzig.

"Frankly, Muller, the most unsettling part of the process is the score-
settling going on. Goebbels crowed about killing the Bavarian official who
arrested Hitler in the beer hall putsch back in 1923. They even shot the
music critic of a Munich newspaper. No one knows why." He shook his
head. "My wife was shopping in the market yesterday and she overheard
someone calling it *German Murder week*."

"So is it over?" asked Muller.

Von Radowitz shrugged. "If I learn more, I'll let you know." He stood
to show Muller out. "By the way, I think it would probably be a good idea if

all of us forgot about the conversation we had at my dinner party last month."

***

Lester and Muller shared information that evening over drinks at the residence. After hearing Muller's report, Lester observed that Rauschning had reacted even more strongly to the spate of killings in Germany. "He was furious," said Lester. "He said committing wholesale murder was simply unacceptable behavior by a head of state. He made no secret of his opposition to Hitler's acts. He told me that he was a Nazi Party member and a believer in Germany's need for a strong leader. 'But not for a murderer,' he told me. So what he's decided to do is to take steps here in Danzig to distance NSDAP rule from Hitler's behavior in Germany. He's decided to take on Forster directly.

"Last week, Forster put out what Rauschning described to me as an especially crude and offensive Party circular. Here's a copy." Lester pulled the paper out of his breast pocket and handed it to Muller, who translated.

"To a National Socialist, there are no decent Jews. All the distress and misery that we are experiencing are contrived by this people. The Jew must be eliminated wherever possible. Any generosity to the Jew is wrong. Catholics of the Centre Party make use of the clerical robe and church to oppose us. The black brethren believe we cannot get at them. They think we are too decent fellows to touch them. They're wrong. They must be taught that their day is over and that our struggle for National Socialism is death for them."

Muller looked at Lester. "Commissioner, that's worse than anything we've experienced here before."

Lester nodded. "Rauschning doesn't' know if this new belligerent tone is tied in some way to the violence in Germany or if it's Forster acting on his own. Either way, he's decided to try to put an end to it. Tomorrow, he's going to issue a formal statement rebutting Forster. He's going to publish it under his signature as President of the Senate, without formal Senate approval. He's still working on the text, but the message will be that the Constitution of the Free City of Danzig protects the rights of all citizens regardless of race, religion or ethnicity. It's a courageous step—especially in light of Hitler's murderous attacks."

The next day, Rauschning's statement was headlined by the opposition press. Opposition leaders praised the Senate President's "level-headed support of fundamental constitutional rights." The NSDAP newspaper *Verposten* criticized the "bourgeois fuzzy thinking of the Senate President who," it said, "spoke only for himself and not for the Senate or for the majority of Danzigers who support the State against the Jew and the priest."

Lester sent Rauschning a hand-written letter commending his action.

***

Ten days later, on July 13, Hitler gave a speech to the Reichstag which was broadcast across Germany and picked up by the Danzig radio station. Muller listened on the large Telefunken console in his boarding house sitting room, making notes so he could give a report to Lester. Hitler made no attempt to play down the bloodshed or distance himself from the violence:

"In this hour I was responsible for the fate of the German people, and thereby I became the supreme judge of the German people. I gave the order to shoot the ringleaders in this treason, and I further gave the order to cauterize down to the raw flesh the ulcers of poison in our domestic life. Let the nation know that its existence—which depends on its internal order and security—cannot be threatened with impunity by anyone! And let it be known for all time to come that if anyone raises his hand to strike the State, certain death is his lot."

Lester listened grimly as Muller read from his notes. They sat together silently for a few moments. Finally, Lester rose and walked to the sideboard, uncorked a bottle of Scotch and poured large dollops into two glasses. Returning to his desk, he handed one to Muller and they silently toasted one another.

"I'm nearly at a loss for words," Lester said. "That the leader of a nation like Germany would actually go before the public and brag about being a murderer." He shook his head and took a long swig of Scotch, staring out the window.

"Here we sit in Danzig, representing an international institution dedicated to peaceful resolution of conflict, and we now find ourselves confronted by a murderous dictator who openly threatens to kill any opponent and whose party seems bent on destroying my office.

"I'd be lying, Muller, if I told you this isn't frightening. Among other things, I've got a wife and three little girls here. I'm scared for them.

"And I'm scared for you too, Muller," he added. "All of us could become targets; maybe not today–but if this isn't stopped, then someday, possibly someday soon." Lester finished his drink and looked at Muller.

"I've nothing to add, Commissioner," Muller said. The threat is real. Forster is cut from the same violent cloth as Hitler. But I think I know what you're going to say next, and I agree with you on that point too."

Lester looked at him with the hint of a smile. "And what am I going to say next, Muller?"

"That you'll be damned if you're going to be driven out of Danzig by a bunch of jerks."

Lester laughed aloud and slapped his knee.

"You've gotten to know me pretty well, Muller. That's precisely what I was about to say–though I probably would have called them 'thugs' rather than 'jerks'. I don't like to be threatened and I'm not about to back down."

"I feel the same way, Commissioner," Muller said. "I'm afraid that what we're witnessing serves only to underscore the importance of your role here.

"I want you to know that I'm sticking with you."

Lester rose from his chair and walked around the desk to where Muller was sitting. They shook hands.

"Thank you, Paul," he said solemnly. Then he smiled. "Do you recall that a month before we left Geneva I asked you to inquire at the League's Office of Administration about whether we should seek special insurance coverage for our assignment here?"

"I do," Muller replied. "They told me, no, because we weren't assuming any serious risk."

"Another example of just how well-prepared the League seems to be for the task ahead," said Lester sarcastically.

CHAPTER 9

July – December 1934

A week later, Lester was invited to a reception that Rauschning was giving for a group of Polish officials visiting Danzig from Warsaw. Muller accompanied him. As they approached the nearby Senate Presidential Residence they saw a detachment of uniformed Gestapo officers stationed near the front entrance. An officer demanded to see their papers. Lester politely declined, stating that he was the High Commissioner of the League of Nations and was entitled to unencumbered access to all destinations in the Free City.

"We are under orders to inspect the papers of all visitors to this residence," said the officer. "You will wait here," he ordered.

"We will wait for one minute," replied Lester, ostentatiously pulling out a pocket watch from his vest. The officer marched across the cobble-stoned roadway to a superior officer, who looked over at Lester and Muller, then slowly made his way toward them, flicking a swagger stick against his uniformed leg.

"Commissioner, of course you may proceed," he said with exaggerated courtesy. "But you will understand that we need to be careful that no enemies of the State are permitted to visit the Senate President's residence."

He stepped aside gracefully and motioned Lester and Muller toward the entrance. Lester returned his watch to his vest pocket, ignoring the officer, and walked to the doorway.

Rauschning greeted them in the garden. "Commissioner, Mr. Muller, welcome," he said. "I assume you have made the acquaintance of my new contingent of Gestapo guards, who are sent to protect me from being bothered by undesirable elements of the Danzig community." He smiled. "Nice of them to be so solicitous."

"When did this begin?" asked Lester.

"Two days after publication of my statement defending the Constitutional rights of Danzig's citizens," Rauschning replied. "I assume the timing was just coincidental." He rolled his eyes.

"It's occasionally annoying, as they tend to search people leaving the building after meeting with me and confiscating any papers they find. It makes getting work accomplished decidedly more challenging–as I'm sure it was intended to do."

Lester was introduced to the delegation of visiting Poles, one of whom told Lester in English that he had lived in the United States–Milwaukee, actually. As they spoke in English to one another, Papee, the Polish Consul, came over to Muller, shook his hand and led him aside.

"We're still trying to sort out the implications of *Reich Murder Week*," he said, smiling but sounding very serious and speaking quietly to avoid being overheard. "However, we have taken the precaution, of advising our friends in Berlin that if any disturbances were to occur in Danzig that threatened the independence of the Free City, we would not hesitate to defend Polish interests vigorously. We have also let it be known that repeated provocations by the Senate, taken at the insistence of the Gauleiter, Mr. Forster, do not contribute to the kind of harmonious relations between

Germany and Poland that our non-aggression pact is intended to encourage.

"I'll let you know if we get a response." Then he grinned, "Looking for someone to trounce you handily on the tennis court this weekend?"

Toward the end of the reception, Otto von Radowitz, the German Consul, dropped by, taking care to greet the Polish guests with smiles and warm handshakes. Muller was glad to see him looking normal again. As he neared Muller he lifted a flute of champagne from the tray of a passing waiter and said quietly, "Could you stop by the Consulate late tomorrow afternoon?" Muller said yes, and von Radowitz turned to engage another guest.

***

Von Radowitz welcomed Muller to his office the next afternoon, then ushered him outdoors onto the adjoining terrace.

"Thank you for coming, and sorry for the guarded invitation; I didn't want to call attention to it."

Von Radowitz ordered a bottle of Marchandel gin and two glasses, commenting on fine weather until the waiter had left them. He poured them each a full glass. "Prost," he said and Muller responded.

"I'm feeling less uncomfortable than when we last met. Von Beckmann was actually promoted when he arrived back in Berlin. That's encouraging, of course, but no one is certain about what role the SA will play now or how much influence it will have. Hitler has appointed a new SA Commander, but he is not well known in the organization and he's laying low. So the jury's still out on the SA. But that's not the reason I wanted to see you. You and the Commissioner know that Rauschning is under surveillance," von Radowitz said.

Muller nodded. "We were asked for our papers last evening by the Gestapo guards outside his residence."

"It's even worse in his Senate Office," said von Radowitz. "His secretaries have been changed and staff members have been reassigned. Presumably everyone working for him now reports to Forster. So, on a pretext, he came to the Consulate this morning to prepare a confidential memorandum for me to send to Berlin which Forster couldn't block. He didn't want to risk contacting Lester about it, but he wanted Lester at least to know what's going on. So, I agreed to have you stop by so I could brief you.

"For better or worse, Muller, you and I have both become pipelines" he said cheerfully. "You're the pipeline to Lester and the League; I'm the pipeline to von Neurath and the Wilhelmstrasse." He smiled and poured them both another gin.

"I'm not going to show you Rauschning's memorandum," von Radowitz said, "but the message is one you'll easily understand." He glanced at what Muller took to be the text of the memorandum in his lap.

"Rauschning spelled out in detail the rationale for Germany to pursue a policy in Danzig that avoids conflict with either the League or with Poland," von Radowitz said, then decided to read the text. "'Even though Germany has quit the League, there is no German advantage in provoking the League over Danzig. At this stage, the League can place obstacles in Germany's path; German interests lie in biding our time and avoiding a fight.

'The same pertains to Poland,' he went on. 'We've just scored a major coup with the non-aggression pact. It would be foolhardy to provoke a crisis in Danzig which Poland—without any doubt—will treat as threatening Polish rights and lead them to react aggressively and to Germany's disadvantage.

'The only prudent course,' he concludes, 'is to follow a policy which respects the Danzig Constitution. Attempts to impose totalitarian rule–which the leadership of the NSDAP is aggressively encouraging–are bound to provoke the very confrontation that Germany ought to avoid'."

Von Radowitz looked up from the memo. "Consequently, he urges Berlin either to remove the current NSDAP leadership in Danzig or to place them under strict orders to conduct government policy in conformity with the Danzig Constitution. The memorandum was sent by wire this afternoon. I added a short message stating my concurrence. I hope to get a prompt and favorable reply."

Von Radowitz smiled, grimly. "Rauschning has made a decision to have it out with Forster and his acolytes. A lot of us think he's absolutely on target–including von Neurath and the Wilhelmstrasse. Despite the recent violence, they remain a powerful influence. We'll have to wait and see."

***

In Mid-August, the Senate ordered the *Danziger Landeszeitung*, the newspaper of the Catholic Centre Party, to be closed and its premises seized for a period of three months as punishment for publication of an article critical of the expenditure of City funds to expand the Sportshalle. The article had observed that the proposed expenditure greatly exceeded the current year's budget, which was already seriously over-stretched, and would be used to expand facilities at the Hall mainly used for NSDAP rallies. It also objected to calls for naming the Facility 'Forster Sportshalle', noting that Albert Forster was no more than a local party leader and was not even a citizen of Danzig.

Lester had Muller prepare a note requesting Rauschning to visit him at the Commissioner's office. There was no reply for several days. Then Arthur Greiser sent a note saying that Rauschning was traveling and that he,

Greiser, was occupied with other more important priorities and would be unable to attend to the Commissioner's request until some later date.

Erich Brost had become a regular visitor to the Commissioner's office. He was the leader of the opposition Social Democratic Party and Editor of the *Danzig Volkstimme*, the SDP newspaper.

"This latest outrage is really juvenile," Brost said to Lester. "It has all the earmarks of an ego trip by Forster. Overspending the budget for a project to be named for him, then shutting down the Catholic paper for reporting what he'd done. It doesn't make it any less of an outrage, of course; but it's very petty."

"I fully concur," Lester replied nodding. "And what's more, I can't get the Senate to address the matter. Greiser sent me a dismissive message back to my request for a meeting about it. There's really no excuse for that kind of behavior."

Lester added, "In fact, I was discussing this very subject with Mr. Muller just before your visit. There's a meeting of the League Council coming up in September and if the opposition were to submit a petition complaining about this matter, I'd be prepared to recommend that it be added to the Council's agenda so they could see what's going on here."

Brost rubbed his hands together. "I was hoping you'd say something like that, Commissioner. I was just about to tell you that we're planning to tell the Catholic Party that we'd join them a petition to the Council to protest this business."

"We'll have a document in your hands within a week." Brost smiled broadly.

***

The following Monday, Rauschning sent a note to Lester requesting a meeting that same afternoon. He appeared at the appointed hour, trailed by

Greiser. Rauschning apologized for the response to Lester's earlier request to meet, explaining that he had in fact been out of Danzig on a short vacation trip. He then looked at Greiser, who, on cue, mumbled words of regret for not reacting more positively to Lester's message. It was clear that he was speaking under orders and was unhappy at being obliged to do so.

The preliminaries dispensed with, Lester calmly and carefully recounted the facts as he understood them and explained the obvious contradiction between the Senate's action and the rights to publish and speak freely embodied in the Danzig Constitution.

"This kind of behavior by the Senate is simply unacceptable," Lester said firmly. "You both know that, but you issued the order to shut down the paper anyway.

"Well, I'm afraid you're going to have to face the consequences of your misconduct. The SDP and the Catholic Parties are preparing a petition to the League Council meeting in Geneva. I've told them I will recommend that their petition be added to the Council's agenda."

Rauschning took all this in, casting a withering glance in Greiser's direction. "Commissioner, thank you for your quite clear explanation of the issue. I was not present in Danzig when the Senate decision was taken. I wonder if you might allow me 48 hours to see if a resolution can be found to solve the problem without taking the matter to the League Council?"

"President Rauschning, I will allow you 24 hours for the Senate to vacate its order." Lester replied. "I think you'd better get started right away."

Rauschning sent Lester a formal notice stating that the Senate order had been withdrawn and the *Danziger Landeszeitung* premises had been turned back to the publisher.

Muller handed the note to Lester.

"For the life of me, I can't understand why they take these very stupid actions which they know they're going to have to reverse," Lester said. "I'm sure Forster was behind all this, not Rauschning; but Greiser's the one who's got egg all over his face since he's the one who issued the order."

"The disarray in the NSDAP is becoming pretty obvious," Muller said disgustedly.

Lester sighed. "I'm afraid you have to advise Ernst Brost to stand down on the petition. The Council's not going to waste time on a complaint where the Senate made the necessary corrections."

Muller had begun meeting regularly with Otto von Radowitz for drinks and sometimes for dinner. They met the following night and von Radowitz chortled as he described the scene when Rauschning and Greiser returned to the Senate from the meeting with Lester.

"He had Greiser find Forster, then sat them both down in his office and told them in no uncertain terms that they had acted very stupidly and created a potentially serious risk to the Senate's governing authority.

"He said that suspending and shutting down the *Danziger Landeszeitung* on such petty grounds was laughable. The actions were in clear contradiction of the Constitution, he told them. If the petition is filed, it would be an invitation for the League Council to throw the book at the Senate. 'And all because of a dumb building project with your name on it, Forster', he said. 'You'll be a laughing stock, and you risk compromising the Senate's authority. We need to fix this now and get that petition killed."

"Forster didn't like it one bit," von Radowitz said. "But even he could see that he had miscalculated. So he proceeded to blame the whole thing on Greiser, told Greiser to cancel the actions, then he stormed out of Rauschning's office."

"It was almost too easy," said von Radowitz. "I'm afraid this is about to become a grudge match."

***

The next day, Lester asked Muller to join him in his office. He had papers spread in front of him on his desk. "I've been trying to decide what to do about the upcoming League Council meeting in Geneva," he said, "and it struck me that we haven't sat down together to assess how we're doing so far. We've been here for nearly eight months now, can you believe it? So much has happened and it's such a hectic pace that time just seems to disappear.

"What do you think we have to show for our efforts?"

"We've survived, at least," Muller said with a grin. "That's no small thing these days.

"I confess, I hadn't thought much about measuring our success either; it's been hard enough just getting through each day." He paused, "But I suppose the best way to describe it is that we've preserved a standoff. We surely haven't converted the NSDAP to become supporters of constitutional democracy, but somehow we've managed to prevent them from impinging too much against the rights we're here to protect.

"Standoff," mused Lester, staring out the window. "That's a good characterization, I think. My office and the League mandate continue to command respect, so I've been able to compel them to climb down from some of their more egregious programs. This business of Forster shutting down the Catholic newspaper because of an editorial criticizing his pet Sportshalle project is a case in point. Even Forster wasn't prepared to risk being censured by the League Council if I'd brought the opposition's petition to Geneva.

"The conflict with the Catholic Youth Organization continues to fester, and they're still importing judges from Germany who are inclined to issue rulings along party lines. But even there, the threat of being called on the carpet by the League acts as a deterrent. It makes them think twice."

Muller nodded. "Part of that is attributable to the relationship you've been able to forge with Rauschning, Commissioner. The fact that the two of you can communicate in English has been good."

"The common language has no doubt helped," Lester replied. "But mainly it's the fact that Rauschning is educated and knows something of the world–unlike Forster and Greiser, who are neither intelligent nor informed. They're a couple of ideologues incapable of doing much more than parroting Nazi slogans.

"And it certainly looks now like they're determined to force Rauschning out of office. If that happens, we're going to have a harder time maintaining our standoff."

He began gathering up the papers on his desk. "For now, though, I think we can safely avoid adding any items to the Council's agenda. Eden will no doubt be delighted. I've been keeping Secretary General Avenol generally informed about our activities and he seems satisfied too. So I guess for now, we can stand pat."

He stopped, then looked directly at his assistant. "But Muller, how about you; how are you doing? I'm very pleased with your work as my Secretary and interpreter. But your schedule doesn't leave you much time for a life. Are you okay? Elsie and I were speaking about this the other evening and we're concerned."

Muller found himself amused at Lester's expression of concern; clearly it was Elsie who had prompted his comment. Lester was all business all the time and expected no less of him. Muller smiled.

"I'm fine, Commissioner," he said. "Thank you for your compliment about my work and your concern for my well-being, but this is what I signed up for and, frankly, I'm enjoying it."

He decided to leave it at that. It was true; he was enjoying the work. And his schedule did not in fact leave much time for 'a life', as Lester had put it, by which Muller assumed he'd meant having a girlfriend. But he'd come to realize that in a community as small as Danzig there was no way that he could present himself as an eligible bachelor. 'Oh and by the way, I'm Secretary to the High Commissioner.' Not exactly what a young woman, let alone her family, wanted to hear. That had been made pretty clear to him by a couple of the single women in the Police Orchestra chorus. So he'd simply decided to ignore the subject. There had been a couple of flings earlier in the summer at Zoppot with women from the cruise ships, but hardly anything serious.

He did enjoy corresponding with Eirene Jones. They traded 'Jerusalem' messages that he hoped weren't being opened by prying authorities and they were planning to see one another over the Christmas holidays.

Anyway, there was no way he could pursue her now. They were separated by five hundred miles and were immersed in separate careers. He felt comfortable 'seeing where it would go'. Though it would be nice to have a little sex now and then, he thought.

Ah, well.

As he expected, Lester moved on to the next piece of business. But it was nice of Elsie to be concerned on his behalf, he thought.

***

One cloudy, misty day in late November, Otto von Radowitz sent an urgent message to Muller asking to meet alone at 3 PM that afternoon at the Oliwa Gate. The message was labelled 'Highly Confidential' and he had underlined the word 'alone'. At lunchtime, Muller went back to his apartment and changed into warmer clothing; it would be cold if they were to meet at the Oliwa Gate. He speculated that 'alone' meant 'be sure you're not followed'.

Leaving himself ample time, he boarded the #9 tram, riding alongside Hindenburg Allee, then out past the airfield, in the direction of Brosen, the beach resort just beyond Oliwa. The tram pulled into the siding by Saspe Cemetery and stopped, waiting for the tram coming the other way from Neufahrwasser-Brusen to pass. He could see the approaching tram growing larger as it crept toward them, its single headlight gleaming in the mist. Muller thought he had been the last person to board the last #9 tram car, but when the oncoming tram passed and his conductor rang the bell twice signaling their departure, Muller pushed the exit button and stepped off the tram, watching it depart. He did not see anyone craning back to find him.

He stepped into the cemetery. It appeared to be abandoned; old headstones covered with moss and lichen were tilted at odd angles, inscriptions no longer legible, and ancient pine trees, stunted by years of high winds, grew along the rear wall. Muller pushed a rusting gate and walked down a pathway to a flat, grassy depression. He could look across at the Brosen resort in the distance. It looked strangely desolate now, refreshment stands boarded up, bright flags packed away for winter, empty booths appearing lonely.

Fifteen minutes later he heard the next #9 tram arriving. When it had pulled onto the siding, he walked to the first car. He had to knock on the window of the tram door to get the conductor's attention. The man opened the door and looked quizzically at Muller as he boarded and paid his fare. Muller ignored him and sat in the rear of the nearly empty car, on the far right side. When the oncoming tram approached, Muller bent down to retie his shoes. He would not have been seen by anyone on the tram as it passed next to them.

Oliwa Gate was the second stop. It was the entrance to the Oliwa Garden which, in summer, was thronged with families visiting the Castle Park, with its goldfish and white swans and the Whispering Grotto. Now it was empty and looking forlorn as brown leaves scattered in the breeze. Muller stood with his back to the ornate ironwork gate. He was confident no one had followed him. It was 3 PM; his timing was just right, but he didn't see anyone. Ten minutes later a door opened toward the end of a dark, shabby, building to his right that looked like a utility shed. Von Radowitz stepped outside and motioned Muller to join him.

He led Muller into what appeared to be a workroom, with benches and stools. The room was gloomy in the approaching twilight. "Sorry for the unusual arrangements," said von Radowitz. "And thanks for coming alone. But we thought it best to be careful." Von Radowitz did not identify who the 'we' might be, but Muller could see from half-filled ashtrays and abandoned paper cups, that others had been there—perhaps still present, but in another room.

Von Radowitz pulled a half full bottle of Marchandel gin out of a bag at his feet, located two fresh paper cups, and poured them both a generous helping. "It's gotten cold; this'll help," he said, raising his cup and toasting Muller before they drank.

"Here's the story, Muller," he said. "We're about to launch a coup within the NSDAP and change the Party leadership. We don't plan on killing anybody," he added quickly. "This is not another Murder Week. But Forster and Greiser need to go. We have secured support within Germany to make the change. The SA in Danzig will be neutralized and we have enlisted the support of the Danzig Police to prevent any unrest. The Catholic Centre Party is—formally, at least—still in coalition with the NSDAP and they will lend support. And we can count on Kasimir Papee, the Polish Consul to tamp down any reaction by Poland.

"I'm not going to tell you any tactical details. We are not asking for any reaction on your part. But we wanted the Commissioner's office to be informed. This will happen soon," he added.

Muller lit a Gitane, and blew the smoke in the direction of a dirty window. "Your June dinner party was a kind of dress rehearsal," Muller said.

Von Radowitz nodded. "The upheavals in Germany a few days later caused us to delay. But now we're ready to act."

Muller finished his gin, ground out his cigarette and stood to leave. Speaking loudly for the benefit of any others in adjoining rooms he said, "I want it known that the Commissioner's office will have no part in any extra-legal paramilitary actions in the Free City of Danzig."

Muller went to the door without shaking hands with von Radowitz. "This is crazy. I'm leaving."

Muller walked back to the tram stop by the Oliwa Gate and boarded the next tram toward Danzig when it arrived a few minutes later, not bothering to check and see if he were being followed.

Muller fumed on the short return trip. How could they expect the Commissioner to be complicit in a hare-brained scheme to oust Forster and Greiser? He assumed the plan was to snatch the two of them, bundle them off to the bridge at Marienburg and hand them over to von Brauchitsch's Command to put them on ice somewhere in East Prussia. Mobilizing Danzig forces to mount a party coup was blatantly illegal; how could they expect the Commissioner to accede to their plan? What if Hitler were to object? What if the local NSDAP were to resist with force? Muller had no confidence that contingencies had been covered.

Upon his return, Muller went directly upstairs to Lester's office and gave him a full account of what had transpired. Lester was even angrier than Muller had been. He telephoned Rauschning's office and was told that Rauschning was 'indisposed at his residence'.

"Put your coat back on," Lester said to Muller. "We're going to pay a house call."

They walked the few blocks to the Senate Presidential residence. Paying no heed to the Gestapo surveillance team, Lester marched up the entryway steps and opened the door without bothering to ring the bell. Inside, he told a surprised staff member that he needed to see President Rauschning immediately. They were shown into a large sitting room and Rauschning appeared moments later. He was pale and looked somber.

"Hermann," said Lester, deliberately using his Christian name to underline the seriousness of his message. "This business of a coup to remove Forster and Greiser must be stopped." He paused for emphasis. "Now!

"As High Commissioner, I refuse to countenance taking illegal steps to change the political leadership of this City. If you do not call off this attempted coup, I shall promptly advise Forster and Greiser of the information about it that was conveyed to Muller earlier today. And I shall issue a public statement condemning it as unlawful."

Rauschning straightened in his seat. "Commissioner," he replied formally. "This is an internal NSDAP matter that need not concern your office. The Party is entitled to determine its own rules of succession. In this instance, we have concluded that policies being pursued by Messrs. Forster and Greiser are a threat to the legitimacy of the Party's majority rule and that they must be replaced. We are simply acting to implement this change in party leadership."

Leaning forward and gazing intently at Lester, he added, "Sean, you can scarcely imagine how bad it's gotten. Forster's demanding that we arrest Catholic priests, shut down Jewish businesses, close the opposition press, and more. These steps would be completely illegal. Plus, he's demanding that we launch a new wave of public works projects to create jobs and win political support. But we don't have the money. If we do what he's demanding, the City will go broke.

"He's not an elected official, or part of the Senate. He's just a Party leader and he needs to go," he said vehemently, his posture now erect and defiant. "Forster is a menace–to the Party, to the City, to the League–to everyone and has to be removed."

"Hermann," said Lester softly, "Everyone knows that you've tried before to persuade authorities in Berlin to re-assign him. And you've failed. For whatever reason, the leadership of the German Nazi Party that appointed him Gauleiter here nearly five years ago won't move him."

"The leadership in the Wilhelmstrasse is behind us," Rauschning interrupted, "And the Reichsbank too. The Danzig government is sustained by subsidies from the Reichsbank. They understand better than anyone that the Germany Treasury can't afford to pay for Forster's extravagances. So we've got strong backing."

"But not strong enough to get Forster reassigned," said Lester firmly. "You haven't persuaded the Nazi Party leadership to do what you want. So you've decided to take it into your own hands, asserting your authority as President of the Senate to use Danzig police and other government resources to kidnap the NSDAP leaders–including your own Senate Vice President, by the way–and spirit them off to East Prussia. It's flatly illegal; if you were to do that to the leadership of the SDP or one of the other opposition parties here, I'd haul you in front of the Council in a heartbeat.

"In addition, it won't work, Hermann," Lester pointed a finger at Rauschning. "A coup that sends Forster and Greiser to East Prussia will be seen by everyone as defying Berlin and the Nazi leadership. You've told me yourself that Forster has access to Hitler directly, and Hitler's certainly made it pretty clear that he won't tolerate any opposition. It is likely to provoke a reaction that could jeopardize the city. It's madness to proceed. Among other things, you and your friends are probably putting a pistol to your heads."

Lester rose to leave. "You need to stop this whole business, Hermann. I'll give you forty-eight hours before taking any action."

Rauschning announced his resignation two days later, on November 24, 1934. The Senate promptly elected Arthur Greiser to replace him as President of the Senate.

The next day, Greiser called on Lester to present his credentials. It was an awkward meeting and, as he translated their remarks, Muller could sense the unease of both men. Greiser was plainly nervous, conscious of his new importance as Senate President, and his tone became truculent as he recited familiar Party litany justifying suppression of minority actions that threatened to provoke disorder and disfavor among the NSDAP majority.

Lester was in no mood to be hectored. "Mr. Gresier, I need not remind you that the government of the Free City of Danzig, which you have now been appointed to lead, is obliged to conduct itself in a manner consistent with the terms of the Danzig Constitution, which is guaranteed by the League of Nations, of which I am the representative. It is my practice not to involve myself in issues of local governance; you are now head of a freely elected government and you will have my support. But that government owes its existence to the Danzig Constitution. We both have a responsibility to uphold the rights it embodies."

Muller could sense Greiser backing away from confrontation. "Thank you Commissioner," he said. "I would like to avoid any conflict."

"Then see to your responsibilities," Lester replied in a firm voice.

"Two points need to be addressed now," Lester continued. "By-elections are to be held in ten days in two rural constituencies of the City.

My office has received complaints of campaign irregularities and intimidation of opposition parties by NSDAP supporters. My first request is that your office take immediate steps to halt this misbehavior.

"Second, you are aware of petitions filed with my office by the Catholic Church and the Centre Party. The Senate has not responded to my repeated requests for information regarding these subjects. I intend to forward the petitions to the League Council to be taken up in the January meetings in Geneva. I think the interests of the Senate would be well-served by promptly replying to my inquiries, so that I am not obliged to report to the Council that the Senate has simply ignored my communications on these serious issues.

"Greiser, we've had our differences. Let's resolve to get off to a better start and to work together."

Greiser mumbled some cordialities and shook hands as he departed.

After showing Gresier out, Lester returned to where Muller was gathering his notes. "God, he's a crude bastard," said Lester, "coarse and stupid. We'll have our work cut out for us going forward. I wonder if he even knows about the plans for the coup and how close he came to getting snatched."

***

In mid-December Lester threw a Christmas party for the Danzig Consular corps and their wives. It was a merry gathering, featuring a very potent punch that Lester had personally prepared from a 'secret recipe'.

Kasimir Papee, the Polish Consul, pulled Muller aside. "Well, that was some adventure watching Rauschning being pushed over the side. We're not happy about it. Greiser's never bought into the Polish–German détente that Rauschning was responsible for starting. Forster either. At one point, the Wilhelmstrasse was going to get rid of both of them in some kind of coup that would have preserved Rauschning's position. They approached me about keeping Poland from reacting to their little plan. I pushed back hard. We're not about to stand by while officials get detained and then disappear for a while.

"So we're stuck with Greiser," he said. "And remember I told you what a charmer he can be when he's had a few drinks? Have a look." He directed Muller's gaze across the room where Greiser had his arm on Elsie Lester's shoulder and the two of them were guffawing together.

"Merry Christmas," Papee said, grinning and heading for the punchbowl.

Otto von Radowitz invited Muller to join him after the party for a drink at the Eden, the upscale hotel on the bluff overlooking the railroad station and the Central Square. There were no recriminations about the failed plans for the coup. "Everybody lost their nerve," he said, pouring them both glasses of Marchandel gin.

"I didn't know it at the time, of course, but the Wilhelmstrasse had already backed away from the plan by the time we met at Oliwa. Von Neurath decided he was sticking his neck out too far, so he went to Goering and asked his help in getting Forster transferred. Goering flatly refused. He told von Neurath that he knew Forster was a hothead and difficult, but he said that Forster was 'one of them'. He wouldn't hear of kicking him out and he knew Hitler would never approve. He told von Neurath he would have a word with Forster to follow the Wilhelmstrasse line. So they dropped the coup idea.

"I think I'm not cut out for cloak and dagger stuff," he said ruefully.

That's for sure, Muller thought. He wondered if von Radowitz even knew that Papee had refused to give him cover with the Polish government. He doubted it.

"Greiser's actually gotten off to a decent start," von Radowitz continued. "Before the meeting with Lester, he was told to cooperate and he appears to be doing so. He issued orders to cut out the bullying, so the rural by-elections were pretty clean and the results were a huge success for them—something like 87 percent voted for the NSDAP, so he and Forster are thrilled; they got the outcome they wanted and they can say they cooperated with the Commissioner."

They finished their drinks. "Let's hope next year is not so contentious, Muller; Merry Christmas."

The next day, Lester began preparing his first Annual Report to the League Council as High Commissioner. He was writing it himself, working from extensive notes. "I'll share it with you when I'm ready, Muller. The key question is what kind of action we want the Council to take. The meeting isn't till January 18, so we have time. But we should both ponder that subject over the holidays."

He went on to say that he and Elsie had decided to remain in Danzig for the holidays with the three girls; they had given up their apartment in Geneva and it was too complicated to go to Ireland. "We've got this really splendid residence and we'll be well fed by the staff. We'll get a Christmas tree and put up decorations, and Ellie has found a lot of things for us to do as a family at Zoppot and in town. It should be a nice time. We'll be fine, so you go visit

CHAPTER 10

Winter 1935

When Muller returned to Danzig on January 4, 1935, a deep freeze had descended on the City. A smoky haze hung in the air as furnaces and chimneys worked overtime to keep the frigid temperatures at bay. Disembarking from the overnight train, Muller shivered in the passport control line at the end of the platform; he was pleased that officials were giving travelers' papers only cursory attention so they could quickly return to their warm offices. He took a taxi to his boarding house, washed up, changed into clean clothes, adding a warm sweater, and took the short, cold tram ride to the office.

The central heating system in the Commissioner's building was doing its job and Muller found his office warm enough to remove the heavy sweater he'd added. Lester greeted him cheerfully. They exchanged pleasantries, then Lester handed him a thick file with his draft Annual Report for the League.

"Have a look at all this and let's meet in the residence for a drink around 6:00 this evening to discuss it,"

When they met that evening, Lester was in a garrulous mood. "I hope your Christmas holiday in Zurich was good," he said smiling.

Muller responded that he had enjoyed Christmas in Zurich with his family, but that he had spent New Year's weekend in Paris, "with a friend."

Lester threw back his head in laughter. "Serious, hardworking Paul Muller slips off to Paris for a romantic weekend; I never knew you were such a Romeo, Muller! Bravo! So you return to us refreshed–but not rested." He laughed again, slapping his knee.

To his surprise, Muller found himself blushing. "I did sleep most of the trip over from Paris," he said a bit shamefacedly, as Lester continued to enjoy his evident discomfiture. He was not about to reveal the excitement and passion he and Eirene had shared in their large room on the top floor at the Hotel Plaza Athenee, overlooking the Place de l'Alma and the Seine. The memory of it now warmed him. So to change the subject, he reached into his briefcase and extracted a sheet of paper which he handed to Lester.

The document bore the title A NATIONAL DECLARATION ON THE LEAGUE OF NATIONS AND ARMAMENTS in large block letters.

"This is what the British are calling 'the Peace Ballot', Commissioner," he said. "My friend is active in the League of Nations Union, the organization that is the sponsor. She tells me they have recruited over a half million volunteers across the country to act as canvassers, asking voters to cast ballots, voting 'yes' or 'no' on the five questions you see on the ballot. The volunteers will go house-to-house distributing and collecting the ballots. Voting is beginning now and will take place over the next six months or so. There is considerable newspaper coverage–even the BBC is following it; the organizers believe they can attract five million voters and they'll use the Ballot to press the government to promote peaceful policies." He didn't add anything about the ballot-stuffing intimacies he and Eirene had shared in their bed. He simply added, "She's very keen on the project."

Lester cast his eyes over the five questions on the ballot:

DANZIG

Should Great Britain remain a Member of the League of Nations?

Are you in favour of all-round reduction of armaments by international agreement?

Are you in favour of an all-round abolition of national military and naval aircraft by international agreement?

Should the manufacture and sale of armaments for private profit be prohibited by international agreement?

Do you consider that, if a nation insists on attacking another, the other nations should combine to compel it to stop—
by economic and non-military measures:
if necessary, by military measures:

Lester studied the ballot for a few moments before handing it back to Muller. "It seems doubtful that many people would choose to vote No on any of these questions." he said. "Doesn't it look a little too well stage-managed?"

Muller smiled. "I have the same reaction, Commissioner," he said. "I confess I didn't share those sentiments with my friend."

Lester laughed. "I should think not, Muller," he said. "No indeed; there were much more important subjects at hand, I'm sure." He continued chuckling.

Muller decided not to mention how naïve he had found the ballot questions and how he had found Eirene's breezy commentary on British Appeasement policy suddenly so much less persuasive. It had been over a year since their tryst together in Annecy; he had felt comfortable with her enthusiastic embrace of British appeasement; but now he found it deeply troubling. He had spent this last year in Danzig, a city ruled by a Nazi Party and deeply influenced by Hitler, whose menacing state was just next door. On the train back to Danzig from Paris, when he wasn't sleeping, he had reflected on how much that experience had changed his perspective. He had not said much to Eirene about it; he didn't want to spoil their weekend–and certainly their appetite for lovemaking together had not been diminished by the passage of time. It had been quite a splendid few days on that front.

But he needed time to think through the implications of what he had suddenly come to recognize as his own changed view of British policy. League attitudes toward Danzig were heavily influenced by Britain: Eden was Rapporteur for the Council on Danzig; Stevenson was running Whitehall's Danzig policy planning staff. Muller wasn't worried about his relationship with Eirene; they'd be fine, he told himself. But he wondered if he would remain confident in British leadership–if he would still see eye-to-eye with Eden and Stevenson. That was a subject needing further reflection.

"I've read Greiser's New Year's statement that you included in the file," Muller said, changing the subject; "it certainly is irritating. He offers the customary upbeat sentiments for the New Year, but they're all couched in terms of advancing the NSDAP agenda. He just can't resist taking verbal swipes at the opposition–'saboteurs' he calls them."

Muller paged through the statement, selecting excerpts. "'Traitorous machinations', 'noxious elements', 'the vital forces of our National Socialism will bring them down'."

"Happy New Year," Muller added sarcastically, looking up and smiling weakly. "They are so damned confrontational. And it's apparent that they're reading their big December by-election victories as a re-affirmation of their political power. I don't see any new policy pronouncements where we can call them to the mat before the Council; it's all rhetoric. But what rhetoric: 'our party is steeped in German blood and German soil'; 'the political sources of National Socialism derive from the deep well-springs of true German character'. Reading the words on the page, you almost have to suppress a giggle; it really is outrageous. But they *mean it*. And that makes it all a little scary."

Lester nodded. "There's really nothing we can do about it. But it certainly sets a confrontational tone for the New Year."

Lester refreshed their whiskies and they spent some time discussing the Annual Report and the upcoming Council meeting.

Muller complimented Lester on the text of the Report. "The best part is the detail it presents on the struggle we've been having with the NSDAP-controlled Senate, which is something new for the Council. They need to have a flavor of the tense environment here. Have you decided on what you want Eden's Report to say?

Lester shook his head. "We need to see how the debate over the petitions plays out," he said. Both the Catholic Church and the Centre Party have presented very credible cases. They'll put Gresier on the defensive. It will be his first time sitting at the Council table; I'm betting he'll overplay his hand.

"I think you ought to come to the Council meeting too, Muller," Lester added. "I'll probably need to communicate with Greiser and I'd like you there. I'll book rooms for us at the Hotel de la Paix beginning on the 17th the day before the Council meetings begin."

Two days later, Greiser sent a formal message to Lester's office finally responding to Lester's demands for information relating to the petitions he had sent to the Council. But instead of responding substantively, Greiser's message said simply that he was authorized by the Senate to advise the Commissioner that he was prepared to undertake negotiations with the petitioners seeking "an acceptable settlement of all outstanding disagreements" upon his return to Danzig following the upcoming Council meetings, and requesting Lester to forward his message to the Council. The message reaffirmed the Senate's pledge always to conduct its affairs in full compliance with the Danzig Constitution.

Lester was suspicious of the offer to negotiate, but told Muller he had no choice but to forward the message to the League as Greiser had requested. He also forwarded it to representatives of the petitioners. Predictably, they were outraged, accusing Greiser of flagrant hypocrisy, but publicly they felt compelled to welcome the invitation to enter into negotiations.

The next day, an event occurred on the other end of the continent that rocked Danzig.

The Territory of the Saar Basin, the highly-industrialized coal mining region located on the Western-most border of Germany, had been placed under League of Nations administration by the Treaty of Versailles in 1920. The arrangement was intended as a form of reparation to France, whose coal mines in Northern France had been destroyed by the Germans during the War. The Treaty provided that a plebiscite was to be held after fifteen years to determine if the Saar should be returned to Germany, become French or stay under League Administration. The plebiscite was conducted on January 12, 1935 and the results were announced the next day. More than 90 percent of the voters favored returning the Saar to Germany. Less than .05 percent favored becoming French.

NSDAP leaders in Danzig were electrified by the news. They immediately declared a public holiday and organized marches and rallies—even in the bitter cold—to celebrate the Nazi victory. Greiser issued a triumphal message: 'Danzig voted in December, the Saar voted in January. National Socialism is everywhere ascendant!'

After Muller translated the message; Lester glanced out of his office window at bundled-up crowds heading to a rally in the Central Square. "It certainly doesn't appear that they're in a very conciliatory mood at the moment," he observed wryly.

***

Their train arrived in Geneva at the Gare de Cornavin just before dinnertime a day later. Lester and Muller boarded a tram for the short trip down the hill from the station. They crossed the Mont Blanc Bridge and alighted at the entrance to the Hotel de la Paix, which was situated at the East end of the bridge, facing the lake and the pier where the lake steamers were firmly tied up for the winter. Muller had wired ahead to Stevenson, who had invited him to dinner at the Hotel d'Angleterre. He checked in at the front desk and asked the concierge to put his bag in his room. Exiting the hotel, he crossed the street and boarded a tram heading back over the bridge.

He found Stevenson, as expected, at a busy table in the lobby pub. He didn't see Carole with an 'e' in the crowd, but thought she might make an appearance before the evening was over. Stevenson rose and greeted Muller heartily, introducing him to the others at the table as "an intrepid guardian of the League in Danzig."

Over dinner, Stevenson quietly thanked him for the "wine stems" he had sent earlier in the year.

"It was valuable information," he said. "The Polish attitude toward Danzig that your source predicted is certainly manifesting itself. Beck has made it known that he has no interest in having the Council involve itself in the internal affairs of the Danzig government. Upholding the Danzig constitution has no appeal for him. His only interest is to ensure that Danzig does not become German."

"Well maybe he ought to pay a little more attention to what the Danzig government is doing to encourage a 'Return to the Reich'," Muller replied snappishly. "Every speech Forster and Greiser make is cast in terms of 'German blood', 'German destiny', 'German this and German that'. They already think of themselves as an extension of Nazi Germany. It's a struggle every day for the Commissioner to keep them from running roughshod over the opposition, the churches, the courts—everything.

"You've read the Commissioner's Annual Report," Muller went on, "menacing speeches, repeated acts of intimidation; if anything, the Report understates the state of crisis that exists. If the League lets them have their way, they *will* become part of Germany and Beck ought to recognize that. His Consul General there understands it. He's telling Beck that the Commissioner and the League are the only things standing between the Danzig Senate and Hitler; Beck needs to start listening."

"Muller, you need to be a little calmer," said Stevenson. "Diplomacy takes time and patience. Eden's bending every effort at reducing tensions, but it's hard, painstaking work."

Muller responded in a testy toe. "Tensions are not diminishing, Stevenson. You need to understand that; Eden, too. The situation's getting worse, not better.

"Stevenson, they have the bit in their teeth. That overwhelming vote in the Saar coming on the heels of their big by-election victories last month set them off like a Roman candle; they haven't stopped marching and singing all week long.

Muller leaned toward Stevenson. "Let me tell you what happened just this week. Greiser announced he's' coming here for the Council meeting, so the Party organized a big send-off for him: A full dress parade at the airfield; too cold for the band to play, but they gave him a twenty-one gun salute. Then a German Fokker aircraft touched down—big swastikas on the fuselage and the tail—I didn't think the Germans were supposed to have an air force, by the way. Anyhow, Greiser steps aboard, waving at the crowd from the doorway of the aircraft like a film star; the plane takes off, does a swoop over the cheering crowd and heads off for Berlin where Greiser is supposed to meet with Hitler.

"Danzig seems always to be on edge; it is not a relaxing environment," he concluded.

The waiter brought their meal and Muller rubbed his hands in anticipation. "Now this is more like it," he said, wanting to break the tension. Venison was his favorite winter fare in Geneva, noisettes de chevreuil, with puree of chestnuts and small red les airelles berries.

Muller smiled as he savored his first bite.

Stevenson eyed him and paused, waiting for the waiter to depart. "I want to talk to you about the Saar vote, Muller. I think you know that Eden is Rapporteur for that matter too."

Muller nodded, his mouth full of venison.

Stevenson continued. "Sir Geoffrey Knox, a British diplomat, was President of the Governing Commission there; it's a position roughly equivalent to Lester's in Danzig. In the run up to the plebiscite, Knox detected increased Nazi infiltration of the Territory and he began to suspect they were planning a coup of some kind to scuttle the vote. Knox came to Geneva in November and warned Eden about the threat. Eden took the message seriously and obtained Cabinet approval to deploy an international police force to maintain order and oversee the plebiscite. He brought it back to the Council and got approval—the Germans aren't here to object, of course. So by mid-December an international force of 3,000 men composed of Italian, Swedish, Dutch and British soldiers entered the Territory, and the vote took place without incident.

Stevenson then added, "Of course, the irony is that the result was so overwhelmingly one-sided. To be sure, the Nazis mounted a huge campaign, flooding the territory with speakers and propaganda of every kind. But I think even they were astonished by the magnitude of their victory.

"The point I want to leave you with, though—and I'll come back to it—is that the Council intervened forcefully and quickly in that instance.

"And that brings us to Danzig," he continued. "I can understand how the Saar vote energized the NSDAP there; it's a big deal. It's the only free election that the Nazi Party has ever won. They're ecstatic in Germany and I can well understand the frenzy it unleashed in Danzig.

Now it was Stevenson's turn to lean toward Muller, using his fork for emphasis. "However, in answer to your question, yes I've read the Commissioner's Annual Report. I think it's a good document. Also, since Eden is given copies of the periodic letters Lester has sent to the Secretary General describing your activities, I've seen them too; so I have a pretty good idea of what you're up against. It's evident that there is a fundamental incompatibility between the NSDAP agenda and the Danzig constitution. You're watching it play out in countless ways, large and small, and believe me, we understand the daily tension that generates for Lester—and for you too."

Muller narrowed his eyes as he watched Stevenson. Something told him he was being set up, but he decided to remain silent.

"We have a plan," Stevenson went on. "Eden will share it with Lester, and I want you to hear it too. We start with a premise that we think is accurate, that Hitler does not want to create a showdown over Danzig. We are engaging him on a number of fronts—along with our allies—to achieve a far-reaching agreement that would settle most if not all of the outstanding issues between us. So he doesn't want to rock the boat any more than we do. If we can accomplish this overall settlement, Hitler will have achieved the security goals he claims to be seeking. We calculate that at that point, German pressure on Danzig will subside.

"This is part of the overall British policy of appeasement, is that it?" asked Muller.

"Exactly," said Stevenson. "What we need for now is a holding action in Danzig by the Commissioner and the League while we pursue this overall settlement.

"There is no doubt in our mind that Lester's actions over the past year have been a deterrent to the NSDAP's agenda. We need him to continue his firm and effective diplomacy, even in the face of continued NSDAP provocation. That will hold the status quo and gain us the time we need to reach agreement with Hitler. We consider Lester's active defense of League interests in Danzig to be a vital linchpin in our policy."

The waiter cleared their plates and opened another bottle of St. Emilon. Stevenson proffered his lighter as they lit up, then continued.

"I assume you are saying to yourself, 'that's all very nice, but we're getting beaten up every day by these guys; give us some help'."

"You're darned right," said Muller. "We need a stronger hand to play."

"That's fair enough," Stevenson replied. "We understand that and here's what we're planning.

"Lester has submitted the two petitions for the Council to act upon. They both present obvious violations of the Danzig Constitution. No one on the Council—not even Beck—is prepared to defend the Senate on these issues. 'But we're not a court; we can't impose damages for the misconduct. I suppose we could direct the Senate to reinstate the newspaper. But the newspaper's suspension has already ended and it's back in business. So that would mean that the mighty League of Nations Council would be reduced to issuing a directive allowing some Catholic kids in far off Danzig to wear uniforms."

Stevenson made a face. "That doesn't strike us as a very muscular show of force," he said.

Muller leaned forward to take sip of wine. "So what do you have in mind then?"

"Something very different," Stevenson replied. "And that's why I began this conversation by telling you what happened in the Saar.

"We've seen the statement that Lester forwarded a few days ago in which Greiser committed to enter into negotiations with the petitioners after the Council meeting and pledged the Senate to abide by the Constitution. He's obviously hoping the Council will do what it did a year ago and issue a report that simply puts the ball back in his court."

Muller nodded. Clearly that was Greiser's objective.

"Eden's inclined to do that," Stevenson continued. "But do it in a way that puts the screws to Gresier. He's scheduled a private meeting with Greiser; Eden speaks fluent German, so not even an interpreter will be present. He'll offer Greiser two choices. Alternative one is a report by the Council that is a broadside condemnation of the Senate's repeated illegal actions and its attacks on the Constitution during the past year. Eden will tell him that he is prepared to issue a report that will hold the Danzig Senate up to shame before the world and will directly criticize his Senate leadership.

"Now, Muller, the reality is that Eden can't get the Council to do that; Beck wouldn't be the only one to object. But Greiser's not going to know that and, believe me, Eden will present this option in a way that will scare the pants off him." Stevenson paused with a smile, refilling their glasses with the last of the wine as they stubbed out their cigarettes.

"Then he'll tell Greiser that there's another option—the one we've just discussed, that would essentially be a holding action and toss the ball back in Gresier's court. But—and here's the important part—he will preface that offer with a detailed description of the steps he initiated to introduce an international police force into the Territory of the Saar when local authorities threatened to flout the terms of the Versailles Treaty. He will tell

Greiser in no uncertain terms that he is prepared to do the same thing in Danzig if the Senate persists in its pattern of unconstitutional behavior.

"Now, you should understand, Muller, that a report authorizing deployment of an international police force in Danzig–like the broadside critique of the Senate in option one–would also not be approved by the Council. The behavior of the Senate hasn't been so egregious as to warrant that kind of League response. At least it hasn't gotten to that point yet." Stevenson paused and smiled.

"Gresier may be smart enough to figure that much out. But he's not going to know where Eden and the Council will draw the line. The prospect of the League deploying an international police force is a serious threat to his power; it's going to rattle him severely. And we think it's going to give Lester's authority a boost in his dealings with the NSDAP."

Muller lit another Gitane and leaned back, trying to weigh how he should react to what he'd been told.

Eden will first threaten a broadside critique that he can't deliver, then a police intervention that he can't deliver, and finally a free pass that he *can* deliver–and which Greiser will take, he thought to himself; two canards and a pass.

Shit, he thought. He signaled the waiter for a whiskey to gain a few moments more to reflect.

His instinct was to react angrily. But it was very obvious that this was no proposal that Stevenson was floating to seek his comment; this was a decision that had been made and was simply being delivered. Britain had bigger fish to fry with Hitler than Danzig; this was Eden's way of 'not rocking the boat' and maybe, just maybe, providing Lester the possibility of some greater leverage.

It wasn't much, but it was the best they were going to get, Muller concluded. Was there anything in it that he and Lester could influence?

Probably only the wording of the 'pass' Greiser was being offered—and that only at the margin.

He took a large sip of whiskey and turned to Stevenson. "Thanks for the briefing," he said, evenly, trying to appear suitably grateful. "I don't have an alternative to suggest and obviously I haven't had a chance to talk to the Commissioner. Just reacting now, my only suggestions are to be sure some safeguards are written into Eden's report."

"Like what?" Stevenson asked a little brusquely. It was apparent that the document had already been prepared.

"I assume it will include language instructing Gresier to enter into the negotiations he promises to begin with the petitioners. It would be helpful to tell him to begin 'promptly', instruct him to negotiate 'in good faith' and 'in keeping with Danzig's Constitution'," he ticked off the elements with his fingers. "And it should also direct him to conduct the negotiations in the presence of the Commissioner."

"Do you really think all that is necessary?" replied Stevenson. It was more a statement than a question.

"Yes," said Muller. He would try to get the Commissioner to insist on language to this effect when he met with Eden.

"And one more thing," Muller added. "The Commissioner should be in that meeting between Eden and Greiser. Gresier needs to see that the Commissioner is at Eden's side when he gets this stern lecture. That would boost the Commissioner's standing," he said. "If, the Commissioner is left out, Gresier can assume that the Commissioner is not being taken into Eden's confidence and may not even be privy to what Eden's telling him."

"Out of the question," said Stevenson. "That's just not the way Eden operates.'" Stevenson signaled for the bill; the meeting was evidently over.

"Think about it," said Muller as they got up from the table.

They shook hands. "I'll see you tomorrow afternoon at the Council meeting," Muller said. "I'm actually excited about attending. I won't have a seat at the big horseshoe table," he added. "But sitting right behind it with the other senior staff should be fun."

He clapped Stevenson on the shoulder. A comradely gesture that would be taken as such, Muller hoped. Stevenson grinned at him and gave him a return clap on the shoulder as he departed.

Teammates, thought Muller.

Rather than waiting for a tram, Muller took a taxi back to the Hotel de la Paix. He called the Commissioner's suite from the house phone. "I hope I didn't awaken you, Commissioner, but I think we need to talk."

"It's fine Muller, come on up. I'm just getting ready for bed."

The suite was spacious. Lester opened the bar, producing a bottle of Dewars scotch whiskey. He proceeded to pour them both a generous helping.

"So what did you learn?" Lester inquired, waving Muller to a seat on the couch.

Muller reported the conversation with Stevenson. "God, it's disappointing, Commissioner, and it looks like it's the best Eden's willing to do."

"You do seem to have a way of extracting information late at night, Muller," Lester said with a smile.

"Eden's invited me to breakfast at this suite tomorrow at 8AM. Let's see if I get the same story from him. Assuming I do, I'll press him to include me in the meeting with Greiser. Oh, and do me the favor of writing out the language you proposed for the report."

Muller took a piece of hotel stationery out of the desk and wrote 'prompt, good faith negotiations, consistent with the Constitution, conducted in the presence of the Commissioner'. He handed it to Lester. "This should help to keep Greiser's feet to the fire," Lester said.

Lester showed Muller to the door. "The Council meeting is scheduled to begin at 2 PM. Let's meet at the Palais around noon. We can revisit the charms of the Secretariat's cafeteria for lunch."

***

Muller awoke the next morning to find Geneva in the grip of the Bise, the fierce northwest wind that whistles down Lac Léman, strengthening as it nears Geneva, pinned between the Jura Mountains to the West and the Alps to the South. Heavy waves broke on the lakefront and the steamers tied up on the quai strained their lines. Pedestrians bundled up and leaned into the gale. Muller regarded the scene as he ate breakfast in the airy hotel dining room; heavy weather was not the best omen for the upcoming meeting. Maybe it'll blow itself out by afternoon, he thought to himself.

Mainly he wondered how the Commissioner was making out in his meeting with Eden.

He boarded the tram and scrambled into the interior away from the wind as everyone else tried to do too. Entering the Palais, he went to the third floor office of the Danzig Sub-Section and spent time conversing with Frederick Krabbe, the Danish Sub-Section chief who seemed competent and knowledgeable, but had never even visited Danzig. Muller recommended that he schedule a trip, though perhaps a little later in the year when the weather was not quite so daunting.

Because of the Bise, the cafeteria was especially crowded; no one wanted to leave the building. Muller and Lester had to share a table and couldn't converse privately, so they ate quickly then walked through the corridor connecting the Palais with the annex housing the Council

Chamber, which was large enough to accommodate meetings of the full League Assembly as well as the Council.

They found seats in the spacious reception area just outside the Chamber entrance.

"Eden delivered essentially the same message to me that you heard from Stevenson," said Lester. "He's under no illusions about Greiser. He respected Rauschning and realizes that Greiser is both more antagonistic and a less capable leader. So he said that he intends to be 'very direct' with him." Lester paused and smiled. "Apparently the term 'very direct' is about as severe as Eden's diplomatic vocabulary gets.

"He refused to invite me to the meeting with Greiser. He believes that, as Rapporteur and de facto director of the Council session, he needs to have some space between himself and the contending parties. I said I thought he and I were on the same team, both of us acting for the League. He waved me off. Disappointing, but Eden's accustomed to getting his way. I also handed him your language and asked him to include it in his report. He said he'd take care of it following his meeting with Greiser. So, we'll see."

People were beginning to arrive for the meeting, so, with Lester leading the way, Muller made his first entry into the Council Chamber of the League of Nations. He stopped and took in the scene.

The Chamber was three stories high, made to seem even larger by a skylight canopy over the center of the hall. A dozen floor-to-ceiling windows with loose white curtains faced the lake, and even on a stormy day like today, the room was full of light. With its back to the windows, a long raised dais held thirteen seats intended for use by the judges of the Permanent International Court of Justice when it was in session. In front of the dais was the famed semi-circular, horseshoe-shaped table. The Permanent Members of the Council were seated around the outside of the horseshoe, with interpreters and stenographers seated within it. A long table was placed in front of the horseshoe, facing it and the dais. Around the horseshoe, on three sides, rows of seats were lined up next to one another, for use by Secretariat staff and observers. A public balcony at the rear of the room overlooked the Chamber.

This was the room Muller had seen in newsreels and photos, where the world's most powerful leaders met to decide momentous issues. He drew in a large breath, full of wonderment at being in this august Chamber.

Lester staked out two seats directly in behind the table facing the horseshoe. "I'll be sitting at the table with Eden when Danzig is raised," he explained. "You'll be nearby if I need something."

Muller nodded.

The Chamber was rapidly filling up. Eden entered the Chamber, trailed by Stevenson and other aides. As Eden made his way to the Rapporteur's seat at the table facing the horseshoe, he stopped to greet Lester, then seeing Muller, extended his hand with a smile and acknowledged him. "Nice to see you again, Mr. Muller," he said. He re-arranged the files his staff had spread at his place. A short, stout, balding man came up and stood next to him, and they conferred briefly, Eden nodding at him to take the seat on his left. Before sitting, though, Eden took the man by the elbow and turned back to where Muller and Lester were seated.

Eden made the introductions. "Commissioner Lester, I wanted you to meet Sir Geoffrey Knox, who has been serving as President of the Governing Commission of the Saar Territory," said Eden. "You both bear some battle scars incurred in serving the League in challenging locations. I thought you should at least meet one another."

Lester and Knox shook hands as Eden continued genially, saying, "Sir Geoffrey is here to deliver formal notice to the Council of the results of last week's plebiscite. In light of the vote, the Council will announce its decision today to terminate the mission of the Saar Commission and return the territory to Germany."

Muller gasped. The first order of business for the Council before turning to Danzig would be to pass the Saar back to Germany? The Germans desperately want Danzig back, and we start a meeting on preserving the League's mandate there by giving them back the Saar? The symbolism would be a disaster. What was Eden thinking?

Eden and Knox took their seats at the table.

Muller leaned over to Lester whispering, "This is awful timing, Commissioner."

Lester grimaced. "I had no idea. It's probably Beck's doing; but Eden should have stopped it." He shook his head.

As Poland held the presidency of the Permanent Council, Polish Prime Minister Beck occupied the seat at the top of the horseshoe. He gaveled the room to silence.

"I declare the 83rd Session of the Council of the League of Nations to be in session," he said in French. An interpreter repeated the statement in English. "The first order of business this afternoon is the status of the Territory of the Saar, which has been under administration by the League during the past fifteen years under the terms of the Treaty of Versailles. Mr. Eden, as Rapporteur, will you kindly introduce the subject?"

Eden delivered a crisp, professional summary of the League's involvement in the Saar. Muller was pleased to note that he laid stress on the international police force that the Council had ordered into the Territory to counter the threat of disorder, complementing the nations whose troops had participated in the exercise. He then introduced Knox, who delivered a very brief statement describing the plebiscite and formally notifying the Council of the results.

"In conclusion, Mr. Chairman," Knox said, "as President of the Governing Commission, I recommend that the Council declare the League administration over the Territory of the Saar to have been successfully completed and that it order the Territory returned to the Republic of Germany, effective immediately."

A raucous cheer went up in the balcony holding the Public Gallery, as a crowd rose and began chanting, 'Seig Heil', 'Seig Heil', waving their arms, and offering Nazi salutes. The Chamber looked up at the noisemakers. Muller, to his astonishment saw Greiser standing among them, shouting and shaking his fist wildly. Good God, he thought to himself. He has no dignity at all; what a fool. He nudged Lester, who had also seen Gresier and was shaking his head.

Beck, taken by surprise by the outburst, was not amused. He gaveled the table and shouted 'Order' several times, quieting the crowd. "Order," he commanded, "or I will clear the Gallery." The room grew quiet again.

Eden took the floor. "The Secretariat has distributed the Rapporteur's report recommending that the Territory of the Saar be returned to the Republic of Germany effective immediately." Beck rapped his gavel. "The Chair will now ask for the Council's decision. All in favor?" All fourteen members raised their hands. "The vote to return the Territory of the Saar to the Republic of Germany effective immediately is recorded as unanimously approved." He rapped the gavel. "The Council stands in recess for thirty minutes."

This time there was no silencing the gallery. They shouted and yelled and jumped up and down, then burst into the Horst Wessel song, all standing with right arms in stiff Hitler salutes. Gresier was right among them noted Muller.

As the gallery celebration finally wound down and Council members and staff milled around the Chamber during the recess, Muller spotted

Stevenson and walked up to him. "That was an awful piece of timing," he said.

Stevenson nodded in agreement. "It was Beck. Eden told him that Knox was in town to give the Council formal notice of the results of the plebiscite. So Beck decided to put it on the agenda for this afternoon. We had almost no notice and had to get Eden's Report ready at lunchtime for the Secretariat to distribute before the meeting. Somehow the Nazis got wind of it and rounded up a crowd of supporters. A very bad show in my opinion. And you saw that Greiser was right in the middle of it?" Muller nodded.

"What a fool," Stevenson said in disgust.

"That's what I said too," replied Muller, smiling.

"Oh and Muller, because we had to scramble to get the Saar Report to the Secretariat for distribution, we had no time to add the changes that you wanted in the Danzig Report. I'm sorry; Eden told me this noontime that he'd agreed to the language, but we simply ran out of time. We have to have the reports in the hands of the Secretariat before the Council convenes. I'm sorry," he repeated.

"Shit," said Muller. "This is not turning into a very good day."

He went back to find Lester and give him the bad news. Lester shook his head wearily. "They aren't making it any easier, are they?" he said.

Lester and Muller were standing with Eden near the table when Greiser came up to them, huffing and puffing, perspiring heavily, still obviously keyed up by the gallery celebration. "Won't it be wonderful one day when we can have the same kind of result in Danzig as we accomplished today in the Saar?" he exulted.

Eden, who was at least a head taller than Greiser, drew himself up to his full height and proceeded–literally, Muller noted–to look down his nose at Greiser and responded haughtily, "That is not an outcome to be expected." He then ostentatiously turned his back on Greiser.

Eden really does know how to deliver a put-down, Muller thought to himself. I have to give him that at least; it must be in the genes.

Beck gaveled the Council back into session and invited Eden to introduce the Danzig agenda. Eden requested the Council to acknowledge Lester's presence at the table as Commissioner and he praised Lester's "tireless efforts" on behalf of the League during the past year. He quoted several passages from Lester's Annual Report, including his observations concerning the tensions between 'the legitimate goals of the NSDAP in advancing the ideals of National Socialism' on the one hand, and the League's role in 'preserving the protections guaranteed by the Danzig Constitution' on the other hand. Eden said that Lester's firm diplomacy had contributed to an improving situation which still merited close scrutiny by the Council.

He then introduced Greiser as the newly-elected President of the Senate making his inaugural appearance at a Council meeting. Turning to the subject matter of the two petitions, he directed the Council's attention to Greiser's recent message stating a desire to enter into negotiations with the petitioners and his pledge to conduct the affairs of the Danzig government in accordance with the provisions of the Danzig Constitution. He declared that in his view, the best course was to postpone any action until the next Council meeting pending the results of the contemplated negotiations. He added, "It would clearly be the best solution if an agreement can be reached locally and one that would naturally be in conformity with the fundamental principles of the Danzig Constitution."

Greiser asked for the floor. He expressed satisfaction at postponing consideration of the petitions, as it would place the Senate "in the agreeable position of achieving during the interval a local agreement removing any need for action by the Council." He repeated that the Senate "scrupulously observed the letter and spirit of the Free City constitution," but he added, "It has often been difficult to achieve the aims and objective of a very large majority of the inhabitants within the limits of that constitution."

He then went on, defiantly, "The council witnessed earlier this afternoon the solidarity of the inhabitants of the Territory of the Saar with Germany; I want the Council to know that the National Socialist majority in Danzig has an equally ardent bond with our Teutonic brethren in Germany. Let there be no mistake that our goal is to return to the Reich at the earliest time possible"

Eden refused to be drawn into a response. Ignoring Gresier's statement, he requested the Council to approve the report circulated by the Secretariat. Beck called for the vote and upon unanimous approval gaveled the meeting to a close. Gathering his papers, Eden rose, once more turning his back to Greiser, and offered Lester a warm handshake. In a loud voice, obviously aimed at Greiser, he said, "Commissioner, you are doing an excellent job in Danzig. The Council wishes you continued success, and I do so personally too. Thank you for your tireless efforts." Then, without so much as a glance at Greiser, he strode out of the Chamber, followed by his staff.

Muller gathered up his own papers, then took a final glance around the large Chamber. He wished Eirene were around tonight to share his pride at taking part in important proceedings in these august surroundings.

CHAPTER 11

Winter and Spring, 1935

When Lester and Muller arrived back in Danzig two days later, they were confronted by more of Greiser's mischief. He had issued a statement that characterized Eden's report to the Council as an endorsement of the Senate's position.

"The negative reaction to the Opposition's activity is shown in the League of Nations report by the British Representative, Mr. Anthony Eden. In this report the opposition is told that questions must first be elucidated in Danzig with the Senate before they are referred to Geneva. The lack of political respect for the Senate which the opposition has always shown is thus confirmed by the respected and distinguished Englishman."

When the opposition press ridiculed Greiser's remarks, the Senate retaliated by shutting down the SDP's *Danziger Volkestimme*. Greiser then infuriated the Catholic clergy in a speech calling them 'liars' and he attacked the Centre Party as 'undisciplined children needing to be taught a lesson by their elders'.

"Commissioner, I don't think you should let Gresier get away with this," Muller said, translating the latest exchanges for Lester. "It's as if he's taunting the League's authority. Why not send him a message offering him a choice; either he recants or you'll issue your own statement accusing him publishing of blatant falsehoods and demanding that he fulfill his commitment to negotiate with the opposition."

Lester agreed and he next day, at Lester's instructions, Muller personally delivered the message to Greiser.

Gresier made Muller wait in his anteroom for nearly 45 minutes before seeing him.

"I expect the Commissioner to make a call on me personally, and not sending his secretary to deliver his messages," Greiser said truculently, not bothering to offer a handshake.

"President Greiser," Muller replied evenly, "the Commissioner sent me to deliver this message in the hope that a lower key exchange might offer a way to calm things down. There is no advantage to be gained in misrepresenting the Council's report or in ignoring your commitment to the Council to negotiate with the opposition on the issues raised in their petitions. The Commissioner hopes that a friendly reminder might lead you to adopt a more conciliatory tone and begin the process of negotiations that you promised in Geneva. He thinks that would be more productive than having him issue a public statement refuting your misstatements of the Council's actions and your solemn commitments to begin negotiations."

Greiser's face grew red, and he slammed his fist on desk.

"Don't you speak to me like that Muller," he said angrily. But then he straightened up and paused, glancing out the window a moment before turning back to Muller and addressing him in a calmer tone with a tight smile. "You are a mere messenger, Muller, and not worth using up any of my energy. You can simply inform your Commissioner that if he wants to engage in a public fight over Council rules and pronouncements, he's welcome to start one. We have our own agenda which we will announce in our own good time. In the meantime, we need no instruction from the Commissioner on how to conduct ourselves."

Greiser turned and sat down behind his desk dismissing Muller with a wave of his hand. "Now get out!"

The next day Lester reacted by issuing a statement rebutting Gresier's statements point-by-point. True to his threat to Muller, Greiser and his allies in the Senate disputed Lester's arguments and there ensued nearly two weeks of exchanges, Lester always expressing himself in a temperate, low key tone, while Greiser became increasingly vitriolic.

"It would have been helpful to have the Council report include that language you proposed about expecting the Senate to begin 'prompt negotiations in good faith'," Lester observed at one point to Muller. "Greiser's simply stonewalling."

The rationale for the hardline attitude was soon revealed. On February 12, 1935, Greiser, in his role as President of the Senate, sent a letter to the members of the Volkstag calling a snap election on April 7 and telling them that new elections would announce to the entire world the wishes of the people of Danzig to embrace the NSDAP agenda.

As Muller translated the document for Lester, he was struck by the cavalier manner in which Greiser brushed aside the petitions. "The Senate considers that it cannot yield to the opposition's desire for amendment of a whole series of laws without damaging its own work of reconstruction and sabotaging the wishes of the majority of Danzigers."

So, it went on, instead of conducting negotiations with the opposition, as Greiser had pledged to do in Geneva, it expressed confidence that the results of the election would demonstrate overwhelming popular rejection of the opposition's complaints.

Muller and Lester met that afternoon in Lester's office to evaluate Gresier's latest move.

"Well this certainly explains why Gresier was so willing to start of fight with me and with the League. It's all part of his strategy to take full control of the Free City," Lester said. "What's really behind his call for a snap election, is trying to win a three-quarters majority in the Volkstag. That would be enough to empower them to amend the Constitution. If they did that, they could simply remove the current democratic protections in the Constitution and eliminate any Constitutional barriers to complete NSDAP control."

Muller nodded. "I think you're probably right, Commissioner."

"They'd also have to win a local vote on the changes–which they could probably do if they get the two-thirds majority to make the changes in the first place," Lester continued. "Then the League Council would need to approve them. They'd probably get that too. I don't see the League having the stomach to disapprove Constitutional changes that have strong popular support even if the purpose is to gut the Constitution of basic democratic rights, which is what this is aimed at doing. They're smart enough to understand that, so they've decided to roll the dice and force the issue. It's a pretty clever move, don't you think, Muller?"

Muller nodded. "They're following the rules. The Constitution says that a 75 percent majority of the *Volkstag* can change the Constitution. That's what they're after."

Lester stood, and paced, alongside his large conference table. "This is where it really gets dicey for us, because the test is going to come in the conduct of the election campaign. If the vote is free and fair and they win the super majority, then good for them. Not the outcome I'd like, but..." He shrugged.

"That would mean the effective end of the mandate and your role here," said Muller.

Lester nodded. "It certainly would. There wouldn't be any democratic rights left for the League to protect." Lester paused, reflecting, "Here's nothing to say that an electorate can't vote itself out of business and turn the Danzig government over to the NSDAP. But that kind of outcome would spell very big trouble for lots of people here in Danzig; I don't expect them to roll over willingly."

Lester then turned to face Muller. "I think, Muller, that we're facing a real test of strength. Forster and Greiser are bullies; we've seen them repeatedly break the rules when it suits them. They'll have the entire apparatus of the state at their command during this election and, given the stakes, I have to assume they'll try to do whatever they can to overwhelm the opposition. I don't have a lot of weapons at my command, but I'm going to stake out a clear position insisting on free and fair elections."

"Greiser's letter calls for the formal campaign to begin on March 16," said Muller.

"Then we don't have much time," Lester replied.

***

Muller and von Radowitz had a dinner scheduled that night. They met at Ostbahn Franz Malthesius Restaurant. Muller ordered his usual Koenigsburg dumplings and decided to add a helping of pork kidneys with vinegar sauce. Von Radowitz decided on smoked eels and Kassler ribs with sauerkraut.

"You need to try Danzig's smoked eels sometime Muller," von Radowitz said. "They're a real specialty. You know how they catch them don't you?"

Muller said no; he'd always thought eels were repulsive and he couldn't imagine anyone actually eating them.

"Well, let me tell you how they do it," von Radowitz said mischievously. "Maybe that'll change your mind about them."

Muller looked doubtful, but von Radowitz continued, smiling broadly now.

"The first thing you do is find a horse that's just died and cut off its head. You tie up the severed head with a really strong piece of rope and you carry it out to the end of one of those big jetties that jut out into the Baltic. This is all a little messy, of course, so you'll want to be wearing really old clothes that you don't mind getting smeared with horse blood and brains."

"Radowitz!" said Muller looking disgusted.

"Once you get to the tip of the jetty," von Radowitz continued, "you swing the horse head around then fling it as far out into the ocean as you can and let it sink to the bottom. Then you wait for about ninety minutes. Maybe you've brought a book along that hasn't gotten too badly smeared, so you sit there contentedly and wait; probably some nice poetry would be suitable."

Muller eyed him suspiciously.

"Then you put the book away and you begin hauling on your rope to bring in the horse head. Oh, I forgot to mention, you've also brought along a potato sack half full of coarse salt, and that's sitting next to you on the jetty. So you haul the horse head up on the jetty and, voila! Every orifice of the hose head is filled with fresh, squirming, wiggling eels; hundreds of them. They're in the horse's ears, his nose, his eyes, his mouth, his brains…"

"Radowitz, I'm about to throw up," said Muller.

"You grab those eels and pull them out of their warm nesting places in the horse head and you toss them into the potato sack. They squirm and wiggle themselves to death in the salt. Then you throw your potato sack over your shoulder and you sell the fresh eels to a guy in the market. He cleans them off with dark peat then hangs them in smoking barrels over beechwood for an hour or so, and the result is a gastronomic delight called smoked eel that you will see being served to me in a few moments."

"God, that's disgusting," said Muller. "Is that really what they do?"

"Absolutely," replied von Radowitz assuredly. "You can share my order."

"Not on your life," said Muller, taking a last swallow from his large beer mug. "But I'll take more of this."

The waiter brought more beer and their first courses. The smoked eels didn't appear as awful as Muller feared they would, but he waved away von Radowitz's fork offering him a bite.

"Well, the fight is on," said von Radowitz. "This snap election is all about Forster making his move. He was annoyed at Goering pressuring him into line after he toppled Rauschning. He figures he's the Party Gauleiter here and he's determined to run things his way. So he's largely ignored what the Wilhelmstrasse has been telling him about not rocking the boat. Since Gresier got back from Geneva, Forster's gone on the offensive."

"We've noticed," Muller said.

"They're ecstatic about the Saar election results and the huge victories they ran up in the rural by-elections late last year. They've decided that they can pull off a big win in April, then amend the constitution and pressure the League to accept the changes. After that, they figure they won't have to put up with any more petitions—or with any more interference from Lester. They've decided that a big victory will destroy his authority—and the League's—so they're going for broke."

Muller nodded. "The Commissioner sees it the same way. But he's determined to make sure the elections are 'free and fair', as he puts it. He's not going to allow Forster and the Party to run an illegal campaign and steamroller the opposition. He's sending a message to the Senate tomorrow, directing them to issue a public proclamation defending constitutional protections of free speech, secret voting, party assemblies and so on. He'll remind them of their responsibility to maintain public order, and will tell them that he's prepared to bring in outside forces if they fail to do that. Finally, he's telling them that if the elections are fraudulent, he'll recommend that the Council invalidate the results."

Von Radowitz nodded. "I was hoping to hear you say something like that. Von Neurath remains very influential in Berlin. I know he doesn't want a crisis in Danzig with all the other things he and Hitler are pursuing at the moment. I'll pass him this information. Maybe he can use it to calm Forster down."

***

Lester drafted his message to Greiser and had it delivered, together with a request that both Greiser and Forster meet with him a day later in his office. The two men appeared at the appointed hour both dressed in full Nazi party attire, Forster in his black Gaulieter uniform with gold piping and Greiser in his brown shirt with polished high jackboots. Both wore red swastika armbands on their left arms. Muller could see Lester stiffen when they were escorted into his office; it was a clear breach of decorum to visit the League's High Commissioner in full uniform.

He gazed at them silently. Then Forster spoke up, his face brimming with confidence and wreathed in smiles, unapologetic. "Commissioner, we wanted to be prompt for the meeting you requested, but we have been conducting vital business for the NSDAP that necessitated us being in formal party attire. So rather than be late, we decided to come as we were."

"So I see," Lester replied unsmiling. "I will overlook the diplomatic error on this occasion. It is not to be repeated."

He did not offer to shake hands and motioned them to be seated at the conference table. Lester did not take a seat, but instead strode to the head of the table and remained standing, looking down at the two officials. He began to speak, motioning Muller to stand beside him and conduct his translations in short direct sentences.

"Mr. Greiser," he said, "the Danzig Constitution empowers you, as President of the Senate, to call for new elections. It also requires you to ensure that any election is carried out with full respect for the democratic right of all parties to assemble, the right of all citizens to engage in free speech and the right of a free press to report the proceedings.

"I charge you to ensure that these rights are fully protected and that nothing interferes with the conduct of free, democratic voting procedures in the Free City."

He then turned to Forster. "Mr. Forster as head of the NSDAP you lead a party with a parliamentary majority. Not a large one," he added, "but a majority nonetheless. I charge you, as party leader, with responsibility for respecting the rights of minority parties to contest this election freely and fairly."

Lester paused and leaned forward, placing his hands on the table, and fixing them with a stern regard. "Kindly confirm that you accept these obligations."

Muller could see Greiser glance nervously at Forster. Forster had a flat face, with large fleshy cheeks and narrow close-set eyes, an appearance at odds with his volatile personality, Muller thought, and he wondered how Forster would react to Lester's peremptory remarks.

To Muller's surprise, Forster leaned back in his chair, casually crossed his legs and languidly laid an arm on the table.

"Why Commissioner, of course. We both absolutely confirm what you just said. Our party has always conducted itself in full accordance with the

Danzig Constitution and we shall continue to do that in this election." He then smiled serenely at Lester.

Lester did not return the smile. He turned to Greiser. "President Greiser?"

"Yes, I concur," Gresier replied.

Lester straightened. "I shall issue a public statement reporting this meeting and advising that I have received from both of you strong assurances that the upcoming election will be conducted freely and fairly."

"We certainly hope you will do so, Commissioner," said Forster, rising slowly to his feet, still smiling broadly. "We expect to win a decisive victory in April. The German people know in their hearts and in their heads that they are one with the Reich. They will act decisively in this election to advance that goal. We will be pleased to employ constitutional means to achieve our victory."

As he bowed stiffly to depart, he added, "Oh, and Mr. Greiser has decided that that business in Geneva about negotiating with those petty petitioners can wait until after the elections results are in—which will show that Danzigers decisively reject the weak arguments that the petitioners have advanced."

***

"What was that all about?" asked Muller as they strolled back into Lester's office. "They're not very credible playing the role of choir boys."

Lester snorted. "I sense they are supremely confident that they're going to win a huge victory in April. So it's in their interest to kick off the campaign on a positive note. They're sure to pick a fight at some point. This just isn't the right time."

He paused. "They're no choir boys. And how interesting that Forster was the one to speak. Greiser's clearly frightened of him. Delaying negotiations with the petitioners is Forster's doing. I wonder if he even told Greiser before telling me. Probably not. He's a menace, parading in here with those damned uniforms on, grinning like a werewolf and just oozing contempt. He was lying through his teeth the whole time and seemed to be enjoying it. Almost as if he were playing with us.

"But at least we laid down a marker, Lester said grimly. "The hard part is going to be making it stick."

***

A few days later, Muller decided to pay a visit to the *Volkstag* to watch the parliamentary proceedings. Newspapers had been carrying reports of unruly behavior and he thought it would be interesting to observe firsthand what was happening.

The *Volkstag* building was a massive work of Baltic architecture featuring a wide three story façade with tall windows and a recessed pediment that emphasized the vertical lines. Above it was a soaring slate roof topped by a small decorative tower. Two wings on either side, each a mirror image of the other, rose to crow-step gables. Oddly, there was a large round tower attached on the left wing which didn't seem to fit the rest of the structure's disciplined architecture. On an earlier visit, Muller had been told that long ago it had been used to incarcerate convicted members of the nobility. Those who could pay occupied the upper floors in apartments with light and windows; the rest were held in a deep, cold, underground crypt.

A couple of inattentive policemen stood by the building entrance and didn't even bother to ask for Muller's credentials, so he just walked in, admiring the great hall entranceway. The parliament chamber was directly ahead, but Muller knew the public gallery was a floor above, so he climbed the broad stairway, opened a tall wooden door with decorative carvings and entered the gallery taking a seat toward the rear.

He had a clear view of the raised speaking podium, situated in front of floor-to-ceiling windows, which faced a semicircle of seats for the parliamentarians. At the moment, there was a lot of milling around in the aisles and the well before the podium, as knots of men gathered, talked and moved to another group. But a divide was evident; many men wore Nazi uniforms or suits with red swastika armbands. They circulated mainly around the left of the podium. On the other side—clearly the opposition—all the men were in suits, but with no identifying symbols. The two groups did not mix with one another.

Finally, a short, heavyset man wearing a Nazi armband ascended the podium, banged the gavel and began reading from a document. The parliamentarians paid no heed and continued mingling with one another until suddenly, as if on some signal, they took their places and the chamber fell quiet.

An older woman sitting next to Muller in the gallery leaned forward, putting her arms on her knees, and said under her breath, but audibly, "Now we'll see if they let anyone speak."

Muller looked at her inquiringly. Seeing his glance, she said quietly, "The governing party has spoken. It's time now for the opposition. But they always shout us down."

The presiding officer announced, "Brandt, Social Democrats, one minute thirty-five seconds." A parliamentarian on the opposition side rose—that must be Brandt, Muller supposed—but as the man began speaking, members of the government party across the aisle began shouting, blowing whistles, even beating cowbells, making such a din that no one could hear a word of what Mr. Brandt had to say. Then abruptly, as if on cue, the noise stopped and the presiding officer intoned, "Time expired, Mr. Brandt. Next

Krueger, Center Left party 45 seconds." Another parliamentarian rose, presumably Krueger, and the same thing happened. Muller looked on in astonishment as the same procedure occurred twice more, with the opposition now angrily heckling the government side and proceedings deteriorated into chaos.

"Those bastards," said the lady next to Muller, banging her fists against her thighs. "They do it every time. They're monsters!"

The presiding officer pounded his gavel and shouted above the din, "Next, Mr. Murovski, Communist Party. 15 seconds." An elderly, portly man with a shock of grey hair and a walrus mustache rose to his feet, but as he did so, a group of muscular men in Storm Trooper uniforms converged on him, dragged him to the well of the chamber and began punching him, shouting, "Bolshevik Jew, Communist scum."

The man fell and his attackers began kicking him. At this point, the chamber exploded in complete pandemonium as members of the opposition waded into the attackers to rescue their colleague and fistfights broke out among parliamentarians who fought one another across the aisle.

Muller watched the unfolding spectacle in disbelief. The lady next to him was now on her feet screaming, "That's my husband; save him, save him." She scrambled past Muller to the gallery doorway and ran toward the stairs, presumably to help her husband.

Suddenly, Muller spied Arthur Gresier, standing in the chamber but off to the side, smirking, hands across his chest. Then he watched as Greiser stalked toward the press gallery, reaching up to grab the necktie of a man in glasses busily scribbling notes. Greiser yanked the man to the rail of the press gallery, shouted something at him, then grabbed the sheaf of notes that the man was holding. Releasing the man's necktie, Gresier stood back a step and pointed toward the press gallery exit, shouting at the man and apparently ordering him to leave. The man cringed, clearly frightened, then turned and ran up the stairs and out the door.

Muller decided he'd seen enough and thought that it was probably a wise time for him to leave too. As he descended the staircase, he saw the reporter curled up on the bottom step, apparently in tears. Muller bent down, putting a hand on the man's shoulder.

"Are you all right? Who are you?"

The man looked up at Muller, he was young and obviously in shock.

"Stephan Kreutzer," he said taking a deep breath, "*Danziger Volstimme*, the SDP newspaper. President Greiser ordered me out and took all my notes. He said I'd be floating in the river if any word of what happened is published." Kreutzer put his head down on his arm and began sobbing.

Muller stood. Making a rapid decision, he reached into his pocket and pulled out a business card which he handed to Kreutzer. "Maybe we can help."

Muller turned toward the main entryway where he had entered and saw Arthur Greiser striding toward him, his face an angry red and his eyes blazing.

"Muller, what are you doing here? Get out. You have no business being here. You're a stooge for the League of Nations and a mouthpiece for Lester. Get out," he repeated pointing to the doorway. "And don't interfere with these sniveling traitors masquerading as journalists."

"President Greiser, I was just leaving," said Muller levelly. "But what I have just witnessed seems to be a very strange way to implement the commitment to free speech that you made to the Commissioner a few days ago."

"Muller, you're a little shit," Gresier exploded, "and getting too big for your britches. The *Volkstag* is an organ of the government of Danzig and it is empowered to operate according to its own rules without any interference. So don't you level any accusations. We're going to crush the opposition and get rid of you and your Goddamned Commissioner once and for all. Now get out before I have you thrown out!"

Muller strode toward the doorway, but over his shoulder he said, "I'll tell the Commissioner you sent your greetings."

Back at the Residence, Lester chuckled and shook his head as Muller related what had occurred. "I probably stuck my neck out a little too far, Commissioner," Muller said ruefully. "It's not my place to get into an argument with Greiser. If I've compromised myself, I'll certainly resign so you can get more suitable replacement."

Lester waved him away. "Don't even think about it Muller," he said. "You were a passive observer when all Hell broke loose. It's hardly your fault that the *Volkstag* erupted or that Greiser assaulted that reporter. It might have been better if you hadn't given the man your card, but that's hardly disqualifying." He shrugged, then looked sharply at Muller. "The real question we have to ask ourselves is whether this is the beginning of a campaign to completely flout the election laws, or is it just a symptom of their deceit.

"If they go for broke and try to just steamroll everything, I'll have to go to the League Council for sanctions." Lester paused, then continued. "They know that and I'm pretty sure they don't want to push things that far. Moreover, I think they're cocky enough to believe they really *are* going to win a landslide victory without having to pull out all the stops.

"We'll just have to see. Meantime, you may want to keep your head down for a while. I don't want you to become a target for any of their gangs."

Muller didn't tell the Commissioner that he had thought about the same thing walking back from the *Volkstag*. He'd felt terrible about watching helplessly as the storm troopers beat up the Communist parliamentarian. But he knew there were a lot of NSDAP brawlers who would think nothing of beating him to a pulp if they were ordered to do so. It was not a prospect he relished.

***

A week later, attending a reception at the Italian Consulate with Lester, Muller ran into Papee and they agreed to a weekend tennis match. "Incidentally," Papee said, "have you seen the report about the new British rearmament program?"

Muller reacted with surprise. "Really? I hadn't heard. It's hard to get foreign news here."

"The Polish press has been giving it a big play," said Papee. "The British Foreign Office apparently released a White Paper, approved by the cabinet, committing the government to increase spending on the navy, the air force and coastal defense. It said they still want to negotiate arms limitation agreements in Europe, but they're no longer willing to engage in unilateral disarmament. The paper was released yesterday, just as the Foreign Secretary and Anthony Eden were heading for Berlin to meet with Hitler. So it seems they're sending him a message. A little surprising, wouldn't you say?"

Across the room, Lester beckoned Muller to his side to translate a conversation with another guest, so Muller couldn't reply. But yes, it was a bit surprising he decided later as he reflected on Papee's news.

March 16 was the formal beginning of the election campaign. But local preparations were immediately overtaken by Hitler's sudden and dramatic announcement that Germany was renouncing the disarmament provisions of Article V of the Treaty of Versailles. In a strident speech in Berlin, Hitler laid out a program to begin conscription for an army of 36 divisions and plans to build a large military air force.

The news struck Danzig like a thunderbolt. The NSDAP was jubilant. This was a vindication of long-awaited ambitions; a big army, a new air force. Rallies that were planned by the NSDAP to launch their campaign took on a martial air and Party members donned uniforms and helmets. Morale soared. Torchlight parades snaked through the City Center and the NSDAP staged boisterous rallies in Zoppot and other communities. Brown shirts marched in formation, bellowing Nazi songs and detachments of the *Schutzpoliezei* deployed in front of municipal buildings with firearms on full display.

The opposition parties, cowed and uncertain of what to expect, postponed their own rallies. But their leaders came together in a crisis meeting. Putting aside years of rivalry, they decided to campaign on a single electoral list in a show of unity opposing the NSDAP.

Hearing the news, Lester observed to Muller that the stakes had suddenly gotten even higher.

"Commissioner, why is it that Hitler seems to trump every move the British make?" Muller exclaimed. "He seems to have taken Britain's rearmament announcement in stride—and then proceeded to up the ante, scrapping the Treaty and *really* rearming! It makes the British look weak and it absolutely emboldens the NSDAP here. Does Eden have any understanding of this do you think?"

Lester sighed. "It's certainly discouraging, isn't it? Germany and Britain now seem to be sparring directly with one another; their bilateral maneuvers are even sidelining the French."

"Right," said Muller, "and they're ignoring the League entirely. 'Collective security' was what the League covenant was supposed to promise. We surely aren't seeing much of that on display these days, so we?"

Muller sensed that Lester didn't want to be drawn into the subject much deeper since it seemed pretty clear that Eden's appeasement policy was deliberately bypassing the League, its sights firmly set on an Anglo-German bargain that he hoped would set the terms for peace in Europe. Muller understood that Lester didn't want to get into an argument over Eden's approach; for better or worse, Eden was Lester's principle ally and Lester had no place else to go for help.

But Muller himself had come to the conclusion that Eden didn't really care that his approach undermined the authority of the League; almost certainly he didn't care that it weakened the authority of the League's High Commissioner in the Free City of Danzig.

Muller decided to let the subject drop, but said to himself, we deserve better here.

That night, Muller was dining alone, which was unusual, as he normally was busy with dinnertime translations for the Commissioner or his own busy meeting schedule. He returned to the Ostbahn Franz Malthesius Restaurant, studiously avoiding any smoked eels, savoring his favorite dumplings and a nice bottle of a 1930 St. Estèphe. As he relaxed, his mind wandered back to the weekend in Berkshire Abbey in the summer of 1933. It had been only twenty months earlier, but it seemed much longer ago. Actually, he decided, it seemed so remote as to be almost other-worldly. He thought of them–Eirene, Robert, Gladys and the others–sitting around those white linen tables laden with good English fare propounding on the virtues–no, the inevitability–of disarmament and planning how to do away with national air forces. Ha, he thought, Hitler certainly put paid to that idea!

He recalled his own outburst in support of the League's role in replacing conventional diplomacy with multilateral negotiations in Geneva. He sighed. How different it was in fact. Eden's appeasement policy was a direct repudiation of the position he had advocated. Instead of using the League as his principal tool for taming a resurgent Germany, Eden was treating the League as little more than a sideshow. In the case of Danzig, he just wanted the League–and the Commissioner–to buy time while he, Eden, armed with British might, negotiated a deal directly with Hitler, wholly outside of any League connection.

And here I am, Muller thought, relegated to helping the Commissioner implement Eden's policy. What a disappointment that's turned out to be. Did he have any real alternative, Muller wondered? He decided no; the League itself seemed to have acquiesced in handing the reins to Eden and was counting on him to bring Hitler to heel. I should be upbeat, Muller thought. I'm playing a small but very real part in executing high diplomacy; I've succeeded to an extent that I could hardly have foreseen at Berkshire Abbey. But somehow he couldn't muster much enthusiasm.

He wondered where Duncan Elliott was now–the only one at that summertime event who'd advocated a tougher line against Germany. What would he say about Appeasement?

Muller's reverie was interrupted by a crash of broken glassware as a large table near the far window was overturned and a pushing and shoving match ensued among men obviously arguing about the election. Most of the other patrons went back to their meals, but men and women at another table, this one closer to Muller, stood up shouting insults, then joined the melee. They were all wearing Nazi armbands and they were clearly determined to have it out with any opposition supporters. Muller took a last gulp of wine, threw down 25 Gulden for the waiter and bolted for the door. A taxi was standing outside; Muller jumped in the back seat, giving the driver his address and made his escape before the police arrived.

***

As if on signal from the restaurant brawl, the election campaign quickly became disorderly and NSDAP supporters began to display their muscle. The Party began using SA storm troopers to disrupt opposition rallies. Party supporters pinned wreaths on doors of opposition supporters with decorations reading 'Here Lives a Traitor'. The local radio station broadcast strident programming attacking the opposition and supporting NSDAP candidates; it refused airtime to the opposition. Danzig's post office distributed NSDAP pamphlets but confiscated opposition mailings. At one point, Ernst Brost, the SDP leader told Muller, a German airplane dropped twelve thousand yards of swastika banners into a nearby field so as to avoid paying Polish tariffs. "Employees of the Danzig fire brigade and telegraph office promptly collected them," said Brost and proceeded to put them on display, decorating houses, street cars and public buildings.

Lester's office received dozens of complaints about NSDAP misconduct from Brost and many other visitors. As the Commissioner lacked staff there was no means of verifying them. In meetings with opposition leaders, Lester was reduced to sympathizing with them and urging them to document whatever abuses they encountered.

Gresier and Forster played a cat and mouse game with Lester, criticizing his 'naïve willingness to encourage groundless opposition complaints', then issuing public calls for strict enforcement of election procedures–all the while running an increasingly corrupt campaign. A week before the election, Forster issued a threat to terminate any opposition civil service employee and the Senate issued orders suspending the opposition press. Both men made fiery speeches belittling the Commissioner's authority.

Frustrated and angry, Lester demanded that Forster and Greiser pay him a visit. By contrast with their earlier meeting, this one was decidedly not cordial. But at least, Muller noted, they were not in uniform this time.

Greiser opened the meeting by saying, with a smirk, "Commissioner, I hope you're enjoying the 'quiet and serene' campaign environment. You need, to relax and not take so seriously the 'frivolous whining' of the opposition."

Forster chimed in, saying, "President Greiser's right. You need to stop being a doormat for the opposition."

Forster threw back his head and laughed, his cheeks quivering, but his close-set eyes glittered, Muller noticed.

Lester reacted sharply. "Your party's behavior has been highly disruptive. We have a long list of complaints that show a clear pattern of abuse. Moreover, your own statements have been highly offensive. Mr. Forster your threat to fire any civil servant associated with the opposition is patently illegal and President Greiser your false accusations against the League and my office are unacceptable."

"But Commissioner," Greiser said in an unctuous tone, "we've repeatedly admonished all sides in the contest to respect the constitutional rules."

"All the while doing whatever you can to undermine them," retorted Lester. "And now you're importing leaders from the German Nazi Party to lead rallies here in Danzig. They are foreigners; they have no business interfering in elections in the Free City."

Forster bristled. "We are National Socialists and we are Germans," he fairly snarled. "We align ourselves with the leadership of the new German Reich and we welcome Herr Goering, Herr Himmler and Germany's Vice Chancellor Rudolf Hess to our city in a firm demonstration of Teutonic brotherhood."

Greiser said in a menacing way, "You'd better be careful, Commissioner. Remember the fate that Knox, the League's man in the Saar faced."

Muller watched Lester's face as it flushed and hardened. He had never seen him look that way.

Lester crashed his fist on the table and leaned toward Greiser. "Don't you *ever* threaten me, Gresier," he said evenly and very slowly, his eyes flashing in anger. "You may think that you're riding high right now. But this isn't over. Your conduct will have consequences."

Lester stood in a gesture of dismissal. "You are public officials. See to your responsibilities." He motioned for Muller to escort them to the door. They did not bother to shake hands.

***

That evening, as Muller queued up for the tram to return to his apartment, there was a disturbance as three young men began a pushing and shoving match. He wasn't paying much attention until one of them bumped into him and slipped a note in his hand before shoving one of his compatriots to the ground and the three of them ran off. Muller didn't react, but put the hand holding the message into his coat pocket.

When he got to the apartment, he drew the shades and turned on the lights, then pulled the message out to read.

The Shivet Pub 9 PM. Important. A friend.

***

Muller removed his coat and sat in his easy chair. Absently, he began rubbing his forehead, as he tried to concentrate and quell his anxiety. He knew where the Shivet Pub was located, south of the Center, along Wiebenwall toward the Mottlau River before it flowed into the Vistula. He remembered he'd been there last summer. He had been walking to a concert in the area when a sudden downpour sent him scampering for cover and he'd found himself in a smallish, rather dark basement pub. It was called the Shivet and he'd only stayed long enough for a beer while the shower passed. He tried to recall the place. On the plus side, it had not appeared to be an NSDAP hangout; there were no banners displayed and he'd encountered no uniforms or Nazi armbands among the patrons, though it was early in the evening and not very crowded.

On the minus side, it was off the beaten track, well outside the Center. If someone wanted to ambush him there wouldn't be many people around to see or to call on for help. Not reassuring.

But he was intrigued. 'Important' the note said.

Making up his mind, he dressed in dark clothing and put on a short wool coat that was warm but not bulky. He opened his trunk and removed the trail knife that he often wore at his belt when hiking in the mountains. It wasn't much, but something at least. Maybe I ought to buy some brass knuckles, just as a precaution, he thought to himself. He fingered the blade of the knife and was glad that he had sharpened it not so long ago. Looping the knife holder on his belt he checked to make certain that the wool coat covered it, but that he could get at it quickly if he needed to. Then he quickly drank the bowl of borscht and ate half the baguette he'd bought at the corner, but decided to wash them down with water instead of a glass of wine.

His first stop was the bar in the Nue Deutsches Hotel, where he was known. He beckoned Emil the bartender to join him at the end of the bar.

"What do you know about the Shivet Pub?"

"It's okay," Emil replied, shrugging. "A little small and dark, but if you like that sort of place..." He smiled and spread his arms.

"Political hangout?" asked Muller.

"Not that I know of," said Emil, "but hard to find a place in this town that's not connected somehow or other."

Muller passed him a coin and waved as he departed.

It was still only 8 PM but Muller decided to leave early so he could case the location ahead of time–and maybe upset any plans that someone might have made for him. He crossed over to the Ladoud Canal and followed it South, noting the looming Commerzbank building on the other bank, displaying large Nazi banners. His route took him past the Polish Central Bank building, another of the large Baltic-style structures that adorned the city, and the High Gate, still adorned with the symbols of Prussia alongside the Free City symbol of the Golden Crown above two white crosses. The road began to narrow into a residential neighborhood and the street lights became fewer and feebler. Muller kept to the shadows, stopping periodically to listen for other footfalls. Occasional cars swept by, but none slowed or seemed to show any interest in him. A cat screeched behind a stone fence and Muller jumped, but it was nothing.

A few long blocks further and Muller spied the sign over the entrance of the Shivet Pub. He checked his watch. It had taken him less than fifteen minutes to get there and nothing had seemed out of order. He found a comfortable corner hidden in the shadows across the street and settled down to watch the entrance to the pub. It was not very busy; occasional customers would enter or leave, usually alone. He remained alert.

Suddenly, an automobile sped down a side street and careened to a skidding stop in front of the pub. The driver and two other men jumped out of the car and opened the rear car door facing Muller's hiding spot. Whoever was sitting in that seat was obviously injured.

"Shit, he's still bleeding."

"Careful, get him out of there–easy for God's sake."

Two men supported the injured man on either side as they helped him out of the car. The third ran to open the pub door and they all disappeared inside. Muller's heart was pounding. Then the pub door opened again and one of the men ran back to the car, closing the back door where the injured man had been removed and opening the driver's door. As he started the car, another of the men bounded out of the entrance to the pub.

"Put it back by the alley in case we have to get away fast," he hissed at the driver who nodded and put the car in gear, backing it into an alley leading behind the pub where it disappeared from Muller's view.

Muller remained hidden in the shadows. Moments later another car, this one with NSDAP markings, drove slowly toward the pub from the same side street as the first car had come. Someone in the passenger seat of the car was shining a flashlight from side to side, apparently looking for something. Muller shrank back as the car glided slowly by and continued on in the direction of the Center, along the route Muller had taken. He glanced at his watch, just visible in the distant street light. Ten minutes before 9 PM. If he had been on time, he would certainly have been visible to the NSDAP car. Somehow, he thought, that probably would not have been a good thing.

Muller remained in his hiding spot. Shortly after 9 PM someone opened the door to the pub and came up the stairs, looking around—as if he were searching for someone. The man looked at his watch, put his hands on his hips and glanced around again.

"Muller?" the man said quietly. "Muller?"

Muller stepped out of the shadows and came up beside the man. "I'm Muller. Why are you looking for me?"

The man was startled and backed away. Then, recovering, he said, "We're glad you're here. Come inside quickly."

The interior of the pub was dark, as Muller had remembered. The bartender and the handful of patrons seemed to pay no attention as the man led Muller through a back door which led to another door that the man opened with a key.

Muller blinked at a well-lit, small meeting room, with folding chairs arranged in front of a small stage. A man had been laid out on the stage. He had a bloody bandage around his head and as Muller approached he could see the man's face had been badly beaten and was still bleeding, with small pools collecting on the stage floor.

With a start, Muller recognized the man as the reporter from the *Volkstag* event a few days earlier. Kreutzer, he remembered; Stephan Kreutzer, the opposition SDP journalist.

"Mr. Muller, thank you for coming tonight," said the man who had led him into the pub. The other two men stood aside to allow Muller to approach the reporter. "You will understand that it's best if we don't identify ourselves. We hadn't expected Stephan to be beaten up, so matters are a little more difficult then he'd planned. But he has a message he wants to pass to you. He arranged this rendezvous. It's a hall that the SDP occasionally uses and so far as we know, it's safe."

"You need to get Kreutzer to a hospital," said Muller.

"We're going to do that, but first he needs to pass you some important information," said the man. "He insisted that we bring him here."

"Stephan, Mr. Muller is here. Can you talk?"

Kreutzer tried to raise his head. One eye was swollen shut and his face was covered with cuts and bruises. "Mr. Muller?" he said, wincing at the effort. "Thank for accepting my message. I had to make unusual arrangements to deliver it."

Muller could see him attempt to smile.

As Muller stood closer, Kreutzer slowly moved one arm, digging into his pocket and extracting a small piece of paper which he handed to Muller. The paper was blood-soaked, but as Muller unfolded it he could make out three names. They meant nothing to him.

Kreutzer closed his eyes and began speaking softly. "I have a friend—actually, my lover," he said, his voice cracking. "He's in the Gestapo here, communications. He hates what they're doing and we have secret sympathies." Kreutzer paused, then opened his eyes and continued. "He learned that Berlin has sent an assassination team to be on standby here until the election. They have a list of potential targets. Opposition leaders, but most important, it includes the Commissioner—and you too, Mr. Muller. The names of the assassins are on that piece of paper. We don't know who's giving them orders. But we're frightened and since I had your business card, I thought I should pass the information to you. Please take care of yourself."

Kreutzer closed his eyes, seemingly drained of energy.

"How did he get beaten up?" Muller asked the man who had led him into the pub.

"It happened only an hour or so ago," said the man. "Stephan and his lover had gone to a small hotel just off Vorsaditche Strasse that apparently caters to that kind of thing. As they left the hotel, some Brown Shirts decided to attack them. Stephan's friend was able to escape somehow, so they concentrated on beating up poor Stephan. Fortunately some of our SDP trade unionists were walking home from work and were able to chase off the Nazis. I live nearby and two of the SDP guys," he motioned toward the other two men, "got me to bring my car so we could get him to a hospital. He insisted we bring him here first because he had set up this meeting and he had an important message he needed to give you."

Muller nodded, his mind working. "Is there a back exit from this room?"

The man nodded, "Two of them in fact," he said pointing to doors at either end of the hall. "That's one of the reasons we chose this place as a meeting hall; two ways to get out fast if trouble arrives."

"You parked the car near one of them?" asked Muller.

"That one." The man pointed. "We'll take Stephan out that way and drive him to the hospital. You probably should leave by the other exit."

"I saw a car with NSDAP markings drive by right after you brought in Kreutzer," Muller said. "I don't know if they were following you, but they were looking for something with a flashlight as they drove along."

"Then we'd all better be careful," said the man. "You're able to find your way, Mr. Muller?'

Muller nodded. "Yes. Thanks and tell Kreutzer I'll plan to visit him."

Muller went to the door and opened it slowly, then slipped out into the darkness. He stood stock-still waiting for his eyes to adjust and listened for any sounds. Finally, he could see enough to begin slowly edging along the wall of a narrow alley. After about a hundred yards it ended at a dark street with only a dim, distant streetlight offering any guidance. Muller decided to go in the direction away from the light, hoping that the darkness would protect him. Walking carefully and stopping to listen, he worked his way along the street, finally coming to an intersection. Looking to his right he could see the reflections of lights and he realized it must be the Mottlau River. In a few blocks he found the riverbank and proceeded north, feeling reassured as he neared Langgasse and the marketplace. He was now only about a mile from his apartment and began to relax.

An assassination squad; he slowed and began to think through what Kreutzer had told him. Should he go directly to the residence to warn the Commissioner? Then he had a better idea.

Glancing at his watch, he saw it was not yet 10 PM. Cafes and restaurants were still open. He glanced at a café on his left and saw it had a call box on the wall in the rear. Entering, he asked the cashier sitting just inside the doorway if he might use the telephone. She shrugged. He dialed the operator and asked for the Danzig Police Headquarters. The desk sergeant who answered told him that Franz Schiller was expected back soon. Muller left his name and asked the sergeant to advise Schiller that he was coming to the station and would Schiller please wait for him.

Going back outside, he was able to get a taxi and a few minutes later pulled up in front of Police Headquarters. The desk sergeant told Muller that Schiller had not yet arrived back and pointed to a bench where Muller could wait.

Muller sat down and drew a deep breath, leaning his head back on the paint-chipped wall behind the bench and closing his eyes.

An assassination team.

With a hit list, which included his name and the Commissioner's name.

Muller snapped back to attention, sitting up straight and trying to absorb the information. Just then, Franz Schiller walked into the station accompanied by a couple of policemen. Schiller stopped and looked at Muller, startled.

"Muller," he said smiling. "I didn't know we had a rehearsal tonight." He came up to shake hands and Muller rose from the bench to greet him.

"I'm afraid it's a little more serious than that," Muller replied.

Schiller looked at Muller and nodded. "Give me a moment." He turned to the policemen, gave them terse instructions, then took Muller by the elbow and led him down the hall. "Let's go to my office. You look like you swallowed something nasty tonight."

CHAPTER 12

Winter and Spring 1935

Schiller's small office was remarkably neat and tidy, with only a few stacks of paper on the windowsill and a handful of file folders in his inbox and outbox. He gestured Muller to sit in a round-backed chair and took his place behind the desk, firmly closing the door behind him. He then reached into a desk drawer and extracted a bottle of schnapps. He inspected two small glasses, wiped them both with his tie, and filled them from the bottle, handing one to Muller. They clinked glasses and drank deeply.

Schiller placed a notebook on his desk, unscrewed a handsome fountainpen and looked inquiringly at Muller. "I'm all ears."

Muller told him the whole story, starting with the events in the *Volkstag* where he had first met Stephan Kreutzer.

"Yeah, we were called in that day, but nothing came of it," said Schiller. "The guys who beat up the Communist deputy were themselves parliamentarians so they were immune from prosecution." Schiller shook his head, smiling faintly. "Another uplifting example of democracy at work."

When Muller revealed his information about the assassination squad, Schiller put down his pen and leaned forward, arms on his desk, unsmiling and listening intently. Muller handed him the blood-smeared paper Kreutzer had given him. Schiller stared at it. Then he took up his fountain pen and carefully wrote the name in his notebook. He removed an envelope from his top drawer, wrote the date and Muller's name on the front, then placed the note in it.

"I'd like to keep this for evidence," he said.

"Certainly," Muller replied.

Schiller then took Muller back through his story, questioning him closely to be sure he had covered everything. Finally, he sat back and crossed his hands behind his head. "Sweet Jesus," he said softly. "Assassination as a political weapon."

He sat up straight again looking levelly at Muller. "I can assure you that the Chief, and this department, will take this information very seriously, Muller. Coming straight to me was a smart thing to do. I'll have you escorted home tonight and I'll contact you tomorrow at the Commissioner's residence. I need to give some thought to what precautions should be taken to protect potential targets, including both the Commissioner and yourself."

Schiller stood to escort Muller back to the front desk of the station and they shook hands. "I think it would be in order for you to have a couple of brandies before you go to bed tonight," he said in friendly fashion, "and don't put the Brahms Requiem on the Victrola."

Muller did as Schiller suggested, but still didn't sleep much before rising early to go to the residence. Muller took the stairs two at a time, hurrying up to the Commissioner's office. Lester was seated at his desk with a cup of coffee, already immersed in the morning paperwork.

"Muller, you're early today," he said smiling and shaking hands.

"I'm afraid I have a disturbing report to make, Commissioner," said Muller as they took their accustomed seats. He proceeded to tell Lester about the night's events.

Lester listened intently. He visibly stiffened when Muller described the presence of the reported assassination team, but he did not interrupt. When Muller finished, Lester put his elbows on the desk and regarded him intently.

"You've had time to think about this, Muller. Do you think this puts Elsie or the girls in danger? That's my first concern."

"I did think about that Commissioner," he said. "I knew it would be your immediate reaction. My answer is, I don't think so. We don't know who's behind this scheme, but it gives every indication of being political, not some plan for mass murders. I can't see any political rationale for an attack on Elsie or the girls; they're just not politically relevant. They have no connection whatever to the campaign beyond their relationship to you. So I don't see any immediate threat to them, though I confess I didn't raise it with Schiller; I thought about it later when I was turning things over in my mind."

Lester grunted, turning to gaze out the windows toward the Central Square. "I hope that's right. It sounds plausible.

"But I'm damned if I'm going into hibernation because of this threat. Frankly, it just makes me angrier at what going on. Moreover, what would be the political advantage of killing me?" he added. "That would be seen as targeting the League of Nations itself. It would generate intense scrutiny, none of which would be favorable to the NSDAP. Actually, as I think about it, killing me would be about the stupidest thing Forster and his cronies could do. It would make the NSDAP look very bad to most of the world and here in Danzig it would scare a lot of people into supporting the opposition who might not otherwise do so.

"That's it Muller," Lester said, laughing hard. "All I have to do is invite that Gestapo gang to come kill me and that would guarantee getting rid of the NSDAP government and bring the opposition to power. Ha! Some strategy."

An hour later, Franz Schiller paid Muller a visit. After greeting him in the entry hallway, Muller led the way up the broad staircase to Lester's office. "I know the Commissioner will want to hear what you have to say."

After introductions, Lester invited Schiller and Muller to sit with him in the easy chairs arranged beyond the conference table in the spacious office.

"It was an eventful but, I think, fruitful night, Commissioner," said Schiller. "With the information provided me by Mr. Muller we were able to track the three individuals to an NSDAP-run residence over near the docks. As they hadn't committed any crime, we couldn't issue a warrant for their arrest. Instead, we advised them that we were taking them into 'protective custody'. It was rather easy to do; two of the three were so drunk they could barely stand; our officers actually had to half-carry them to our vans. The third guy was sound asleep and had no interest in making trouble when we woke him up. After we took them away, a couple of NSDAP higher-ups tried to intervene, but the Chief–I told him about the matter and he took charge personally–told them to fuck off.

"It didn't take long to get the men to talk. They are in fact officers in a Berlin Gestapo unit and have specialized in arresting and, from time to time, killing persons opposed to Nazi rule in Germany. They were told to come to Danzig and await orders. They only arrived yesterday morning. The man they were to report to here works directly for Albert Forster. Surprise!" said Schiller, interrupting his report and smiling sarcastically.

Muller and Lester also smiled, exchanged knowing glances.

Then Schiller continued, serious again. "Early this morning, the Chief paid Mr. Forster a visit. He told Forster that he was to get those three agents in a truck on their way out of the Free City within an hour. He also told Forster that if any political or diplomatic figure in the Free City were assaulted or killed, he–the Chief–would see to it that Forster would be arrested and charged with the crime. He told Forster that we know all the dirty tricks he's pulling to win this election, that we had documented them and would not hesitate to use them against him if it seemed appropriate to do so.

"He then did what the Chief can do perhaps better than anyone else I know. He picked Forster up by his lapels and slammed him against the wall of his office so hard that a bunch of pictures fell down with a crash, and with his nose not two inches from Forster's, asked him if he understood. Forster said he did.

"So Commissioner, I think this unpleasantness is now safely behind us."

After Schiller departed, Lester said to Muller, "I think we needn't bother mentioning this episode to Elsie...Or to anyone in Geneva."

***

The final days of the campaign became a blur of Nazi flags and uniforms, squawking loudspeakers and marching bands. As promised, Hess, Himmler, Goering and other German leaders visited the City, addressing loud rallies with fiery rhetoric and attacks on 'enemies of the Reich'.

Muller ventured out to see what was happening. Mindful of his own vulnerability, he'd decided that the best way to get a feel for the atmosphere, without exposing himself to the roving bands of storm troopers and Hitler Youth gangs, was to ride the tram system. There was plenty to see: NSDAP members marched around wearing sandwich board emblazoned with election signs; billboards were slapped on walls all across town; every building, it seemed, was draped in Nazi banners; and storm troopers were on the march. But surprisingly, as he rode the #3 tram along the docks and shipyards in the sections of town closest to the harbor, the displays were for the opposition and there were no signs of marching storm troopers.

Reporting later to Lester, Muller said, "It wasn't like there was some demarcation line, but the Nazi symbols just petered out and instead I saw the Danzig flag and symbols along with trade union and Catholic Party billboards."

Lester was intrigued. "I wonder if Forster's overplayed his hand?"

As Muller left the residence for dinner on election eve, he was handed a statement that was being distributed by opposition runners. Glancing at it, Muller was shocked to see it was a statement signed by Hermann Rauschning, the former President of the Senate who had not been seen in public since his humiliating removal from office.

Muller jogged after the runner who'd handed it to him. "Where did this come from?"

"Don't know," said the young man, "but Mr. Rauschning sent it to our leadership earlier today and since our press has been shut down, they duplicated it and got lots of us to spread out across the city to distribute it by hand. Want some more to hand out to other people? We've got lots of copies."

Muller shook his head, "No thanks. One's enough," He turned back toward the residence to show the document to Lester.

***

Muller began scanning the document while Lester poured them drinks. "Rauschning is saying that he is issuing a statement in his role as 'a responsible citizen and voter in Danzig'," he translated for Lester.

Muller marveled as he read on. The document said he was rejecting both the program and the doctrine of the NSDAP as being in direct conflict with fundamental principles of constitutional democracy.

"This is pretty amazing, Commissioner," Muller exclaimed as he continued reading and translating.

"Dismissing the NSDAP agenda as 'empty propaganda', Rauschning endorsed 'full civil equality' for all Citizens of Danzig before the law. He denounced Forster by name, accusing him of imposing 'an unlawful and arbitrary system of absolute power, lacking integrity or morality'. He closed by declaring himself opposed to NSDAP's Electoral List and he urged voters to support the opposition and the rule of law."

When Muller had finished translating it, he and Lester sat back staring at one another.

"What an extraordinary act of courage," said Lester softly. "I hope he's taken steps to protect himself. If his message actually gets out to the voters, it will have an effect."

He offered his glass to Muller and they silently clinked them in a toast.

***

Election Day was a Sunday and the weather was fine for Danzig in early April, with clouds, a chill breeze off the Baltic, but no rain or snow. Muller walked around the city to watch the voting. Things seemed orderly enough; he noticed some new NSDAP posters had been plastered overnight on several building walls, Members of the Hitler Youth, in full uniform and wearing sandwich boards bearing Nazi slogans, hung around many of the polling places, but Muller saw no signs of violence. He took the #9 tram out to Zoppot and walked around, again seeing nothing amiss. He had a late lunch at the Parrot Restaurant, which was crowded with people dining after church or after casting their ballots.

Muller decided to listen to the election results that night on the large Telefunken console radio in the sitting room of his boarding house. A broadcast was expected around 10 PM. Muller fortified himself with a bottle of Marchandel gin and a crossword puzzle listening to the marches and patriotic songs being played as the station awaited the announcement. But 10 PM came and went; Muller dozed in his overstuffed chair. Around 11 PM an announcer made a brief statement that despite the delay, the results would be announced soon. Muller awoke again with a start shortly after midnight, martial music still playing. Something was amiss.

He took a generous swallow of gin, put on his coat and walked toward the *Volkstag* where the radio station's small studio operated in cramped basement corner. Loudspeakers in the street continued to play the repetitive marches. Muller quickly saw he was not alone and that quite a large crowd was converging on the *Volkstag*. As he neared the building, the music on the loudspeakers, abruptly stopped. "Albert Forster, Gauleiter of the NSDAP will announce the results." Loud static. Indistinct voices could be heard. A long silence. Then the music started again.

The crowd at the entrance to the *Volkstag*, now numbering nearly a hundred, began muttering to one another and looking around in frustration. Then people began exiting the *Volkstag*; Muller could see groups departing by side exits, obviously trying to avoid being seen by the crowd in front. Finally, someone burst out of the front entrance and shouted, "NSDAP has won a resounding electoral victory, winning 59 percent of the vote." People in the crowd reacted with disbelief, turning to one another, everyone seeming to talk at once.

"What? What? 59 percent?"

Some reacted in laughter. "This is the best they can do?"

Others reacted angrily and pockets of men began pushing and shoving one another. Muller moved to one side, but he was close enough to hear one of the men leaving the building talking to a nearby group of men.

"Look, I'm just an engineer here, so don't quote me."

"Come on, Klaus," several in the crowd urged him on. "What the Hell happened?"

The engineer looked around, finding himself surrounded by anxious faces.

"All right," he said. "Here it is. We spent the night playing this boring music just waiting for the bosses to come down and make the announcement. We were as annoyed as anyone at the delay since we had to sit around and just play marches."

The engineer, now seeing that he was the center of attention of a growing crowd, became more animated. "So finally a couple of guys from the Senate came down to the studio to make sure we were ready to go. 'Sure', we said, so they disappeared again and then a new bunch arrived with papers they were shuffling. It was all very confused."

Muller watched with amusement as the engineer began preening himself while his audience grew.

"Finally Gauleiter Forster was escorted into the studio," the engineer continued in a louder voice. "Forster's been on the radio before, but had me show him where he should stand for the microphone and everything. He clears his throat a few times and says 'testing, testing,' shifting around. Finally he says he's ready. One of the Senate guys hands Forster the script from which he's supposed to speak and announce the results."

The engineer paused for effect.

"Forster looked at the paper and went white," the engineer paused. "He was speechless. His hand holding the script began shaking like a leaf. He opened his mouth, but nothing came out. Then he turned around without a word, tossed the script at one of the staff and walked out of the studio. No one knew what to do, then someone told me to put the marches back on and that's what I did. And that's the story. Who'll buy me a drink? I need one."

Muller recounted the entire episode to Lester the next morning.

"I'll bet he just shit his pants," Lester said laughing heartily. "Serves him right. And Greiser too...Maybe this will take some wind out of their sails," he added quietly.

Later that day, Greiser tried to put a brave face on the result by issuing a statement vindicating the absolute NSDAP majority, saying that 'by soundly defeating the opposition,' the Citizens of Danzig had clearly rejected the opposition's maneuvering and whining in their petitions.

The opposition, however, was ecstatic. A delegation of opposition leaders asked to meet with Lester a day later.

"Commissioner, we would certainly have won a fair election; as it is, we barely lost a rigged one," said Ernst Brost, the SDP leader. "This is a huge victory for our united opposition. It demonstrates how deeply unpopular the NSDAP has become with most of Danzig's voters. Even by their own tally, they only gained two seats in the *Volkstag*. They pulled out all the stops—and even with a corrupt vote, they gained almost nothing.

"This is the beginning of the end for those bigmouths," Brost said disdainfully. "We also want to let you know, Commissioner, that we are collecting extensive documentation of the flagrant misconduct committed during the campaign." He held up a thick folder. "It will take us a little time to organize, but we will be submitting petitions to overturn this election backed by incontrovertible evidence." He slapped the folder on his knee for emphasis, and proceeded to spill most of the papers on the rug. Amid general laughter, he and two of the other opposition members got down on hands and knees to recover them.

"We'll do a better job of organizing them than that," Brost said with a smile.

Lester thanked them for their visit. "I can't make any promises on how I'll deal with your petitions, but you certainly have the right to present them." Then he paused before adding, "Actually, I'm rather looking forward to reading them."

Muller expected that matters would quiet down as the NSDAP licked its wounds, but a day later, the Senate shuttered the SDP newspaper again and the next day ordered the arrest of four opposition members of the *Volkstag*. Lester and Greiser exchanged tart messages, with Greiser finally lifting the ban on the newspaper and ordering release of the parliamentarians.

"They're immune from arrest by the rules of the *Volkstag*," Lester groused to Muller. "He didn't have a shred of justification for locking them up. It's almost irrational."

***

Then, as things began to get back to normal, Danzig was jolted by yet another crisis. On May 2, 1935, with no warning, the Senate announced a devaluation of the Danzig gulen by 43 percent. Coming only three weeks after an election campaign in which the NSDAP had bragged about the City's strong economy and ridiculed opposition accusations of mismanagement, the announcement was shocking and generated immediate outrage. Greiser tried to blame Polish customs policies and opposition foot-dragging on employment measures. No one was buying the story. Rumors had been rife for years that the German government had been secretly subsidizing the Danzig budget through transfers from the Reichsbank; the consensus in the business community, at least, was that the Germans had pulled the plug and the City was out of money.

Muller decided to tap into the expertise of his fellow boarder, Viktor Truczinski, who was manager of a large sawmill situated in the industrial zone in the port. Frau Scheffler, his landlady, had only two other boarders in addition to Muller, Truczinski and a Frenchman named Jean-Claude Charlet, who was in the cosmetics business and was rarely in Danzig, but who kept the apartment for the sake of convenience. The last apartment, the one in back, remained vacant, much to Frau Scheffler's disappointment.

Muller and Truczinski saw each other occasionally at breakfast, the only meal that was offered; Truczinski tended to run later than Muller in the morning, but they had become friendly and several times during the past summer, they had gone out together to Oliwa and the beaches at Glettkau and Brosen. Truczinski was a native Danziger and part of a Polish community that had lived and worked there for generations.

Muller invited him for drinks the next evening and Lester asked them to join him in his spacious office, opening a fresh bottle of Distillers scotch for the occasion. "I don't want to butt in on your conversation with Muller," Lester said as they settled in chairs with their drinks, "but when I heard you were dropping by, I asked Muller if it would be all right to at least eavesdrop so I can get your perspective on this economic hole we seem to have fallen into."

"It's a pretty deep hole," replied Truczinski in fluent English. "I'm happy to talk about the mess these guys seem to have made for me—and for most of the people who live here."

In response to Lester's inquiry, Truczinski explained that he had been brought up speaking German and Polish at home and learned English, "so I could continue the family business."

"You ought to tell the Commissioner about the business," said Muller. "It's interesting. I'd begun to describe it, but we got interrupted and you'll tell it better anyway."

"All right," said Truczinski, "the short version, then." He smiled.

"My family owns a sawmill business that we've operated here for a long time. My great grandfather worked in the business; his son, my grandfather, was able to buy the mill and my father took it over after his death and continues to run it. Our customers are lumber merchants in Europe, mainly London and Antwerp. They buy boards from us and sell them, mainly to manufacturers of high end furniture. Good hardwood is scarce, so we have a ready market for our boards, since they're sawn from virgin timber. My father and brother run the sawmill; my job is to handle marketing and sales. That's why I spend a lot of time in Europe—mainly speaking English to our customers."

"Tell the Commissioner how you get the logs," said Muller.

Truczinski nodded. "Nowadays, we get them from Bialowieza, a remote, swampy part of Eastern Poland." The woodsmen go into the forests of the region in winter, when everything's frozen. They fell the trees, then transport the logs by sledge to the banks of the Nymen river to await the spring floods. When the river gets high enough, we send teams of raftsmen up there. They assemble the logs into rafts composed of more than twenty logs all lashed together, often as many as a dozen big rafts.

"All the rivers in the European plain run South to North; everything goes "down" to the Baltic. But if you look at a map, the rivers flow from the bottom of the page toward the top; it's as if we float the logs 'up' to our mill.

"Anyway, when the ice melts, the raftsmen maneuver the rafts into the current; they use long staves to steer and push them along. They bump and thump and glide their way down the Nymen to the Bobr, then into the Bug as far as Modlin, where it flows into the Vistula, and finally after a trip of a month or six weeks, they arrive at our yard, where the Mottlau and the

Vistula come together. You've probably seen the sawmill area, right across from the Schichau shipyards. That's where we are."

"Those raftsmen ride the log rafts all that way?" asked Lester.

Truczinski nodded, smiling knowingly. "Not for the faint of heart. They build reed huts on the rafts that offer a little protection, not much, and they try to pull over to the riverbank at night to cook and sleep. But it's hard, hard work."

He shrugged. "Back in the old days, we used to source logs as far south as Kiev. My father can recall lumberyards there with huge logs stacked eight or ten high where my grandfather would make his purchases. They'd float rafts down the Dnieper to the Prypet, through the canal to the Bug and connect to the Vistula; it could take as long as three months."

He paused. "We haven't been able to do that trip since Stalin shut down the Soviet border, but we still have contacts along the old route and they're telling us terrible stories about famine in Ukraine in the last year or so. Even the tightest borders have leaks, and every now and then a handful of Ukrainians–scarecrows, most of them–find their way out and talk about towns and villages with entire populations dead of hunger. Stalin followed through on his threats to kill the landowners–kulaks, he called them–and he imposed collective farming. The resulting shortages have apparently been catastrophic and caused wholesale famine."

Truczinski shook his head. "The Soviets are tight-lipped about almost everything–including this. But the stories we've been told are very scary...That's a longer story about our sawmill business than I intended." His expression brightening. "But Muller told me you wanted to discuss the devaluation, so let me tell you how it affects us."

Muller could see Lester lean forward expectantly.

"We pay for our Polish logs in zlotys–the Polish currency," said Truczinski. "We have to buy the zlotys with our Danzig gulens. Well, thanks to the devaluation, it now costs us almost twice as many gulens to buy the same number of zlotys. So our raw material costs have doubled. We're luckier than most Danzigers, because we sell our finished boards against letters of credit in hard currencies—mainly British pounds and Dutch guilders. So we can recoup some of our losses. But we have to spend a lot of that hard currency to buy the machining equipment we depend upon to produce our boards. Specialized sawblades are crucial. If we can reduce the thickness—the kurf, it's called—of the sawblade even by as little as a 64th of an inch, we increase our output by that fraction. It doesn't sound like much, but multiply it by a million board feet per year and it adds up to real money. We buy only the best sawblades, mainly in Sweden. We use a lot of them and they're expensive. So poof," he opened his palms, "there goes our hard currency, and we're left with raw material costs that have doubled. I calculate our income will shrink by a minimum of 25 percent this year.

"Suppose you run a restaurant here," he went on. "Danzig's not a big farming community, so you have to import most of your fruits and vegetables and your meat and poultry from somewhere in Poland—now at nearly *double* the cost in gulens. And your customers pay for the meals you serve them in gulens. So the only option you have is to raise prices. But your customers don't have more money to pay those higher prices; they've been hit by the devaluation too. It becomes a vicious circle."

"So what happens now?" asked Lester. "Does the situation just stabilize at those levels?"

Truczinski sighed. "A lot of us are old enough to remember the runaway inflation we experienced a decade ago. It ruined nearly everyone. People are afraid that this devaluation is the first step back down that road. They're scared and angry. The NSDAP was clearly lying about this currency crisis during the campaign and people are fed up with it. I'm no politician, but I'll tell you, if that ballot took place next week instead of last month, the Party wouldn't win 25 percent of the vote."

Lester was relishing the conversation. He refilled their glasses a third time and sent to the kitchen for canapes to sustain them further.

"We need fuel to sustain us in this important inquiry," Lester said, only a little facetiously.

"The new Polish port at Gydina is relevant to the story too," Truczinski continued. "I took Muller out to Zoppot last summer, Commissioner. If you stand on the breakwater at Brosen – the big mole there–and look to the right, you can see the port of Danzig; if you turn the other way and look left, you can see the port of Gydina. It's just over the border in the territory of the Polish Corridor; the two ports are only about fifteen miles apart. The situation makes absolutely no sense commercially or economically. But beginning in 1924, using French capital, Dutch dredgers and Danish engineers, the Poles transformed what was just a marshy fishing village into a world-class port with modern cranes, warehouses, and multi-tracked railway connections; they operate steamship lines to Europe–even to New York. Gydina now has a population of about 50,000, supporting big new hotels and restaurants; it clearly outstrips the port of Danzig, which has fallen into disrepair and doesn't have the same modern facilities."

Muller proffered cigarettes and his lighter, not wanting to interrupt.

"And here's the irony," Truczinski went on, "the whole idea of the Treaty of Versailles, with the Free City tucked inside the Polish Corridor, was to provide Polish access to the Baltic. But the Poles hardly use Danzig at all; Gydina has become their access to the Baltic.

"Danzig had been German for over a hundred years," he went on. "Danzigers hated being stripped out of Germany and they certainly didn't want to become dependent upon Poland–a country that hadn't even been in existence during that same hundred years. So they continued to think of themselves as German and they've made no effort to integrate themselves with the Polish economy. As a consequence, Danzig's become steadily more isolated and its economy has grown progressively weaker. The Reichsbank is subsidizing Danzig's budget; otherwise Danzig would be broke."

Lester nodded. "The subsidy's been more or less an open secret. But I confess I didn't realize the weakness in the Danzig economy. You certainly wouldn't have known that from the speeches by the NSDAP leadership. Their campaign story was all about how good things were and how they were only going to get better."

"One of the reasons Hermann Rauschning was popular with the Danzig business community was that he wanted to change things," said Truczinski. "He understood that Danzig needed to increase its revenues, and had to integrate better into the Polish economy. He also suspected that there might come a time when the Reichsbank subsidies might slow down, or even stop altogether. Forster, of course, vehemently opposed Rauschning's approach. First, he's stupid and has no concept of economics; second, he hates Poland and the Poles and he wanted no part of any integration effort; all he wants is to get Danzig back into Germany. So he engineered Rauschning's ouster and is undercutting better ties to Poland– and any hope for improving our economy."

Truczinski took a cheese tart. "These are good," he said, reaching for another before resuming.

"Forster and his allies cheered when Hitler announced he was going to build a big army and air force, but they didn't think to ask how he was going to pay for his new military playthings. It looks like one of the ways he's doing it is to cut down on some other expenses–like, for example, the payments going to support Danzig. All of a sudden those subsidies seem to have become a lot less important in Berlin. So the word came down:

'Devalue!' and Forster sent Greiser out to make the announcement. It is a devastating confirmation of a failed policy that had been followed for years. And the NSDAP is getting the blame–which they richly deserve."

Lester absently swirled his whiskey with his finger, gazing out at the gathering twilight. "What you're telling me, Mr. Truczinski," he began, "is that if the Germans don't keep up the subsidies, Danzig will become insolvent, so it seems pretty clear the Germans will conclude that they have no choice but to keep the subsidies flowing–maybe not at the same level, but enough to keep the City afloat. Assuming that's correct, the key question is which power base in Berlin will call the shots. The Wilhelmstrasse? The Finance Ministry? The Reichsbank? And how will this new leverage affect the behavior of Forster and the NSDAP? Will they be ordered to call a halt to the harassment or will they just ignore the crisis and keep pushing their agenda?"

"I don't know," said Truczinski. "But think we'll learn the answer pretty soon."

"This situation is also certain to alarm the Poles," Lester said. "They're very sensitive about preserving every aspect of their Treaty rights in the City. If they sense that Germany will try to use the financial crisis to assert more influence over the City, they'll react. I'm not sure how, though. Will they try to punish the City, for example by imposing border restrictions and cutting off exports? Maybe; they've done that before. Or, will they decide they can improve their position by throwing the City a lifeline, say in the form of a loan? That's certainly plausible, and maybe smarter."

Truczinski looked at his watch. "Commissioner, I'm truly sorry, but I've got a dinner appointment and I'm afraid I need to leave. This has been a very pleasant conversation and I'm pleased finally to meet Muller's boss."

They stood and finished the last of their drinks. Lester thanked Truczinski for coming and they shook hands warmly, agreeing to meet again soon.

"That was interesting, Muller. He helped clarify my thinking," Lester said. "There's another point that I didn't want to bring up while he was here, but that you and I need to consider, and that's whether this financial crisis gives the League Council new leverage that we should try to persuade them to use. The June Council meetings are only six weeks away. We need to give that question some close attention."

***

Shortly after the meeting with Truczinski, Lester received a message from the President of the Danzig Bank, requesting an urgent audience with the Commissioner. Gustaf Grundgen was Danzig's central banker. He didn't preside over a very large institution, but the Danzig Bank was fortified by laws, enacted in 1920, giving it broad authority over financial matters affecting the City.

Arriving punctually for the meeting a day later, Grundgen came quickly to the point.

"Commissioner, the City of Danzig is in urgent need of funds. The government's annual expenditures are running at 80 million gulens per year; our revenues are 60 million gulens per year. The source that has been providing payments to make up the difference is no longer available, at least at those levels."

It was evident that 'the source' he referred to was the Reichsbank, but as the subsidies were meant to be secret, he couldn't identify it.

"Negotiations are continuing," Grundgen went on, "but it is incumbent upon my Bank to find alternative sources of financing. Therefore, I am formally requesting you, as High Commissioner for the

League of Nations, to use your good offices to seek a five-year loan to the Free City of Danzig from the Bank of International Settlements in Basle in the sum of ten million Swiss francs at an inter-bank interest rate to be agreed. We stand ready to provide the appropriate documentation. The Bank of International Settlements is independent of course, but it's an integral part of the League of Nations fiscal structure. As the Free City is a mandate of the League, My Central Bank governors and I believe financial support to the City from the Bank is entirely appropriate."

Muller translated for Lester and the Commissioner inquired if the President of the Senate, as head of the City government, agreed to this request.

"Herr Greiser has been informed of my plan," Grundgen replied evenly, then added, "And he has agreed to the request that I have just made."

As he translated the reply for Lester, Muller thought he'd bet Greiser had to grit his teeth to say yes.

Lester responded that he would communicate Grundgen's request to the Secretary General of the League and would advise him of the League's reaction.

After Grundgen's departure, Lester looked at Muller. "Well that was unexpected."

Muller agreed, then added, "Commissioner, I probably need to tell you that the President of the Bank of International Settlements is one of my family's closest friends. Nicholas Odier was a classmate of my father's in school. His family runs a private bank that's very similar to ours. We've all hiked and skied together, celebrated birthdays and anniversaries together; I've literally known him my entire life. He took a leave from his family's bank two years ago to become President of the BIS. So, while I agree that you need to forward Grundgen's request to the Secretary General in Geneva, there is also an option available to approach Odier directly."

Lester looked at Muller and smiled. "Muller, you do seem to have a knack for this job."

He paused. "Let's hold off on your option for the moment, though. I'll get off a letter to Geneva and we'll see how they react. I think the loan is a good idea; there's no doubt it would give us a stronger hand here. Maybe we can get Eden on board."

***

The very next day the Polish leader, Marshal Jozef Pilsudski, died. Lester and Muller paid a visit to the Polish Consulate to sign the mourning book. Kasimir Papee, the Polish Consul General, motioned for them to join him in his office. He waved them both to seats and pulled out a bottle of the Danzig Gold Wasser, pouring them each a generous helping.

"Our formal condolences," said Lester lifting his glass.

Papee acknowledged the toast. "Nothing but the best for our beloved Marshal." He tossed down the drink and refilled his glass. "It's nice to see you both," he said, smiling, "I needed a break from the crowd of local mourners."

"How do you assess the impact of the Marshal's death?" asked Lester. "You've said he's been more or less a figurehead because of his infirmities."

Papee smiled thinly. "The body's hardly cold, but the maneuvering has already begun in Warsaw. Beck is there, of course; he's roundly disliked by a lot of the other ministers and party bigwigs, so I don't think they'll agree to have him replace the old man. But he's got a lock on the Foreign Ministry; he'll probably be content to continue running Polish foreign policy and

243

ignore the rest of them. That's what he's done during Pilsudski's infirmity over the past year.

"Despite Beck's embrace of Germany in the wake of the non-aggression pact, he's a little nervous about this devaluation business," Papee added. "He doesn't want to have Berlin interfering here anymore than they already do. So I'm to approach the President of the Danzig Central Bank and sound him out about negotiating a loan from our Treasury, or a couple of our big banks in Warsaw; that would provide him financing while they get their house in order here.

"I expect Forster will resist the idea," Papee continued. "He doesn't want any constraints on his 'Nazification' agenda. But of course, that's one of the reasons we rather like the idea. I'll keep you posted."

Lester and Muller strolled back the Commissioner's residence, enjoying the springtime afternoon. "Well, the financial ball seems to be in play," said Lester.

CHAPTER 13

Spring, 1935

A day later, the opposition filed suit in the Danzig Supreme Court asking the court to declare the April election void because of pervasive fraud and intimidation.

The SDP's Ernst Brost delivered a copy of the opposition's complaint to Lester.

"We decided to try first to get the election invalidated here by our Supreme Court, rather than petitioning the Council," he said. "We've put together a very convincing case; the misbehavior in the rural districts was particularly brazen. They didn't even try to hide it and we've got a lot of very persuasive documentation we'll present to the Court."

He handed a copy of the document to Lester. "I think you'll find this interesting reading—when Mr. Muller can get time to translate it for you.

"Sorry it's so long, Muller," he said, looking at Muller and smiling.

"Our newspaper intends to report the suit tomorrow," he continued. "We're hoping it isn't shut down again and that none of the complainants gets arrested. Some of them have parliamentary immunity, but that hasn't stopped Forster in the past. I thought I'd give you this notice so you can try to intervene if we run into trouble.

"Also, we're beginning to plan for a new government," he continued. "If we can force a new election, the NSDAP will be defeated. People are very angry about the devaluation and how Gresier and Forster lied about it during the campaign. Prices are going up everywhere and they're hurting; the NSDAP has become deeply unpopular. In fact, several of us have begun talks about bringing Hermann Rauschning back as President of the Senate in a new coalition government that we'll try to form. He seems amenable to the idea."

"I was worried about his safety in the wake of the statement he issued on election eve," said Lester.

"So was he," Brost replied. "He sent his wife and five daughters to Gydina, which, of course is in Poland, and then joined them himself as soon as he sent out the statement. He received a number of threats; one of his household staff members was beaten up and his farm was vandalized. But he came back a month or so ago, and he hasn't encountered any trouble. He's careful, but determined not to be cowed."

"Please convey my personal best wishes," said Lester. "We became good friends before he was deposed."

He then grinned at Brost. "An opposition government with Rauschning in charge would certainly be a change. It would make my life a lot easier. But in the meantime, I hope that Greiser doesn't overreact to your suit."

An hour later, Franz Schiller paid Muller a surprise visit.

"Sorry to drop by so suddenly," Shiller said as they shook hands, "and I wish the subject was choral music. But it's urgent business.

"You'll recall how furious my Police Chief was about Greiser's attempt to sabotage the concert and embarrass the Department last year—and how much the Chief despises 'Little Arthur Motorboat'?"

Muller smiled. "I do indeed."

"The Chief's felt obliged to follow Greiser's orders for the most part; he's the President of the Senate and head of Danzig's government, after all— even if he's a jerk. So, the Department has had to do his dirty work: arresting politicians, seizing newspapers and the like—actions that we knew perfectly well were illegal and that no self-respecting police department should be asked to perform. But, as I've said, the Chief decided that he needed to play along. However, nearly always, our actions prompted someone to complain to the Commissioner. The Commissioner would then intervene and take Greiser to task; Greiser would huff and puff for a few days, but finally he'd back down and tell us to remove the padlocks from the newspapers and release the prisoners. He would then issue a statement justifying his actions to make himself look good. Meanwhile the Police Department would be left holding the bag and made to look like a bunch of chumps."

Muller nodded. "What's your point? Has something changed?"

"Muller, the Chief's tired of playing the game, and that's why I'm here," Schiller replied. "The opposition filed suit today in the Danzig Supreme Court to invalidate the April election."

"I know," said Muller. "Erich Brost just dropped off a copy of the complaint for me to translate."

"Good," Schiller replied. "But we're being told that Greiser's in the process of preparing orders directing the Chief to shut down the *Danziger Volkstimme*, the SDP daily, for reporting the event, and to arrest half a dozen of the complainants, including a couple of parliamentarians who are supposed to have immunity. Greiser's going to make his usual assertion that the report and the individuals 'pose a threat to disorder', which we all know is nonsense and is just his usual excuse for exercising censorship."

"Brost told us he was afraid Greiser was going to do just that," said Muller.

"Well, the Chief doesn't want to play along this time, Muller," said Schiller. "He's sick and tired of being the fall guy. And there's another reason too–an important one. The opposition's complaint is based in no small part, on testimony and affidavits of individual police officers who witnessed acts of fraud and intimidation, and often took action to try and stop them. As you know, Muller, a lot of policemen aren't NSDAP; a lot of us are Catholics and support opposition parties–and are still trying to do our jobs the right way. So when the complainants asked for help in getting up their court papers, individual officers agreed to step forward and tell their stories. The Chief sanctioned all this, of course. And you'll remember that when the Chief confronted Forster about the assassination team, he told Forster that we knew all about their dirty tricks in the election and that we'd use that documentation against him."

Muller nodded, smiling. "If I remember it right, that was just before he put Forster up against the wall."

Schiller grinned back. "Correct. So he's damned if he's going to go around arresting people and shutting down newspapers because they filed a lawsuit which cites police testimony. But rather than take on Greiser frontally–which of course means taking on Forster again too–the Chief had the idea of a more subtle approach."

"Such as?" Muller asked. He was trying to figure out where Schiller was going with this.

Schiller smiled. "Hear me out Muller. The Chief would like to suggest that the Commissioner send a message to Greiser–this afternoon–telling Greiser that he, the Commissioner, was advised by the Danzig Chief of Police that the Chief was expecting to receive orders from Greiser to shutter the *Danziger Volkstimme* and arrest a half dozen persons for reporting that the opposition had filed a lawsuit to invalidate the April election. He proposes that the message would then go on to say that the

Chief had advised the Commissioner of the Chief's conclusions that the reports were accurate, since such a lawsuit has in fact been filed, but that it posed no risk of disorder within the community.

"Then finally he suggests that the message state that the Commissioner has no intention to intervene in an issue of local law enforcement, but that he felt duty-bound to report this communication promptly to Greiser, so he, Greiser, could take it into account in determining his course of action. That's it; nothing more," Schiller concluded, looking at Muller and smiling, opening his palms wide.

"Go on," said Muller, beginning to get the idea.

"So," Schiller said, "let's do a little play-acting. Let's assume that I'm Greiser and I get a message like that from the Commissioner. I'm under pressure from Forster to shut down the paper and order the arrests. I know that I really don't have proper grounds to do that and, if I do issue the order, the Commissioner's going to be up in arms about me acting illegally–again–and will threaten to report me to the Council in Geneva. And this time, the Commissioner's going to be able to say–and maybe say publicly–that he warned me, before I issued the order, that the Chief of Police had told him that that the reports I'm trying to block are factually correct and pose no risk of provoking disorder. So ultimately I'm going to have to back down–again–and look weak–again.

"How to find a way out?" Schiller continued, warming to his role. "Aha! I can decide not to issue the order and tell Forster that I didn't do it because the Police Chief had tipped off the Commissioner ahead of time. He cut the ground out from under our pretext for the order. So we can't issue it. Forster will be angry–he's always angry–but he'll have to agree."

Muller smiled encouragingly at Schiller.

"One more thing, Muller, I'll also tell Forster that I'll lay down the law to the Chief–well, maybe a better choice of words. I'll say, I'll show the

Chief who's the boss and let him know this is never to happen again. Of course, I'm not going to do that. I'm scared to death of the Chief. And the fact is, the Chief *can* do this again–more or less anytime he wants to. So, I'll have to make a deal with the Chief. Forster won't have to know. That's how I'll play this." Schiller grinned broadly and directed a small bow in Muller's direction.

Muller clapped politely and chuckled aloud. "Very clever, your Chief."

"Two final thoughts," said Schiller. "The Chief thinks the NSDAP would lose a new election, so it's a good time for a nod to the opposition. Finally, I'm to tell you privately that the Chief won't abuse this arrangement. Barring something quite extraordinary, this is a one-time request."

Muller smiled and drummed his hands on the table as he considered the proposal. "All right, Schiller; wait here." Muller went into Lester's office. About five minutes later, he returned, accompanied by Lester.

"Commissioner, you will remember Detective Franz Schiller. He's come with a message for you from the Danzig Chief of Police." Schiller rose from his chair and proceeded to deliver his message. Lester looked at him with a straight face but with a twinkle in his eyes.

"Thank you Detective Schiller and thank the Chief for this information. As Commissioner I have no authority to intervene in an issue of local law enforcement, but I feel duty-bound to report this communication promptly to President Greiser, so he can take it into account in determining his course of action in the matter." They shook hands solemnly.

As Schiller took his leave, Lester guided him to the stairway, winked at him with a smile and said, "Always a pleasure to see you Detective Schiller."

Returning to his office, Lester laughed heartily and slapped Muller on the back. "This is more fun than I've had in weeks. Let's get that message off to Greiser."

The *Danziger Volkstimme* printed overnight and was distributed the next morning, leading with a headline about the lawsuit; there were no arrests. Later that day, Lester received a response from Greiser acknowledging receipt of his message.

***

There was not much time to savor the small victory. The NSDAP daily, the *Verposten*, announced a sudden and unexpected visit to the City by the powerful President of the Reichsbank, Hjalmar Schacht, two days later. It would be Schacht's first visit to the City and it provoked a flurry of activity by the government and the Party.

Muller called the visit to Lester's attention. "This may be the answer to your question the other day to Truczinski about who would be calling the shots in this new financial environment, Commissioner."

"We'll see," Lester replied. "I wonder if I'll be invited to the meeting?

"Somehow I doubt it." He smiled.

A large NSDAP rally was organized to greet Schacht upon arrival at the Central Station. The Square in front of the station was crowded with Black SS and Brown SA uniforms and a throng of Party members wearing armbands and other Party decorations. Nazi bunting and banners hung from every rooftop and balcony–except the Continental Hotel, which displayed a Polish flag as usual.

Muller persuaded Papee to get him access to a room in the Continental facing the station so he could get a good view. He wanted to see Schacht, who was a famous and rather mysterious figure in banking circles. Muller's father had had dealings with him a decade or so earlier when Schacht was at Danatbank in Dresden; something to do with financing I. G. Farben, the chemical manufacturer. He had always described Schacht as among the least likeable men he had encountered in his long banking career and he'd shaken his head upon learning of Hitler's appointment of Schacht to head the Reichsbank.

Schacht's train pulled into the Central Station before noon and, as he was escorted to the podium that had been erected for the occasion, the crowd, on cue, broke into the Horst Wessel Song followed by chants of 'Seig Heil' and stiff Nazi salutes.

Schacht looked the part of the native Prussian, with his perpetually erect posture, pince nez glasses (he was amazingly short-sighted, according to Muller's father), short, stiff hair and formal morning-coated attire. He also wore a pugnacious scowl, which Muller's father said never left his face; he always seemed to be angry at someone or something.

Muller couldn't catch much of what Schacht said in his short speech; the wind blew his words toward the Baltic. But according to press reports (for once, Muller noted, all the papers seemed to agree), he had preached the virtues of austerity and the crowd, Muller could see, lost enthusiasm for the speech and disappeared rapidly after he concluded. After a formal luncheon and brief meetings with leaders of the Senate and the *Volkstag* (and, Muller assumed, with Forster) Schacht boarded the train without fanfare to return to Berlin.

The next day, Otto von Radowitz proposed to Muller that they dine that evening at the German Consulate. After extracting a promise that he would not be served Danzig smoked eel, Muller accepted.

"Smoked eel?" inquired von Radowitz as he poured them chilled Marchandel gin. The weather was fine and von Radowitz had organized cocktails and dinner in the garden. Muller told him Papee's tale of the horse head and the eels.

Von Radowitz laughed. "I've never heard about that," he said. It sounds like a dish to try sometime."

Muller grimaced.

"Tell me about the visit from Mr. Schacht," he said, changing the subject. "I assume you were at the luncheon given for him."

"Yes," von Radowitz said, "and fortunately seated nowhere near him. He is a decidedly difficult man; he scowled the entire time and made everyone uncomfortable. His message was also downbeat. He said Danzig is living beyond its means and must reduce expenditures. He dismissed Forster's beloved public works program as folly and said work should stop immediately. He also criticized the failure of the government to increase revenues, clearly signaling encouragement for better commercial relations with Poland. He said that the Reichsbank would 'continue to support Danzig'–an obvious reference to the secret subsidies that everyone knows about–but said the level of support would have to decline significantly."

"It sounds like a downbeat affair," said Muller sympathetically.

"But later in the lunch, he began to hold forth enthusiastically about next summer's Olympics in Berlin," von Radowitz continued. "He almost lost his scowl describing the scale of the construction projects underway at the Reichsportsfield: a massive stadium large enough to accommodate 110,000 people, a hockey stadium, an equestrian facility, a vast swimming complex, a gymnasium and so on, everything clad in natural German stone, plus separate projects for sailing at Kiel and rowing in Grunau. He made clear that all this work was costing tens of millions of Reichsmarks. He also made it pretty clear that these expenditures took priority over subsidies for Danzig."

"So what's your impression?" Muller asked. "Where do things go from here?"

"Schacht referred several times to the Fuehrer's decision to rearm and he made it clear that, despite improvements in Germany's finances, there was not enough money to pursue full economic growth and rearmament at the same time.

"For me," von Radowitz continued, "the clear implication was that Hitler's choice of building an army and an air force–not to mention the Olympics–is leading to an economic slowdown. Schacht didn't actually use the word 'hardship'–and maybe I read too much into his remarks–but I gained the impression that he believes the German economy is in for a rough patch–rougher than people are expecting. That was a little surprising, frankly," von Radowitz added, "because all the news coming out of the press organs in the Reich is very positive. If we hit a serious economic downturn, it will be a very unpleasant surprise for a lot of Germans." He shook his head.

After pausing a moment, he continued. "What's clear is that the Danzig subsidies are on the chopping block and Schacht's the guy wielding the knife. My impression is that he'll keep subsidies going enough to keep Danzig afloat. Certainly that's a Wilhelmstrasse priority–and we assume a priority for Hitler too. So Schacht isn't going to shut us down–though he'd probably like to; but he'll keep us on short rations."

"Did you know that the Bank of Danzig has formally requested the Commissioner to seek a loan from the Bank of International Settlements?" interjected Muller.

Von Radowitz nodded. "We heard about that. I have to assume that Schacht would welcome it, although the Wilhelmstrasse is cool to the idea and certainly Greiser and Forster don't like it. Do you think the Commissioner can get the money?"

"I've no idea." Muller replied. "The Commissioner's only just sent the request to Geneva and we haven't gotten any reaction."

He was not about to share with von Radowitz his private access to the head of the Bank of International Settlements.

"We've also received a message from Poland offering a loan," von Radowitz said. "That makes everyone nervous; we don't want to get tied down by loan covenants to the Poles, so I think that's probably off the table."

They finished the gin and took their seats at the table where the staff had laid out plates of poached salmon with potato salad and two bottles of chilled Riesling. The sky was still bright as they approached the summer solstice.

"It's been a tough couple of months for our friend Greiser," von Radowitz said, pouring their wine. "He's tired of being pushed around by Forster, so he's enlisted my help in trying to get Forster removed or re-assigned somewhere. As you know, I think Forster's a liability too, so I've gone to von Neurath to see what he can do."

"I've heard this record before," said Muller, thinking of the meeting in the shed at Oliwa in November. "What's changed?"

"The botched election in April and the devaluation are two clear black marks against Forster," von Radowitz replied. "Both were failures and everyone knows that Forster was responsible. So that's one big change. The other change is that Greiser has come to fear your Commissioner almost as much as he does Forster."

Muller cocked his head and waited for von Radowitz to continue.

"Greiser sees the Commissioner holding the threat of action by the Council in Geneva like a Sword of Damocles over his head. He knows that he doesn't have any real legal justification for most of the punitive actions he's being ordered to impose by Forster. He's come to dread meetings and communications with the Commissioner because Lester is always so calm, so diplomatic, and so firm—and generally right. Greiser still buys into all the NSDAP sloganeering and so on. But he's been the President of the Senate for six months now, and—weak as he is—he's come to realize that, as the head of government, he has real responsibilities to discharge.

"He's also smart enough to understand that the popularity of NSDAP has plunged and, if a new election were held today, they'd almost certainly lose their majority. That would be a disaster–both for the Party here and for the Nazis in Germany–and he realizes that he'd be the fall guy."

Gresier as a responsible government leader, Muller thought. That would certainly be a new role.

"He feels like he's walking a tightrope," von Radowitz continued, refilling their glasses. "He has to toe the NSDAP propaganda line, but he also has to respond to Lester's critiques and his unrelenting firmness. Greiser knows that if he goes too far, Lester has the power, potentially, to bring down the house by getting the Council to act. And he's never sure where the line will be drawn and the Council *will* act.

"Think about it, Muller," he said. "Germany quit the League, so there's no one on the Council that Greiser can count on for protection. He's the only person there to defend himself. He's seated at the table beside Anthony Eden, who is intimidating and a powerful potential adversary, and seated at the table next to Eden is the Commissioner, another formidable presence. Let me tell you, it's a very lonely and uncomfortable position for a man like Greiser with little education and experience. It makes him very uneasy."

"So now he'd like to get rid of Forster?" said Muller. "I find that a little far-fetched, I'm afraid. Besides, we all know that Forster's position as Gauleiter is controlled by the Nazi Party. That means someone like Goering–or even Hitler himself–would need to order his removal.

"Is that a realistic expectation?"

Von Radowitz shrugged. "We hope so. Today's rumor is that Schacht is assigning someone from the Reichsbank to oversee Danzig's finances– unofficially, of course; the subsidies are secret after all."

He smiled. "But if we can't get rid of Forster, maybe this guy can at least force him to quiet down for a while."

Muller thought that, in a contest between the Party leader and a Reichsbank functionary, he wouldn't put his money on the banker. But he kept his own counsel and accepted another glass of Riesling.

***

In late June, Secretary General Avenol sent a response to Lester's inquiry about seeking a loan to the Senate from the Bank of International Settlements. It was brief and to the point. "Kindly be advised that Mr. Eden and I disapprove the proposal. No work should be undertaken on it."

"I guess that settles that," said Lester, showing Avenol's message to Muller. "I think it's a missed opportunity to get more leverage here. Or maybe Eden wants Berlin to have to keep subsidizing Danzig. But I think we have to drop the idea of sending you to Basle; too bad."

"Incidentally, Elsie's persuaded me to take the family on a short vacation cruise to Sweden in two weeks. Things here seem to be under control; our standoff seems to be holding. But it's been a very busy couple of months; you ought to think about taking some time off yourself."

"Actually, Commissioner, I have a friend who's planning to visit me here for a week in early August; we decided a vacation in Danzig would be fun, as she's never traveled here before."

"Splendid," said Lester. "Elsie and I will look forward to meeting this mysterious friend whose identity you've so carefully guarded.

CHAPTER 14

Summer 1935

Eirene swung down the steps of her compartment and waved gaily to Muller who was waiting just beyond the platform where immigration officials were stamping passports. He could see her handing coins to a porter who collected her trunk, placing it on his cart and moving directly to the passport table, ahead of travelers without porters. She was wearing a light blue sleeveless blouse and flowered skirt, and her dark brown hair was topped with a large, floppy, straw-colored hat that looked summery.

She stuffed her passport back into her handbag and ran toward him, smiling broadly. Muller held out his arms to embrace her, but she stopped, stood up straight and said, "Ready?"

Muller nodded.

"Je-ru-sa-lem," they sang together, and fell into one another's arms laughing.

He had booked a large, airy room on the 7th floor of the Eden Hotel. "Sorry, sir, the staff is assigned to the 8th floor," he was told. Rather unusual, he'd thought, but the clerk assured him the 7th floor room was among the hotel's finest, and indeed, it did have a nice view overlooking the Central Square and the railroad station's clock tower, facing in the direction of Hindenburg Allee with its stately chestnut trees and the tram line running alongside.

After tipping the bellman, they locked the door and began tearing at one another's clothing, rolling onto the bed. Making love excitedly, they suddenly climaxed, still tangled in the bedclothes, then collapsed in laughter, breathing hard and squeezing each other in pleasure.

"Welcome to Danzig," Muller said in a formal tone of voice.

"My pleasure sir," Eirene replied, "and it was–is–a pleasure," she added giggling.

"I've missed you Eirene," said Muller adjusting his arm over her breasts.

She turned and kissed him saying, "I'm already glad I made the trip."

Then she stretched. "Now I'm going to draw a bath; I have almost three days of travel grime all over me. It's a very long trip from London to get here. So you get dressed and go to work. Come back for me at around 1:00 for lunch," and she strode, without a stitch of clothing, into the large bathroom, firmly closing the door, where Muller could hear her starting the tub as he dressed.

Returning as instructed, Muller suggested they take lunch in the garden restaurant at the Eden and they were promptly seated at a table shaded from the sun by a large red umbrella. He ordered two glasses of chilled Marchandel gin. "It's a local drink that's widely served here," he said. "I've become very fond of it. Cheers!" They clinked glasses and took a swallow.

"Oh, I think I'm going to like it here," offered Eirene, her tongue licking the gin on her upper lip. "This is good."

"We have only one official obligation during your entire visit," said Muller, "but it's this evening. The Commissioner is hosting a reception for a dozen senior officers from the German Battleship *Admiral Scheer* which is paying an official visit to Danzig. The diplomatic community will be there along with government officials. I hope you'll come; it's only a two-hour event, then around 8, when it's over, the Commissioner and his wife Elsie have invited us to dine with them. They're very anxious to meet my 'enchantress', as the Commissioner has begun referring to you."

"Paul," she said sternly, "tonight? At 6 PM? Good Lord."

She rose and stalked toward the hotel lobby. "No, no, you sit still," she said, motioning him to remain in his seat. Fifteen minutes later, she returned. "Fortunately, I was able to get an appointment with the hairdresser at 3, I'll have a manicure and pedicure at 4, my dress will be pressed by 5, so, yes; I'll accompany you."

She shook her head. "Do you really have a sister? Don't you know anything about women?"

"Mathilda is a lot younger," he said sheepishly. "Sorry."

"Another of those gins and you'll be forgiven," she said, enjoying his discomfiture.

"I'll even give you the gift I brought along for you." Eirene reached into the large handbag she had placed on an adjoining chair and extracted a narrow, rectangular package with bright blue ribbon tied around patriotic British wrapping paper. She handed it to him.

Inside was a framed copy of the Peace Ballot. But someone–he assumed Eirene–had filled in the results.

A NATIONAL DECLARATION ON THE LEAGUE OF NATIONS AND ARMAMENTS

Should Great Britain remain a Member of the League of Nations?

Yes: 11,166,818 No: 357,930 Doubtful: 10,528 No Answer: 104,790

Are you in favour of all-round reduction of armaments by international agreement?

Yes: 10,542,738 No: 868,431 Doubtful: 12,138 No Answer 216,759

Are you in favour of an all-round abolition of national military and naval aircraft by international agreement?

Yes: 9,900,274 No: 1,699,898: Doubtful: 15,175 No Answer: 322,740

Should the manufacture and sale of armaments for private profit be prohibited by international agreement?

Yes: 10,489,175 No: 780,350 Doubtful: 15,157 No Answer: 355,414

Do you consider that, if a nation insists on attacking another, the other nations should combine to compel it to stop—

by economic and non-military measures:

Yes: 10,096 No: 639,145 Doubtful 27,639 No Answer: 862,707

if necessary, military measures:

Yes: 6,833,803 No: 2,366,184 Doubtful: 41,058 No Answer: 2,381,485

Eirene was excited. "Can you believe, we received a total of over *11.6 million* ballots! Remember I told you we were aiming for 5 million voters? We more than doubled our goal! And look at the results: An overwhelming affirmative vote for each of the five questions."

"Well," said Muller a little hesitantly, then recovering, continued appreciatively, "that's really quite remarkable, Eirene."

Eirene was bursting with enthusiasm. "We announced the final results at the Royal Albert Hall at the end of June. Uncle Robert presided. The press coverage was just huge and overwhelmingly favorable." She pulled a wrinkled clipping out of her purse.

"Listen to this from the *Spectator*:

"The verdict is decisive and impressive. The immense proportion of the votes in favour of the League, armament reduction, and collective sanctions is what anyone with his finger on the pulse of the country might have expected; but few would claim to have foreseen that so many millions of persons would have responded to the appeal, and in doing so revealed the intensity of national feeling which these international issues evoke. Henceforward there can be no reasonable doubt about the conviction of the mass of the people of this country; no Government will dare to flout public opinion by slighting the League, or by refraining from efforts to secure agreed disarmament and collective sanctions against peace-breakers."

"It really is all that we had hoped for—even more in fact, given the size of the vote. So, my dear Paul, as you labor in the vineyards of the League, you can feel confident of the strong support of the British people."

Muller held the framed display, continuing to read it over. Eleven and a half million votes was impressive just as a feat of organization, he thought. But how persuasive would the results be outside Britain?

As if reading his mind, Eirene went on excitedly, "Anthony tells me he's already using the results to pressure the Italians over their threat to invade Abyssinia."

"That's really quite splendid, Eirene," Muller responded, wondering to himself if Eden would use the ballot results to bolster the League's position in Danzig.

Somehow, he didn't feel much confidence on that score.

Their meals arrived and the conversation turned to other things, a bit to Muller's relief.

After lunch, Eirene made her way to the hairdresser, instructing Muller to pick her up in time for the party.

***

It was a perfect midsummer evening for cocktails in the Commissioner's garden. Two well-stocked bars had been set up at either end, with white linen tablecloths and white-jacketed bartenders. Several tall, round tables were spaced casually on the green lawn with ashtrays and plates of olives and there were small seating arrangements along the edge, close to the flower beds.

"How splendid it all looks," said Eirene as Muller introduced her to Sean and Elsie Lester.

"And how lucky we are," Elsie replied, "Danzig weather is notoriously unreliable, so let's enjoy it while we can." She took Eirene by the elbow and led her into the garden, leaving Lester and Muller behind.

"I would say that *she* looks splendid," Lester said to Muller with a wink.

She really did, thought Muller, admiring the fitted white dress with black piping at the neck and the flat-brimmed hat perched just to one side on her dark hair. Very stylish. And the dress was short enough to show off her very feminine legs.

The German naval officers arrived punctually, clad in dress whites with gold braid and colorful medals, each with a red and white ribbon at his neck bearing a black swastika. The commanding officer led the men into the garden where Lester stood. "Commissioner," he said standing at attention and saluting, "Admiral Otto von Plotz at your service. Allow me to introduce my officers." As he did so, each one stepped forward, stood at attention and saluted.

"Gentlemen, welcome to my residence," Lester said and introduced Elsie, then led the Admiral to the nearest bar. He introduced Muller as his translator.

"No need, Mr. Muller," the Admiral said in fluent English, "I've competed in regattas with the British since I was a boy. I'm a regular at Cowes," he said smiling, "and I have some silver to show for it."

Muller took the opportunity to return to Eirene, who was employing serviceable French with several of the diplomatic wives. The garden filled up rapidly. Greiser arrived with several other members of the Senate and, carrying a large glass of beer, he genially greeted other guests. Von Radowitz and Papee were there with their wives and Muller made it a point to introduce Eirene to them. The naval officers began to relax and seemed to mingle easily. Lester rapped his glass, asking for quiet and delivered brief welcoming remarks that were reciprocated by the Admiral.

As Muller completed his translation and the cocktail chatter resumed, he noticed a commotion on the other side of the garden. Something was clearly going on. Muller turned to look and saw Greiser, loudly beckoning his entourage.

Suddenly, Greiser banged his beer glass down with a loud crash on one of the tables. Surrounded by his Senate supporters, he pointed to where Hermann Rauschning, who had just arrived, was standing in friendly conversation with the Lesters.

Greiser's party all cast baleful stares at Rauschning, then Greiser gathered them, ordered them to turn their backs on the garden, led them across the lawn to the doorway without even a glance in Lester's direction and proceeded to stalk out. Muller could see several members of the *Volkstag* follow suit.

The remaining guests exchanged inquiring looks, but most simply shrugged, continuing to chat with one another and with the naval officers, who seemed unaware that anything had transpired.

Rauschning smiled ruefully at Lester. "What's that saying about the skunk at the garden party?" he said as he prepared to depart soon after.

"*You're* not the skunk," said Elsie, offering farewell kisses on both cheeks.

The Admiral and his staff took their leave, thanking Lester profusely and suddenly it was just the four of them. They refilled their drinks and found seats beside a row of bright yellow lilies as the staff began to clean up.

"What an awful boor," Elsie exploded. "With manners like that, he must have been brought up in a pig sty. Sean, I'm so sick and tired of their nasty rudeness; I can't wait to get on that boat to Stockholm tomorrow and get away for a while."

Lester mused, "It doesn't look like they've forgotten about Rauschning's election eve statement does it?" Then he smiled. "Enough of that though. Eirene, we're looking forward to getting acquainted over dinner. Muller's being a very tight-lipped Swiss about the two of you."

***

The warm summer weather continued. Muller bought tickets for *The Flying Dutchman* at Zoppot's Opera-in-the-Woods Festival and they decided to make a day of it, boarding the # 9 tram after breakfast with a host of other holiday-seekers. They strolled through Oliwa, making certain to visit the Whispering Grotto, and lunched at the Starfish, where they shared a slice of five layer buttercream cake for dessert. The promenade led them to the beach at Brosen and the giant breakwater jutting out into the Baltic. They decided on the North Beach and rented separate bathing cabins to change into their suits. A beach attendant led them to two adjoining wicker beach chairs, and arranged towels for them.

"They're called strandkorbs," Muller explained as they settled into the chairs. "Everyone uses them here. I'd never seen one before either, but they offer some protection from the wind off the ocean, which is usually chilly, so you can turn them as you like to face the sea or the sun–and they keep you off the sand."

They swam, then lay back in their strandkorbs and napped in the sun. After another swim, they showered off the ocean salt and applied Nivea Cream to Muller's sunburned legs before getting dressed and walking to the casino for a few futile passes at Roulette.

Muller chose the Parrot for dinner before the opera, then they filed into the vast amphitheater and slapped at the pesky mosquitos as Wagner's music soared into the summer night. Muller found himself transported. Wagner was always a little bombastic, some said even vulgar; but he had such a keen ear for melody and intertwined his leitmotifs so cleverly that Muller always found his operas hugely entertaining.

He was also feeling very good about having Eirene seated next to him, their bodies warmly pressed together. And, for once, it was a night when politics and intrigue could be put aside. He realized that it had been a very long time since he'd felt so relaxed.

The next morning they awoke to a wind-blown rain beating against the windows of the 7th floor bedroom at the Eden. They agreed it would be a good day for a visit to the Maritime Museum, so, after a leisurely breakfast, they boarded the #5 tram, switching to the #4 tram at Holtz Market which would take them toward the Welchsel. The museum was housed in a graceful mansion with an elegantly decorated stone facade reaching up toward Gothic gables in colorful, choreographed steps. The interior was decorated with tall wooden panels and a spiral staircase led up to the right.

Strolling through the museum, they were treated to displays of colorful engravings illustrating sieges and sea battles, trophies of long-forgotten wars and paintings of wealthy merchants and fierce-looking sea captains. The clerk who gave them their tickets said they should not miss the 'Niobe' exhibit, but that they needed to keep their fingers crossed in her presence.

Muller translated the very short written description they were handed. Niobe, it seemed, was a figurehead from a large Florentine Galley that had been captured by pirates in 1473 who proceeded to kill the crew and bring the vessel to Danzig. The figurehead had been removed from the ship and re-sold many times, but, according to legend, disaster always followed in her wake. The pirates who captured her were soon killed and the first ship to which she was affixed caught fire, burning dozens of other ships in the harbor—but not Niobe. Her comely features seduced other new buyers who inevitably encountered mutinies, lightning strikes, failed expeditions and other calamities. At the beginning of the 19th century, about the time

Danzig became part of Prussia and Poland disappeared, she was deposited in the basement of the Prison Tower, 'in a torture chamber', where she had been forgotten, until suddenly making a reappearance at the museum's opening in 1922. But calamities resumed, including the death of the museum director that had fetched her out of the Prison Tower; his successor had died too.

Undeterred, Eirene and Muller entered the exhibit space.

"It really is a bit spooky," said Eirene, taking Muller's arm. Muller had to agree as they approached the figurehead.

Niobe was a voluptuous green woman, carved from wood, her arms fetchingly crossed over her breasts and her amber eyes gazing emptily into the distance. She was large too and in the gloom of the rainy day, she looked almost as menacing as her legend. They regarded this now rather forbidding creature and the exhibit guard whispered that they should be careful, as a priest had suffered a heart attack right here not a year ago and recently the bodies of four students had been discovered, slashed with daggers and swords from the nearby exhibits.

Eirene smiled as Muller translated under his breath, rolling his eyes.

Muller turned back to the guard. "So how do visitors to Danzig, like the two of us, break this unlucky spell and avoid misfortune?

"Well, sir," said the guard, his lugubrious features suddenly wreathed in smiles, "the best way is to visit the Fritzpub in the next block along Brotbackengasse and tell them Heinie from Niobe sent you; they'll give you a shot of something that will do the trick."

They found the restaurant and ducked in the doorway out of the rain. Muller ordered a bottle of Marchandel gin and two plates of sauerkraut and sausage. He told the waiter they'd come at the recommendation of Heine in the Niobe room. The waiter winked and brought two small shots of Gold

Wasser, which they drank quickly and, after drawing deep breaths, agreed that no curse could survive it.

After a moment, Muller turned serious. He leaned forward, his arms crossed on the table between them. "I've been reluctant to bring up the subject of Eden," he said. "I know you're friendly with him, Eirene, and I don't want to say anything critical that might be annoying. But I'm bothered and I thought you might be able to help me."

"Certainly," she said. "And I'll be discreet—especially after all that secret agent business with Stevenson last winter."

"I do owe you an explanation about that; it partially involves Eden," Muller said. "He's been very supportive of the Commissioner's performance here, making sure that the Council formally takes note that he doing an effective job. And that's no trivial thing; if our adversaries thought for a moment that the Commissioner was on shaky ground with the Council, he'd be unable to function. By the way, I think Eden's right, and that the Commissioner *is* effective. The problem is Eden's willingness to push off any Council decision until the next meeting and then pushing it off yet again. He seems unable to take action or bring anything to closure and it's hampering the Commissioner's effectiveness."

Eirene sipped her gin and Muller lit their cigarettes as they awaited lunch.

"Anthony's carrying a heavy load," she said. "He's in the Cabinet now as Minister for the League of Nations. Hoare is Foreign Secretary, but members are looking mainly to Anthony on foreign policy matters.

"Look what happened this spring," she said. "The Government issued a White Paper announcing rearmament. Eden went to Berlin, and Hitler turned the tables entirely by renouncing Article V of the Treaty and unveiling a program to build an army and an air force. Our embassy in Berlin also learned they were starting to build U-Boats again. Much handwringing at Whitehall and in the House. But Anthony took up the challenge. 'All right,' he said, 'if they've renounced Article V then let's replace it with something else'. He then proceeded to negotiate the Anglo-German Naval Agreement in June which stipulated a tonnage ratio in our favor."

Eirene paused and looked at him mockingly. "See? Your favorite League of Nations Union representative knows her stuff. I've actually done some work on this issue. In fact the actual tonnage ratio is 35:100. Their new limit is a lot higher than we'd like it to be; but at least there's a limit. And the agreement sets a precedent for future limits on military aircraft. That's a key goal, as everyone is convinced that aerial bombing would be a catastrophe."

Muller had the thought that Eirene's pet theory of eliminating national air forces and establishing a League air force was now hopelessly out of reach, but he held his tongue as Eirene continued.

"So my reading, Paul, for what it's worth, is that Anthony's still embarked on his quest for an overall settlement with Germany. I don't know how Danzig or the League fit into all this, but I'm persuaded Anthony believes he can do a deal that will enable Germany to discard the excesses of the Treaty, accepting limits that we all can agree on, and finally take her rightful seat at the grownup's table in Europe."

The waiter brought steaming plates heaped with sauerkraut and different kinds of sausages; they dug in hungrily.

"Eirene," said Muller between mouthfuls, "that's all very well. But it's also all very unilateral. Nothing that you've described has involved the League at all. As we hear it, Eden didn't even bother to tell the French about the Anglo-German naval agreement until after it was signed, and the League's Disarmament Conference hasn't met since last year. So, for all the publicity and support for the League generated by your ballot–which, as

I've told you, is genuinely impressive–Eden seems to going his own way, without involving the League or even his most important ally."

"Paul, that's not fair," she responded with a shake of her head pointing her fork at him. "Anthony has been deeply involved in the League's negotiations to solve the Italian–Abyssinian dispute. He's been working with French Prime Minister Laval and there have been numerous League Council meetings devoted to the issue. We imposed an arms embargo on the Italians in June–I warrant that was unilateral, but it was done in full coordination with the French and the League.

"I think you're mistaken," she went on. "Anthony's using all the resources at hand. Putting Italy in the League's dock is a big step; they were one of the victors at the table in Versailles. And it seems to be working; Italy seems to have responded to the diplomatic pressure that Anthony's leading."

Muller nodded. "I do have to concede that Eden and the British delegation seemed very distracted by the Italian–Abyssinian issue during the June Council meetings. Incidentally, I always get confused about why people keep referring to Ethiopia as Abyssinia. Any idea why they do that?"

He smiled quizzically, then continued, "And you make a fair point that the League is actively trying to head off Italian aggression there."

They decided the meal needed beer, so Muller signaled for two large steins. When they arrived, he continued. "But I want to bring us back to Danzig. It's not as big as taking on Italy, but it's important and it's an issue I think Eden can use as leverage. But he just keeps deferring and delaying."

What the Hell, Muller finally decided; if I can't be candid with her, this relationship can't go any further. His frustration with Eden's inaction had been gnawing at him. Lester was sympathetic to the constraints Eden was operating under; he had rebuffed Muller's criticisms. But Muller was convinced that Eden's foot-dragging was a serious error. So he decided to plunge on.

"Eirene, he just won't *do* anything! The formula is always the same. Petitions are placed on the League Council agenda that Eden controls, since he's the League's Rapporteur. The petitions uniformly document conduct by the Danzig Senate that flouts the constitution which the League has the mandate to uphold. There's never any doubt that the conduct they're complaining about is clearly illegal. Greiser comes to the table–"

"Who's Greiser?"

"Sorry, he's the guy who stormed out of the Commissioner's reception. He's President of the Danzig Senate–head of the government, and, by the way, a real troublemaker.

"Anyway," Muller went on, "Gresier's allowed at the table in the League Council meetings. He always stands up and strikes a pose of innocent misunderstanding, pledges always to operate in harmony with the 'letter and spirit' of the Constitution and promises to work out solutions with the petitioners through negotiations back in Danzig. Eden's response is to simply accept Greiser's assurances and the Council then proceeds to adopt a meaningless report, couched in impenetrable diplomatic prose, putting the issues off till the next meeting. But Greiser never does anything back in Danzig to deal with the petitions. He stonewalls, or worse; and Eden pays no attention."

"Surely you're overstating, things, Paul."

"I'm not," Muller responded, maybe a little too sharply, he thought. "Eden did precisely what I've just described in the June Council meetings, even though Greiser had clearly failed to keep the promises he'd made back in January and had engaged in new acts of high-handed conduct in the interim–including, by the way, conducting an election thoroughly tainted by fraud, which Eden never even referred to. That omission was particularly vexing, I have to tell you."

"Paul, don't you think—"

"It's very frustrating. I didn't intend to vent like this to you. The Commissioner defends Eden too and maybe I'm too hard on him. I know you admire him and there's no doubt he's carrying heavy responsibilities. Still, I think he's badly mishandling the Danzig issue."

Muller pushed aside his unfinished plate, still heaped with uneaten sausage. "No one could eat all that," he said, smiling and wanting to change the tense tone he'd used. There was no point in getting angry. But it was very frustrating!

Muller took a deep breath and a swallow of beer before continuing.

"And that brings us back to Stevenson, who, as you know is Eden's principal assistant on League issues. I have issues with him now, too, for all the reasons I've just stated, since he's the one who efficiently implements what I believe is Eden's feckless approach. But I do owe you an explanation about the wine glass missive I sent you to give him."

Muller brandished his lighter for their cigarettes.

Eirene pulled out a pack of Regatta's and selected one. "I like this local brand better than your Gitanes," she said, accepting his light.

"I needed to send him some confidential information between meetings," Muller continued. "We have to keep our distance officially from Whitehall, so I couldn't send it to him directly. Also, I was worried that my message might be intercepted. We can't trust the mail here; the Commissioner and I assume it's being opened—or at least some of it is. You were the safest courier I could think of. So, voila, wine glasses to Eirene, with a note to Stevenson, sent via ocean-going freight that doesn't dock in Germany. So thanks," He smiled broadly at her.

"Was it really secret stuff?" asked Eirene mischievously.

"Not as secret as the ballot-stuffing that's been going on," he replied with a grin.

She punched his arm, blushing. "I should hope not."

They returned to the Hotel in a driving rain that seemed even colder. The reception clerk handed Eirene an envelope. Tearing it open, she let out a little squeal of delight.

"Paul, Elizabeth Wiskemann is in town. We must see her. She's a famous and terribly energetic journalist and a good friend. May I invite her for dinner?"

Understanding that his consent was a formality, Muller nodded, bowing briefly in Eirene's direction.

***

That evening, they scurried through the rain across the Square to the Nue Deutsche Hotel where Wiskemann was staying and where they'd agreed to meet for dinner. She looked, Muller decided, like a journalist; slightly disheveled and not entirely pulled together, but fairly pulsating with energy. Wiskemann had traveled widely in Europe for most of the past five years and she regaled them with tales from Poland, Yugoslavia, Czechoslovakia ("Benes and Masaryk are my two favorite national leaders") and from Germany, where she had lived during the late Weimar years and witnessed Hitler's seizure of power.

"It was frightening how quickly and how savagely it all happened," Wiskemann said. "Within sixty days of becoming Chancellor he abolished the Reichstag, crushed the trade unions, imprisoned his political opponents and replaced the police with his storm troopers. Seemingly overnight, he became a dictator and Germany became a police state. I still visit there because I'm a journalist and I need to go. But it's uncomfortable."

She closely questioned Muller about the politics of Danzig and relations with the League. He was surprised at the range of her knowledge and inquired how she was so well-informed.

"Two reasons, Paul," she replied. "I'm persuaded that Danzig is a vital piece on the European chessboard. It's a microcosm of the continent; a contest of wills where the Nazis and the League are facing off against one another. What happens here is likely to determine what happens in the larger European contest. So, first reason: it's important and I keep abreast of it.

"The other reason is that the situation in Danzig is widely reported in the British press and it's regularly the subject of parliamentary debate. If you know where to look for it, there is a lot of information available and I've made it my business to stay informed.

"This is my first visit; I'm frankly a little ashamed at not getting here sooner, but I've decided to get back here regularly to stay in even closer touch."

"Not too close," purred Eirene. Wiskemann gave her a dirty look.

By the end of the evening, Muller had extracted a promise that nothing he said that evening was for publication, but Wiskemann, in turn, had extracted from him promises to arrange on-the-record interviews with Lester, upon his return from holiday in a few days, and with Rauschning.

CHAPTER 15

Summer and Fall, 1935

The next day was Sunday; the weather had cleared and the sun shone brightly in a brisk blue Baltic sky. After a late brunch, Muller said he wanted them to stroll over toward the Sportshalle.

"There's an NSDAP rally scheduled this afternoon that I want you to see," Muller said. I think you'll find it an educational experience."

Muller didn't say much as they walked along Elizabethwall, past the Commissioner's residence and through the central square in front of the railway station. He watched out of the corner of his eye to see Eirene's reaction as trams packed with uniformed party members glided toward Hindenburg Allee and brown-shirted, middle-aged storm troopers with wives wearing Nazi armbands and children dressed in Nazi regalia began filing alongside them as they approached the parade ground.

The grandstand was bedecked with Nazi bunting and flags as it had been when Muller attended a similar rally over a year earlier. Bands played the same marches and uniformed SS troops with shiny helmets directed traffic toward the grandstand and the rows of seats in front that were rapidly filling with eager spectators.

Muller took Eirene's hand and slowed as they neared the rally. It wouldn't be wise to get too close, he thought. As they veered off to the side, Eirene inadvertently bumped into a plump woman in full Hitler Matron attire, knocking her uniform hat to the ground.

"Oh, I'm so sorry," Eirene said, picking up the hat, knocking off the dust and handing it back.

"What did she say?" the woman asked her companions, who all stopped and stared at Eirene, suddenly aware that she and Muller were the only ones not wearing Nazi identification.

"Some kind of foreigners," muttered one of the men.

"What the Hell are they doing here?" asked another.

Muller sensed an angry mood brewing.

Breaking into a big smile, he clapped one of the storm troopers on shoulder. "What a great day for a party rally. And how fine you all look in your uniforms! I told my English cousin that she should come down to the parade ground this afternoon and see how real Germans gather to salute their leaders." He smiled at the group. "She doesn't speak German, but she wanted to see a real Nazi parade. So we're happy to be a part of your rally."

The woman Eirene had bumped now put her hat back on and smiled, patting Eirene on the back. "Well, good for her," she said. "We're going to put on a good show this afternoon. She can tell all her friends back in England how we German Nazis will lead the way in restoring our nation."

She pumped Eirene's hand. "Enjoy the show, my dear."

As the party members continued striding toward the rally, Muller led Eirene across the street and they retraced their steps back toward the railroad station. They stopped at a nearby Café and enjoyed a mocha with pastries. "That might have gotten ugly," Muller said. Eirene nodded, her eyes wide. Muller noticed her hand shaking as she raised the mocha cup to her lips.

"Ugly is right. I was scared," she said quietly.

That evening, Eirene announced that she had changed her departure plans, deciding to return to London via steamship instead of the long train trip through Germany and France. "It's not that I'm nervous about traveling in Germany; with their Olympics only a year away, they're hardly going to terrorize a British tourist like me. I just need time to think, and I've decided the salt air on an ocean voyage will help me to sort things out." She turned directly to Muller, her expression serious. "Among other things it will me help sort out my thoughts about you; about us."

"And what about us?" Muller asked lightly, returning her gaze, not sure what to expect.

"I enjoy everything about you, Paul," she said. "I think I'm probably in love with you, in fact. But I've also been thinking very seriously about standing for Parliament. It's become a passion, and I'm feeling horribly torn because my two passions—you and Parliament—are pretty incompatible, I'm afraid." She paused.

Muller looked startled. Parliament? That was a bit of a wild card.

"Sorry; I didn't mean to blurt that out quite so directly," Eirene said. "The last thing I want to do is to put a damper on our delicious holiday together and our ballot-stuffing events. I want to enjoy every minute together. But I also hope very much that you'll understand that I'm feeling very torn. I don't know if an ocean voyage will help, but I need to try something."

They were sitting in a restaurant over lunch and he reached across the table and took her hand. "I'm thrilled to be at least one of your principal passions," he said. "Let's see what happens; I'm still comfortable with that."

I don't seem to have much choice, do I, he thought. He smiled warmly at her.

Later, sitting in the hotel lobby catching up on the newspapers, Muller reflected on their conversation. Eirene had told him she'd loved him. Well, he said to himself with an unexpected rush of emotion; no one's ever said that to me before. But did he love her, he wondered? He realized he'd never really thought about it, at least not in that way. When she'd arrived a week ago, she'd teased him for not knowing much about women; maybe she's right, he thought. I certainly enjoy her company and she was really sexy, no doubt about that. And they certainly had a common interest in politics and current events. That was a big plus, though he wondered if they were still on the same wave length politically.

Muller sighed. He was fully committed here in Danzig; the reality, as he'd admitted to Lester, was that he didn't have time for 'a life' here. She was busy in England, and if she stood for Parliament, and especially if she were elected, it seemed pretty likely that she wouldn't have time for 'a life' either.

Christ! Why do we have to complicate things? He shook his head and returned to the newspapers.

Over dinner that evening, Eirene looked at Muller playfully. "You were reluctant to bring up the subject of Eden; I've been reluctant to tell you about Daddy's trip to meet Hitler."

"So he did wangle the invitation after all?" said Muller.

"Ribbentrop–Hitler's advisor–arranged it as he said he would. He even organized an airplane to fly Daddy to Berlin; his first flight ever. But then Hitler's chauffer suddenly died and Hitler went to Munich for the funeral, so Daddy and Ribbentrop flew to Munich together. They were met at the airport by a big open Mercedes car and driven directly to Hitler's personal flat in the city, which Daddy described as being 'solid and Victorian'. He said Hitler was dressed in his Sunday best, all fresh from the laundry, and they proceeded to converse together for nearly an hour–and-a-half. He said it was very amiable and he found Hitler entirely reasonable, with none of the impatience or speeches monopolizing the conversation that one hears about. Hitler said he wants good relations with Britain, expressed the desire to meet with Baldwin; he even signed copies of some of his speeches for Daddy to take back and present to Baldwin."

Muller watched with amusement as Eirene told the story—animated, and obviously proud of her father.

"Well, Daddy was thrilled," she went on. "He went right around to tell Baldwin all about the discussion. But, of course, Baldwin showed not the slightest interest in meeting Hitler; Daddy couldn't budge him. The man is hopelessly lethargic."

"Sorry," Muller said, more to show he was listening than in real sympathy.

"So Daddy couldn't save the world as he hoped," Eirene said, looking crestfallen. "I guess I don't really mean 'save the world'," she continued, "but he wasn't even able to make an impression—not even a man of his influence." Her voice trailed away.

"Well perhaps..." He wasn't sure of an appropriate response that wouldn't sound sarcastic.

But she continued, frowning. "I'm also finding it hard now to reconcile Daddy's sunny, upbeat attitude with what I've experienced on this trip. A week here with you, seeing all the swastikas and the Brown Shirts strutting around, hearing your descriptions about their behavior—and of course listening to Elizabeth's stories the other night—all of that leaves me feeling a lot more uneasy about the situation. I'm going to have to think about that on my trip home too. Especially the frightening encounter with those Nazis during the rally; it's different when you're actually present and can feel their aggression."

Muller looked at her fondly. "Maybe we should call this a learning experience," he said, hoping to strike the right note.

Eirene smiled wanly.

That night as they lay in one another's arms, Eirene wept and made fierce love to him. "God, this is so good," she groaned. Then as they lay together she wept again. "I'm sure there'll be an election this fall," she said, "and the Tories have a safe seat they want me to stand for. I desperately want to do it, and to be one of only a handful of women in the House. How can I do that with a Swiss lover–or even a Swiss husband?"

Muller decided to respond by stroking her and arousing her to another passionate climax, before they both fell into a deep sleep in one another's arms.

The next morning, Eirene wouldn't let him accompany her to the ship. "I'd make a terrible scene tearing myself away," she said wrapped in his embrace as they said goodbye. "I've loved all this, and loved being with you–and I'm feeling so, mixed up." She wiped away tears. She kissed him lightly and followed the doorman to the waiting taxi.

Muller went back to work.

***

As Muller had feared, the September 1935 Council meeting followed the now all–too-familiar pattern of issues being sidestepped and pushed harmlessly forward to the next meeting. Lester and Muller had journeyed to Geneva in an upbeat mood. The June Council meeting had referred several of the long-pending petitions to the League's Committee of International Jurists for review. Three Jurists, all distinguished judges from League member nations, had deliberated in Geneva for several long days in late July and proceeded to deliver their opinions, in each case favoring the petitioners and criticizing the Senate. The opinions weren't binding decisions; they were advisory. But they seemed to form a basis for concrete Council action. Several other new petitions had also been added to the agenda, arising from Senate actions taken since the June meeting. Taken together, the moment seemed ripe for the Council to confront the Senate and force it to take remedial actions.

But it was not to be. Greiser arrived in Geneva accompanied by an array of Senate advisors and began aggressively challenging all of the agenda items. Greiser himself embarked on an energetic round of talks with Council representatives, including Eden, whom he was able to meet, following Eden's practice, without Lester being present. Stevenson had cancelled his trip to Geneva because of the death of his mother, and Muller found himself unable to engage Stevenson's staff.

Lester vainly attempted to persuade Eden to take a strong stand and write a report directly challenging Senate misconduct.

"He's unwilling to do it," Lester told Muller over dinner. "Right now, he's paying a lot more attention to the Abyssinian problem than he is to Danzig."

Muller told him that Eden's staff had seemed preoccupied with the Abyssinian crisis, too. "Maybe Stevenson could have forced them to spend time attending to Danzig if he had been here," said Muller; "without him, they clearly weren't interested."

"Abyssinia's become an issue that's consuming them," responded Lester. "Eden told me that earlier this month, he and French Prime Minister Laval persuaded the Council to issue a report exonerating both Abyssinia and Italy of culpability for the so-called Walwal conflict that set off this whole dispute. He thought that would settle things. But now, he's hearing reports that the Italians are massing troops along the border and there's apparently an imminent risk they'll invade. The British Parliament has already come out for imposing League sanctions against Italy in the event of war, so Eden's trying to prevent hostilities from breaking out and, if the Italians do attack, then getting the League to order sanctions.

"Frankly, I had a hard time trying to focus him on our struggles in Danzig," Lester went on, "He's very complimentary about my efforts and sympathetic to our difficulties, but he doesn't want the League to take on another fight while it's struggling with this Abyssinian crisis. I tried to persuade him that Council action confronting the Senate would actually *strengthen* the Council's hand, showing the world that it had the will to stand up in defense of its mandate. I told him that could help stiffen the League's resolve to act in Abyssinia–and elsewhere if needed."

"That's the point, Commissioner," Muller injected. "League action in Danzig would be a show of strength; doing nothing is an admission of weakness."

"Eden heard me; he understood. But he was unmoved," said Lester.

He hesitated before continuing. "Part of me suspects that he's reluctant to have the League tweak Germany about Danzig at the same time it's exerting pressure on Italy, because he doesn't want to drive them into each other's arms. That is a legitimate concern; but I don't think it should control our proceeding tomorrow. I've prepared some fairly tough remarks to deliver if I feel they're needed. I'm not going to remain silent."

***

The Council convened on September 23 to take up the Danzig agenda. This time, Muller was much less awed by the august surroundings of the Council Chamber and the assembled League representatives. He had grown weary of the Council's timid reluctance to act even in the face of hard evidence of Senate disregard for the League's mandate.

Beck opened the proceedings and Eden, as Rapporteur, summarized the issues. He did not downplay the Jurists' opinions nor minimize the allegations in the new petitions that had been submitted, but neither did he declare that the record warranted Council action. Muller noted that Eden's comments made no reference to Greiser's failure to meet the commitments he had made to the Council in June–and before that, in January–to resolve petitions locally.

Beck then called upon Greiser, who made a lengthy speech discounting the accusations against the Senate. Striking a truculent note, he disputed allegations that the Senate had failed to protect constitutional rights and then returned to the familiar theme of pledging full Senate support for working within the framework of the Danzig Constitution. Again he preached the virtue of seeking additional time to address these local issues locally.

Muller, sitting behind the table with his hands across his chest, swore to himself.

Beck turned the floor back to Eden who recommended that the Council issue a report acknowledging that, while serious charges of misconduct had been levied against the Senate, the Council expected that the Senate 'would take the necessary steps to bring its legislation into conformity with the Danzig Constitution' and report its progress back to the Council through the Commissioner. Beck thanked the Rapporteur, expressing his hope that the Senate would comply with the Council's wishes but agreeing that they be provided ample time to do so. After the ritual unanimous approval of Eden's report, Beck was about to gavel the session into recess when Lester rose to speak.

"As the servant of the Council, I accept and will do my best to implement the Council's decision," he said. "But I think that the Council is owed my candid observations at what I deem to be a crucial juncture."

The representatives around the horseshoe table fell silent and stopped packing their briefcases at Lester's unexpected intervention; they gave him their full attention.

Lester reminded them that every Council meeting since his appointment had concluded the same way as today's meeting had ended, with a referral of contentious issues back to Danzig's Senate, accompanied by an expression of confidence that the Senate would resolve the issues locally. He noted that if the Senate had acted cooperatively, as it always promised to do, the problems would no longer remain on the agenda. But the Senate had not acted cooperatively and had not met its commitments, he said. Relations between the Commissioner and the Senate had been unsatisfactory. Cooperation, he said, should mean more than expecting the Commissioner–and the Council–simply to accept the Senate's unwillingness to act.

"While the Senate has made declarations of loyalty to the Council," Lester said, "there have been too many declarations showing hostility to the constitutional principles the Council is mandated to protect." He then itemized the Senate's record of arbitrary arrests, newspaper closures, discrimination against minorities, and countless attempts to impose majority views on political opponents.

He concluded, turning directly to Greiser, seated next to Eden.

"I make an earnest appeal to President Greiser. Sir, you tried to obtain from the people of Danzig a popular mandate empowering your party to change the Constitution. You failed. I insist that you now agree to accept the Constitution as it was written and now exists, and that you do so not only in the letter of that document but also in its spirit. The Senate should concentrate on helping its citizens address the serious financial and economic hardships they confront that would surely bring more benefits to the members of the community of Danzig than repeated conflict and confrontation with political opponents.

"You occupy the seat of power in your government. I implore you to exercise it for the common good."

Yes, Muller said to himself; good for you Commissioner.

Lester sat down.

No one reacted. The Chamber was silent. After several moments, Beck banged the gavel in adjournment. Eden turned to Lester, and spoke loudly enough to be heard by the Council members as they prepared to depart, and most importantly by Greiser seated next to him. "Well said, Commissioner. Those are sentiments that we can all embrace."

Muller sat disconsolately. Not one member nation representative had spoken out in Lester's support or insisted that Greiser reply to Lester's challenge. Just silence; until after adjournment, when Eden voiced his encouragement, knowing it would be off-the-record.

It was another disappointing outcome. Muller sighed.

As they prepared for the journey back to Danzig, Lester told Muller he wanted him to get copies of all the actions taken by the Council relating to Danzig since he'd become High Commissioner.

"We don't have transcripts or the formal reports in Danzig, Muller," he said. "In my remarks to the Council, I was going to read off the record of petitions, the commitments made by Greiser to resolve them and the list of unfinished outstanding issues that the Council has ignored. But I realized I didn't have the records at hand and I didn't have the time to organize them—even here, where they're available. I want to be sure we have them in Danzig from now on, so I'd like you to arrange with the Secretariat to provide us official copies of everything, including today's proceedings."

Muller nodded and set off to make the arrangements.

***

Ten days later, on October 4, 1935, Italy invaded Abyssinia. Upon hearing the news, Lester turned to Muller glumly and said, "I'm afraid we are now hostage to this crisis."

Relations with the Senate had been quiet after they returned from Geneva. Von Radowitz told Muller over dinner that Greiser was annoyed by Lester's closing remarks, but was relieved at the Council's decision to afford him more time.

"He knows that he dodged a bullet," von Radowitz said. "He returned here by way of Berlin where von Neurath told him to avoid any new controversy, so he's been trying to lay low, though apparently Hitler told Forster to ignore the League. So the lull probably won't last."

One morning shortly after their return from Geneva, Lester told Muller that he had stayed later in the office than usual the prior evening and had heard strange noises outside his office window. He said that he looked out the window and didn't see anything, but the noises continued, so he went downstairs to the door to the garden and, upon opening it, spied a group of men in the bushes, apparently digging something. "I was so surprised I asked, in English, what the hell they thought they were doing. They jumped when they heard my voice, then picked up their shovels and ran away. I took a torch out to look and what I saw seems to be a trench leading under my window. Let's have a look in daytime together."

They walked outside into the garden and there, indeed, was a partially dug trench, just as Lester had described. There was also some wire and equipment that the men had evidently left behind when they fled. "Some kind of listening device?" wondered Lester.

Muller called Franz Schiller at the Police Station to come have a look.

"Give us a few days," said Schiller.

A day later, Schiller came to Muller's office. "We found the four guys the Commissioner chased away," he said. "They're part of a new surveillance unit the SA has just set up, and, as the Commissioner suspected, they were trying to install some kind of listening device. I think we've put the lid on them, but I'm afraid you'll need to be alert to other possible intrusions. These guys were pretty inept and their equipment isn't very good; but they're becoming more aggressive."

"So they were SA men," Muller said. "Locals or from Germany?"

"Germans, but evidently assigned here," Schiller replied. "Now that we've identified them, they'll probably be sent back."

"And if the Commissioner were to confront Greiser on this business, Greiser would claim total ignorance, am I right?" Muller asked.

"I'm sure that's correct," said Schiller, "and it might even be true; the SA has its own command structure that isn't always accountable to Greiser, or even Forster."

"So this is different than that earlier assassination team incident," said Muller.

Schiller nodded. "We can't pin this on anyone directly.

"Incidentally, Muller, the individual who gave them access to the garden is the Commissioner's butler, a man named Schmitz."

"Rudi Schmitz," said Muller shaking his head. "He's been the butler here since before we arrived. The Commissioner will certainly have to dismiss him."

"I don't think you'll see him again," replied Schiller. "We're told he has just been made chief bartender at one of the clubs that the SA owns on the other side of town, over by the NSDAP headquarters. By the way, if you're looking for a candidate to replace Schmitz, maybe we can offer a candidate."

"And who would he be spying for, Schiller?" Muller replied smiling.

Schiller smiled back, "Well, I suppose you could take your choice, given the amount of intrigue here."

"I'll speak to the Commissioner," said Muller as they stood to shake hands.

"Oh, by the way," said Schiller, "Ernst Stieberitz has fixed the program for our Christmas concert next month. The feature will be the Bach Christmas Cantata, which will be fun to sing if we can get through all those fugues. But he's been told to eliminate 'Hark the Herald Angels Sing' from the carol-singing portion of the program. It was composed by Felix Mendelsohn, and he's a Jew."

"I hope that's a bad joke," said Muller.

Schiller shook his head.

"Craziness," said Muller, then added, "Well, they better check up on 'O Tannenbaum' too. That sounds like a Jewish name to me."

Schiller looked at him in mock seriousness. "Right; can't be too careful."

***

In early November, Lester told Muller he had started to keep a diary.

"I've never done one before," he said, looking a little sheepish, "but Elsie persuaded me that I ought to keep some personal record of our time here in Danzig. I'm not sure exactly what to record. At a minimum, I suppose I can keep a running score of the daily reports we receive about people getting beaten up or arrested and journals being banned and so on. Last week, I described the incident of the plainclothesmen you and I spotted following us when we went out to meet the Bulgarian Consul General. Those sorts of details ought to capture a little of the tense climate we're living in."

"I think that's a really good idea, Commissioner," said Muller. "An insider's report of what it's like to live through this business. We really are making history here," he continued, "or I suppose that's what we're doing. If nothing else, at least you'll have a record for yourself to reflect on in retirement." He smiled.

"Well, speaking of history Muller, today I decided to acknowledge history being made—though not here. I saluted the fact that on November 2, 1935, the League of Nations imposed economic sanctions on a country it declared to be an aggressor.

"Think about it, Muller," Lester said, gesturing expansively. "Fifty nations cutting off trade with Italy, one of the largest economies in the world, because it invaded Abyssinia in violation of the League's Covenant. For the first time ever, 'collective security', that grand phrase that's bandied about so readily, has actually been invoked and will take effect in two weeks. So I decided to write a little tribute to the League as my diary entry today."

He paused. "We better hope those sanctions work, Muller. The League's prestige is on the line; if it falters, we'll feel the impact here."

Muller agreed.

***

The next day, Muller received a telegram from London,

Elected Stop Joy Stop Sadness Stop Jerusalem

Muller held the message in his hand and stared at it for a long time.

Then he folded it neatly and placed it in the top drawer of his desk.

We both agreed to see where things led, he thought. I guess now we know: to the House of Commons for Eirene; stuck here in Danzig, for me.

Muller sighed. It was one thing to think about that kind of separation when Eirene was here and they were together. It was a little different to confront the reality of it delivered by telegram.

This would take some getting used to, he decided.

CHAPTER 16

Fall 1935

The post-Geneva lull in Danzig was shattered on November 14 by publication of a decision by the Danzig Supreme Court in the case filed by the opposition seeking to invalidate the April 7, 1935 elections. The seventy-page opinion managed to infuriate both the opposition and Senate and the fallout engulfed Lester and Muller.

Translating the document for Lester, Muller could see the court struggling to reach its verdict. On the one hand, it declared that the election had been characterized by pervasive misconduct under Danzig's election laws. It contained detailed accounts of witnesses that it declared to be credible (including numerous Danzig policemen, Muller noted), describing instances of voter intimidation and electoral fraud. It also strongly criticized government actions that had overtly favored NSDAP candidates and discriminated against the opposition. It even cited actions by Forster as NSDAP Gaulieter in fomenting the illegal behavior. But then, in what Muller found to be an almost eerie contradiction, it declared that the law did not empower it to annul the election entirely and that that the April results would be allowed to stand, except for removing one seat from the two-seat gain the NSDAP had claimed and assigning it to the SDP.

This result meant that the NSDAP majority remained secure. Muller concluded that the judges, even though convinced that the opposition had proven its case, were unable to muster the courage to unseat the government.

The decision provoked an immediate outcry and Lester and Muller were caught up in multiple meetings with representatives of the contending parties. The opposition began work immediately on a petition to the Council seeking an order requiring new elections. Ernst Brost, the SDP spokesman, made their case to Lester.

"The decision not to invalidate the election is squarely in conflict with the findings of misconduct that the court documented," Brost said.

"We know for a fact that some of the judges were threatened. The Chief Judge is named Haagen; his mother was half-Jewish, so that makes him one-quarter Jewish and under the German Nuremburg laws, he's deemed a non-person. We don't have the Nuremburg laws here in Danzig— at least not yet, thank God—but that didn't prevent Forster from threatening him with exposure and expulsion from the bench. Then there are the judges that were appointed from Germany. They're all Nazis and we don't have any confidence in their integrity.

"So," he said, "what we're going to do is bring this whole record to Geneva and lay it out for the Council members. They'll see for themselves that, by any fair reading, the number of votes infected by fraud was more than enough to swing the majority to our list. So the election results are completely invalid and need to be annulled. We're going to demand that the Council force a new election."

Lester's meetings with Greiser were equally emotional.

"Those so-called findings of illegal conduct are almost laughable," Greiser said. "Obviously the opposition bribed the judges to write this silly nonsense. I can tell you, for instance, that the statements attributed by the court to the Danzig police are complete fabrications. This kind of judicial interference and use of perverted legalisms against the rise of our Party is a perfect example of what's wrong with the opposition."

Greiser also rebuffed Lester's insistence that he follow through on the commitments he had made in Geneva to negotiate solutions to the pending petitions. "We will not be pressured to act hastily or dismantle programs we have instituted in pursuit of our National Socialist goals, Commissioner. The sniveling petitioners may try to curry favor with you and the League Council in Geneva, but they will not—nor will you or the Council—distract us from steadfast adherence to National Socialism."

After another especially fruitless session with Greiser, Lester threw up his hands in frustration. "I know Forster has his boot on Greiser's neck, but he's just become insufferable. I've made a decision to send the opposition petition on the election to the Council for the January meeting. Greiser's been saying I can't do that, because the court has rendered its decision and the Council has no authority to overturn a Danzig Supreme Court decision interpreting Danzig law. Well, I think the Council does have that authority. I'm sure he'll throw a fit. But I'm fed up with being hectored by a man who lacks neither the courage to stand up to Forster nor the integrity to fulfill his promises in Geneva."

"Actually, Commissioner, I suspect that part of Greiser's erratic behavior is a result of being scared to death that you *will* send it to Geneva," Muller observed. "When you do refer it, he'll find himself squarely in the cross-hairs."

"Well, he's brought it on himself." Lester set his chin firmly.

On November 27, a day after Lester's announcement that he was sending the opposition's petition to the Council, Greiser delivered a ferocious speech before the *Volkstag*.

He accused the opposition of crimes against the 'German people' of Danzig and warned that leaders who continued to stand in the way of National Socialism 'place themselves beyond the pale of the German national community'. He accused the League of causing the economic hardship that Danzig was experiencing, saying 'friendly cooperation' with the League had cost Danzig nearly 20 million gulen. 'If we were not condemned to such expenditures, devaluation would never have been necessary.' He accused the League of 'meddling' in the affairs of the City 'creating risks to security and civic order.' The Commissioner, he said, was 'biased against the majority of the City'; he had become 'an outspoken advocate of denying to citizens the fruits of their own election' and was nothing more than a 'tool' of Geneva and the 'faceless League'.

He concluded with a direct challenge. "Political power in Europe has been fundamentally changed in the years since we were severed from our Motherland. Germany was weak then, it is strong now, and under the leadership of our Fuhrer we shall no longer submit."

Muller had never seen Lester more incensed.

"The arrogance, the recklessness; it's as if he's become unhinged. Muller, this has the trappings of a coup; it certainly is an invitation to the NSDAP and the Volkstag to overthrow the Constitution."

For the first time since they had arrived in Danzig nearly two years earlier, Lester placed a long-distance telephone call to Avenol in Geneva. "We are in crisis," he told the Secretary General. "I'm coming to consult the Council at the earliest time possible. Kindly alert Eden."

Turning to Muller Lester said, "I want a message prepared to Greiser advising him that his remarks to the Senate are an unacceptable affront to the authority of the League of Nations and the Office of the High Commissioner. Advise him that I am reminding him of his solemn duty under the laws to perform his Constitutional responsibilities and inform him that I am departing for Geneva forthwith to consult with the League Council."

"Let's hope that will suffice to hold the fort while we take this up with the Council," he added grimly.

Lester then Summoned von Radowitz to his office. He told him that German interference in Danzig affairs was no longer tolerable.

"I have no doubt that Greiser's speech was written in Berlin, not Danzig," he angrily told the German consul. "This must cease."

Lester dismissed von Radowitz's protestations. "Just deliver the damned message," he said. Next he called in Papee and warned him that Greiser's harangue placed Poland's interests in the territorial integrity of Danzig–and perhaps even in the Corridor itself–at risk.

"I agree, Commissioner," replied Papee. "The speech is very threatening. I've already sent a message to Beck urging him to defend the interests of the League in Danzig; that's the only way to protect Polish rights under the Treaty–which are indisputably our most important priority."

After Papee departed, Lester turned to Muller with a conspiratorial glance. "So, Muller, it looks like we'll get to see Beck's true colors pretty soon. Will he decide that Papee's right, that we're the only thing standing in Greiser's path, and act to defend us at the Council, or will he do what Papee predicted to you in that first meeting the two of you had, and abandon us?"

Muller nodded in agreement. They were definitely going to provoke some action, he just wished he had more confidence that Beck would see the error of his earlier ways.

A day later, von Radowitz asked for an urgent meeting with Lester. He arrived earlier than the appointed hour and appeared uncharacteristically agitated.

"I've been instructed to reassure you that no one in Berlin wrote Greiser's intemperate speech," he said. "It was a speech that is contrary to Germany's wishes and we were astonished at the attacks upon you and the League. We understand how offensive both the tone and the content must seem to you. Von Neurath is very annoyed about it and he has instructed me to issue a personal invitation for you to visit Berlin at the earliest possible moment so he can reaffirm German support for your role."

"Impossible," replied Lester. "Germany is no longer a member of the League. It would be entirely inappropriate for me to call upon the Foreign Minister of a non-member state–especially one that, frankly, has interfered with the League's work here."

"Commissioner, I understand that this is a delicate issue," von Radowitz said. "I am instructed to assure you that the meeting would be conducted in strictest secrecy."

He paused and looked at Lester before resuming. "Von Neurath actually telephoned me this morning urging me to persuade you to come. I was surprised, as we all know how insecure telephone lines are. He's very serious. I hope you will give it further thought, Commissioner; the trip could help to ease the tensions here."

"I've made plans to travel to Geneva next week for consultations," said Lester, "so it's quite impossible."

"But Commissioner, you could have the meeting en route to Geneva," said von Radowitz eagerly. "Unless you're planning to fly–which is risky given the weather at this time of year–your train will pass through Berlin anyway. You could conduct the meeting–entirely off-the-record–then get back on a later train the same day. No one would need to know and it would be a chance for you and von Neurath to have a serious conversation. I also gained the impression that other Nazi Party leaders may be invited to participate in the discussions," von Radowitz added, smiling enigmatically as Muller translated.

*****

"The Poles aren't going to like it at all," said Lester to Muller later. "And of course they'll find out even though it's supposed to be a secret. But I've decided von Radowitz is right; it's time I had talks in Berlin. So tell them to set it up."

Two days later, Lester and Muller boarded the early morning train south to Dirschau where they could catch the East-bound Koenigsburg–Berlin express and arrive just after lunchtime. There was a 6 PM overnight departure from Berlin that would get them to Geneva the following morning. That left a four-hour window in Berlin for the meeting.

Upon arrival, they were met by a diplomatic delegation and whisked by motorcade into Central Berlin. They drove down the Unter den Linden, turning south toward the junction with Friederichstrasse, where the Wilhelmstrasse was situated. Their chief escort, an elegantly-tailored diplomat who introduced himself as 'Max', explained, in flawless English, that, while the term 'Wilhelmstrasse' referred to the elegant building they were approaching, it was also the name of the street they were following. "The Wilhelmstrasse–the building, that is–used to house both the Foreign Ministry and the Chancellery," he said, "but our Fuehrer ordered a new Chancellery to be built there." He pointed, "You can see it there to the South. So we moved the Foreign Office into the former Presidential quarters and Party leaders took over our space while their new ministries are being built."

As they exited the large Hoche limousine, Muller looked up at the three-story façade, with its tall windows, topped by a slate roof. The lines were clean and efficient and lent the structure an unexpected fin de siècle air of graciousness.

Mounting a broad marble stairway, they entered a vast second floor reception hall with overstuffed chairs and damask-clad walls displaying large oil paintings. They were immediately ushered into von Neurath's large corner office with its heavy wooden desk, polished to a high sheen, and fireplaces at either end. Von Neurath welcomed them and led them to a comfortable sitting area close to one of the crackling fireplaces. He was a heavyset man with prominent jowls and a high forehead, accented by thinning hair that was swept back. A neat mustache lent him an almost dapper look.

Von Neurath spoke heavily-accented, but quite fluent English, so Muller became note taker. The Foreign Minister complimented Lester's work as Commissioner, acknowledging the difficulties he faced and expressing admiration for his diplomatic demeanor. Von Neurath candidly criticized the behavior of Forster and Greiser and accepted German responsibility for at least some of their misbehavior. "It is not uncommon for nations to speak with more than one voice," he said. "We have our challenges in Germany with respect to articulating a consistent Danzig policy."

Then he launched into a lengthy discourse on Germany's determination to remove the penalties inflicted on it in the Versailles Treaty. It was not a truculent statement and it praised what he called 'genuine efforts' on the part of the British to formulate an agreement that would meet Germany's needs, but he made it plain that securing the return of Danzig to Germany remained a firm German goal and a necessary part of any overall settlement.

"Minister," Lester replied, "with all due respect, the kind of comprehensive settlement you describe doesn't seem imminent, nor does any arrangement to return Danzig to Germany; indeed, we both know how strongly Poland would object to that.

"I'm facing an immediate issue, not some future conjecture. I'm endeavoring to protect a League of Nations mandate that the Nazi Party Gauleiter in Danzig and his puppet head of state are actively trying to undermine. Last week President Greiser made a speech containing threats that I interpret as an invitation to a coup d'etat. That is unacceptable. I had expected to receive assurances from you that Germany intended either to replace the Gauleiter or rein him in. Forster's crude belligerence does your government no good and it will provoke a response from the Council."

A secretary entered the room and handed von Neurath a note.

"Well," he said smiling as he read it, "with his usual perfect timing, Reichminister Goering has just asked if you would pay him a visit. I told him you would be our guest this afternoon; I think it would be informative for you to meet him."

Lester looked at his watch.

"His office is just down a flight of stairs in another corridor of the building," said von Neurath. "I'll have Max escort you and Mr. Muller."

Hermann Goering was a strikingly handsome man in his early 40's, with strong features, a shock of light brown hair and a once-muscular frame, now giving way to corpulence, but still very much a presence, Muller thought, observing the leader that he had seen in so many photographs. Goering had been catapulted to fame as one of Germany's most successful fighter pilots during the war and had been at Hitler's side since the early 1920's, even suffering wounds in the famed Beer Hall Putsch when Hitler had been arrested in 1923. He had founded the Gestapo secret police organization in 1933 and was among the most-feared members of Hitler's close inner circle.

When Lester and Muller entered Goering's office, they found him lying back on a brocade couch, dressed in a military tunic weighted with colorful decorations, grey riding breeches and one pink stocking; his other foot was propped in a large tub with ice and water. He didn't make any attempt to rise or shake hands, just waved them to leather upholstered chairs to his left.

"Kicked by a horse this morning," he offered by way of explanation, seemingly willing to let Muller translate, even though a heavy-set blonde woman seated behind him appeared to be the official interpreter. Even though he was half-reclining on the couch Goering projected strength. No, Muller thought, not just strength: raw power.

"So, Commissioner, I've heard much about you; not always good, mind you, but I'm pleased at least to meet you."

"And you, Reichminister," said Lester evenly.

"We think of Danzig as an open wound," Goering began. "We sometimes have to pick at it, just to remind the rest of the world, that it remains our wound." He said this smiling broadly, obviously enjoying the disquieting image. "That's what Forster does for us from time–to–time; he rubs the wound. Now, I know that probably makes your life a bit more difficult, Commissioner, but that sometimes happens when you're trying to manage a field hospital." He laughed aloud at his characterization.

Lester was not amused. "Reichminister, Danzig is a Free City, not a field hospital and Forster is crude and coarse. He is not a citizen of Danzig; he is your Gauleiter there, and he damages both your policy and your image in the City."

Goering threw back his large head in laughter. "Bobbie–that's what Hitler calls him; 'our Bobbie'. It's a nickname from the days when he was a student of Hitler's sister years ago."

Lester remained silent.

"So you think 'our Bobbie' is crude and coarse? Why, of course he is; it comes naturally to him. That's why we put him there and why we'll keep him there." Goering guffawed. "The masses, our followers, love him; he's one of them. Look, we know he's small-bore, but he's useful and he's ours."

"Reichminister, I have no interest in interfering with your Nazi Party affairs," said Lester. "You can do what you like with the Party—unless it interferes with the Danzig government in a way that threatens the constitution that the League and I have a mandate to uphold. When that happens—and it has occurred too frequently of late—I am duty-bound to object. You can have your Bobbie do his Nazi cartwheels at Party meetings and rallies. Just make sure he keeps his hands off the Danzig government."

Goering raised his eyebrows and gazed sharply at Lester. "Nazi cartwheels?" he said, his face darkening. Then, apparently having thought better of retorting, he said, "I've decided to take that as a compliment, Commissioner."

He looked levelly at Lester. "Part of what you've said is fair enough," he said. "In Germany, the Party and the government are the same, so there would be no difference in Forster's roles. I acknowledge that's not the case in Danzig—at least not now. So maybe we can have a word with him on that score; I know von Neurath feels his excesses are hurting us too. But don't expect him to be replaced. Bobbie will remain our Party Gauleiter for as long as our Fuehrer wants; and he wants to keep him there."

Goering waved his hand, dismissing the subject.

"Now on to more important business. Commissioner. I understand that you are a serious fisherman." The two men then began swapping fishing stories and compared notes about techniques and equipment, which Muller had a hard time translating as he didn't know the terms. Finally Goering laughed and pointed to Muller, saying to Lester, "You need to take that young man out and show him how to fish so he can learn how to translate better for us when we next meet." He heaved himself into a half-sitting position and shook Lester's hand as they departed.

Von Neurath was encouraged by Lester's description of Goering's apparent willingness to temper Forster's interference with the Senate. "We can exercise reasonable control over Greiser," he said. "If Forster backs off a bit maybe we can make things work better there."

"Do I have the commitment of the German government that they will use their influence to prevent an attempted coup d'etat by Forster or Greiser?" asked Lester bluntly.

Von Neurath gave Lester a measured look. "I do not think a coup d'etat is in the cards."

Lester said, "I interpret that as a 'yes'."

They stood as Lester prepared to depart. "I'm glad I accepted your invitation to meet," he said to von Neurath. "I'm expecting this to improve things." They shook hands.

The motorcade drove Lester and Muller to the station to catch the Express train to Zurich and Geneva, with Max and his delegation escorting them to their compartment and drawing the curtains before leaving. At Lester's direction, Muller summoned the porter and arranged for a bottle of Distiller's Whiskey and a plate of cheese and crackers to be delivered.

Muller offered a mock toast: "To Nazi cartwheels," he said smiling broadly. "I'm glad he decided to take that as a compliment."

Lester nodded. "A hard man."

***

When they arrived in Geneva, they found the League in an uproar. Word had leaked a day earlier that British Foreign Secretary Hoare and French Prime Minister Laval had negotiated an agreement granting Italy control over large swaths of Abyssinian territory in return for ending the fighting and committing Britain and France to removing the League's sanctions against Italy. Arriving at the Palais after checking into the Hotel de la Paix, Lester and Muller watched as officials and clerks scurried about. Frantic meetings were being held and participants, after dispersing, reconvened, then dashed off to still more meetings.

Lester shook his head in wonderment. "I've never seen the League in such disarray."

The first floor press section of the Palais was crowded, but Muller was finally able to collect copies of the *Guardian* and the *Telegraph*, both of which expressed outrage over the pact. 'It is insupportable to reward Mussolini's aggression,' the *Guardian* editorialized. 'Hoare Must Go!' thundered the *Telegraph*. Parliament had apparently exploded in strident opposition when word of the pact leaked out. Both papers reported that the Government, having finally owned up to the deal, was deluged with sarcastic taunts from Conservatives and Liberals–and even from its own backbenchers. The common theme seemed to be disgust with undermining the League's collective security program. According to the Guardian's editorial writer, 'The League guards the peace; how can we abandon the League?'

Reading the heated reports, Muller thought about Eirene, doubtless fully caught up in the crisis–almost certainly backing the League and calling for Hoare to resign. When she was advocating for the League, did she think about him and his mission in Danzig, he wondered? Probably not, he decided resignedly.

After three fruitless days in Geneva seeking to call attention to their Danzig crisis, Lester and Muller conceded defeat. They dined together at the Hotel de la Paix and prepared to depart early the next morning.

"I've managed to see Eden alone for less than an hour," confessed Lester. "No chance of convening the Council on our business; everyone's consumed by the fallout from Hoare-Laval to the exclusion of everything else."

"Eden says he wasn't involved in negotiating the Pact at all; apparently it was all cooked up by Hoare and Laval in Paris, when Hoare stopped by while heading off to a holiday. But now that the deal's exploded in their faces, Eden's the one left to pick up the pieces. Hoare will certainly be forced out and Eden seems likely to be named Foreign Secretary in his place, so he's forced to spend time treating cabinet issues in London and dealing with angry member state representatives here. He's entirely consumed by the crisis.

"I tried to explain that we have our own crisis in Danzig and I described Gresier's threat to simply take over the Free City. I even laid out a strategy for using the new petition to annul the April elections and force a new vote. I explained that the opposition would almost certainly win a majority and described the impact of a Nazi party defeat in Germany and elsewhere in Europe."

Lester toyed with his wine glass frowning in frustration. "I couldn't get him to address any of the issues. He said that my plan to order new elections would need cabinet approval and there was no chance of that occurring in the midst of this crisis, then he dashed off to another meeting.

"Avenol was even worse," Lester added. "I think our Secretary General would be very happy to see Danzig just disappear."

Muller reported that he had found Stevenson to be equally pre-occupied and indifferent to Danzig's problems. "But he did share some insights into what Hoare and Laval were trying to do. He said that the Italian military is simply overwhelming the Abyssinians in the war. Not quite machine guns against spears, but something pretty close to it; they've even used mustard gas against them and the slaughter is apparently terrible. So, what Hoare and Laval were thinking was to give Mussolini most of what he wants and preserve at least some semblance of an Abyssinian state; at least that would stop the killing."

Muller leaned forward, dropping his voice so as not to be overheard. "The most interesting part was the underlying political intrigue. According to Stevenson, what really drove both Hoare and Laval was the goal of ending the confrontation with Italy for fear of driving it into Hitler's arms.

"They feared that keeping the pressure on Mussolini would leave him nowhere else to go for support but Germany. An alliance between the two of them would change the whole European chessboard. So, Muller said, "to Whitehall, Hoare's move made perfect sense; sacrifice a meaningless little country in East Africa to Mussolini and thereby remove the threat of a German–Italian alliance. The Pact was about removing a potential obstacle to the goal of negotiating a peace agreement with Germany; Abyssinia was just a pawn in that larger game."

"Well," Lester responded, "if that's accurate, then the League itself was just another pawn too. The Pact committed Britain and France to overturn an historic resolution, adopted by the members of the League of Nations less than a month ago, to impose sanctions against Italy for violating the League's solemn Covenant. We talked about it together in Danzig."

Muller nodded. "I remember it well."

"The first time a collective security program had ever been instituted," Lester continued, angrily "And the two of them simply said, 'we'll get rid of it'."

Lester gesticulated with a wave of his hand; "Just like that! No consultations, no negotiations, just a bilateral declaration to remind the world that Britain and France remain the Great Powers and will decide what needs to be done. The pretty clear message to the League of Nations was 'do as you're told; you don't make the rules, we do'."

"No wonder the place is in an uproar," Lester added. "It's a complete humiliation; Eden's trying to minimize the damage. But there's no doubt the League has suffered a serious setback."

Lester took a long sip of wine. "It's going to have an impact on us too, Muller. I hope Danzig doesn't become the next Abyssinia, but I don't have a lot of confidence that we can avoid the same fate."

He sighed. "Muller, we'll need to re-calibrate our plans for the January Council meetings; the next 30 days are going to be busy. I'm going to need you in Danzig, so why don't you take a day or two now on the return trip to see your family in Zurich. We're going to have a working Christmas in Danzig."

CHAPTER 17

January 1936

Muller translated Forster's New Year's message for Lester: "I wish all Danzigers good courage in the New Year and a firm belief in Adolf Hitler."

"And a Happy New Year to you too, Bobbie," replied Lester, smiling sardonically. "That's certainly a discouraging note on which to begin."

Upon Muller's return to Danzig a few days before Christmas, he and Lester had debated strategy for the upcoming Council meetings. Ultimately, Lester had decided against recommending a specific course of action to the Council.

"Elsie's like you," he had told Muller. "She wants me to squarely back the opposition's election petition and insist that the Council order a new vote. I've decided I can't do that. There's no doubt in my mind that that would be the best outcome. But I don't have confidence that I would prevail if I were to insist on it. Moreover, it would offer Greiser an opportunity to accuse me of bias in favor of the opposition and strengthen his hand.

"Instead, I want to write a detailed Annual Report which captures life in Danzig under the NSDAP and distribute it to the Council ahead of the meetings. I want to describe the pressure: the violations of the constitution

309

and attacks on the League, the glorification of Nazi doctrine, the beatings, the arrests, the censorship, the verbal assaults, the broken promises; all of it.

"None of the Council members have ever visited Danzig to see it for themselves. I want to convey the reality of what's happening here. If we can do that persuasively, the Council will see that something needs to be done. Once they get to that point, we can try to influence the outcome. But first we've got to lay the foundation.

"So, Muller," he concluded, "let's get to work."

And so they did. Over the next week, swapping drafts back and forth and conversing with one another late into the evening, Muller and Lester labored to prepare a document that met the standards Lester had laid out.

By the time they finished, the Report ran to more than forty pages with nine annexes. Muller found himself frustrated by Lester's unwillingness to employ colorful prose and his insistence on language that Muller called 'diplomatic dullness'. Still, the Report did not pull any punches.

It reminded the Council of the litany of broken promises made by Greiser in Geneva. Two full sections were devoted to criticizing Forster's role, liberally quoting his bloodthirsty declarations and attacks on both the Danzig Constitution and the League mandate. The report described the displays of Nazi flags and banners on public buildings, revealed the active roles of German Nazi leaders, enumerated repeated interference with opposition newspapers and the clashes with Catholics and political minorities. All in all, Muller decided, it was a powerful document.

He and Lester also made sure that it featured the opposition's election petition and its request to annul the fraudulent outcome and to order new elections. Lester allowed himself to advise the Council that in his considered judgment, "there must be a complete change in the attitude of the local government or a change in the machinery through which the League's guarantee is made effective." It was not as far as Muller wanted him to go, but in context, it was an obvious invitation to the Council to appoint an oversight committee and order new elections.

Lester and Muller arrived in Geneva on January 17, 1936. The Danzig portion of the Council meetings was scheduled for three days of debate beginning on January 22. There was a feeling of anticipation in the atmosphere ahead of the meetings that Muller had not sensed before. The Commissioner's Annual Report had caused a stir when it was distributed a few days earlier and foreign correspondents had arrived to report on the upcoming proceedings.

Lester told Muller that Avenol had waved the Annual Report at him when he visited the Secretary General upon arrival.

"'This is literature,' he said. I asked, 'is it good politics?' He responded, 'Not only good literature but good politics too'." Lester smiled in satisfaction.

Eden had arrived in Geneva, but there were regular bulletins about King George V who was reported to be near death. Lester fretted to Muller about, "yet another diversion from our agenda. Last year it was rearmament that interfered, then it was Abyssinia—will a Royal funeral interrupt us this year? Since Eden is now Foreign Secretary, he will certainly need to go back if the King dies; but he's still Rapporteur for Danzig and his departure would throw everything into a cocked hat."

Stevenson told Muller that Eden had the same concern, so he intended to convene a preliminary session informally. Greiser was not yet in town, so Eden had instructed Stevenson to fetch him. While awaiting Greiser's arrival, Stevenson asked Muller to participate in a meeting of Foreign Office personnel and the Secretariat's Danzig Sub-Section staff to discuss the text of the Rapporteur's report.

Krabbe, the Sub-Section Chief, reported that member state representatives were strongly influenced by Lester's Annual Report. He said they seemed prepared to take affirmative steps to protect the League's Danzig mandate rather than simply accepting Greiser's assurances and pushing the issues forward to the next meeting. "They're all persuaded that enough is enough. But there's no consensus about what to do," Krabbe concluded.

The meeting ended inconclusively. Muller had resisted the urge to intervene and encourage the staff to embrace the option of annulling the elections and ordering a new vote. He sensed this was not the time. As they gathered their papers and began to leave, Stevenson invited Muller back to the Hotel d'Angleterre.

"I've got a dinner in an hour," he said, "but let's have a drink together."

Ordering large neat whiskies for them both, Stevenson grinned at Muller. "You bit your tongue all afternoon, didn't you," he said teasingly. "I know you want to go to the election option; Hell, if I were in your shoes, I would too. But you were right not to push it this afternoon."

Stevenson went on, in a new authoritative tone that Muller noted with some irritation. "We need to see how the politics of this meeting develop," he said. "Eden's out of patience on Danzig; he's going to insist on some action. But he hasn't decided yet what it should be. It's a dicey time—since he's now Foreign Secretary. He's decided he has to rely on the League; the government really has no other choice, given the popular outcry over Hoare's attempt to go around it."

Muller resisted the impulse to remark that working with the League would probably be a novel concept to Eden, after having ignored it so often. He contented himself with a smirk.

"The League's biggest commitment now is to the Abyssinian sanctions program," Stevenson went on. "Eden's going to try to add an oil embargo to strengthen it. But that will be hard to do since the Americans will be happy to sell the Italians as much oil as they want. Then there's Poland; Beck is still in love with his non-aggression pact with Germany. Any League action regarding Danzig will need strong Polish cover, because Britain has no interest in new commitments to Eastern Europe. But Eden isn't at all certain that he can count on Beck to bring Poland along. So there are a lot of moving parts and he has to proceed cautiously."

Always thinking about the big picture, Muller thought. Why won't he concentrate on Danzig?

"Stevenson, think about the Saar Plebiscite," said Muller. "Eden organized an international police force there and forced the Nazis to keep their hands off the vote. The League looked strong and came away with a victory. Why not do the same in Danzig?"

"But the Nazis won 93 percent of the vote in the Saar," Stevenson snorted. "What kind of a victory is that?"

"They wouldn't win in Danzig if a new vote were taken now," Muller replied sharply. "Inserting a League force like Eden did in the Saar would completely change the dynamics. The local NSDAP wouldn't be any match for even a small League of Nations presence and the local police would cooperate.

"A new vote would bring a new government to office that would remove the crisis," He added. "Think about it—actually winning an issue for once. Wouldn't that be a nice change?"

Muller leaned toward Stevenson, gesturing for emphasis. "Stevenson, ordering a new election and overseeing it would strengthen the League's reputation at a moment in time when it needs a boost. Look, I know coming to an overall settlement with Germany is Eden's highest priority," Muller's eyes locked in on Stevenson's. "My argument is that ordering a new election for Danzig can help him achieve that goal. If the NSDAP were to lose a new election—as it surely would—most of us estimate they would be lucky to get even 25 percent–that would puncture Hitler's reputation and help persuade him to accept the kinds of limitations Eden wants to accomplish.

"This is an *opportunity* for Eden; he should seize it."

"I like your fire, Muller," replied Stevenson, smiling faintly, "but don't get too far ahead of yourself."

"Don't you patronize me, Stevenson," Muller replied heatedly.

Stevenson raised his hands slightly in mock surrender, throwing a few francs on the table. "I need to leave. We'll have time to return to this subject as the week unfolds."

As Stevenson strode to the elevators, Muller ordered another whiskey, annoyed at himself for his testy outburst–but also annoyed at Stevenson for being condescending.

He was not expecting a kiss on the cheek as Elizabeth Wiskemann slipped into the seat next to him.

"I was hoping you'd be here, Paul," she said smiling at him. "This should be an exciting week. Maybe the Council will even *do* something for a change."

Muller laughed and ordered fresh drinks, "With you here to offer them guidance, surely they'll do the right thing, Elizabeth," he said, smiling at her. He found himself glad to see her again. Eirene had sent him clippings of the stories she had written last summer after visiting Danzig and Muller had found them surprisingly insightful.

They exchanged news and chatted comfortably. In tacit agreement, neither mentioned Eirene's election to the House and its implications for Muller.

Elizabeth had no dinner plans, so Muller invited her to join him at the Restaurant de Simplon, close to the railroad station and only a short taxi ride away. As they worked their way through generous helpings of filet des perche washed down with chilled Muscadet, Muller found himself unburdening himself and sharing his frustrations over the League's handling of the Danzig issue. Then a thought occurred to him.

"Elizabeth, I don't know the rules about talking to reporters, but if I had an idea about how to achieve an important breakthrough on Danzig, how could I communicate it to you in a way that you could publish the story without implicating me or mentioning my name?"

"Paul, it's called 'going off the record'," she smiled. "It's done all the time in London. When politicians or officials want to influence debate on some issue or other by revealing confidential information, they pass it to a friendly reporter who writes the story without attribution."

She looked seriously at him. "We can do that if you want to. I'm your friendly reporter; if I like the story, I'll write it without attributing it to anyone and get *The Statesman* to publish it. Just so long as it's not something covered by the Official Secrets Act."

"No, no," said Muller, "it's not even secret; it's just an idea for how to achieve progress in Danzig and strengthen the League that I think needs to be publicized. I want senior people here in Geneva and in member nation capitals to think seriously about it. Everyone here tends to defer to Eden on these things, and he plays his hand close to his vest. I'd like to get this idea out in the open so people have to deal with it. I can't do that myself and I'd almost certainly be sacked if I'm discovered to be your 'source'—is that the term? But sitting here tonight, I suddenly came to the realization that you could put the idea on everyone's breakfast table while the Council is meeting, and they'd at least have to face it."

They looked around to see if they were being observed. Satisfied they were not, Muller ordered another bottle of Muscadet and began to speak. Wiskemann began taking notes.

***

On January 22, 1936, as the League Council prepared to go into session on the Danzig agenda, *The Statesman* led with a story headlined **"Council Nears Decision to Overturn Danzig Election."** It carried the byline of Elizabeth Wiskemann.

Geneva, January 22, 1936. The League of Nations Council meets today to decide the fate of the Free City of Danzig, which the League has a mandate to protect. As it convenes, it has in hand the Annual Report of its High Commissioner, a respected and determined diplomat, which describes, in graphic terms, a record of repeated attacks on basic constitutional rights of Danzig's citizens perpetrated by the local governing body. That government, called the Senate, is controlled by the Danzig Nazi Party (NSDAP) which won a paper thin victory in an election held in May 1933 and, since assuming power, has repeatedly sought to subvert the Danzig Constitution. The Council has previously admonished the Senate to change its laws to conform to constitutional norms; but promises to do so by the Senate's leadership have been broken.

The Senate claims to speak for all German Danzigers, asserting that its Nazi policies override minority rights. Ordering a snap election in April 1935, the Senate attempted to win a supermajority and amend the constitution; instead it won only another narrow victory. And now the Danzig Supreme Court has ruled that election was riddled with fraud and misconduct. In effect, it said, the NSDAP stole the April election.

Danzig's brave opposition has petitioned the Council to annul the April results and order new free elections. NSDAP mismanagement has decimated the local economy and Nazi bullying has alienated the voters. The opposition is confident of a decisive victory in a new election. So as the Council convenes today, it possesses a new powerful weapon to promote democracy: the chance to order free elections to be held in which Danzig citizens can unseat the NSDAP and bring an end to Nazi rule.

A Nazi party turned out of office by German voters in Danzig! What a thunderclap that would provoke, not just in Danzig, but across all of Europe. Danzig is a small provincial city on the Baltic, but it is a seismograph for all of European politics. Danzig is where democracy and totalitarianism are facing off against one another under the watchful eye of the League, which has an international mandate to protect democratic rights. What a triumph it would be for the League to achieve a clear victory for democracy in Danzig, and how that victory would echo across Europe. It would puncture the image of invincibility that Herr Hitler seeks to project and it would offer hope to other minorities seeking vindication against fascist domination in Austria, in Czechoslovakia—even in Germany itself.

History is waiting for the Council to act.

Muller read the article with admiration; he thought that Elizabeth had captured both the tone and the substance to put the issue in sharp relief. He looked forward to the upcoming meeting with an unaccustomed sense of optimism.

Beck gaveled the Council into session and called on Eden, as Rapporteur. Eden proceeded to summarize the Commissioner's Annual Report. Muller thought he did so quite fairly, quoting from the text—including some of Forster's wild assertions—and listing both the issues carried over from previous meetings that remained unresolved despite Greiser's assurances and issues raised by the new petitions, including the election petition.

When Eden was finished, Beck opened the floor to debate and, in stark contrast to earlier sessions, numerous Council members rose to make statements, all of them critical of the Danzig Senate's behavior. Muller noted that many of them referred to the election petition and expressed support for ordering a new vote; he smiled to himself as he observed copies of *The Statesman*, headlining Elizabeth Wiskemann's story, among the papers strewn in front of most members as they sat around the horseshoe table.

When the session reconvened after lunch, Greiser was first to speak and he delivered a lengthy speech trying to rebut the Commissioner's Annual Report. He belittled the election petition as being 'rife with error' then continued, "Let me be very clear, any attempt by the Council to interfere with the results of the Danzig election would be entirely unacceptable and outside the competence of the Council. The election was challenged locally by sore losers alleging fantasy misconduct. The Danzig Supreme Court has reviewed this baseless claim and rendered its decision. The election stands and the results are confirmed. That ends the matter definitively." He then concluded with a reaffirmation of his—and the Senate's—commitment to the League Council and the Danzig Constitution.

But this time, the Council wasn't buying it, and members intervened to record their disagreement.

The Spanish representative directed a question at Eden, "Mr. Rapporteur, we have just heard the opposition's election petition challenged as being 'outside the competence of the Council'. My question, sir, is whether the Rapporteur will advise us whether or not the Council's scope of authority under our mandate extends to the election petition. My government wishes the Council to take up this issue. Some of the rest of you will have seen the article in today's newspaper dealing with the subject." He held up a copy of *The Statesman*. "I find the proposed course of action worthy of the Council's attention."

Eden looked impassively at the Spanish representative, "Minister de Madriaga, I'm afraid I do not have the leisure to peruse the press, so I am unaware of the newspaper story you refer to," he said archly. "But the subject of the election petition is included as part of the Danzig agenda and is a proper subject of Council discussion and decision."

From his vantage point behind the table where Greiser and Lester sat on either side of Eden, Muller could see Greiser's neck redden and the hand holding his cigarette quivered.

There then followed an hour of disjointed Council discussion, only some of which related to the election petition. Toward the end of the afternoon, Beck gaveled the session into adjournment to allow time for the Council to address a brief item of unrelated business involving a claim by Uruguay against Hungary. Eden beckoned to Greiser to join him in his Palais office on the top floor. As was his custom, Eden excluded Lester from the meeting.

As Stevenson followed Eden out of the hall, he glanced toward Muller and gave him a dirty look.

Greiser had been assigned a small office on the third floor of the Palais, adjoining the Secretariat's Danzig Sub-Section for his delegation to use during the Council session. Viktor Boettcher, Greiser's Foreign Secretary, Muller thought the title wildly exaggerated, headed a team of four aides who had accompanied Greiser. Both Lester and Muller disliked Boettcher, who was Forster's man. He was a slender, dark-haired young man; Lester had remarked to Muller that he had the appearance of a Jew, except for his penchant for spewing Nazi slogans.

Muller decided to take a seat in the Danzig Sub-Section suite to keep an eye on things. After an hour, Greiser came down from his meeting with Eden and slammed the door of his delegation's small office. Even from his seat several offices away, Muller could hear Greiser and Boettcher shouting at one another. Finally, they opened the door and went to find Krabbe, the Section Chief, asking him to request postponement of the scheduled morning Council Session 'to allow for consultations', they told Krabbe. As he departed, Greiser caught a glimpse of Muller and turned toward him, his face reddening. Then he changed his mind, looked away, and strode to the elevator.

Probably just as well, Muller thought. If Greiser had accosted him, Muller was ready to respond in kind—and not necessarily in a diplomatic manner.

The next day was a blur of meetings and hurried drafting and re-drafting of Eden's report to the Council. Polish emissaries from Beck's top floor suite hurried up and downstairs from Greiser's small office carrying papers and messages back and forth. Greiser was called to the Hotel d'Angleterre to meet with Eden's staff and returned looking dejected. Late in the day, Muller learned that Greiser had been summoned by both Eden and Beck.

Stevenson later told Muller what had happened. "Eden read Greiser the riot act and told him that unless he committed formally to enacting legislation resolving all of the petitions left over from previous meetings, he and Beck would insist upon a Council resolution accepting the election petition, annulling the April results and ordering a new vote within 60 days. Beck told him that Poland was ready to provide troops in Danzig to ensure a fair election—like the Saar Plebiscite—even though he had absolutely no intention of doing so; he and Eden cooked up the bluff together.

Great, Muller thought to himself, another canard, his heart sinking. His face must have betrayed his emotions because Stevenson smiled and held up his hand, continuing his account.

"According to Eden, Gresier turned white and protested that he needed to consult with 'his superiors', whom Eden assumed to be someone in Berlin. They gave him an hour. It didn't even take that long; he was back in thirty minutes, a changed man, all wrapped in smiles and bonhomie. He told them he was fully prepared to make the commitment they had demanded and that he thought it was a 'just and fair' outcome. He said that he assumed that upon his agreement, the election petition would be put aside.

'Adjourned', Eden responded.

"They broke out the champagne," Stevenson added. "Then Greiser asked Eden, as a personal favor, to remove language from his draft report that criticized Forster by name. Doing so, he said, would make it easier for him to implement the formal commitment he was making. Beck said he thought that was acceptable and Eden decided to agree.

"So everything was settled," Stevenson concluded.

Without Lester's participation, Muller thought.

Stevenson then looked at Muller levelly. "I don't know who was behind that piece in *The Statesman*," he said. "It angered Eden when he read it; he doesn't like to be pushed in a direction that he doesn't want to go. But in the end, he decided to use it to pressure Greiser. So it turned out much better than it might have done." He winked at Muller and departed.

The Council session that was gaveled into order the next day was pre-arranged and anti-climactic. Eden's report retained language deploring the failure of the Senate to resolve the outstanding petitions but noted satisfaction that the Council had received "a formal and binding commitment by the President of the Senate to enact legislation to resolve the petitions in favor of the petitioners, working in full cooperation with the League's High Commissioner." It declared that the Council had decided to "adjourn" the election petition. And while the report incorporated language critical of actions taken by the Senate that flouted the constitution, it did not name Forster or any of the other individuals responsible for the misconduct.

The report was quickly approved and the session adjourned.

Muller arranged to meet Elizabeth Wiskemann late that afternoon at a small bar called La Rouge, situated on a side street behind the Beau Rivage Hotel. It was frequented by prostitutes and they agreed it was sufficiently discreet that they were unlikely to be observed.

"We could always say I'm your pimp rather than your source," Muller joked. Wiskemann smirked. She was not pleased with the Council's report.

"They missed the boat," she said bitterly. "A decision annulling the vote and ordering a new election would have reverberated through the whole of Europe. Your vision—my story—was absolutely correct and it could have changed the whole framework of negotiations. Confidence in the League is eroding; this was its chance to make a show of strength. The fact they let it slip away is now just another measure of its weakness."

She shook her head. "I'm afraid that's a new reality we'll have to factor into our thinking; we can't rely on the League any longer."

"I'm afraid you're right," Muller replied. "Lester is satisfied that Eden squeezed a genuine commitment out of Greiser and thinks the Council showed enough backbone to force the Senate to be more cooperative. Certainly most of the press is treating it as a victory for Eden and the League. I'm not persuaded; but I hope I'll be proven wrong."

He looked at her. "You wrote a great story, Elizabeth; it made a difference."

"But not enough," she said.

Muller stood to leave, but Elizabeth motioned him back into his seat. "You should know that I received a long cable from my publisher this morning," she said.

"You mean the publisher of *The Statesman*?" Muller asked.

Elizabeth nodded. "Apparently my article on Danzig annoyed some very important people in the Foreign office," she said. "A senior Whitehall mandarin—that's what they're always called when they don't want anyone to see their dirty laundry" she said disdainfully–"anyway, whoever it was telephoned to say that the article had been very unhelpful to Britain's policy of appeasement. He made it plain that His Majesty's government expected a journal of *The Statesman's* stature to discuss 'sensitive pieces like that' before just publishing them willy-nilly."

"You're placed on some kind of probation?" Muller asked incredulously.

Elizabeth nodded. "That's exactly what seems to have happened. All very neatly and surgically done, of course; no fingerprints or resort to veiled threats. But a message nonetheless quite clearly delivered," Elizabeth said.

"This nice little message they delivered makes me even more disappointed that the Council didn't take the bull by the horns and order a new election," she said angrily.

Then she looked Muller in the eye.

"No one knows about your role in all this except me," she said quietly. "But I'm afraid the message is directed as much at you as at me," she said quietly, "and at anyone else who might try to interfere with what His Majesty's Government believes its policy prerogatives to be."

Muller returned her gaze.

"Well, fuck them!" he said, smiling broadly.

***

Lester and Muller returned to Danzig on January 30, a day before the third anniversary of Hitler's ascent to power in Germany. The NSDAP sponsored a large evening rally to celebrate the occasion with a long torchlight parade of goose-stepping SS and SA storm troopers and fiery speeches by Forster, Greiser and others. A stunning display of fireworks lit up the frigid night sky to cap off the event.

Gresier made an appointment for breakfast with Lester a day later. Muller observed that usually Greiser preferred to do business only after plying himself with alcohol; was this early morning appointment a harbinger of change?

Over fried eggs, sausage, toast with jam and black tea, Greiser quickly came to the point. "Commissioner, I wanted to tell you directly that the Senate will complete work within two weeks on revising legislation to resolve the petitions and to meet my commitment to the Council."

Lester replied evenly, "Given your commitment to the Council, I would have expected nothing less."

Muller could sense that Lester was not going to give Greiser a pass.

Gresier lowered his head momentarily, acknowledging Lester's point.

"But more broadly Commissioner," he continued, "I hope we can put aside the differences that have divided us and work cooperatively in the weeks ahead. I know both the Party and the Senate have placed difficulties in your path. I intend to see to it that henceforth the Senate will operate in a manner that observes the constitutional limitations that you and the Council have insisted upon."

Lester replied that he would welcome a better relationship, "But I did not detect any moderating language in the intemperate speeches made at the NSDAP rally a few nights ago."

Gresier bit off some toast and chewed it, then looked across the table at Lester.

"Commissioner, I think it will not come as a surprise if I tell you that Gauleiter Forster and I are not always in accord on all matters and that our tones of communication sometimes differ." He smiled.

"That difference seems generally to be magnified at Party functions like that rally the other night. Forster plays a role at these events that he relishes and that Party members expect; I find myself, of necessity, echoing that role a bit more enthusiastically than I would always like."

He then put down his knife and fork and with elbows on the breakfast table looked squarely at Lester.

"When we were in Geneva, I had occasion to place a telephone call to Reichminister Goering. He advised that I should cooperate with the Council and with you, as he did not want any trouble in Danzig. He also said that you and he had met in Berlin in December and that you had urged him to limit Forster's activities to performing his Party responsibilities. He told me that he would take care of that. So I am now hopeful that Forster will not interfere with my duties as President of the Senate."

Gresier resumed finishing his breakfast. "I would like to get off on the right foot in a better relationship by extending an invitation to you and your wife to dine with Gretel and me and a small group at the Rathaus on Friday night. I have arranged the Red Room for the event, which was no small thing; the Rathaus warden said ladies were never permitted to dine there. But I persuaded him, after some hesitation, that this was time to make history.

"So," he concluded with an uncharacteristic flourish, "I hope you will join me in a fresh start and a history-making dinner."

Lester replied that he would welcome a fresh start and accepted the invitation gracefully.

***

The Danzig Rathaus, or Town Hall, was a splendid gothic structure dating from the 14th century with a soaring filigree tower housing a carillon that could be heard around the City ringing the quarter hours. Mounting the carved wooden staircase and entering the Red Hall beneath an elaborately decorated city emblem, the Lesters and Muller were struck by its elegance: a lavishly decorated ceiling with paintings set in richly carved woodwork and old master paintings adorning the walls. A tall white alabaster partition rose above the fireplace highlighting a large rendering of the red Danzig crown and white cross emblem, offset by decorative gold leaf, and all of it set aglow by dozens of flaming candelabras. The effect was stunning and dignified. The guests were all dressed in formal white tie and gowns; no uniforms–and no Nazi banners, either–Muller noted with satisfaction.

The evening proceeded smoothly, with lively conversation over a meal featuring boar and venison, accompanied by fine wine; a Moselblumchen 1928, Muller observed. Toasts were exchanged, politics was adroitly ignored; conversation flowed and laughter seemed to come easily.

After thanking their hosts, the Lesters and Muller took their leave, driving back together along Langestrasse toward the residence, Elsie observed that it had been the most entertaining and relaxed evening since they had arrived more than two years ago. "Perhaps this really is a new beginning, Sean," she said hopefully. "Maybe that awful Council meeting in Geneva really did make a change for the better."

Seated beside her in the Daimler, Lester squeezed her hand. "It was a very pleasant evening," he replied, evidently not prepared to respond to Elsie's hopefulness.

***

Greiser was as good as his word–better, in fact, completing legislation to resolve the petitions in only a week –and the tension that had seemed so palpable for so long began to lift. Lester decided to take Elsie and the girls on a short ski holiday in the Harz Mountains.

"Someone told Elsie about the Techmannsbaude," he told Muller. "It's a mountain hotel at 800 meters just above Krumhubbel in the Reisengebirge. It sounds a little rustic–all wood, with German proverbs painted on the wall. After sleepless nights for most of January, I'm looking forward to it."

When Greiser learned of Lester's plans he immediately offered an SS van to drive them to the resort. Lester politely declined, thanking Greiser but saying that the rail connections they had booked were part of the adventure. He told Muller that Elsie had looked aghast when he reported the offer. He laughed, "She said traveling in an SS van would feel like being herded off to one of those concentration camps."

While Lester was away, Muller and von Radowitz met for one of their regular dinners, this time at Speishaus, where they played billiards, downing shots of Marchandel gin for every missed shot. Finally von Radowitz racked his cue. "I'm having trouble seeing the balls," he said, laughing as they slid into one of the booths ordering sausage and sauerkraut and another bottle.

Between mouthfuls, von Radowitz gossiped about the political infighting on the German side. "That little shit Boettcher came back from Geneva acting like he had single-handedly saved Greiser's bacon and playing up to Forster."

"Lester said he looks like a Jew," said Muller.

Von Radowitz guffawed loudly. "A fucking Jewish Nazi! That's rich."

"By the way, you know that Greiser called Goering from Geneva," he added.

Muller decided to look non-committal to see what von Radowitz would reveal.

"According to von Neurath, when Eden and Beck put the squeeze on Gresier either to resolve the outstanding petitions or face an order for new elections, Greiser panicked and telephoned Goering directly asking what he should do. On an open line," von Radowitz chuckled. "Goering told him to agree to resolve the petitions and do whatever was required to avoid new elections. He told Greiser he'd handle Forster. According to von Neurath, he told Gresier, 'we'll take care of Danzig when we're ready. For now, your job is to remain in power and keep it quiet."

"So, Gresier's following orders and being nice." Von Radowitz added as he finished the last of the gin.

"Muller, let's get out of here. I need more gin. Liesl's away in Berlin visiting her mother, so let's go out to the dancehall in Ohra. We can listen to the music and maybe find a couple of girls."

Von Radowitz drove a little unsteadily, but Ohra was not far, along Hindenburg Allee on the right, just before Langfur. The dancehall was called The Racetrack and a gaudy neon sign out front made it easy to find.

The room they entered was smoky and crowded, with heavy red drapes covering the walls and setting off the bandstand where a dance band was noisily playing the latest hits, most of which sounded like American jazz to Muller's ear. Tables were crowded together on three sides of a small dance floor. The crowd was mostly male, but Muller noticed more women joining the throng from behind the bandstand.

A working evening, thought Muller. Well, what the hell.

Muller and von Radowitz smoked and drank more Marchendel Double Noll, laughing and cheering on the band. Two striking women approached their table; von Radowitz invited them to take seats and had just poured them generous helpings of gin when Muller noticed the first signs of trouble. When they came in he had observed a group of young blonde SS troopers on the far side of the room, boisterously drinking and whistling at the women. Now he saw that an even larger group of SA troopers had taken tables directly behind where they were seated and had begun taunting the SS table. They suddenly found themselves between the two groups of rowdy storm troopers who were now on their feet yelling at one another.

Bad place to be, thought Muller.

He turned quickly to von Radowitz and the two girls and said, "Let's dance." But as they stood to go to the dance floor, an SA trooper hurled a heavy glass ashtray at the SS table, where it struck an SS man on the neck, opening a wound. A melee ensued as the SA and SS storm troopers charged toward one another and began fighting. Muller was knocked to the ground and crawled toward the near curtain to regain his feet. He saw von Radowitz struggling in the grip of an SA trooper and edged toward him. Muller hit the Brown shirt with a chair, knocking him down, then grabbed von Radowitz, pulling him toward the doorway.

Von Radowitz' temper was up, but Muller finally wrestled him outside.

"We've got to get out of here! You get the car, I'll find our coats inside."

Von Radowitz shook his head as if to clear it, then nodded. Muller leapt over the coat check counter inside the entryway, located their coats and bounded outside as von Radowitz pulled the car up. Muller jumped into the passenger seat. By now the fight was spilling outside and von Radowitz had to dodge clusters of men fighting, finally gaining the highway and speeding back toward the City.

Breathing hard, but laughing with relief, Muller clapped his hands on both knees. "I can just see the headlines, 'German Consul and Commissioner's Secretary Arrested For Brawling With Nazis in Night Club'." He guffawed. "We'd have to get Greiser to suspend publication."

CHAPTER 18

January–May 1936

Smooth cooperation with the Senate continued after Lester's return from his ski holiday and he and Elsie embarked on a determined effort to further improve diplomatic relations by hosting a series of successful dinners and luncheons. Lester began to express cautious hope to Muller that the Council's January decisions really had achieved a breakthrough.

The weather in late February turned bitter cold with temperatures dropping fifteen to twenty degrees below freezing, accompanied by wind-blown snowstorms. On the last Sunday of the month, Muller and Viktor Truczinski took the #9 Tram out to Zoppot for lunch. Bundled in their warmest clothing they walked out on the breakwater where closely packed ice floes extended as much as four hundred yards into the sea, seeming to stretch to the horizon. People cavorted on the icy surfaces, shouting and laughing.

Later, dining in warmth near a fireplace in the Parrot, Truczinski told him that in the outskirts there was a vast ice-harvesting effort underway. There hadn't been much ice on the freshwater ponds, so people had begun forecasting expensive ice next summer. But yesterday, traveling up from Dirschau he had seen carts converted to sledges hauling ice blocks into storage in stone caves. Even though the Vistula was widely known as an ice-free port, he said he had seen ice-breakers at work steaming upriver to keep shipping lanes open. Gydnina, he said, was completely shut down because of the freeze.

He told Muller that the business community was pleased with the apparent truce between the Senate and the Commissioner. He said that initially, there was disappointment that the Council had not ordered new elections, as it seemed certain that the NSDAP would be voted out of office. Economic conditions continued to be hard, he said; the devalued gulen remained a burden on shopkeepers and others. But at least the specter of a confrontation with the League, and the threat of Polish intervention that would likely follow, seemed to have faded.

"Long term though, I'm not optimistic, Muller," he said. "Germany, Poland and the League all have competing interests in the City which are fundamentally incompatible. There's a reason Danzig is being portrayed in the press as the powder keg of Europe."

"But the goal of British appeasement policy is to wrap everything into a single package that will bring all those issues into alignment as part of an overall European peace plan," replied Muller. He thought it wouldn't hurt to inject a little optimism into their conversation. "Eden seems committed to that goal."

Truczinski looking very skeptical nonetheless nodded. "He certainly seems to be." He paused, then added, "We all better hope that he can get there."

***

A week later, on March 7, 1936, another stunning event began to unfold. At 9:30 AM a squadron of nine Luftwaffe planes roared over Cologne, Germany, circled above the spires of the great cathedral and headed West, across the Rhine, in flight formation. As thousands in the street crowded forward to watch, German army cyclists, wearing steel helmets and rifles slung over their backs, rode into the square, followed by nineteen battalions of goose-stepping infantrymen and thirteen artillery battalions, who marched across the bridge over the Rhine and entered the industrial heartland of Germany, called the Rhineland.

The Rhineland had been declared a demilitarized zone by the Treaty of Versailles. It comprised all German territory west of the Rhine to the French border as well as areas east of the Rhine that included the cities of Cologne, Dusseldorf and Bonn. Thirty minutes after German troops crossed the river, the German Foreign Minister, Constantin von Neurath, summoned the British, French and Italian ambassadors to the Wilhelmstrasse and handed them a note declaring that Germany had "restored the full and unrestricted sovereignty of the Reich in the demilitarized zone of the Rhineland."

At noon, Hitler called the Reichstag into session and announced his decision to re-militarize the Rhineland. The Assembly broke into wild cheering and shouts of 'Seig Heil'. At the close of a bellicose speech invoking Teutonic blood and swearing never to capitulate, Hitler extended an olive branch: "We pledge that now, more than ever, we shall strive for an understanding between European peoples, especially for one with our Western neighbor nations. We have no territorial demands to make in Europe! Germany will never break the peace."

The news electrified Danzig. The NSDAP newspaper *Verposten* hurriedly printed a special edition reporting the events under a banner headline 'Treaty Defied; Rhineland Rearmed' and the local radio station broke into its patriotic music programming to announce the news with feverish excitement. The Senate decreed the rest of the day a holiday and Forster hastily assembled an NSDAP rally in the Central Square.

Muller gathered what information he could and translated the news to Lester, who received it more calmly than Muller himself.

"The major qualm I have is whether the French will over-react and create a crisis," he said. "I frankly hope they will not. This is a case of Germany re-occupying a part of Germany, after all. It's not as if they invaded some third country."

"But Commissioner, this is the second time in less than a year that Germany has unilaterally violated the Versailles Treaty," Muller replied. "Isn't that grounds for alarm?"

"It is," Lester nodded. "Hitler's tactics certainly are alarming. But in this case he simply took something that was going to be offered to him anyway in any sort of peace settlement."

Lester then looked at Muller adding, "Actually, it is a little scary that Hitler just seems to take what he wants. I have to confess that Elsie and I have had a conversation about what the family should do in the event some spark should ignite war. I think it's unlikely," he shrugged, "but these are unsettled times and journalists keep saying that we're sitting on a potential powder keg here."

"What did you decide to do?" asked Muller, not telling Lester that he had been wondering about the same thing.

"We talked about trying to catch a steamer to Scandinavia," Lester said. "But we didn't get much beyond that. It's a little hard to plan for the unknown.

Lester shrugged, and turned back to the business at hand. "Let's see what our friends Papee and von Radowitz have to say about the Rhineland when they get back from their capitals."

Papee called on Lester the next day after returning from Warsaw, saying that he had lots of good tidbits of information to share. "About the only advantage of being related to Beck," he said, "is that sometimes I get more information than I would otherwise. That was certainly the case on this trip."

"We're all ears," said Lester, inviting Papee and Muller to be seated in the comfortable chairs alongside the big conference table.

"It seems Hitler sent Goering to meet with Beck two days before the re-occupation took place," Papee began, "asking Poland to remain neutral if the French were to declare war. He sent a separate emissary to Mussolini on a similar mission, asking him to keep Italy on the sidelines too, but said that he intended to keep France and Britain completely in the dark about his plans and present them with a fait accompli.

"Well, you know Beck, Commissioner," Papee continued. "He loves the diplomatic dance; food and champagne were brought in to fortify them as they negotiated back and forth, and apparently Goering proceeded to get quite drunk. Beck said that Goering began perspiring profusely, admitting that he was terribly nervous about Hitler's decision and even going so far as to reveal that it had been taken against the Army's advice. Goering kept referring to France's 100 divisions on its frontier with Germany, saying that the paltry force of 30,000 lightly armed soldiers Hitler was proposing to send into the Rhineland could simply be swatted away by the French and leave Germany's western border defenseless against a French invasion. If Poland were to invade from the East too, he said, the Reich would be doomed. According to Beck, Goering got very overwrought and practically begged Beck to commit to Polish neutrality."

Translating for Lester, Muller pictured the image of Goering Papee was describing; certainly very different from the forbidding presence they'd met in Berlin a few months earlier, Muller thought to himself.

"Beck can be very cunning," Papee went on. "He told me that he had been closely following reports from our embassy in Berlin detailing the seriousness of the economic crisis Germany is suffering. Apparently there are long lines to buy food, serious shortages of shoes and items of clothing and increasing popular discontent. He said that during Goering's handwringing performance, it suddenly dawned on him that Hitler's Rhineland occupation gambit was just that; a stunt. If it succeeded, it would distract attention away from the dismal economy and rekindle patriotic support. If it failed, well, he was in big trouble anyway—maybe even at the end of his rope. So he decided to roll the dice. Forget the army's advice; it was a moment to be bold."

Lester was paying close attention, Muller noticed, clearly intrigued by Papee's account.

"So," Papee continued, "Beck said his decision was easy. He told Goering that Germany could always count on Poland's neutrality and support, especially in light of their bilateral non-aggression pact that he, Beck, had initiated. He said, he put a happy Goering back on his plane with a fresh bottle of champagne and sent him on his way.

Later he told me 'I'll get full credit for backing Hitler if he wins his bet. But if he loses, and the French invade, Hitler's probably finished, so at that point, I can simply change my mind and invade from the East if a good opportunity presents itself. I win either way,

"But Beck also told me that he didn't think the French would do anything about the re-occupation, and it looks like he's right," Papee concluded. "Much as I hate to admit it, the stalwart French that we've counted on for so long seem to have lost their nerve."

"What does this mean for Danzig?" Lester asked.

Papee shook his head. "I'm sure Hitler doesn't want to create any new tensions in the wake of his re-occupation. I think we're safe for the time being—though I'm not sure how long that will last. Hitler's got to be feeling pretty good about himself at the moment: he's just thumbed his nose at the Treaty, he's shown that he's smarter and braver than his generals, he's cowed the French, the British just want to keep talking, and the League is silent. What does he do for an encore, I wonder?"

"Anyway, Beck believes he aced it," Papee said, standing to leave and turning toward Muller. "Much as I will ace you, Muller when we get back on the tennis court again sometime soon."

Muller accepted the challenge and they agreed to a match in two days' time.

Von Radowitz returned a day later from Berlin and came to see Lester. His analysis was strikingly different. He said that von Neurath had been the brains behind Hitler's decision. "The key to this puzzle was Locarno," he said.

Seeing Lester's quizzical look, he added, "I was a little vague about that too, so here's the background.

"In October 1925, Germany, Britain, France and Italy signed agreements in Locarno Switzerland;" hence the name, he added, smiling. "The agreements provided that the Rhineland would remain de-militarized permanently, and Britain and Italy would guarantee the German and French borders against any 'flagrant violation' by one against the other. It was quite an important deal at the time, being widely understood as an agreement by Germany to voluntarily accept a de-militarized Rhineland, essentially replacing the terms imposed on her by the Treaty.

"In 1930, British and French troops withdrew from the Rhineland and the French began building their Maginot Line. From our standpoint, getting French troops out of the Rhineland was important, because–notwithstanding guarantees by the British and the Italians–we always feared that if we took action the French didn't like, they'd simply annex the Rhineland and there wouldn't be anything we could do about it. The Rhineland was a kind of collateral that the French controlled. When they left, that changed things."

Changed things positively for the Germans, but negatively for the Poles, Muller thought, remembering how upset Papee had been in relating the same tale from a Polish perspective.

"So, picking up the story," von Radowitz continued, "once Hitler assumed power, and even as he railed against the Versailles Treaty, von Neurath was careful to have him always promise to respect any treaty Germany had willingly signed–like Locarno–*but only so long as the other parties also abided by it.*" Von Radowitz emphasized his words and gestured to underscore their importance.

"I hadn't been paying much attention, but last year the French negotiated a Mutual Assistance Pact with the Soviet Union. Germany objected that the agreement was an unacceptable plan to encircle Germany. The French government dismissed the German objections and submitted the treaty for approval by their National Assembly last month. That was the opening von Neurath was waiting for.

"He gave Hitler a series of briefs he had been busily preparing, arguing that the Franco-Soviet Pact was in clear violation of the Locarno Treaties. Hitler could then declare to the world that since the French had breached their Locarno obligations, Germany would no longer be bound by them either, so Germany was lawfully entitled to re-occupy the Rhineland.

"It was perfect cover and hoisted the French on their own petard."

"Clever diplomacy," Lester said, reflecting on von Radowtiz's statement. "Muller, in translating Hitler's statement to the Reichstag for me, you read me something he said about Locarno, am I remembering right?"

Muller nodded. "That's correct, Commissioner, Hitler accused Britain and France of violating the Locarno Agreement."

"Which I didn't pick up on," mused Lester.

Then Lester turned back to von Radowitz. "Very interesting. Please continue."

"A real struggle arose internally," said von Radowitz. "The military chiefs were all opposed to Hitler's plan, fearful of French invasion. By contrast, von Neurath was confident in his analysis and certain that the French would not react. In the hours before the order to march was given, the German Chief of Staff, General von Blomberg, pleaded with Hitler to call it off and Goering was in despair. Hitler ignored them and gave the order. You've read what happened," he concluded. "It was a masterstroke.

"So the Wilhelmstrasse is riding high at the moment," von Radowitz said with a smile and a touch of pride. "As we predicted, the French haven't moved a muscle, and they won't. Eden gave a speech in the Commons saying something to the effect the 'the future is more important than the present'. So he's not going to make any trouble. We know he's keen on negotiating some kind of overall settlement in Europe. Now that our influence with Hitler is decisive again, maybe Whitehall and the Wilhelmstrasse can come to agreement. At least that's our hope," he added.

Lester decided those sentiments warranted a toast with good Scotch whiskey.

After von Radowitz departed, Lester refilled their drinks, and sat back down, reflecting, twirling the whiskey in his glass and gazing out the window. He sighed and shook his head.

"We live in strange times, Muller. I have no idea how to reconcile the two accounts we've gotten from Papee and von Radowitz. They sounded so different, but maybe they're both accurate; I can't tell."

He paused again. "I think one lesson we have to draw from this is that Hitler seems able to do pretty much what he wants in Germany. There don't seem to be any constraints. He can apparently override his military leaders, ignore objections from insiders like Goering, seize on a plan by his Foreign Minister, and simply roll the dice, risking war with France; his choice and his alone. And, we saw last year that he's prepared to murder anyone standing in his way. How do you deal with a leader like that?"

***

A few days later, Lester requested Greiser and members of the Senate to visit his office. The cordiality that had prevailed since the January Council meeting continued. Lester was pleased to note that interference with the press had nearly ceased, and, during the meeting, the Senate agreed to remove a number of objectionable propaganda programs in the schools. Lester was especially pleased to reach accord on his long-standing insistence that only the Danzig flag, not the German swastika, should be flown above public buildings in the City.

Greiser remained after the other Senate members had departed. It was evident that he was seeking assurances from Lester that he would introduce no Danzig issues at the Council meetings scheduled for May 11–13 in Geneva. Lester told him that cooperation the two sides had shown since January was heartening and he could see no reason to burden the Council with any issues from Danzig.

"Commissioner, I can see no reason for any change in the excellent relations we've established," Greiser said. "We still want to return to the Reich, but we've got to face the reality that Danzig is likely to remain a Free City for many years to come. I've heard some of our supporters predicting that a Rhineland coup of some kind will take place here too, but I tell them that's mad; everyone knows that Poland would fight an attempted takeover in Danzig.

"It's one thing to reassert control over German territory as the Fuhrer did in the Rhineland; trying to recover the Free City, with its League mandate, would be an entirely different matter and would very likely provoke war. That kind of talk isn't productive and I've discouraged it."

"I'm glad to hear that," Lester replied. "That's certainly my view too. But Greiser, if you're really looking for ways to improve conditions here, why not try reaching out to the opposition? You're all Germans, here. You represent roughly half of them; but the other half feels excluded. You may have to bend some of your National Socialist principles a bit, but why not put out peace feelers and try and draw at least some of the others into your camp? God knows the economy is a mess and needs all the help it can get."

"Commissioner, that's one of my goals," Greiser responded enthusiastically. "The longer I hold this office, the more I feel a sense of responsibility to all Danzigers. And you're right, that would entail redirecting some Party goals. That makes it a challenge," he said ruefully, "but a worthy goal nonetheless."

After Greiser left, Lester looked quizzically at Muller. "Is this the new Arthur Greiser?" he said, "or is he just following Goering's orders and doing a great job of play-acting? I suppose we'll find out soon enough. But I certainly like this new persona better than the old one."

***

The 90th Council meeting convened on May 11 1936 and was among the shortest and least contentious to date. The only excitement occurred at the opening, when the Ethiopian delegate was invited to sit at the table for an agenda item involving the Italian sanctions program. The Italians had formally annexed Abyssinia by that time and the Italian foreign minister, Baron Aloisi, objected to the Ethiopian delegate's presence, arguing that since 'Abyssinia or Ethiopia—or whatever you want to call it' no longer existed as a state, it was not entitled to have a delegate at the Council. He then marched out of the Hall attended by journalists and photographers. Five minutes later, when the agenda item was finished and the Ethiopian delegate departed, the Baron reappeared and took his accustomed seat, wreathed in smiles and bonhomie.

Lester and Muller were sitting behind the table watching the performance. Lester spoke out of the side of his mouth, "Italians seem to have a special affinity for arrogance."

During the trip to Geneva, Lester had told Muller that he expected to be offered an extension of his appointment beyond January 1937, when his assignment was scheduled to expire. "If I receive sufficient support from the League and the member nations, I'm prepared to accept another twelve months, until January 1938. I hope you'll agree to stay."

Muller readily agreed. He was enjoying the work and he and Lester got on well. There were no immediate prospects for 'a life', as Lester had delicately put it earlier. He had no interest in trying to resurrect his relationship with Eirene– at least not at the moment. So, yes, why not? With all of its frustrations, the Danzig puzzle was a compelling process and he was playing a real role. Still, he was curious.

"I didn't know this was under discussion Commissioner," Muller said.

"I kept it under wraps," replied Lester. "I didn't even speak of it to Elsie until very recently.

"The subject first came up during that tense January meeting when I let it be known that I might be forced to resign unless the Council acted. Eden and Avenol wouldn't hear of it, but somehow Beck found out and began promoting the idea of replacing me with a Polish High Commissioner.

"One of the very few amusing moments of that session was laughing to myself about how–if that were to come about–the Germans' own stupidity would have produced the worst result they could have conceived. Ha! Can you imagine how the Wilhelmstrasse would have reacted to the prospect of a Polish High Commissioner?" Lester smiled at the incongruity of it all.

"Anyway, last week Avenol wrote me to say that he and Eden wanted me to stay on for another year and that they had persuaded Beck to agree. I decided I wanted to stay to see this out. Elsie readily agreed, and Muller, I'm glad you will remain my reliable right hand."

The next day the Council met privately. Members roundly applauded Lester's performance and there was strong support for a one year extension of his appointment. Even Greiser, who had been invited to participate, supported the appointment, praising Lester's 'professionalism'.

With Eden presiding, Beck himself made the motion for the extension. It was unanimously approved.

Later, Muller was able to corner Stevenson for an hour in the bar at the Hotel d'Angleterre. He shared the conflicting information he and Lester had received on Hitler's Rhineland occupation.

Stevenson grunted. "We've received various reports too," he said. "We weren't shocked by it. In fact, we were in active discussions with them about a military aviation agreement as part of a general settlement, and returning the Rhineland was one of the incentives we had on offer. But it was Goddam cheeky of them just to snatch it like they did."

Stevenson heaved a big sigh, and ran his hand through his hair.

He was clearly under heavy pressure, Muller thought.

"Eden's come to the view that Hitler will violate any agreement he decides he wants to," Stevenson said quietly. "So what we need to do is get him into a new overall agreement, as soon as we can, but one that will have enough tradeoffs so he'll have to stick to it. That's what we're working on now. But the French are not on our side. They're furious at Hitler for just thumbing his nose at the Treaty again. We leaned on them pretty hard not to react militarily, though I don't think they were ever really going to do anything anyway. But relations between us are very strained right at the moment. That's making it very difficult to reach a common position that we can use to negotiate an overall deal with Germany.

"They've got elections coming up later this month. If what we're hearing is correct, the Popular Front is likely to win the majority and form the next government. Can you believe Leon Blum, a Jew, as Prime Minister, heading a French government composed of socialists and even Communists?" Stevenson shook his head disbelievingly. "But ironically, those guys may be more inclined to align with us than the merry-go-round of more conservative governments we've had recently. We'll have to see."

Then he turned brightly to Muller. "Meanwhile you didn't need that new election option you and that reporter tried to railroad through the Council back in January did you? What was her name?"

"I have no idea what you're talking about," said Muller with a straight face.

"Well, no matter," said Stevenson. "It seems to us that the Senate received the Council's message loud and clear and has been behaving itself just like we expected it would."

Muller returned Stevenson's grin. "Right; it's all due to the Council's leadership," he said, keeping the straight face and concealing the sarcasm he intended.

"By the way, Lester asked me to stay on during his extended term and I've agreed," Muller added.

"That's good," Stevenson said. "If things remain calm like they are now, we should have plenty of time for tennis in September."

"But they don't generally seem to do that, do they," Muller replied as they shook hands.

***

On the return trip to Danzig, Lester was relaxed but pensive. He told Muller he was reassured by the strong show of support he had received from the Council.

"It's difficult being so far away from Geneva and so isolated in the peculiar atmosphere of Danzig," he said. "Every day brings new issues that I have to decide with no rulebook to guide me. I try to do the right thing, but inevitably I second-guess myself. You've been a big help, Muller. But it's very reassuring to find the Council so strongly in my corner. Greiser behaved impeccably. I think we really did turn a corner with the Senate in January." He paused, then continued, "But I've never seen the League so disorganized, Muller. The Italians simply defied the rules and the League's sanctions have proved worthless. Now they've taken their seat in the Council as if nothing happened; but of course, something *did* happen, and there appear to be no consequences. The League can't even decide whether, or when, or how, to end the sanctions—which are now largely being ignored anyway."

Lester gazed out the compartment window at the passing countryside. "The League's prestige has been severely damaged. If it can't get the rest of the world to enforce collective security in a blatant case where one country invades and conquers another country, who's going to take it seriously in some other smaller dispute?"

"You mean, like enforcing constitutional rights in Danzig?" asked Muller.

Lester smiled at him wryly. "I'm afraid I do. The reality is that our hand has been seriously weakened."

***

The first morning back in Danzig, Lester called Muller into his office and handed him a letter to read. "I've gotten my share of strange messages from the United States," he said, "but this takes the cake."

Under the letterhead of The Shoe Club of America, New York City, the letter asked Lester for his help "in adding to our collection of worn shoes from notables all over the world."

Muller read further in amused disbelief. "Having completed our collection of worn shoes of statesmen and notables from all walks of life in the United States of America, we are now seeking to add to our collection the worn shoes of similar personages in other countries. The Shoe Club feels that a collection of shoes that have been worn by men of renown will be an inspiration to the younger members of the industry not only in craftsmanship, but to show them that their livelihood is a service to mankind of which they can be proud."

It closed by asking Lester to "bespeak his graciousness by sending an old pair of shoes and completing the enclosed autograph form."

"Wait till I show this to Elsie," Lester chortled. "She'll finally realize how important I *really* am."

"The Shoe Club," he said to himself again chuckling.

***

A day later, a letter arrived from Greiser, 'I would like to express on my own behalf and on behalf of the government of the Free City my hearty congratulations and my special pleasure at your reappointment. I hope that your further term of office will be under a lucky star and that your selfless mediation will in the future work out for the good of the Free City.'

"Well," said Lester. "Things have come a long way since January."

CHAPTER 19

Summer, 1936

As Danzig approached the summer solstice, the daylight lasted longer, but the atmosphere began to darken.

The first incident came as an unwelcome surprise.

Franz Schiller had invited Muller and about twenty other members of the Police Band and Chorus to a picnic at his uncle's farm in the hills west of the city, close to the border with the Polish Corridor. It was the first Saturday in June and a warm sun and soft breezes lifted everyone's spirits. Schiller had organized two minibuses for the 30 minute trip and all of the guests had brought along food or drink to contribute to the event.

Muller found himself sitting with Guste and Pyotr Starbusch. Guste was a soprano in the Chorus with whom Muller had become acquainted. She introduced her husband who was a Polish Post Office employee, proudly showing off her swelling belly as she did so.

"Only a little over a month to go," she said merrily. "We hope it'll be a girl this time."

Pyotr explained that they had a two-year-old boy whom they'd left with his mother.

"Constantin is walking now," he said laughing, "and into everything."

"It would definitely not be relaxing to bring him along today," Guste added. "This is probably our last little holiday junket for a while. So to celebrate, we left Max at home and brought along some of Pyotr's mother's special summer sausage." Guste pointed to a basket at her feet.

"Special?" asked Muller.

"Very special," responded Pyotr. "It's actually my grandmother's recipe. Pork, beef, garlic, mustard seed and smoked for a couple of days. Very special," he repeated.

"I'm looking forward to trying it," Muller replied smiling. "It sounds much better than smoked eel."

Their buses followed a narrow country lane for the last mile or so, then turned left into a short dirt trail that delivered them to a neat farmhouse with a heavily thatched roof and a barn that was visible off to one side. In front of the farmhouse was a grassy field that sloped gently down toward the country lane. As everyone disembarked, Muller could see that, at the top of the slope, a long table had been fashioned, using wooden planks nailed to saw horses and covered by sheets of red and white checkered oil cloth. Large platters were already laid out with potato salad and sauerkraut alongside bowls heaped with early lettuce. At one end, he could see a keg of beer was ready for business. Off to one side, a fire pit had been dug and a pig was being roasted, skewered over hot coals.

The guests added their gifts—Muller had brought along a bottle of his favorite Stobbes Marchendel Double Null gin—and soon everyone was chatting and drinking merrily. One of the band members, Rudy, a colleague of Schiller's and a formidable trumpeter in the band, had brought along an accordion; he began playing folk songs and soon everyone was singing along. After a while, the pig was declared to be done and Schiller removed it from the pit, slicing juicy pieces that he put on a platter which people passed around.

Guste made certain to add several slices of the 'special summer sausage' to Muller's plate and after trying it, he declared it a winner.

"Special," he said, smiling.

Schiller's aunt had brought out several large blankets which she laid on the grass and people sat down with heaping plates and mugs of beer, laughing, talking and enthusiastically consuming what everyone agreed was a splendid feast.

Suddenly there was a loud honking. Two trucks bedecked with Nazi banners were slowly driving past the farm with a dozen or so young men hanging onto slats on the flatbeds. They began shouting curses at the picnickers, one of them even dropping his trousers and pointing his bare fanny up the hill.

"Commie bastards, Fucking Bolsheviks"

"You're all traitors. Get the fuck out of here."

Honk, Honk. Then the trucks were past them, disappearing behind a copse of trees.

The laughter and chatter had stopped. People sitting on the blankets stared at one another.

Schiller's uncle walked among the blankets with a large pitcher of beer, refilling mugs. "Sorry, my friends. That was part of an SA troop from the village. We have a bit of a disagreement with one another. They criticize me because I'm not a Nazi and I tell them to mind their own business. So every now and then they make trouble." He shrugged, seemingly unconcerned.

Conversation resumed in desultory fashion, but the incident had cast a cloud over what had seemed a perfect picnic. Muller finished his plate, savoring one last bite of sausage, stacked it on the table, and walked over to where Schiller was conversing with his uncle.

"I don't have any jurisdiction here," said Schiller as Muller came up to them, "but I'm trying to persuade Uncle Max to let me go down to the village police station and have a word with the boys there on a cop-to-cop basis and get them to tell those troopers to lay off."

"Won't do any good," said Schiller's uncle. "Most of the cops out here are Party members and those that aren't, don't want to get involved. I've been through this before, Franz. We got harassed during the election too. But I have leverage here. Some of those boys have family members that need to work here during the harvest. That usually keeps things from going too far." He filled Muller's beer mug from the pitcher. "Franz has told me about you, Mr. Muller. It's nice to have a celebrity come to visit."

Muller reddened, "I'm hardly a celebrity, Mr. Schiller. Your nephew is the strong man here; he's been very helpful to us on a few occasions."

"And he's a mean bass in the chorus," Muller added smiling.

The elder Schiller nodded. "We try to take good care of Franz and his family, especially since his parents died a few years ago. I'm sorry you didn't bring Helga and the children out today for the party, Franz; we always enjoy seeing them."

"Fritzie's my ten-year old," Schiller said to Muller, then turned back to his uncle. "Fritizie had a track meet for the Catholic Youth Organization this afternoon, so Helga had to stay back along with Freda. Otherwise they'd have loved to come."

Max Schiller poured them all some more beer, then said to Muller, "This is a bad time for Catholics in Danzig, Mr. Muller. The Party's cracking down on us hard. Frankly, I'm fearful it's going to get worse. I've been telling Franz that he should begin thinking about finding some way out, among other things for his family's sake. But he's stubborn."

The words were no sooner out of his mouth than the honking began again as the two trucks, now filled with even more troopers drove down the lane, this time headed in the other direction. The troopers, some without shirts, began shouting more slurs and curses and then, as the trucks slowed, they began lobbing firecracker bombs in the direction of the picnickers. People jumped back off the blankets and ran up toward the farmhouse at the top of the slope. Guste Starbusch shrieked as one of the small bombs went off next to her and she scurried up the hill toward the farmhouse.

Franz Schiller ran down the slope directly toward the trucks. Muller saw him draw his pistol from his service holster and stop to aim, both hands extended in front of him holding the big pistol. As he fired, the rear tire of the second truck exploded and the truck veered toward a ditch on the far side of the lane, coming to a sudden stop and lurching.

"Get out of that truck," Schiller yelled at the men as they struggled to hang on to the sides of the truck that was now leaning heavily to one side.

"*Out! Now!*" Schiller said walking toward truck pointing his gun directly at the men, who suddenly, realizing they were in serious trouble, quieted down and quickly jumped to the ground, several of them raising their hands.

"Please don't shoot," said one of the men, "we didn't mean any harm; we were just playing tricks."

Schiller fired a shot just over their heads. They jumped and cringed, more of them raising their hands and backing away.

"Take off your pants and boots," said Schiller, his pistol pointed at the men. "Now!"

The men began doing as he ordered, jumping around on one leg, than another, to remove their footwear and trousers.

"Pile them under the gas tank," Schiller ordered.

The men complied.

"Now get in that other truck."

The men ran to the first truck and jumped onto the back.

Schiller stepped onto the lane and opened the empty truck's gas tank. The gasoline ran out onto the clothing the men had heaped there. Letting the tank empty entirely, Schiller stepped toward the truck filled with the men, now thoroughly frightened, his pistol still pointed at them. Without taking his eyes off the men, he pulled his lighter out of a pocket, fired it and tossed it on the gasoline soaked clothing and footwear. They blazed into flame and quickly turned the truck into a fireball.

As the flames burned themselves out, the remains of what had been the truck rolled on its side.

It became deathly still, Schiller still pointing his pistol at the men in the truck, who watched him fearfully.

"Identify your troop," Schiller said.

"Sturmabteilung Danzig Heit 27," several men said together.

"Name and rank of commander."

"Ludwig Magendanz, Oberleutnant."

"Rudy," said Schiller to the accordion player behind him, still without taking his eyes off the back of the truck. "Write that down."

"Yes sir," Rudy responded, pulling out his notebook and a stubby pencil.

Schiller began walking slowly toward the truck, lowering his pistol very slightly.

"I am Detective Franz Schiller of the Danzig Police Department. We have power over the leaders of your Party and will ensure that you are disciplined for your misconduct. This property is owned by my uncle, Max Schiller. If there is any form of attempted retaliation against him or his family, we will know where to find you and punish you. You have been warned."

Schiller continued. "I was going to shoot a couple of you in the kneecap just to illustrate how uncomfortable that can be. But I have decided I will instead let all of you think about how that might feel."

Schiller suddenly fired another shot over the heads of the men in the truck. Several shrieked in terror, one began vomiting over the side of the truck.

"Do you understand that you are under an order to stay away? Answer me!" Schiller shouted.

"Yes sir," the men said.

"Louder," said Schiller. "*All of you.*"

"*Yes sir!*" the men shouted.

Schiller lowered his pistol. "Now get out of here, before I change my mind and begin shooting you sorry scum."

The driver of the truck put it in gear and gunned the engine, sending it careening down the lane, the men in back holding on to avoid being thrown out.

Muller and the other guests had stood transfixed watching the event unfold. As Franz Schiller returned his pistol to its holster and began striding back up the grassy slope, there was a smattering of applause and quiet words of thanks for his quick reaction.

Muller could see that Schiller was still furious. "Those strutting little hoodlums, trying to throw their weight around that way; I just can't abide them."

Schiller's uncle came up and thanked him, offering him a mug of beer. Schiller shook his head. "I'm afraid I'm not in much of a party mood any longer."

Pyotr Starbusch came up and stood next to them putting his hand on Schiller's shoulder.

"That was a nasty thing and we're all grateful for your brave response, Franz. I think none of us feels much like picnicking anymore either. So," he said turning to the others, "let's all pitch in to clean everything up so our gracious hosts don't have more work to do on our account. Then I think we'd better return to Danzig."

The minibuses deposited a disconsolate group of guests back at the Central Square. As individuals thanked Schiller and moved away to return home, Muller hung back. Finally, he and Franz Schiller were alone.

"I know you need to get back to your family, but let's walk over to the Café Werzler over there." Muller gestured. "I'd like to share a thought."

Schiller agreed and they took a table in the sun away from the other guests. They both ordered espresso.

When the waiter had left, Muller turned to face Schiller. "That was a courageous thing you did this afternoon."

"I'm afraid it was rash and stupid," Schiller replied. "I was thinking about it as we drove back on the bus. What I did was effectively to paint a bullseye on my back." Schiller looked across the Square, busy with people out in the sunny weather, most laughing and smiling, seemingly carefree.

"Oh, I can handle things in the short run," Schiller continued. "As a cop, I've got the goods on at least half of the top guys in the NSDAP. I can put the squeeze on them to sit on those young punks and keep them away from my uncle's place. At least for now."

Schiller sighed. "But what happens if those bastards really do take over? They'll probably be able to sack the Chief and I'll be one of the next people they'll target." He shook his head, then smiled faintly at Muller. "In fact, what I did today maybe moved me up on the priority list for removal from the force–and who knows what other consequences."

Schiller took a large sip of espresso. "You heard Uncle Max today telling me I should find a way out of this mess. After today, that's probably even better advice. But where can I go? What can I do? I certainly can't go to Germany and Poland doesn't seem like much of a solution either."

"That's what I wanted to talk about," said Muller quietly, raising his head to look directly at Schiller. "You probably know that my family owns a private bank in Zurich."

Schiller nodded. "I confess I did check your background so I know that much at least." He smiled. "Strictly business, of course."

"Of course," Muller smiled back. "But let me tell you a little bit about Swiss private banking. The business of Muller & Company—and our competitors—is to manage the assets of wealthy individuals and families and to keep their secrets. Private banking started during the French Revolution and the Napoleonic wars, when private wealth across Europe was at risk. Aristocrats and merchants were desperate to preserve their wealth and the secrets that accompany wealth. Switzerland has remained neutral in all the years since and over that time, Swiss banks have built a strong reputation for safeguarding assets and information. Ours is not the oldest or the biggest of the banks, but it's been very successful and enjoys an excellent reputation."

Muller paused to take another sip of his coffee. "My father is Chairman and my elder brother works there, and will one day succeed him. I've never taken a strong interest in the business. I've always wanted to be a diplomat—though, I frankly never expected that profession would entail the kind of violence that I've encountered here." He smiled wanly. "Like you, I'm very unsettled by Hitler next door and the NSDAP Party here. You know better than anyone else that the Commissioner is a target and, by proximity, I'm at risk too."

Schiller nodded, "You are a target; I've heard mutterings that I haven't chosen to share with you. Nothing specific, mind you; but because you're so closely identified with the Commissioner, and because he is so roundly hated by the NSDAP, it rubs off on you too."

"I assumed that," Muller replied. "I'm afraid it goes with the job. I don't like it and sometimes it scares me. But assuming I don't get unlucky and wind up beaten to a pulp by a bunch of Nazi goons, I have a modicum of confidence that the League will protect me and somehow get me out of here if this place explodes—which, I think we both know, is a distinct possibility."

Muller made the now almost instinctive glance around where they were seated to be sure no one could overhear. "But you don't have the same lifeline," he said looking squarely at Schiller.

"That's why I raised the subject of my family's bank in Zurich."

Schiller leaned closer, listening intently. "Go on, please."

"The bank needs a person with your investigative skills and your experience in dealing with the Nazi mentality," Muller said. "Zurich is located next door to Germany; the border runs right through Lake Constance. The cross border issues are serious now and only likely to get worse. My father talks about problems with refugees from the Nazis—mainly Jews—trying to safeguard assets, but there are also newly-wealthy Nazis trying to do the same thing. There are increasing pressures from both the Swiss and German governments affecting the business, some of them covert and underhanded. Swiss people don't like to talk about it, but there's a brisk cross border smuggling trade, most of which involves money and therefore impacts the banks, including Muller & Company."

"I don't understand how this applies to me," said Schiller, cocking his head uncertainly.

"I've spoken to both my father and brother about all this during my visits with them at home," Muller replied quietly. "They're worried; they need someone like you to help navigate all these grey areas and deal with the often sketchy people that come into play. If you agree, I'll speak to them about the idea of hiring you and moving you and your family to

Zurich. Zurich is German-speaking—a little different accent," Muller said, smiling and using his best Zurich sing-song tempo to make his point, "but nothing serious. I'd like you to think about letting me talk to them."

Schiller pushed aside his expresso cup and laid his forearms on the small table, making the same glance over his shoulder before responding in a low voice.

"Muller, I don't need to think any further. I'm at risk here. So getting out with a chance to take on the kinds of work you've just described sounds like a good idea. Helga and I have spoken often about trying to find some way out, but neither of us could come up with a plan. You've just offered one. She'll be just as pleased as I am to jump at it. So, yes talk to them; I hope they like the idea."

"Actually, you've just made the afternoon a lot nicer than it was until a few minutes ago," Schiller said, smiling. "I got pretty depressed during the bus ride back thinking about what I did and what it might mean for my family. I feel much better now."

They stood and shook hands.

"Thanks, Muller. Helga will be furious when I tell her how I confronted those Nazi troopers at Uncle Max's farm; but she'll be thrilled about your idea."

**

Two days later, the NSDAP newspaper *Verposten*, published a photograph showing an opposition figure named Kurt Blavien leaving the High Commissioner's residence. The newspaper reported that the Blavien was a notorious socialist radical whom Danzig authorities had later arrested. What was this 'enemy of Danzig' doing meeting with the High Commissioner, the newspaper wanted to know, inviting readers to submit their own interpretations, and setting off a week-long diatribe of orchestrated attacks on both Blavien and Lester. The *Verposten* added to the controversy by revealing that its photograph had been obtained from the police, who had permanently mounted a 'teleobjective kamera' on the house across the street from the Commissioner's residence to monitor the visits of 'disreputable characters assisting the Commissioner in his anti-Danzig plots'.

A day later the SDP newspaper *Volkstimme* was seized.

Lester complained to Greiser who promised to secure Blavien's release and restore publication of the *Volkstimme*. But reports of beatings of Danzig citizens by NSDAP gangs rose sharply.

Boettcher, the Senate's Foreign Secretary, made an appointment to inform Lester that the police had been instructed to arrest Catholics wearing uniforms in the Corpus Christie Procession scheduled for the next evening and asking Lester to intervene with the Bishop to avoid trouble. Lester replied sternly that the uniforms issue had been resolved after the January Council meeting and told Boettcher that re-opening the issue again now was unacceptable. Boettcher protested that this was a different uniform issue, but Lester curtly dismissed him.

"What a nasty young man," Lester said, "so arrogant and full of himself. Still," he sighed, "I'd better send a note to Bishop O'Rourke informing him of the message. But I'm damned if I'm going to urge him to discourage his people from wearing their uniforms."

Sunday June 12 dawned sunny and warm and Lester took his family out to Zoppot to swim and watch the equestrian jumping competition. Muller had been at the Parrot until late Saturday night with Truczinski and decided he didn't want to go back out to Zoppot that afternoon and deal with the crowd. Instead, he strolled to the Commissioner's residence and spent a leisurely afternoon seated in the garden, napping and reading. He helped himself to Lester's bar for cocktails, then walked back along the

Langgasse toward his boarding house, stopping to enjoy a summer meal of potato salad and chilled poached fish on the terrace of the Café Vaterland. It was strangely deserted for a summery Sunday night that was still brightly lit by the high angle of the sun. But he was enjoying his dinner and his Graham Greene novel, entitled *England Made Me*, was an entertaining tale of suspense and smuggling in Stockholm–and of course he was enjoying a bottle of Stobbes Marchandel gin to which he had become very partial.

Suddenly, he heard shots fired from the direction of the Topfergrasse, near the Commissioner's residence. Quickly paying his bill, Muller hurried back along the Langgasse, hearing more shots, sounds of splintering glass and voices shouting. Turning the corner, Muller saw that St. Josephaus, home to the Catholic Center Party, was being stormed by SA Brown shirts. Uniformed troopers were on the roof, breaking windows and clambering inside. Over the uproar, he could hear a piano loudly playing the banned former German national anthem, *Deutschland Uber Alles*, which suddenly stopped with a discordant crash. Doors had been broken down with axes and fighting could be seen inside the building, now spilling out onto the street. The SA men were wielding clubs and Muller could see the glint of brass knuckles. Injured men and women began streaming out of side doorways, many bloody and all looking wildly around in bewilderment. More seriously injured civilians began to emerge, leaning on one another or being carried to the street curbs where some were attacked again by Brown shirts using clubs and delivering booted kicks.

Police were nowhere to be seen, then whistles suddenly blew and a squadron of black-uniformed police officers charged into Topfergrasse toward the Josephaus. Ignoring the attacking Brown Shirts, the police began hauling civilians away toward waiting Black Maria vans. The melee inside had by now degenerated into small groups attacking one another on the sidewalks and the street. Muller could see what looked to him like

German sailors and dockworkers, evidently supporters of the Catholic Party, fighting back fiercely, stabbing with daggers and frog stickers at suddenly frightened SA troopers. Finally, as police whistles and sirens howled, exhausted men backed away from one another. Wounded from both sides lay on sidewalks and slumped in the gutters.

Ambulances began arriving as the police continued to arrest civilians. Then SA commanders, shouting above the fray, assembled their men and began marching toward Langgasse, near where Muller was standing. He could see many of the Brown Shirts bloodied and limping, but their fierce determination remained on full display as they fell into step and began to bawl the familiar *Horst Wessel* song, swinging their arms in unison, and disappearing around the corner.

In the pandemonium, Muller found Franz Schiller standing with another police officer off to the side, observing events and looking angry.

"Schiller," said Muller breathlessly, "what the Hell is going on?"

Schiller quickly took Muller by the arm and backed him up to the wall of a nearby apartment, keeping his arm on Muller's shoulder. "Careful, Muller," he hissed, "or they'll take you in too. These are not our guys; this is one of those specially trained Schutzpoliezei units I told you about. They're here to complete the dirty work of the SA. One of our informants alerted us to what was about to happen so the Chief sent Kurt and me out to have a look."

Just then, two big policemen emerged from the St Josephaus building carrying a uniformed SA trooper, who appeared to be dead. They lay the body on the sidewalk, then, laying a sheet over it, resumed arresting men and women in civilian clothes. Only a handful of medical orderlies had arrived and Muller moved to help with the wounded. Schiller steered him back to the Langgasse. "Not a smart idea, Muller. You could get hurt. Go home. Then come down to see me at the station tomorrow afternoon and we'll talk."

The next morning, Muller told Lester what had happened. Lester replied that he had returned from Zoppot just before midnight and saw activity near Topfergrasse, only a few hundred yards away from the front entrance to the residence. He said that he'd tried to go out and investigate, but a police detachment had been posted near the entrance and they refused to let him pass, directing him back into the residence.

Lester summoned Greiser, who came to the residence quickly, his face grim.

"Forster's decided to go on the offensive," Greiser explained. "I'm doing what I can to regain control, but this is a crisis and I'm not sure how much authority I'm going to have." He left hurriedly.

Lester and Muller glanced at one another.

"Looks like someone in Berlin has had a change of heart," Lester said.

Muller agreed, wondering to himself if they would target the Commissioner–and him.

That same afternoon, Forster addressed a rally at the Sportshalle, railing against the opposition and aiming especially venomous attacks at Lester, as "a handmaiden of the Bolshevik League of Nations and a friend to enemies of the German people". Squads of belligerent SA troopers marched through downtown Danzig carrying swastika flags and assaulting anyone not returning the Hitler salute. Muller, going to meet Schiller, narrowly escaped a confrontation by leaping aboard a passing tram as an SA contingent approached him.

"A nasty business, Muller," said Schiller. "The Catholic party was holding what they thought was a secret rally, but someone obviously squealed. Forster's apparently declared war on the Catholics, so he decided to send the SA to storm the meeting and he ordered the Schutzpoliezei to arrest whomever the SA left behind.

"Our best count is 13 hospitalized, half a dozen with serious injuries, and another 35 or so treated and released. Only one death, that SA guy you saw them carry out. His name was Deskowski. We know him; a very fat drunk who could never hold a job until he joined the SA. He has a record of heart problems and the coroner said he clearly died of a heart attack. But Forster is pressing for a formal death certificate saying he was killed by the Catholics. So far, the coroner is sticking to his guns. We'll see.

"The Chief's having a tussle with Forster about releasing the civilians arrested last night. The Chief knows he can't touch any of the SA troopers. But he's still got enough muscle to spring the Centre Party people. It is getting dicey, though. Someone's decided to unleash Forster–someone in Berlin, maybe? We're not sure where this ends."

They shook hands. "Give my regards to the Commissioner," Schiller said. "I'm going to have one of my men escort you back to the residence so you don't get stopped by any of the gangs. Oh, and Muller," he glanced around, then said softly, "I hope you can let me know about Zurich soon."

"I will," said Muller.

That night, in a rural section of the Free City, SS Black Shirts attacked a local SDP leader's home. An exchange of gunfire ensued and two SS troopers and the local politician were killed. The NSDAP *Verposten* labelled the SS deaths 'assassination by a cowardly traitor to the Reich'. Translating the story for Lester, Muller was uneasy. This was the first time gunplay had been involved.

A day later, Lester met with opposition figures, including some victims of the St. Josephaus attack. They presented him with an array of weapons used against them. "These are souvenirs, Commissioner; they'll serve as reminders of what we're up against." They told Lester they were preparing to form their own paramilitary militias. "We have to be able to protect ourselves, Commissioner. That guy the SS shot the other night never had a chance. They're using trained killers."

Lester strongly counseled against arming themselves. "Your strength is in your legality." But he admitted to Muller later that given the deteriorating atmosphere, he could understand their position.

On June 14, the NSDAP staged a massive funeral in honor of the SA Brown Shirt Deskowski, whose death the coroner now publicly asserted was attributable to a savage attack by a club or blunt instrument. In death, Deskowski was elevated to 'Hero of the Reich' and an extravagant ceremony honored his 'martyrdom for the Fuehrer'. A thousand goose-stepping uniformed SS and SA storm troopers paraded past a reviewing stand where a swastika-festooned casket lay in state. The leaders of the German SS and the German SA flew to Danzig from Berlin, bearing a funeral wreath from the Fuehrer. The rally was held in the part of the Central Square closest to the Commissioner's residence and loudspeakers pointed in its direction, enabling Muller to hear the incendiary speeches. Forster, who spoke last, threatened to take control of Danzig by force if necessary. In nearly hysterical terms he declared that "patience with those opposing National Socialism is exhausted; within three weeks we will restore tranquility to Danzig and force our adversaries—and the Commissioner who encourages them—back into their holes."

After the service, knots of uniformed storm troopers roamed the streets looking for trouble. Lester instructed Muller that he was not to leave the Residence or return to his boarding house that night. "You will dine with us and spend the night in the guest room."

Muller decided to do as he was told.

With order in Danzig unraveling, Lester summoned Greiser the next morning and told him that current behavior by the NSDAP was inexcusable. "You leave me no choice but to call the Council's attention to this deplorable state of affairs. If I have to bring in foreign troops to restore order, I will do it. But the situation is intolerable."

Greiser was apologetic and said he shared Lester's alarm. "I've arranged to fly to Berlin this afternoon with Forster and von Radowitz," he said. "I'm going to try to fix things. Please hold off sending any alarming messages to Geneva."

Watching Greiser getting into his car as he departed, Lester looked glum. "It's come to a pretty pass when we have to send those three stooges off to Berlin just to keep the peace in Danzig," he said to Muller. "And Germany's not even a member of the League.

"In just two weeks, we've gone from harmony to a virtual state of siege. It's as if somebody pulled a switch somewhere. Is this just Forster suddenly flexing his muscles? Somehow, I doubt it."

Lester turned to Muller, "I'm suddenly feeling very vulnerable."

CHAPTER 20

Summer, 1936

Despite the worsening disorder, planning for the visit of the German cruiser *Leipzig* proceeded smoothly. Diplomatic protocol called for officers of the vessel to be saluted at receptions to be hosted by the Consul Generals of Germany and Poland, the Danzig Senate, the High Commissioner and the Danzig Harbor Board. These were similar to arrangements made the previous summer for the visit of the *Admiral Scheer*. On that occasion, Greiser and his Senate allies had marched out of the Commissioner's reception to protest the presence of Hermann Rauschning, but he had fled Danzig, so that was no longer an issue and the Poles, who had the diplomatic lead, declared themselves satisfied with the arrangements.

The Commissioner's reception was set for June 25 beginning at 6 PM. The weather was not perfect as it had been a year ago; the sky was pewter grey, but it was warm and humid. After the confinement of the long Baltic winter, the uniform practice in summertime was to err on the side of being outdoors. So the Commissioner's garden was once again prepared with two bars, high tables with ash trays and snacks and seating areas next to the flower beds.

Muller observed to himself that an especially significant difference was that Eirene was not at his side for this reception. It was becoming a more distant memory.

The Lesters, elegantly attired, stood on the terrace steps leading to the garden preparing to greet the arriving guests, with Muller–also in formal dress–attending them. Suddenly, a uniformed SA storm trooper marched through the residence to the terrace and peremptorily came to attention before Lester. He stuck out a gloved hand with an envelope, handed it to Lester, then, drawing himself to attention, raised his right arm in the Nazi salute, barked "Heil Hitler," turned on his heel and marched back toward his car that was waiting at the entrance.

Startled, Lester handed the envelope quizzically to Muller, who opened it and stared a moment at the message.

"It's a formal message addressed to you from Greiser," Muller said. "It reads, 'Kindly be informed that no officers of the *Leipzig* will call upon the representative of the League of Nations in Geneva by order of the German Supreme Commander. In light of this order, I have directed that no representative of the Danzig Senate will attend this evening's reception either'."

Lester looked at Muller in stunned silence. He asked Muller to read it again, this time wincing, as if struck.

"Those bastards," Lester said, then more loudly, "bastards!" Straightening, he slapped his hip. "Muller, station someone at the entrance to explain that the reception has been canceled because of unforeseen events. Elsie, you might as well tell the staff to begin shutting down and cleaning up."

Lester strode back inside, where he mounted the stairs to his office and firmly shut the door.

Muller did as he was told, then poured himself a whiskey and sank into one of the padded wicker chairs next to a bed of yellow lilies. Elsie joined him a few moments later, declining his offer to fetch her a drink. Lester came across the garden to join them, carrying two glasses and a bottle of whiskey, which he plunked down on the low table next to them. Filling the two glasses, he handed one to Elsie and topped off Muller's.

"Here's to being snubbed by Hitler," Lester said with a wry smile.

Muller noted that his boss had apparently regained his sense of humor.

"I telephoned Geneva and left a message for Avenol," Lester explained. "I assume that he will agree that this constitutes a serious diplomatic incident warranting a response."

Muller sipped his whiskey waiting for his boss to continue.

Lester sank back in his chair, idly watching the waiters removing the reception tables and the two bars. "I feel as if I've been punched in the belly. This was all calculated to inflict the maximum embarrassment and humiliation."

He reached out and took Elsie's hand in his. "Sorry, my dear," he said, looking affectionately at her.

Elsie returned his gaze and smiled. "Sean, we're Irish. They have no idea how tough we are."

Lester squeezed the hand he was holding.

Just then Papee strode briskly across the terrace toward them. "I just heard what happened. It's an outrage."

Lester invited him to join them for a post-snub drink, but Papee declined.

"Look," Papee said, "I know this whole thing was aimed at you and the League, but let me tell you it is also an unacceptable insult to me and to Poland. *We* are empowered by the Treaty to have exclusive responsibility for the conduct of the foreign affairs of the Free City of Danzig and *we* established the diplomatic rules of engagement for that damned German ship to pay a visit here. Interfering with our diplomatic authority this way is simply unacceptable; I'm on my way now to read the riot act to Greiser. I know Beck will be furious too."

Papee clapped Lester on the shoulder. "Have that drink, Commissioner; you deserve it–several, in fact. You're not in this alone."

Muller awoke the next morning to read a furious personal attack on Lester published by the NSDAP's *Verposten*. It called Lester "superfluous" and "the champion of opposition Bolsheviks, Communists and other vermin." It blamed Lester for the recent violence in the city, asserting that "his campaign of political agitation caused the injury to a half dozen National Socialist patriots and the death of three martyrs for the Fuehrer." The tone of the article then turned threatening, "The League of Nations representative in Danzig must leave us National Socialists alone; do not try to interfere again."

SA and SS contingents resumed aggressive street marches.

Gresier refused to respond to Lester's insistent demands to meet and restore order.

Von Radowitz sent a message to Muller asking him to call on him that afternoon at his consular residence, "Entering via the side entrance, please."

Muller showed Lester the message. "It sounds a little like the cloak and dagger charade he put on last year when he was trying to get rid of Forster."

"You'd better go find out," Lester said. "But be careful."

As the weather was fine, Muller decided to walk to von Radowtiz's residence. He varied his pace, stopping frequently to look about him, trying to determine if he was being followed, but so many people were out strolling in the warm sunshine that he couldn't tell. Frankly, he decided, he really didn't care one way or the other. At least there was no sign of any roaming Nazi gang.

There was no doorbell at the side entrance, so he rapped on the glass pane. Von Radowitz himself opened the door and shooed him in, closing the door quickly behind him and pulling the curtain over the window pane.

"Sorry about the side door business," von Radowitz said, "I'll explain. But let's at least sit in the garden; it's pleasant and no one can see us." He smiled conspiratorially, guiding Muller to the garden where two wicker chairs with bright blue padding were arranged beside a table holding a tray with two glasses and a bottle of Marchandel gin.

After the ritual toast, von Radowitz got down to business. "This whole thing was cooked up by Forster appealing directly to Hitler. The Wilhelmstrasse didn't know anything about it and I wasn't told until about the same time you were. But now we're under strict orders not to have anything to do with the Commissioner until further notice. That's why I wanted you to use the side door. Do you think you were followed?"

Muller shrugged. "I couldn't tell; there are a lot of people on the street today."

"You probably were," von Radowitz said, "but no matter; I'll deal with it. The snub and Forster's attack on Lester and the League is causing us serious headaches; the directive to keep Lester in the dark is not helping, so let me tell you where I think things stand."

Von Radowitz proffered his lighter for their cigarettes, then pocketed it and leaned forward.

"When I flew to Berlin last week with Forster and Greiser, Forster was in a terrible mood. He was angry that Lester publicly pushed back after that aggressive speech Forster made threatening to take control of the streets. And he was angry at Greiser for having agreed to Lester's demands. Greiser was a basket case, caught between his commitments to Lester and the League and Forster's insistence on attacking Lester—and through him the

League. Forster kept pounding on him during entire trip and by the time we landed, Greiser looked like he was ready to have a seizure.

"The plan had been for all three of us to go to the Wilhelmstrasse, but there was a second car at the aerodrome to meet us. Forster announced to me that he had other business, and proceeded to hustle Greiser into the other car with him and off they went. I had no idea where they were going, but figured maybe they'd see Goering.

"We were supposed to meet back at the plane in two hours. I went to see von Neurath, who told me that he and Goering had agreed that Forster needed to tone down his behavior and Goering said he'd take care of it. So I assumed things were under control."

As von Radowitz refilled their glasses, his hand showed a tremor. This is not good, Muller thought to himself.

"I got back to the aerodrome right on time and found Forster and Greiser already in the plane with the engines turning," von Radowitz said.

"They'd have left without me if I'd been late," he added angrily, shaking his head. "It's a short flight but this time the mood was entirely different. Forster was puffed up and all smiles, clearly in charge. Greiser sat mute and didn't say a word; he appeared completely cowed. I knew something must have happened, but I didn't know what. Forster waved away my inquiries and Greiser just stared into space."

"I finally cornered Greiser yesterday alone, without Forster, and demanded to know what had happened," von Radowitz continued. "He told me that he and Forster had been driven directly to the Chancellery and escorted into Hitler's private waiting room. Moments later, Hitler appeared and invited them into his palatial office. Greiser said Hitler was in a lively mood, bantering with Forster as the three of them sat on a comfortable balcony. He said that Forster reminded Hitler of the *Admiral Scheer* reception last summer, when Lester, in Forster's words, 'insulted the

German Navy' by inviting Herman Rauschning to his reception. Hitler apparently reacted strongly, saying that Rauschning was 'a turncoat'. Greiser quoted him as saying 'I took that man into my confidence, speaking to him right here, in this office, then he betrayed me and published that hateful letter, vilifying our National Socialist cause; 'oh yes,' Hitler said, according to Greiser, 'I remember that traitor very well'."

Muller sat quietly, but his stomach sank. It was just as Lester suspected; Hitler considered the Rauschning letter to be a personal insult. And since Lester entertained Rauschning at last year's reception, Hitler had classified Lester as an enemy too.

Muller decided he had to interrupt. "I'm finding all this very disturbing."

Von Radowitz held his hand up, his expression grave. "I'm afraid it gets worse. According to Greiser, Forster then proceeded to tell Hitler that the *Leipzig* was scheduled to visit Danzig during the next week, which would give Lester the chance to insult the German Navy again by inviting– if not Rauschning, who was no longer in Danzig–then other Bolshevik and Communist opposition members to his reception. Gresier told me Hitler's mood turned black as he struck the table in front of him and snarled 'that must not be allowed to happen'."

I can't believe what I'm hearing, Muller thought.

Seeing Muller's shocked expression, von Radowitz nodded as he continued. "And that's when Forster suggested that the Fuehrer personally order the vessel's officers not to attend Lester's reception. 'Good,' said Hitler, according to Greiser. 'I'll order it at the last minute to humiliate him.'

"And that, Muller, is how this episode came about," von Radowitz said grimly.

"Orchestrated by Forster but ordered by Hitler personally," Muller burst out. "Good God, von Radowitz, that's disgraceful."

"Unfortunately, there's more," von Radowitz replied. "Gresier went on to tell me that Forster complained to Hitler that Lester was continuing to block National Socialist progress and he said that the League had extended Lester's appointment for another year in office, so Lester would continue to be an obstacle."

Von Radowitz paused before continuing. "Greiser said Hitler reacted by instructing Forster to 'go after' Lester. Hitler said the League was weak and no longer a threat after its defeat by Italy. He said that he'd had enough interference by 'this Lester', as he referred to him. 'So do what you have to do,' he told Forster."

Muller's head was spinning. This sounded like a declaration of war.

"There's more," said von Radowitz. "According to Greiser, Hitler then turned to him, saying that he had heard from Forster that he was not obeying Party orders and was accommodating Lester and the League. Hitler said he knew that was what the Wilhelmstrasse wanted Greiser to do. 'But that's not what I want any longer,' he said, according to Greiser. 'I want you to follow my orders, Greiser; Bobbie will tell you what to do. I expect you to obey, is that clear?' Greiser told him it was."

"So, said von Radowitz, coming to the end of his report, "the Greiser I saw on the flight back to Danzig was a very unnerved and submissive Arthur Greiser."

"And we've seen the results," he continued, spreading his hands, "Lester humiliated by Hitler's deliberate snub and Forster pouring it on with his newspaper attacks. And Forster may have more up his sleeve. We don't know what else he may be planning."

"And you're ordered to have nothing to do with us, is that right?" Muller inquired.

"Yes, but it's not so simple," replied von Radowitz. "This whole thing has stirred up a diplomatic hornet's nest because the Polish government sees the attacks on the Commissioner as a threat to Polish interests in Danzig. They're up in arms and threatening economic retaliation. You know how precarious Danzig's finances are; a Polish economic squeeze could be very damaging. Consequently, both von Neurath and Schacht are now clamoring for Forster to be reined in. They're trying to persuade Hitler that having Lester remain in office as a Commissioner–even if it cramps Forster's plans–is preferable to a quarrel with Poland that might cost a lot of money."

"I don't know how this tug of war is going to end," von Radowitz concluded. "But I'm urging my Berlin contacts not to cut off relations with the Commissioner. I wanted you to hear the story, in part in hopes that Lester can find a way to co-exist with the Senate in a way that's less confrontational; someone needs to keep the lid on this kettle that's threatening to boil over."

"Forster's the one raising the heat," said Muller, angrily. "I suggest you have a word with him about that."

He finished his gin and stood to go. "I'll inform the Commissioner. Kindly let me out by way of the front entrance."

Von Radowitz did so.

Muller walked briskly back to the Residence. He didn't care if he was being tailed or not. He mounted the staircase and went directly into Lester's office.

"You're not going to believe what I have to tell you, Commissioner," began Muller, as he recounted von Radowitz' disturbing revelations.

Lester listened intently.

When Muller was finished, Lester stood up and walked to the large windows facing the Central Square, open to the warm summer breeze. He remained standing for several minutes, seemingly lost in thought. Then he turned to Muller and spoke decisively.

"We need to get to Geneva immediately," he said. "I'll send wires to Avenol and Eden. You make the travel arrangements."

Muller consulted timetables and proposed they leave from Dirschau after dinner, taking the route through Warsaw, Prague and Vienna to Zurich, then down to Geneva. It would take a half day longer, but it would eliminate the connection through Berlin, which seemed like a good idea. Lester concurred, so they packed quickly and arranged for the car to drive them south to the station in Dirschau in time to dine before boarding the Warsaw leg of the journey.

"I told Elsie everything as I was packing and suggested that this might be a good time for her to take the girls off to Sweden or someplace else, "Lester said to Muller as they prepared to depart.

"But she wouldn't hear of it. Elsie has an aversion to being bullied," Lester smiled. "I guess they'll probably be safe enough while we're away in Geneva," he said, partly to reassure himself. "They're not Forster's target; I am."

Lester and Muller finally reached Geneva on the evening of June 30. As they disembarked and gathered their bags to take the tram down the hill from Gare Cornavin to the Hotel de la Paix, Muller bought a special afternoon edition of the *Journal de Genève* carrying a banner headline, "A Lion Ignored."

The newspaper reported that Haile Selassie, Emperor of Ethiopia, had addressed the League of Nations Assembly that afternoon to lodge a personal plea for justice with the 52 member nations. In what the newspaper described as "an eloquently moving speech," the man who was often referred to as "the Lion of Judah" had reminded the delegates of their responsibilities under the League's Covenant, described Italian aggression, including the use of mustard gas that killed thousands of soldiers and civilians, and asked the Assembly, "What response will the League offer to my people?" The newspaper reported that the Emperor stood at the podium, "a slender, dignified figure wrapped in a dark cloak, waiting for an answer." It concluded, "The response was a thunderous silence. The only audible sound in the hall was that of delegates shifting in their seats in embarrassment."

Lester shook his head sadly as Muller translated the story. "That report doesn't describe an atmosphere here that seems likely to have much sympathy for our plight in Danzig."

Muller was unable to meet with Stevenson the next morning, so he went to see Krabbe at the Palais in the Danzig Sub-Section. Krabbe had visited Danzig earlier in the year where he had been treated badly by members of the Senate, especially Viktor Boettcher, who had lectured him about "improper interference" by the League in NSDAP programs. Krabbe had returned to Geneva very sympathetic to the difficulties under which Lester and Muller labored. He was the one Muller turned to for help in getting copies of the Secretariat's formal documentation on Danzig issues, as Lester had directed.

Krabbe welcomed Muller warmly and expressed his anger at the humiliating snub inflicted upon Lester in the *Leipzig* affair. "I'm pleased that the Commissioner and you decided to come to Geneva. The League is in enough trouble now on other fronts; it can hardly roll over and permit itself to be insulted in Danzig without responding in some way."

Muller inquired what kind of League response was being talked about in the corridors, but Krabbe said that discussion of the precise steps was "still a bit vague."

I'll bet, Muller thought. The League always seemed to get 'a bit vague' when it came time consider actually doing something.

Krabbe, though, took him by the elbow and guided him into the corridor and, looking around to be sure they weren't being observed, surreptitiously handed Muller an envelope. "There's a draft memorandum being circulated among a very restricted group by the Legal Section. It's a rationale for how the League can discontinue its role of protecting the Danzig Constitution. It's still very much in draft and rather controversial, as you would imagine, but I thought you should have a look at it. I'd appreciate it if you and the Commissioner would keep this for yourselves and not disclose to others that you've seen it. It's very sensitive."

"Who commissioned the memorandum?" asked Muller.

"The Secretary General," replied Krabbe, putting a finger to his lips.

Muller thanked him and went in search of someplace private to read the document. Since the Council was not in session, he walked over to the large reception area outside the Chamber where delegates could mingle and converse. Finding it deserted, he purchased a cup of coffee from the small café and selected a leather armchair where he sat down and read the memorandum. It was a tightly-reasoned text written in the lifeless prose of a lawyer who was hermetically sealed off in disengaged analysis.

The gist of the argument was that the League guarantees toward Danzig had not come into force by reason of language in the Treaty of Versailles itself, but rather by means of a formal resolution adopted by the League Council. The Danzig guarantees were "not guarantees *to* Danzig but guarantees *regarding* Danzig, which were adopted by a resolution of the Council of the League, making it an active party in the creation of the guarantee and not a passive entity on which the guarantee was imposed by the Treaty." The italics were the author's. At great length, and in stilted language, the document concluded that since the League Council had created the Danzig guarantees by resolution, it could change them by resolution too. The current situation in Danzig, it observed, where a Nazi-controlled Senate refused to be bound by League guarantees to the Danzig

Constitution, was reason enough for the League to decide simply to abolish them if it chose to do so.

Muller shook his head and returned the memorandum to its envelope. Here was the Secretary-General confronting the Nazi challenge to solemn League guarantees toward Danzig by looking for ways to wash his hands of the guarantees. That's a strange way to pursue collective security, he thought.

Muller finally tracked down Stevenson that afternoon. Predictably, Stevenson's attention was on matters unrelated to Danzig.

"Eden's in shock. We were in Council session this morning dealing with the sanctions issue and suddenly, just to our right, a man stood up—we later found out he was a Czech—shouted something about the League failing to protect small countries, then he pulled out a pistol and proceeded to shoot himself in the head. God, it was awful."

Muller was stunned; the violence of the outside world intruding right into the very Chamber where the League was deliberating how to keep the peace. Another discouraging omen, he decided.

When he was finally able to steer the conversation to the subject of Danzig, Muller found Stevenson only mildly sympathetic to the Commissioner's predicament and seemingly resigned to diminished League influence in Danzig.

"The *Leipzig* incident was very regrettable. I can understand how personally uncomfortable it must have been for the Commissioner. But Germany is no longer a member of the League. How can the League discipline a non-member? Especially when that non-member is Germany, with whom we have much bigger fish to fry. What are we supposed to do, demand that Hitler apologize? He'd laugh in our faces—or more likely just ignore us."

Muller kept his temper. "It was only five months ago that the Council tabled the opposition's petition to order a new election."

"Out of the question," Stevenson interrupted him. "Last week Neville Chamberlain, who's Chancellor of the Exchequer, and a growing power in the Cabinet, by the way, made a speech in Commons flogging Eden for his sanctions policies as imposing burdens on the League beyond its powers to execute. Can you imagine how he—and the Cabinet—would react to the idea of the League trying to police an election in Danzig? And the House of Lords is charging Eden with undermining appeasement by continuing to oppose Germany's legitimate demands. Do you think for a moment they'd support an election in Danzig aimed at embarrassing Hitler?"

"Face it, Muller," he said. "Danzig's a small part of a bigger game, and frankly it's smaller today than it was when you started."

"Hastened by the decline of the League itself," retorted Muller.

Stevenson's manner softened. "I'm afraid that's right. Look, Eden's scheduled to meet with Beck tomorrow to take up Danzig. I'll try to get word back to you on what they decide."

***

Muller and Lester met the next morning for breakfast. Muller handed him the envelope containing the Legal Section's memorandum and briefly described its message. Lester took the envelope but said he doubted Avenol would have much influence over disposition of their issue. "Eden's still the Rapporteur for Danzig and wants to manage it in his own way. I get the sense he wants Poland to take the lead in trying to persuade the Germans to climb down. He and Beck are meeting today and I have an appointment with Beck this afternoon which I'd like you to translate; I find his French damnably difficult to comprehend."

That afternoon, Beck ushered Lester and Muller into his top floor office suite in the Palais. It had a sweeping view facing northeast toward Montreux, overlooking the sun-drenched lake which was dotted with sailboats and Lake steamers. Lester walked to the open window. "Summer days in Geneva always seem so serene, Minister," he said, admiring the view, "especially from high up in the Palais. I'm afraid there's a lot less serenity in Danzig."

Beck was very tall, with a narrow head that was elongated by his receding hairline. He joined Lester at the window.

"I find Geneva dulls the senses to the real world," Beck said. "Someone observed that the League might get more accomplished if it were obliged to function in the third class waiting room of the railroad station in Calcutta; there's some truth in that, I'm afraid."

He gestured for Lester and Muller to be seated around a small conference table.

"Eden and I met this morning," Beck began. "He's still shaken by the suicide in the Great Hall. The man was only 20 feet away. I don't think he felt a sense of personal danger; Eden's a man of great courage. He performed bravely at the front during the war and I'm not suggesting he was afraid. But he's under enormous pressure in his role as Foreign Secretary. I think witnessing the violence so near at hand just underscored the stakes in his quest for a peace agreement."

"Commissioner, on the subject of Danzig, we've scheduled a Council session on July 4, the day after tomorrow. We're glad you took the initiative to travel here, as conditions there seem to have gotten out of hand. We've summoned Greiser to appear before the Council and explain himself."

"That's a start," Lester replied. "But it's pretty clear that Greiser's acting under pressure from Germany–even from Hitler himself."

Beck nodded in agreement. "Eden seems inclined to give us the lead in trying to reason with Germany on this issue. They're no longer in the League, of course, which limits the Council's ability to influence them. My government, on the other hand, is a chief beneficiary of the Treaty provisions dealing with Danzig. In our view, the snub inflicted upon you in the *Leipzig* affair was not only a serious breach of protocol toward you and the League, but also a breach toward Poland and our Treaty rights. We don't want the Germans to get the impression that they can simply ignore legal norms and conduct any policy they like in the territory of the Free City."

"What's the plan?" Lester inquired.

"Probably a Council resolution empowering Poland to negotiate with Germany," Beck replied. "I intend to remind them that Poland will not accept a German takeover in Danzig. We need to reaffirm the League's authority over Danzig. I think you know that I've not always been so keen on that line, but I regard Germany's recent behavior as a grave threat to our interests so I intend to treat the matter very seriously."

"Minister, I mean no disrespect," Lester said, leaning toward Beck, his arms on the conference table. "But I would like to make clear to you that the paramount issue at stake in any negotiation that the Council authorizes Poland to undertake with Germany is the integrity of *the League's* role in defending the protections afforded by the Danzig Constitution. As Commissioner, I will not be party to an agreement that papers over that issue or concerns itself only with bilateral issues affecting *Polish* relations with Germany. A negotiation mandated by the Council to deal with the League's—and my—authority to exercise our treaty responsibilities regarding the Free City must not compromise that authority."

Beck regarded Lester levelly. Muller could see his jaw muscles tightening.

"I will take your comment as an expression of your view concerning your responsibility as High Commissioner," Beck said evenly, "and not as a challenge impugning my negotiating integrity." He looked sharply at Lester. "You have acquired the reputation of being dogmatic and inflexible on occasion, Commissioner. It will perhaps come as no surprise that our embassy in Berlin reports that officials there criticize you as biased and unbending. Eden tells me he is hearing the same from their embassy as well."

Lester's expression remained impassive; he didn't rise to Beck's bait.

Watching Lester, Muller thought that Lester probably took what Beck intended as criticisms instead to be compliments. He stifled a smile as he completed translating.

Beck paused, "I accept that there are fundamental conflicts between National Socialist doctrine and the protections guaranteed by the Danzig Constitution and that defending those protections makes you a target of the Nazis. That appears to be part of your job now. But your obligation is to obey the mandate of the Council in carrying out your responsibilities," he said, "just as it is for me in carrying out negotiations that the Council may direct. Neither of us is at liberty to get ahead of our mandate."

Lester smiled at Beck and offered his hand. "I think we understand one another, Minister."

As Lester and Muller rose to leave, Beck added, "And Commissioner, do not think I am unmindful of the difficulties under which you operate in Danzig. You have an enormously challenging assignment. Papee keeps me regularly informed. He holds you in high esteem and reports you are doing an admirable job. Let's find a way through these problems together."

Lester and Muller went into the reception area outside the Chamber and, after getting coffees, found two seats in a quiet corner.

"I had to fire that shot across Beck's bow," said Lester, smiling. "I'm not going to preside over a sell-out and I wanted to make sure that message got through. I think it did."

Muller nodded in agreement. "I think that's safe to say."

"I told Eden the same thing," Lester said. "Here's what I think is going on. Eden and Beck have set up a two-track negotiation with Hitler. Eden has the bigger agenda, trying to find some formula to achieve arms limitation in Europe. Beck's role is to block Hitler's designs on Danzig. But a tradeoff is implicit and will be obvious to Hitler: If he'll make a disarmament deal with Eden, Beck will agree to concessions in Danzig. In short, we're becoming a bargaining chip in a bigger game."

"It's very clear that I am to subordinate my role to these larger goals," Lester continued. "Greiser's policies and resolution of the *Leipzig* incident are important only in how they influence the big picture. It's going to make life in Danzig even more uncomfortable, I'm afraid. But I want them to understand that I will not give them cover if they negotiate a sell-out. So we're going to have to be on high alert, Muller."

"It'll be hard to get on a much higher state of alert then we're currently on," Muller responded with a grin. "But I take the point."

"Incidentally," Lester said, "I popped into Avenol's office this morning and asked him about that Legal Section memorandum you gave me. He sputtered a bit and seemed embarrassed that I knew about it. But I didn't get the impression that he was planning any action based on the document. The conclusions it reaches are in such direct conflict with so many Council pronouncements that formal adoption of that line of argument would make the Council a laughingstock. What worries me though, is that it provides a rationale for the Council to decide simply to no longer concern itself with defending the Constitutional protections. If it wants to wash its hands of the subject–which it could someday decide to do–it wouldn't need to adopt anything formally to remove its guarantees, along the lines the memo suggests; it could simply decide to ignore them. That's where the risk lies."

"I'm no lawyer, Commissioner," Muller said, "but that's the way I read it too. If that's what they do, our role in Danzig would be finished."

Lester nodded. "I've thought about that, Muller, and you're right. If the Council were to decide to ignore the League mandate, my position as High Commissioner would be untenable. I'd simply become a figurehead."

"At that point, there would be nothing to stop Greiser and Forster from simply taking complete charge," Muller replied.

"I'm afraid that's right," said Lester. "I don't sense that either Eden or Beck comprehend the threat of physical violence that we face. If Hitler unleashes Forster and his gang of thugs, there's a risk that they'll simply take over the city. I'm glad they've summoned Greiser before the Council, but I haven't yet heard any plan to condemn the violence or somehow censure him. It's all very well to task Poland with beginning negotiations, but I'm a lot more worried about a potentially violent takeover by Forster than I am about avoiding German diplomatic snubs. And I just don't sense any willingness to take that on."

"Poland has always said they would fight any attempted takeover by the Germans," offered Muller. "Would they fight a takeover by Forster and the NSDAP?"

Muller and Lester exchanged glances. Lester didn't respond. He didn't need to.

***

The next day Stevenson was not to be found. Checking the Hotel d'Angleterre late in the afternoon, Muller learned that Stevenson was not expected back until late. But surveying the bar, he spied Elizabeth

Wiskemann seated at a table, bent over her notebook and writing intently. He came up behind her and planted a kiss on her cheek.

"My turn to surprise you this time," he said.

She half stood, embracing him,

"Paul, I'd thought you might be here; please join me." She motioned to the chair beside her. "Give me a second to finish this story that I need to telephone in." Finishing her writing, she closed her notebook with a flourish and hurried off to the telephone booths.

"Ten minutes," she said over her shoulder, "no more. Order me a drink."

Sipping his whiskey, Muller watched Elizabeth as she crossed the lobby and, after a few minutes, returned to the bar glancing down at her notebook, checking to be sure she'd covered everything.

He found himself amused as he reflected on her appearance. Elizabeth's approach to clothing was, he groped for the right word, 'practical', he decided. Her hair looked frowzy and her carriage was decidedly steady and unfeminine; but she radiated self-confident energy.

"Sorry to play journalist on you," she said, seating herself and tapping her glass to his. "This sanctions business is just such a compelling story. Were you here for Haile Selassie's speech?"

Muller shook his head. "We arrived that night and read about it."

"It was a dramatic scene," Elizabeth said. "Pathos, really; an eloquent plea for help followed by...deafening silence. Tomorrow the Council meets to simply abolish the Abyssinian sanctions program completely. Admit failure and move on."

"Wait, Elizabeth, did you say the Council is voting to abolish sanctions *tomorrow*?" asked Muller incredulously. "The Council meeting tomorrow is about Danzig; that's why I'm here."

"Danzig is the second agenda item, Paul," she said. "It's right after the vote on ending sanctions. Didn't you know?"

Muller felt a stab of pain in the pit of his stomach. Could it really be true? Was the Danzig issue really to come before the Council right on the heels of the most egregious failure in the entire history of the League of Nations?

That would be awful. Did Lester know, he wondered; did Eden know?

"Paul, are you all right? You look absolutely stricken."

"I had no idea," he said. "It's terrible news for us.

"Look, Elizabeth, preserving the League's mandate in Danzig is going require the Council to take a stand tomorrow. What do you think the chances are that the Council will be willing to act bravely for Danzig right after letting sanctions go down the drain? Not very good, I'd say. What we'll almost certainly get instead is another equivocation, another evasion, another admission of weakness. God almighty."

Muller gulped his drink and slammed the empty glass on the table, drawing stares. He didn't care. He summoned the waiter, handed him some francs without even glancing at the bill, and stood up to leave. "Sorry, Elizabeth, I've got to find the Commissioner."

The concierge at their hotel said the Commissioner had just departed to walk over to the Hotel des Bergues, situated across the Mont Blanc Bridge, on the other bank of the Rhone River as it began its long trip to the Mediterranean. Muller sprinted across the bridge and turned left toward the Hotel entrance. He spied what appeared to be a diplomatic party conversing over cocktails in the garden to the rear of the hotel. Muller handed the bellman a coin, asking him to find High Commissioner Lester and tell him that he had an urgent message in the lobby.

Lester strode into the lobby trailed by the bellman. "Muller, what's the matter?"

Muller told him the news.

Lester nodded gravely. "I know. I heard about it while I was still at the Palais and immediately went to Avenol demanding that he change the agenda. He flatly refused. He said Eden was Rapporteur for both agenda items and had approved the schedule and that was that."

Muller groaned. "But Commissioner..."

Lester held up his hand. "I thought about trying to track down Eden, then decided not to. He's obviously made up his mind and I know him well enough to know that he won't budge. It's a terrible decision. But we're stuck with it, I'm afraid."

Muller stared at him. Was there really no way to change this thing? Muller's shoulders slumped.

"I'm grateful to you for coming to find me." Lester said quietly and gave Muller a clap on the shoulder, then he shrugged, and returned to the party.

Muller walked north along the Quai back to the d'Angleterre. Elizabeth was not in the bar and he got no response when he rang her room. He took a table at the bar and downed several strong whiskies, then boarded a tram back to the Hotel de la Paix and dined alone at a table in the garden overlooking the crowds swarming on and off the Lake steamers that docked across the street.

CHAPTER 21

Summer, 1936

The next day, the League Council was scheduled to meet at 2 PM in the Chamber for the sanctions vote. The Palais was crowded, as member nation representatives and a large press corps gathered for the event. Muller found the mood subdued; a little like getting ready for the funeral of someone important, he thought to himself.

Standing in line at the cafeteria, he saw Stevenson making his way toward him before exiting. "Good idea to grab a bite," he said. "I just did the same thing; it could be a long day." Dropping his voice, he said quietly, "Eden received a cable from our Ambassador in Berlin this morning saying that after being summoned by the Council, Greiser flew directly to Berlin with Forster and the two of them had a long meeting with Hitler and Goebbels." He shrugged. "We don't know what it means, but I thought you should know."

Muller got back in line. Goebbels? The German Propaganda Minister? He's a new player; what does that mean? He puzzled over this development, finished his lunch, then strolled over to the Council Chamber.

Muller lacked credentials for the sanctions session and the public gallery was already packed, so he stood in the reception area outside the

Chamber craning his neck, along with other observers, trying to follow the vote to end the sanctions. It didn't take long; less than thirty minutes later the delegates began streaming out of the Chamber. They didn't linger, Muller noticed. Instead of the usual chatter and comparing of notes, they all just seemed to want to leave–to be almost anywhere else. Reporters tried to stop them for interviews, but no one seemed to want to announce their presence today and they hurried past the journalists.

Muller caught sight of Elizabeth Wiskemann and watched her futile efforts to find delegates willing to talk. Finally, she gave up and Muller approached her.

"Sorry about my abrupt departure last evening," he said.

She waved his apology aside. "I understood. What a mood in there." She gestured towards the Chamber. "It was as if they knew that while the vote was about burying sanctions, they were really burying a big part of the League too. And no one wants to talk about it–especially to a reporter. Danzig is up next?"

Muller nodded.

"Can you give me a scoop on what to expect?"

"Frankly I'm not sure myself," Muller replied. "Let's plan to meet after the session."

"I'd like that," said Elizabeth.

Muller showed his credentials and was admitted to the Chamber where people were milling about, some departing after the sanctions vote and some coming in for the Danzig session. Lester entered and Muller took him aside to tell him the news about Greiser's detour to Berlin and the meeting with Goebbels and Hitler.

"Funny," Lester said, "I was just with Eden and he didn't mention it. He must not have thought it was important."

Beck entered the Chamber and made his way toward his seat, ready to preside and call the Council into session.

Suddenly there was a loud commotion at the entrance and Muller could see Greiser and his advisors in an angry exchange with security officials. Security had been increased after the Czech suicide and the guards were barring Greiser's group from entering without new credentials. Muller watched as Greiser lost his temper and screamed that he was ready "to blow up this dog house."

Beck sent an aide to the doorway and Greiser was finally admitted, followed by Boettcher and three others. Still angry, Greiser stalked over to the table where he slammed his papers down, scowled at the Council and took his seat, failing to greet either Eden, seated on his right, or Lester, seated on Eden's other side.

Muller looked at Greiser and realized the man was drunk. It was not an uncommon condition for Greiser, and Muller knew the appearance only too well; but here, in the Council Chamber? Muller shook his head.

After Beck gaveled the Council into session, Eden, with customary smoothness, noted the circumstances of the *Leipzig* affair, observed that, "as an international incident" it warranted attention and proposed that, in light of its Treaty rights and obligations, the government of Poland be requested to take up the matter through diplomatic channels. Beck spoke briefly to state his government's willingness to assume this responsibility.

Eden then resumed, observing that while the internal situation in Danzig had recently deteriorated, he was confident that, "with the wholehearted cooperation between the Council and the Government of the Free City, a dangerous crisis would be averted and matters would speedily be returned to normal."

Muller shifted in his seat, scarcely believing what he was hearing.

Greiser then abruptly rose to his feet, swaying, then steadying himself. He fumbled with a black notebook, then opened it and began to read from it in a loud voice.

Muller, seated behind him, could see the neatly typewritten text. That was something new, he thought; Greiser's speeches were always clumsily prepared.

Then it dawned on him. *Goebbels*. Greiser's reading a speech written for him in Berlin by Goebbels!

Greiser began his remarks by dismissing the *Leipzig* incident as a dispute between Germany and the Commissioner which the Danzig government had nothing to do with but which, in any event, the Commissioner had brought on himself by his "insulting behavior" during the *Admiral Scheer* reception a year earlier which had "demeaned the honor of the German Navy."

He spoke, Gresier continued, as the governor of 400,000 Germans who were compelled to live under "an alien constitution" forced upon them by the League of Nations, which allowed "a divided and torn minority to terrorize the legitimately elected majority." It was "intolerable" that the League's High Commissioner drew an immense salary "paid in gold and foreign currency" while Danzig was locked in poverty. The Commissioner, he said, routinely searched for "grains of explosive matter" to arouse controversy and he supported opposition terrorists preying on "innocent citizens" who support their Fuehrer. The Commissioner, he went on, "does not understand the German mentality and he does not even speak our language."

Muller felt himself stiffen. This was an outrage; how could Eden just sit there and permit this insulting speech to go on. But Eden appeared unperturbed.

Greiser meanwhile moved to his conclusion. "There can be only two solutions. The Council must either replace the current High Commissioner with a qualified individual who will not meddle in the internal affairs of the Free City, or it must abolish the position of High Commissioner altogether and appoint the President of the Danzig Senate as its representative to preserve order and peace."

Muller snorted in disgust.

Greiser then placed his notebook on the table, came to attention, clicked his heels together flung out his right arm and shouted "Heil Hitler."

Members of the Council were visibly startled by this display and the press section responded with jeers and catcalls, waving their arms in disgust.

Greiser turned to them, stuck out his tongue, and thumbed in nose at them.

Muller looked on in utter astonishment. *What? Thumbing his nose to the press in the Council Chamber? Cocking a snoot?* That's what children do to one another on the playground! Muller rubbed his eyes in disbelief; had he really seen it? He shook his head. Of course he had.

Eden, seemingly oblivious to both Greiser's attack on Lester and his childish behavior, observed that the President of the Senate had been requested to appear before the Council as a matter of courtesy "and not with the purpose of calling into question any actions of the Commissioner or the Danzig government."

He then added that, as the Assembly required the Chamber for several items of business, the Council should stand in recess until 6 PM.

Muller watched in disbelief as in the most nonchalant manner, Beck proceeded to gavel the session into adjournment. Greiser had just committed a series of unforgiveable diplomatic affronts, and no one reacted! Muller shook his head.

Eden stood, bending to ask Lester to accompany him, and strode to the entryway without any acknowledgement of Greiser's presence. Muller noticed that the Council members seemed consciously to avoid Greiser as they departed. Muller trailed after Lester, but he and Eden entered the elevator together and the door closed.

Muller was able to intercept Stevenson in the corridor leading back to the Palais. "Those remarks were an insult to both the Commissioner and the League, but Eden didn't utter a word of censure or come to the Commissioner's defense. That's outrageous."

Stevenson smiled lightly at Muller. "It was obvious that Greiser was making a fool of himself," he said. "Everyone knew it, so there was no need for Eden to say anything."

"But the press will report his accusations and the record will show no reaction by the Council," Muller retorted sharply. "He'll be hailed as a hero in the German and Danzig papers."

"Muller, you need to calm down," Stevenson said. "Nothing Eden could say is going change how the German press decides to play this subject. It makes no sense for Eden to gratuitously criticize Greiser and generate a new controversy."

"Stevenson, you're the one who told me yesterday that Greiser met with Hitler and Goebbels on his way to this meeting," Muller replied. "The remarks Greiser made this afternoon are clearly a message from Hitler to the League. I saw the text of his speech and I'm willing to wager it was written by Goebbels. It's a deliberate slap in the face of the League–and the Commissioner."

"Even if you're right, Muller, what's the point in getting in a public spat about it?" Stevenson said, shrugging. "The Council's going to deputize Poland to negotiate with the Germans and try to sort things out. That's the only way anything's going to get accomplished. A war of words with a lowlife like Greiser doesn't get us anywhere."

Muller moved closer to Stevenson, looking him squarely in the eye. "If it looks like the Council has abandoned its responsibility and left the Commissioner hung out to dry, his life will be in danger. Stevenson, you've never been to Danzig; you've never seen the storm troopers marching around and attacking their opponents with clubs and knuckledusters. If Greiser is allowed to return to Danzig after pissing all over the League and its Commissioner without even a word of censure, Sean Lester will be in serious danger and you can kiss his mission goodbye."

"Easy, Muller," Stevenson said sharply. "We know what we're doing."

Muller was about to explode when Stevenson put a hand on his arm, "I've seen the Nazis marching in Berlin, Muller, and you're right, they are very scary." He paused.

"I take your point. We can't put Lester at risk; let me have a word with Eden about that to see what can be done." He turned and strode to the elevator.

Muller took a seat in the reception area and took a coffee. He was still furious and it didn't help to see Greiser and Boettcher and the other Senate representatives across the room in high spirits and boisterous conversation with one another, opening a bottle of Champagne.

When Lester returned from the Palais, he came over and took the seat next to Muller. He looked weary.

"Coffee, Commissioner? A drink?" asked Muller.

Lester shook his head. "I'm afraid I had a bit of a row with Eden. I told him that I was going to resign. I said that since Greiser—and probably Hitler too—are obviously gunning for me, I had become a distraction and that so long as I remained in office, my presence would hamper the ability of the League to carry out its responsibilities. So I said it made sense for me to take myself out of the picture. Eden wouldn't hear of it; in fact he called Beck to join us. Both of them implored me to stay, saying that my resignation would play right into Hitler's hands. They believe the negotiations that Beck will be having with the Germans at the Council's behest offer the best hope for progress on the Danzig issues—and that progress there may well lead to agreement on broader issues. They were very insistent."

Muller told him of his suspicion that Goebbels had written Greiser's speech and described his exchange of words with Stevenson.

"The Goebbels angle is interesting," Lester said thoughtfully, "and it's plausible. Germany's pressing hard to get me removed. We know from von Radowitz that my invitation to Rauschning for the *Admiral Scheer* reception seems to have stuck in Hitler's craw. So that outrageous performance by Greiser may be part of Hitler's strategy to get rid of me and bully the Council into giving up on the mandate. That's not a pretty picture is it?"

"Commissioner, it's disgraceful that Eden did nothing to rebut Greiser's insulting statements," said Muller angrily.

"Yes, that would have been nice," said Lester, his voice drifting away.

Then he smiled. "Thanks for your statements to Stevenson concerning my safety. It has occurred to me that I might be at some risk. But I'm an Irishman, Muller, and I don't react well to threats. I'll not be bullied."

What about Elsie and the girls? Muller thought, but decided not to say anything.

"Let's see how the rest of this meeting turns out," Lester said, standing to return to the Chamber. "I told Eden that I would not resign now. But I made it clear to him that it remains an option."

When the Council resumed, Eden observed that it was not the League of Nations that had created the Free City, nor the Commissioner—and certainly not the Rapporteur. The Treaty had imposed an arduous duty upon all concerned, and he therefore thought he was entitled to ask that the parties "continue in the performance of that duty in a courteous manner."

As he listened, Muller swore to himself.

Greiser and Forster would not be likely to pay much mind to Eden's plea for 'courtesy'.

Eden then called upon Lester who spoke only briefly. He told the Council that he did not intend to rival "the eloquence" of Greiser's remarks. From the amused expressions around the horseshoe table, Muller could see that Lester's sarcasm was understood by everyone. Lester described the breakdown of order that had occurred during the past month and concluded by observing that he hoped Greiser's belligerent remarks "would give the Council some idea of what its representative was regularly exposed to in Danzig."

There followed nearly an hour of interventions by Council delegates offering praise and support for Lester's conduct in Danzig. Beck's statement was especially complimentary and commended Lester's for "his fortitude in the face of evident provocation."

Greiser, having fortified himself sufficiently during the break, sat silently, smiling a bit like a Cheshire cat, thought Muller.

Now he rose to his feet again.

Greiser expressed satisfaction that Eden had said the Council would entertain the possibility of studying the proposals for change that he had submitted earlier. In light of the Council's deliberate pace in reviewing new approaches, he had expected no immediate action. But, he said, he regarded them "as a first offensive" in the effort "to revise relations between The League of Nations and Danzig. The German people whom I lead expect changes to be made, and made very soon, which would make it possible for the President of the Senate in the Free City to never appear again before the League of Nations."

Gresier smirked in Lester's direction and sat down.

Eden politely thanked Greiser for his suggestions, once more gently observing that the Council was only dealing with its agenda in this session and nothing more.

God, said Muller to himself, can't Eden say *anything* in defense of Lester and the League? Shit!

The Council approved Eden's report appointing the government of Poland to enter into negotiations with Germany with a view to resolving the Danzig issues. As he gaveled adjournment, Beck requested the Council delegates to remain in their seats. "Mr. Greiser, you and your colleagues are excused. I will ask the Council and Commissioner Lester to remain in secret session."

Muller remained in his seat.

When the room had cleared and the doors were bolted, Eden took the floor. "Minister Beck and I have observed with apprehension the menacing remarks made today by Mr. Greiser. Coming as they do in the wake of what appears to have been a breakdown of civil order in Danzig during the past month, the Minister and I wish to raise with the Council our concerns regarding the Commissioner's personal safety and the security of the League's mission when he returns to Danzig. We need to consider what precautions the Council should take, including provision for military protection, should that become necessary."

Muller reacted with annoyance. Why would Eden wait until after Greiser had been excused and the press shooed out before finally saying something positive? He gritted his teeth.

"Before I ask the Commissioner to comment," Eden continued, "I want to say that I am not raising this subject at his request. But the Council should know that the Commissioner has good reason to believe that his telephones are tapped. His mail has been intercepted. A member of his staff was caught trying to install a listening device in his office. A camera has been installed across the street from his building in order to observe visitors. On at least one occasion he has been followed. We witnessed today some flavor of the invective which is directed at him by the National Socialist government that is in power in the City. It is a threatening situation that we have a responsibility to address." He turned to Lester.

Lester rose and gazed around the horseshoe table at the Council delegates before responding. "I thank the Rapporteur for his statement. It is true that the security of my assignment in Danzig has deteriorated sharply in the last month. I believe the Council is aware that the local government in Danzig has mounted a campaign to remove me. This effort was made apparent in the remarks delivered here today by President Greiser. The campaign has the support of the German government. Indeed, Germany may have instigated it."

Lester paused for effect. "I informed the Rapporteur during the interval between sessions today that, in my estimation, I have become a distraction and that my continuing to serve as Commissioner may detract from the Council's ability to discharge its responsibilities to protect the Danzig Constitution. I told him, therefore, that I am prepared to resign in order to permit the Council to appoint another person to serve as High Commissioner. The Rapporteur and the Council President declined to accept my offer to resign and urged me to serve out my term as appointed by the Council."

Here, Lester paused. "I believe it is appropriate for the entire Council to consider whether my resignation would contribute to a solution to the Danzig challenge."

Muller heard most delegates urge Lester to continue his work.

"You must stay," a number said loudly.

Lester regarded the Council, looking around the horseshoe table.

"If I were to return to Danzig as Commissioner, I say frankly to you that I do not know what reception would await me. I am not so concerned for my personal safety; but I am very concerned at the possibility of a National Socialist takeover that would remove constitutional protections and install a totalitarian state. I assume that President Greiser will be returning to Danzig confident that he defied the Council today with impunity. The Council chose not to censure the Senate for its violent behavior in the last month or for Greiser's insolent speech today. While individual delegates challenged his attacks on my conduct in office, the record will show no decision by the Council to criticize the increasingly confrontational behavior of the Senate President."

Good for you, Muller thought. That's laying down a marker.

Lester bent at the waist, placing both hands on the table and looking intently at the faces before him around the horseshoe table. "So if I were to remain in office, I would go back to Danzig in a weaker position to perform the League's responsibilities than I was before. If the Council wants to continue trying to enforce its League mandate–and if I'm to continue to serve as High Commissioner and represent the League–then something needs to happen to strengthen my hand. Otherwise, the League's mandate is likely to be simply overwhelmed by the Senate's opposition."

Lester straightened up and gestured toward the papers stacked before Eden. "Six months ago, the Council had before it a petition to force a new election that would almost certainly have removed the current government. The Council chose to table that initiative. Six months later, the League is now weaker and that government is stronger and even more intransigent."

Rub their nose in it, Commissioner, Muller said to himself, cheering Lester on silently.

Lester paused again before concluding. "If the Council decides to abandon the League's mandate, then I shall resign. If the Council desires to continue trying to enforce its mandate and it wants me to continue as its High Commissioner, then it must decide how it intends to demonstrate its authority and mine."

Lester took his seat alongside Eden.

Beck, as presiding officer broke the ensuing silence. "My government will not consent to abandoning the League's mandate in Danzig! Poland has vital interests that the mandate protects. It is true, as the Commissioner has just stated that the Council has sought to enforce its mandate without unnecessary confrontation with the Danzig Senate."

Beck then turned to Lester with a broad smile. "However, I think it is safe to say, Commissioner, that your firmness in confronting the issues has clearly conveyed the strength of the Council's authority. Indeed, the fact that you have become a target is testimony to your success."

Muller watched as delegates around the table nodded vigorously.

"Hear, Hear," several of them said.

"Now," said Beck, "regarding steps to strengthen the Commissioner's hand. I am prepared to say that my government, in discharging its mandate to negotiate with Germany, will make known to the Germans the Council's unswerving commitment to its mandate for protecting the Danzig Constitution and to insist that they cease interfering. Further, my government is prepared to consider the use of military force to maintain order in Danzig and preserve the security of the Council's mission there if that step should become necessary. I shall make that fact known both in Berlin and to the Danzig government. Do I hear any objections?"

Beck paused, looking around the table. "Hearing none, I direct the Rapporteur to record the Council's approval.

"It is unthinkable that you should resign, Commissioner," Beck continued. "That would convey precisely the wrong message; indeed, it would play into the hands of the Senate and its German allies. So, I ask the

Council to enact a resolution rejecting your offer to resign and expressing its full confidence in your performance of your duties. May I have a motion to that effect?"

The Australian delegate responded, "So moved."

"All in favor?' asked Beck. All the delegates raised their hands.

"So ordered," said Beck. "Commissioner, I invite you to meet with me tomorrow at 10 AM to discuss details concerning the use of military force in Danzig."

As the delegates rose to depart the Great Hall, most of them came over to shake Lester's hand and add personal words of support.

Stevenson came over to Muller and offered a handshake. "I hope this will get things back on track."

Muller decided to put diplomacy aside.

"Stevenson, this was all arranged to be in secret session," he said bitterly. "No one in Danzig or Berlin—or anywhere else, for that matter—has the slightest inking of what just transpired. You buried it. Just like you're getting ready to bury our mission—and maybe the Commissioner and me too."

Muller turned on his heel and strode out of the Chamber.

By the time Muller got back to the Hotel de la Paix, it was late. The concierge handed him a message. It was from Elizabeth Wiskemann, saying that she was departing on an early morning train, traveling first to Prague then to Warsaw. She planned to be in Danzig in about a week and looked forward to seeing him.

Muller realized that he had completely forgotten about meeting her following the Council session. Well, too bad! It had been a long day.

***

Lester and Muller went to Beck's suite at the Palais the next morning. They were invited into Beck's large airy office to await his arrival and Muller gazed out the window at the lakefront below them. Just a mile further along the Quai Wilson, he could see the large, gleaming white marble structure that was to be the new home of the League of Nations, replacing the Palais. After three years of construction, it was now nearing completion and some secretariat offices were already being relocated there.

Muller pointed it out to Lester. "The building seemed so grand–and so fitting–when the plans were announced," he said. "Now it looks almost pretentious."

Lester nodded. "Wouldn't 'white elephant' be the right description?"

Beck arrived, apologizing for being late, invited them to sit around a small table and arranged for coffees to be served. He turned to Lester.

"I'm very pleased that the Council so resoundingly rejected your resignation last evening," he said. "You're the Council's indispensable man in Danzig."

"Thank you, Minister," Lester replied, "but most days I feel more like a bull's eye for target practice by Greiser and Forster–and by Hitler as well. It appears that he's taken a personal interest in my removal from office."

Beck nodded. "I intend on stopping in Berlin on my return to Warsaw. I plan to be very direct with them that Poland would consider an attempt by Germany to annex Danzig as an attack warranting a military response. Herr Hitler may not like you, Commissioner, but I'm very sure that he doesn't want a war on his hands. So I'm confident that I can get them to back off."

Muller translated for Lester, wondering to himself at Beck's breezy self-assurance.

"As for military action required to keep order in Danzig," Beck continued, "we have numerous options available to us. There are three Polish Army battalions stationed in Gydina. If we give the order, these troops can march across the border at Zoppot; they would be in central Danzig within a couple of hours." He smiled. "They could even take the trams from Zoppot and be there sooner. Alternatively, we could load them aboard vessels and steam them right into Danzig harbor. As you know, that would be only about a twenty minute boat ride, since the two ports are so close to one another."

"How would you envision initiating such a deployment?" Lester asked.

"I sent overnight directives for plans to be drawn up for this contingency," Beck replied confidently. "I assume the first step would need to be a formal request from you, Commissioner. I think it unlikely that we would intervene unless you, as the League's representative, were to formally notify us it was necessary. As I said, I've directed the Polish High Command to initiate planning for precisely how this should be accomplished and I will see to it that this is done promptly and communicated to you."

Gathering his papers, Beck concluded, "I shall keep Papee fully informed on both our diplomatic and military initiatives so he can brief you. I shall also use him as an intermediary to deal with Greiser and the Senate on my behalf.

"Commissioner, I think we are prepared to deal with the crisis." Beck stood up, the meeting obviously over.

As they shook hands in departure, Beck said, "By the way, Commissioner, I'm planning a short holiday in mid-July. The Polish Navy has constructed a small but very well-appointed compound on the Baltic close to Gydina which I intend to enjoy for a week or so. I will invite you and we can continue our conversations in a more informal setting."

Lester thanked Beck and he and Muller departed.

They found their now accustomed seats in the Chamber reception area. Lester put his arms on the chair's arms and steepled his hands, reflecting a few moments before speaking.

"I'm afraid I don't believe him," Lester said finally. "He's not about to threaten Hitler with military action. I'm sure he'll visit Berlin to stress Poland's strong support for the League mandate and he'll try to work out some face-saving solution with them. But he won't risk worsening relations with Germany–which he's worked so hard to improve–by telling them he's ready to send in troops to protect Danzig.

"I also think he lied about ordering the Polish Military Command to draw up contingency deployment plans. The Polish military doesn't report to the Foreign Minister; it reports to the Defense Minister. I don't know who that is, but I'm sure that he doesn't take orders from Beck and that he'll have his own ideas about using the Polish military in Danzig."

Muller nodded. "Both resolutions–the one about authorizing Beck to threaten the use of military force and the one commending your conduct in office–were taken during the secret session. So there will be no public announcement about either of them. As far as the rest of the world knows, they simply don't exist."

Lester nodded. "I'm pretty sure that Eden set it up that way. Nothing must interfere with British appeasement policy," Lester added, smiling wryly, "especially a couple of League Council resolutions that will never see the light of day. Despite all those brave words last night, I'm afraid the reality is that we're headed back to the fray, pretty much on our own."

Lester turned to face Muller. "Or at least I am. Muller, you ought to consider whether you want to continue. I've got to see Avenol on some other matters; I'm confident that I could get him to reassign you to a better posting."

"Commissioner, I'm not about to quit," Muller said firmly. "Thank you for the thought, but please put it out of your mind. I'm still in."

Lester stretched his hand out and they shook, smiling at one another.

"I'm glad," said Lester. "If I'm Beck's indispensable man, you're my indispensable man.

"So I'll go meet with Avenol; why don't you go down to the Travel Section and get us tickets for the trip back. I think we should avoid Berlin again and take the longer route."

Muller made the arrangements, then telephoned his father in Zurich and told him they had an hour between trains in Zurich later that evening.

"Your mother and I will be delighted to see you," he responded warmly.

As he prepared to leave the Palais, Muller dropped by the Sub Section offices to pick up the transcripts of the Council meeting. Krabbe handed him an envelope.

"All ready for you Muller," Krabbe said.

"The secret session transcript is there too, I assume," Muller replied.

"No," said Krabbe. "That has to stay here."

"Like Hell, it does," Muller stood up. "Come on, we're going down to the Records Office and you're going to get it for me."

Krabbe protested, "But that's against the rules."

"Frankly, I don't give a damn about the rules," said Muller. "Rules in this sorry organization seem to get broken with increasing frequency these days. So come on, let's go get the document."

The clerk in the Records Office refused Muller's request.

"Not allowed," he said curtly, turning his attention to other matters.

Muller pushed open the swinging door to the office and stepped in, putting his face inches from the startled clerk's, who tried to shrink back.

"I am the Secretary to the High Commissioner of the League of Nations in Danzig, whose mission and very life may depend upon this document," Muller fairly snarled the words. "You will give it to me. *Now.*"

The clerk shrugged. "You want it so badly, you can have it. But you have to sign for it here," he pointed to a register. "It'll be your ass on the line not mine."

Muller signed his name in bold script, took the papers the clerk handed him, checked to see they were correct, then added them to Krabbe's envelope.

"Thank you," he said, leaving the office.

He waved to Krabbe and returned to the hotel to collect his bag for the trip back to Danzig.

CHAPTER 22

Summer, 1936

The train departed from Geneva and ran along the lakefront. Lester and Muller settled into their compartment and watched the late afternoon sun reflect off the sparkling lake, and brighten the towering mountains on the far shoreline.

"I have a very different feeling leaving Geneva, this time," mused Lester as they gazed at the arresting views. "There was always a sense of energy there. You could feel it in the hallways and during the meetings—even the dull ones. There was determination in the air, confidence about accomplishing good things. I realized as I packed to come to the train this afternoon that I didn't feel any of that during this visit. Something's missing, and I decided it was the vitality I had been accustomed to. Something like desperation seems to have replaced it. It's a discouraging sensation."

He paused, still reflecting. "Something similar is affecting us too, Muller. Look at the two of us, heading back to a Danzig that we know well by now. But what can we expect when we get there? What's the Senate going to do? We're in the dark. And we've decided we have to make a detour around Germany because we don't know what to expect there either."

"Things are a lot different than when we arrived two and a half years ago," said Muller in a similar reflective tone, "and they haven't changed for the better."

"I haven't told this to anyone," Lester said, "but I stopped keeping my diary before we made this trip. Who knows if we'll get raided one night; I decided I don't want some Nazi reading my notes to myself, so I decided simply to stop. I carefully wrapped up the pages that I've already written and buried them beneath one of the flagstones in the garden one night after everyone had gone to bed."

He smiled at Muller. "I should probably show you the spot when we get back so you can rescue it if something were to happen to me."

***

Zurich Central Station was the classic railroad terminal, with its high vaulted dome rising above the lines of platforms and tracks below. As the train slowly rolled to a stop and the usual sudden burst of steam announced it had arrived, Muller could see his parents standing on the platform, his father, as usual on any business day, dressed in a dark pinstripe suit with white shirt and muted necktie, his mother wearing a light frock with a fashionable long skirt.

After disembarking, Muller hugged his mother and embraced his father. Lester greeted the Mullers cordially—they had met before on several of these quick intervals between trains—then quickly excused himself.

"I've got seats for us as usual in the First Class Lounge," Karl Muller said as they turned to walk down the platform. "Your connecting platform to Vienna is especially convenient," the rest of his words lost in the noisy departure of a large locomotive on the adjoining track.

Once inside the Lounge, they found seats in chairs close to where fans were stirring the warm summer heat. "I was asking why you're routing your way through Vienna instead of the usual connection through Berlin," said his father. "That seems a little strange."

"Yes, well," Muller responded, a little too quickly, "with Germany no longer being a League member, we thought that might be a preferable route."

"But tell me all the news," Muller said, turning to his mother and changing the subject.

His father gazed at him solemnly. But his mother, seizing the opening, excitedly began telling all about his brother's long expected engagement that had just been announced.

"The party will be in six weeks and everyone will expect you." She went on describing more details of the party and the planning. "Your sister gets back by early July for the summer," she went on, reporting animatedly on Mathilda's experience at the University of Chicago and how much she was enjoying studying physics–and how there had been no reports of any dates with gangsters.

"Well, that's a relief, "Muller smiled. Then he put his hand on his mother arm. "Mum, forgive me, but could I have a word with Father? Could you give us a moment while we speak over by the bar?"

His mother looked quizzically at him, but said, "of course," and his father rose, the two of them stepping over to the bar area where several tables were unoccupied.

"You don't want to go through Berlin, I take it," said his father, a little severely.

Muller looked down a little sheepishly, then smiled. "Perceptive as usual, Father; relations are a little strained at the moment. Actually, more than 'a little', to be truthful," he admitted. "But here's the idea I wanted to put to you."

He explained his plan to have Muller & Company hire Franz Schiller to help deal with awkward cross border problems and other unusual situations that might arise. "I've taken the liberty of writing up a memo with my ideas and a summary of Schiller's experience." He handed over a brown envelope. "I think very highly of Schiller and I think you and Thomas will both like him."

Karl Muller didn't hesitate. "Good. Your brother and I have been talking for the last several months about trying to find someone with precisely that kind of background whom we could trust. We're seeing stranger and stranger things happening, Paul, and we need help."

He reached into his wallet and handed Muller a card. "Give this to Mr. Schiller and have him contact me directly. I'd like to meet him soon. We can arrange to move him and his family here and help them get settled. It's an excellent suggestion.

Karl Muller smiled. "Now go back and pay attention to your mother while I visit the toilet!"

Thirty minutes later, still chatting amiably, they strolled back out to the platform where the Vienna Express was preparing to depart. Muller hugged his mother again, kissing her on both cheeks. "It's so good to see you Mum. Tell Thomas, I was sorry to miss him but that I'll try to arrive early for the big engagement party."

He turned and embraced his father. "Thanks for your support, as always, Father."

Muller mounted the steps to his compartment, leaning out the open window to wave as the train began to glide away.

***

Lester and Muller finally arrived at Dirschau at mid-morning a day later. As they detrained and passed through passport control, they were surprised to see Elsie Lester waiting for them with the Daimler. She embraced Lester with a warm kiss, and gave Muller a welcoming hug.

"Where's our driver?" inquired Lester.

"He's left," she said. "I think the Party forced him to quit. So I drove up to meet you myself. I didn't want you to take the train up to Danzig and arrive at the Central Station. Not after last night's demonstrations."

"What happened last night?" Lester asked.

"Gresier arrived back from Geneva" Elsie said. "He'd taken the train from Berlin through Stettin and got in around 9:00. He was met like a conquering hero; a huge rally with flags, marching bands, goose-stepping storm troopers; all the trimmings. I couldn't make out all of the speeches, but it sounded like everyone was bragging about how he had defeated the League and won freedom for Danzig. I heard a lot of attacks on you, Sean; my German is not so hot, but even I could tell they were insulting you and your office. So, I thought, I 'm going to drive down to Dirschau and get you into the Daimler so we can get to the residence without drawing attention to your arrival."

Muller could see Lester stiffening as Elsie spoke. He hugged her tightly and kissed her cheeks. "Thank you my dear," he said. "Thank you. But I am going to take the train up to the Danzig Central Station. I am going to detrain and I am going to walk to the residence. They can do what they will, but I'll be damned if I'll be intimidated!

"Muller," Lester said, "take our bags and drive Elsie and yourself back to the residence."

Lester turned to walk toward the Danzig train platform.

"Sean Lester," said Elsie sharply, "I think that is a really stupid idea. But if you're determined to do it, you are not going alone." She stepped in his path. "I'm as Irish–and as stubborn–as you are. If you're going, I'm going with you."

Elsie handed the car keys to Muller. "Paul, you take the Daimler back." She crooked her arm inside Lester's elbow and looked up at him brightly. "Shall we go my dear?"

Lester started to protest, then thought better of it. "Yes indeed," he replied, guiding her toward the platform. He smiled at Muller. "Drive carefully."

"Commissioner," Muller started to protest, but Lester waved him off and walked away with Elsie on his arm.

Muller drove rapidly north to Danzig. This was so like Sean Lester, he thought, not willing to bend and determined to perform his duty as he saw it. It was also damned foolhardy; who knew what Gresier and Forster had planned for Lester's arrival? Lester was very courageous–and Elsie too. Muller hoped it wouldn't end badly.

After parking the Daimler in the garage, he entered the Commissioner's residence and hurried up to the third floor drawing room where a tall window overlooked the Central Station.

To his horror, he saw a detachment of Brown Shirts drawn up in formation directly in front of the station. Just what he'd feared.

Shit!

Muller ran down the staircase and tore out the front door toward the Station. He didn't know what he was going to do, but he couldn't just stand at the window and watch what had all the earmarks of a looming confrontation.

Muller's heart raced. Then, as he ran toward the station, he suddenly saw the Brown Shirt detachment marching smartly away from the station and directly toward him. He stopped. The troopers proceeded to march past him and continue up the street past the residence in the direction of the Central Bank building.

Muller almost laughed aloud. The Brown Shirts hadn't been sent to disrupt Lester's arrival after all. They were just marching around, practicing, as they did all the time. Smiling to himself in relief, he retraced his steps to the Residence and got to the window in time to see the train as it looped south along Hindenburg Allee and entered the station.

Shortly afterwards, he watched Lester and Elsie, hand in hand, exit the station, cross the square and stroll along the sidewalk toward the residence without incident, Lester tipping his hat occasionally to passing pedestrians. Moments later, the two of them walked casually through the entrance and into the residence, both wreathed in smiles.

"Ah, Muller," Lester said as Muller descended the staircase. "I'm so glad you got back safely." He winked and gave Elsie a big hug.

***

The next morning, as Muller approached the residence, he was stopped by a uniformed policeman who demanded to see his papers. He handed over his diplomatic passport and, looking around, saw that a police unit had been assigned to cover all the approaches to the entryway.

"I'm the secretary to the High Commissioner," Muller said testily. "Why are you blocking my way and demanding to see my papers?"

"We're ordered to provide protection to the Commissioner by checking visitors to ensure that he's not bothered by unsavory visitors, opposition politicians and the like."

"By whose order?" Muller demanded.

"The President of the Senate," said the policeman, returning his passport. "You may pass."

"This is what they did to Rauschning when they were plotting to get him removed," Lester said when Muller reported what had happened. "It's not quite a declaration of war, but it's pretty close. This is the kind of thing Beck was supposed to take care of during his visit to Berlin."

Muller nodded, "I'll get a message to Papee to come see us."

When Papee arrived that afternoon, he was angry. "I told that police goon to stand out of my way or I'd have his badge pinned on his balls. I said, 'I'm the Consul General of Poland and I have full diplomatic immunity within the Free City. Now get out of my way'. He decided that I probably meant it, so he stepped aside.

"Greiser's playing with fire if he tries to challenge Polish sovereignty here," Papee said, still fuming. "He's also threatening to shut down both the *Volkstimme*, the SDP paper, and the *Danziger Nationale Zeitung*, the German National paper; he claims they're fomenting disorder by reporting the actions taken by the League in Geneva."

"Things are not getting off to a promising start after the Council meeting," Lester said. "What do you hear from Beck? His negotiations don't seem to have borne much fruit."

Papee shook his head. "That's putting it mildly. Beck stopped in Berlin on his way back from Geneva. He saw Goering and apparently was totally rebuffed. He said Goering categorically refuses to issue any apology for the *Leipzig* incident; he lays the blame squarely at your feet, Commissioner, because of the invitation you extended last year to Rauschning, whom Hitler personally detests. He was no better about restraining Forster. Once again he blames you, saying that Forster's opposition to your policies is entirely understandable. So, there's no progress at all to report on Beck's Council mandate."

"Did Beck tell Goering that Poland was prepared to use military force to defend its interests in Danzig against a German takeover?" asked Lester.

Papee shook his head. "Not so far as I know. That kind of language would need ministerial approval. I don't think even Beck would go out on that limb alone. Why do you ask?"

"Because that's what he told the Council he was going to do," Lester replied.

"What?" said Papee, looking at both Lester and Muller in disbelief. "You'd better tell me what happened in Geneva."

Lester told Muller to summarize for him. Speaking rapid French, Muller described the meetings. When he got to the part about Greiser baiting the press, Papee broke out in guffaws. "He actually cocked a snook at the press? Stuck his tongue out and everything? Right there in the Chamber? Really? That's too funny." Papee used a handkerchief to dab at his watering eyes.

"Probably a diplomatic first," he said, blowing his nose.

Papee turned serious as Muller described the secret Council Session and Beck's request that Eden report unanimous Council approval of his proposal to threaten the use of Polish troops to keep order in Danzig.

"This is the first I've heard about threatening to deploy our military," he said. "Are you sure? That's a very serious step."

"Wait here, a moment," said Muller.

He went quickly down the stairway to his office, opened the safe and extracted the Secretariat's transcript of the secret Council session.

Returning to Lester's office he handed the sheets to Papee.

Lester registered immediate disapproval. "Muller, those are documents classified as 'secret' by the Council." He stood to retrieve the documents.

Papee held up his hand, reading rapidly. "Commissioner, I will hold this information in strictest confidence. But I don't think anyone in the Polish Government knows about Beck's commitment. If I'm going to help, I need to know what happened."

Lester hesitated a moment, then snatched the papers out of Papee's hands.

"You've read enough and we've told you enough for you to get to Beck and begin making sense of this," said Lester angrily. "I will not be toyed with on this matter, Papee. If Beck lied to the Council, I need to know it. I told him I would resign if he uses his instructions from the Council to negotiate with Hitler as a cover to sell out the League. If that's what he's done, I shall publicly reveal his misconduct to the entire world."

Lester stood, and handed the papers back to Muller.

"Put those back in the safe where they belong, Muller," he said angrily then turned to face Papee.

"Do your job, Consul General," he said, dismissing him.

Muller returned to Lester's office to find Lester still steaming.

"That was a serious mistake, Muller! We have no authority to share the Council's secret proceedings with anyone."

"But Commissioner, that document is probably the only thing standing in the way of a League capitulation to Greiser," Muller protested. "Beck committed to the Council that he would warn both the German government and the Senate here in Danzig that Poland was prepared to use force to protect the League's mandate here. According to Papee, he didn't tell either one—and didn't even tell his *own* government," he added with a wave of his hand.

"Unless we find a way to force Beck's hand," Muller continued, "we're out of luck here; our mission will have failed and we might as well pack up and leave."

Muller stood defiantly in front of Lester's desk. He'd never had this kind of argument with Lester and he had a decidedly uncomfortable feeling doing it. But damn it, those were the facts and they had to be faced.

Lester smiled faintly and motioned Muller to take the seat next to his desk. He offered Muller a cigarette and fired his lighter for them both to light up.

"What you say is largely true," he replied quietly. "I'm quite well aware of it, believe me.

"But Muller, we can't act independently of the Council. We can't go around spilling the beans about sessions that the Council decided to conduct in secret.

"I know how frustrating it is," Lester added. "But if we take actions that get us in trouble with the Council and we lose the Council's confidence, then things will get worse even sooner." Tapping his cigarette in the big glass ash tray on his desk and leaning back in the desk chair he grinned at Lester.

"I knew exactly what you were doing, when you interrupted your translation and dashed downstairs to get those papers. I could have stopped you even before you left the room. But I didn't. And I didn't stop you because I wanted Papee to see them too. Beck is clearly playing some kind of game and Papee is our best bet to find out what his game is. So I wanted him to see the official, classified, 'secret' documents."

Lester slowly enunciated each word.

"He can go to Beck and say 'I saw the transcript of the Council session with my own eyes, now what the Hell is going on?' or words to that effect. And he can also state–truthfully–that you showed him the documents and I, as the Commissioner, grabbed them away and read you the riot act." Lester's smile broadened.

"So I'm hung out to dry?" Muller responded.

"Less than you would have been otherwise," said Lester, still smiling.

Muller began to smile as well, "that's certainly true," he said sounding, and feeling, mollified. "But we're still in a bind here."

Lester nodded. "We are indeed, Muller. Let's see what our friend Papee learns in the next few days. We'll know one way or another very soon."

***

The next day Muller received a telephone call from Elizabeth Wiskemann saying she had arrived in Danzig after taking the overnight train from Warsaw and asking for an appointment with Lester. They fixed a time for late that afternoon. Muller told her about the police screen and reminded her to bring her credentials. At the appointed hour, he saw her approaching the residence and being stopped by a policeman. She began speaking animatedly to him and Muller moved toward the doorway to intervene, when suddenly she began striding to the entrance, tucking away a notebook. She smiled and they exchanged pecks on both cheeks.

"Did the police give you trouble?" he asked.

"Not really," she replied. "I employed my usual technique. I told him that I was a journalist working on an important story and that if he interfered, I would publish his name and badge number as a troublemaker. He backed away immediately; it works every time." She smiled.

Lester welcomed her into his office and showed off the collection of clubs and cudgels the opposition had given him after the Josephaus assault.

Elizabeth blanched. "God, those are awful. Look, that one's still got dried blood on it. Ugh." She shivered involuntarily.

Lester invited Muller to sit in on the interview. "No translation needed, Miss Wiskemann, but Muller is my right hand here; in fact you should be interviewing him as much as me."

"Well, he did invite me to dinner, tonight, Commissioner," Elizabeth said teasingly. "Maybe I could interview him then."

Muller held up both hands in mock surrender. "Dinner is strictly—what's that term again Elizabeth?—off the record."

***

Later, before going to meet Elizabeth, Muller strolled over to the Café Werzler and used the call box to telephone the Danzig Police Station. He was connected right away to Franz Schiller who agreed to meet him at the Café.

As they shook hands, Muller discreetly pressed his father's card into Schiller's right hand.

"Probably not a good idea to call attention to it," Muller said, as they exchanged greetings. He then related to Schiller the brief conversation he had had with his father. "My suggestion is that you get in contact with him and arrange to visit Zurich soon. He'll pay for your trip. Things here aren't getting any better. I thought it best if I didn't try to visit you at Headquarters."

"Thanks, Muller," replied Schiller. "I'll act promptly. Things are definitely not getting any better. I'll find a way to keep in touch discreetly—for both of our sakes."

***

Danzig was still enjoying midsummer sunlight when Muller picked up Elizabeth Wiskemann at the Neue Deutsche Hotel at 6:30. They took the #9 Tram to Zoppot and strolled along the Brosen Mole, stopping for drinks at one of the outdoor cafés, then went for dinner at the Parrot where Muller was well-known. They were shown to a table by the railing overlooking the Baltic, which was calm and quiet at low tide. He made a point of warning her off the smoked eel—she gagged, but laughed at his story–and they settled for simple grilled fish with potato salad and a chilled bottle of Riesling.

Elizabeth had been in the press gallery at the Council session, so she had witnessed Greiser 'cocking a snook' at them. "I've been a journalist for more than a decade," she said. "I've never witnessed anything like it. The British press had a field day; you should have seen the cartoons!"

"I am to interview him tomorrow morning," she added. "Frankly, I'm not looking forward to it. He seems a vile man."

"Why don't you ask him who wrote the speech you heard him deliver in Geneva," Muller suggested. "There's a rumor it was written for him by Goebbels in Berlin. It's one of those stories that gets around."

"He was given a hero's welcome here when he returned from Geneva last week," Muller continued, "so he's probably feeling pretty full of himself. You've seen the policemen he's stationed around the Commissioner's residence. He's also threatened to suspend publication of most opposition newspapers and he's issued a slew of new directives. For all we know, he's planning a coup. At a minimum, he's decided to take the Commissioner and the League on frontally. This is probably a good time to see if you can draw some indiscreet declarations out of him."

Elizabeth pulled out her notebook and made a few notes.

Later, over a second bottle of Riesling, Elizabeth offered her impressions of France, which she had visited before the Council meeting in Geneva. "French society is just riven. Election of the Popular Front has upset everything. Leon Blum is Prime Minister, but he and his leftist allies have no experience in actually governing; they're professional opposition politicians. They want to make big changes in work rules to help the trade unionists and Communists, but their ministers are so inexperienced, they can't get much of anything done. The business community is up in arms about their program, the Catholics are angry at everyone and there are even some monarchists talking about bringing back the Bourbons. It's just a mess.

"Everyone in France is terrified of Hitler, but no one wants to do anything to stop him. The Quai d'Orsay is furious with Eden and the British, whom they accuse—with some justification, frankly—of ignoring them and going their own way."

Muller gazed at Elizabeth. He found her observations interesting, but a plan began to form in the back of his head.

"Meanwhile, there's a big conflict brewing in Spain," she added, suddenly animated. "There are rumors that the Germans and Italians are funneling support to right wing nationalists who want to overthrow the Republican government—which is turning to the Soviets for help. That would make for a fine kettle of fish wouldn't it? The Fascists against the Communists. I think I'll try to go to Madrid later this summer to see what's going on there."

They strolled back to the tram station. Elizabeth dozed on the ride back, her head on Muller's shoulder. As the tram approached the Commissioner's residence, Muller decided to act on his idea.

Poking her gently in the side, he said, "Wake up Elizabeth. We have more business to discuss." They stood and he helped them both alight from the tram.

She looked at him quizzically as they walked toward the darkened residence.

"Not funny business," he said evenly; "serious business."

Muller let them into the residence and turned left to his office. He carefully drew the curtains before switching on the lights. They both blinked at the sudden brightness.

Muller pulled out a chair for Elizabeth, then turned to open the combination of his safe, extracting the secret Council transcript.

"What I'm about to show you is secret," he said. "The Commissioner would have my head if he knew I was doing this. But I'm going to do it anyway."

He laid the documents in front of Elizabeth. She began to read, then looked up sharply at Muller.

"Paul," she said, "this is labeled secret by the League Secretariat. Why are you doing this?"

"Read the material, then I'll tell you," Muller replied, taking two cigarettes from his case, firing his lighter and handing one to her.

Elizabeth read the transcript rapidly, then re-read parts of it. She pushed the papers back toward Muller and tapped her cigarette in the ash tray. "Has any of this been disclosed to the public?"

Muller shook his head. "None of it. But it needs to get out; that's why I showed it to you."

"Paul, I can't publish any of this," Elizabeth said. "It's all classified as secret by the League and that would make it secret under British law as well. Both *The Statesman* and I would be prosecuted under the Official Secrets Act and the British Foreign Office would put us through the meat grinder. We're already on some kind of probation after my story in January, so there's simply no possibility that I can use this information.

"Sorry," she added, "because it really would be quite a scoop."

Muller nodded. "I assumed you would have to say that."

Then he looked directly at her before continuing. "But even though you can't break the story, as such, the information I've given you can inform your reporting.

"Look," he said, "the fact that the Council held a secret session at the end of the June public session is a matter of record. An enterprising reporter like you can make inquiries among your network of contacts to find out what participants and home offices may be saying about the session and what went on there. There are lots of ways for information to leak–which, frankly, you know about that better than I do. And since you know the facts, I'm reckoning that you'll figure a way to tease it out of someone. Hopefully, before it's too late."

"Why are you doing this, Paul?" Elizabeth asked. "This is a very dangerous business. Frankly, just having read the document makes me nervous. What if I slip up and blurt something out by mistake? It could end my career as a journalist."

"I'm doing it because I'm afraid the League is going to give up on its mandate and let Forster and Gresier and his gang of thugs simply take over Danzig and turn it into a mini Nazi dictatorship. I've spent two and a half years working–with the Commissioner–to prevent that from happening. We're on the brink of defeat, but I'm not prepared to quit without using every available tool to avoid it.

"And I'm not worried that you'll make some inadvertent slip of the tongue," he added. "You haven't gotten to where you are, fighting all the obstacles, without having your wits about you."

"Well," she said with a conspiratorial grin, "I suppose I could ask Greiser tomorrow if he knows what happened during the secret session after he was directed to leave the Chamber.'

Muller grinned back. "That's what I was about to suggest. I wonder how Greiser would answer."

Muller stood and returned the Council transcript to the safe and twirled the combination.

"Big day tomorrow. Elizabeth, I'll see you back to the hotel."

Muller reflected as he walked the few short blocks to his boarding house. Was it a mistake to confide in Elizabeth and show her the document? It was a dangerous business. It was his ass on the line, as the file clerk had told him in Geneva when he signed the register. If he disclosed the document and was discovered, he would have no protection. The Poles would be furious; the Germans as well. The Danzig Senate would gleefully pile on. And he knew how annoyed Eden and Stevenson would be. No help there, for sure. Even the Commissioner would have to disavow him; that would be particularly painful, Muller thought to himself.

But, if it came to that, it would be because all of them–all except the Commissioner–were willing to sell out the mandate. Bigger fish to fry; other priorities to focus on. Who's going to miss Danzig, right?

As he got ready for bed, Muller removed the cork from an open bottle of red wine and took a long swallow.

There might come a point, he thought to himself, where he would have to decide whether or not to disclose the secret information and to show up the cynical maneuvering of the League's politicians for the world to see.

If it came to that, he decided that he was ready to do it, despite all the troubles it might bring down on his head. As he drew up the covers and closed his eyes, he hoped he'd feel the same way in the bright light of morning.

CHAPTER 23

Summer, 1936

Muller awoke the next day feeling more hung over than resolved. He briefly thought that what he should have done last night was to have skipped the detour to his office and instead gone directly to the hotel where he was sure Elizabeth would have taken him to bed. That would have been nice, he reflected.

But after the first cup of strong black tea, he was sure he'd done the right thing. He found a fresh file on his desk containing a half dozen new pronouncements from the Senate all of which, on even quick examination were plainly objectionable. He found it very tedious to translate these documents and then prepare formal objections for the Commissioner to sign and send to the Senate, which the Senate would then proceed to ignore. He wondered to himself what was going on in the minds of the clerks who drafted this rubbish. Did adherence to National Socialism demand skills in writing decrees that dangled hints of free expression before dashing them in language returning to Party dogma?

He was happy to be interrupted by a telephone call from Elizabeth Wiskemann.

"I've completed the interview with Greiser," she said. "You'll want to hear about it. How about taking the train down to Dirschau with me so we can talk before I meet the express to Berlin after lunch?"

"Better yet, I'll drive you," Muller replied. Since Lester had elected not to replace the driver who had quit, the Daimler was available. "I'll pick you up in front of the hotel in twenty minutes."

"Well, at least he was sober," Elizabeth said after stowing her bags in the boot and clambering into the passenger seat. "But what a nasty man. You were right about his self-confidence after Geneva."

Reading from her notes, she said, "Listen to these quotes—on the record: *Danzig's severance from the League as far as her internal affairs are concerned is now complete; Never again will I have to participate in a Council meeting to discuss the internal affairs of Danzig; The will of the people in Danzig will bring about a change in the High Commissioner and a cessation of his attempted interference in our affairs.*" Elizabeth was excitedly waving her arms with her notes.

"He was absolutely crowing, striding around his big office, gesturing and posturing."

"Then I asked him who had written his speech in Geneva," Elizabeth went on, looking up from her notes. "He looked completely undone by the question. Well, he stammered, of course he had written it personally. It had been important *to set the right tone*, he told me, and said that he had spent hours editing it to his satisfaction.

"Then I told him the rumor was that it was written for him in Berlin by Goebbels. You should have seen the look on his face," she laughed. "He sputtered and coughed and got all red. Oh yes, I think that's probably going into my story."

Then, she stopped, putting her hand to her mouth. She turned to Muller and mouthed "Can we talk here?"

Smart. Of course there was a risk that the car was bugged. He shook his head and put one finger to his lips.

Traffic was light so they made good time, arriving at the station a full hour ahead of the Koenigsburg-Berlin Express. While Elizabeth purchased her ticket, Muller bought a couple of wieners and two chilled bottles of beer from a vendor and they walked across the street to a leafy park, finding a bench to themselves where they could speak quietly.

"Those quotes from Greiser are very dismissive of the Commissioner and the League," Elizabeth said, taking a big bite of her wiener.

Muller nodded. "You were in Geneva, Elizabeth. You saw how Eden let him deliver that threatening speech without any word of censure—and not even any criticism of the misconduct here in Danzig that led to the meeting in the first place. He let Greiser essentially thumb his nose at the League."

"Literally," said Elizabeth with a giggle.

"Even that," Muller nodded. "Did you ask him about the Council's secret meeting?"

Elizabeth paused to swallow a mouthful of wiener. "He simply dismissed it," she said. 'It doesn't matter', he said. 'Nothing that the League does matters anymore.' I even followed up, asking him if he wasn't at least curious why the Council would excuse him and go into secret session. He said he could care less, and simply waved the subject away like it was a bug or something."

Muller took his last swig of beer and tossed the empty bottle in the trash can next to the bench. "I guess I'm not surprised," he said, his hands on his knees staring across the street at the station. "The whole purpose of the secret session was to empower Beck to use the threat of Polish military intervention to get Hitler to put the brakes on Forster and Greiser."

"Beck obviously didn't do what he promised to do," Muller continued. "So even that small fig leaf of protection seems to have vanished. Our role here is now at Hitler's whim; if he instructs Forster to get rid of us, we're finished."

"Are you in danger, Paul?" Elizabeth asked in alarm.

Muller paused before responding. "I hope not. The Commissioner and I are accredited diplomats; that ought to count for something.

"But with this crowd, you never know," he added with a shrug.

The Express train had arrived and they walked back into the station and along the platform. Finding Elizabeth's compartment, Muller mounted the steps and stowed her luggage in the overhead rack then stepped down. Elizabeth put her arms around his neck and kissed him warmly on the lips.

She stepped back, then smiled brightly at him and climbed into the carriage, firmly closing the compartment door and lowering the window. "Be careful, Paul," she said, "I'll be thinking about you." She leaned out as the conductor's whistle shrilled; the locomotive engaged and the train began to creep forward.

"I'll send you a copy of my article," she said, cupping her hands and waving back at him as the train gathered speed.

Driving back to Danzig, Muller ran over in his mind the statements Greiser had made to Elizabeth. His declaration that Danzig was now severed from the League and his boast that he would never again be called before the Council were revealing—and disturbing. Greiser clearly now believed that he had a free hand to do whatever Hitler instructed him to do and that the League was too weak to do anything about it. And Greiser was probably right.

Shit!

When he shared the information with Lester, he found the Commissioner agreed with his pessimistic assessment and felt very disheartened about the situation.

"Secretary General Avenol sent me a long message today telling me that hostilities have broken out in Spain," he said. "Apparently a Nationalist general named Franco has mounted a coup against the government that's backed by the Germans and the Italians, while on the other side the Soviets are supporting the Spanish government. According to Avenol, this has the makings of a civil war pitting major outside powers against one another. He says the British and French are desperately seeking some kind of non-intervention agreement and the League is devoting virtually all of its resources to averting a full scale war.

"I've been sending Avenol reports on all the plainly unconstitutional directives we've been getting from the Senate, the reports of Greiser's plans to shut down opposition papers, all the violent rhetoric, and so on," Lester continued. "I wanted him to know just how defiant Greiser's become, and frankly, how exposed we are here. His reply is to tell me how bad things have gotten in Spain."

"In other words, stop pestering me with problems in Danzig?" Muller asked.

Lester nodded. "That's how I'm reading it. Also, we haven't heard back from Papee and Beck hasn't invited me to his vacation compound on the Baltic. It looks like we're on our own, Muller."

"I've decided to send Elsie and the girls back to Ireland," Lester continued. "I'm effectively sitting here in the Residence under house arrest, with the Gestapo screening my visitors. Greiser's screaming for my head. It's a bad atmosphere and I'm apprehensive something could happen to my family. Elsie objected at first, but I've persuaded her to go with the girls."

"You ought to leave too, Muller," he added. "Your name was on that assassination team's hit list a year ago; I'm afraid you're probably even more of a potential target now."

Muller nodded. "I'm afraid we're both targets, Commissioner. You need to consider how much longer to stay as well."

Lester absently lit a cigarette, pocketed his lighter and leaned back in his chair, gazing out the open windows at the buildings across the Central Square.

"The only weapon we have left, Muller, is that secret transcript in your safe," he said quietly. "And we can't use it. At least not now."

"Shall I at least contact Papee and get him to tell us what he's learned?" Muller asked.

Lester nodded, smiling. "He's the only one who's seen our weapon; let's see if it's gotten anyone's attention."

When Muller called him, Papee responded that he had a meeting scheduled the next day with Beck at Gydina. "Tell, the Commissioner that I'll be pleased to meet with him right afterwards. I should have all the answers at that point. But I've reserved a court at the Sportshalle at 5 PM, want to play?"

Muller accepted readily; he needed some exercise.

Papee's car pulled up at the entrance to the residence at 4:30 and Muller jumped in the back seat.

"Nice afternoon for a match," Papee said; "it'll take our minds off this business with Gresier.

I obviously haven't spoken yet to Beck about all this, but I have to tell you that I think any chance of our ministers taking up the question of deploying troops in Danzig evaporated with the news about the fighting in Spain."

Papee turned to Muller. "Poland doesn't have anything to do with what's happening in Spain, and it's a long way off. But our two biggest neighbors seem to be squaring off against one another there. Our embassy in Madrid reports that Germany's shipping arms and sending fighters to the Nationalists and the Soviets are doing the same thing for the Government. Fighting already seems to have broken out between them. That's making us very nervous."

"We're told that the League is very nervous in Geneva, too," said Muller.

"You know that we have non-aggression pacts with both Germany and the Soviet Union." Papee tapped the seat for emphasis.

"Remember the picture I drew on the cocktail napkin that night? When you're a small country like Poland, stuck between two much bigger neighbors who are beginning to shoot at one another–even though they're doing it a thousand miles away–you get apprehensive, and very leery of starting a new controversy, like sending troops into Danzig, for example."

"Look, Muller," Papee went on, tapping the seat again. "I don't know what Beck was thinking when he told the Council that Poland would defend the League's mandate in Danzig with Polish troops. Frankly, I don't believe that was ever in the cards. But it's clearly unrealistic now, in light of the fighting in Spain. We can't risk rocking the boat."

Muller studied the back of the Polish chauffer's bald head before turning to Papee. "Avenol told the Commissioner in a message yesterday that the League is entirely focused on getting a non-intervention agreement to keep everyone out of Spain. He took the message to mean that the League has its hands full and doesn't want to hear any more about Danzig.

"So," he continued, "the League's busy elsewhere, Poland won't stick its neck out and Gresier's declared victory. It looks to me like the mandate we're supposed to uphold in Danzig has become a dead letter."

The car pulled up to the Sportshalle. "On that happy note, let's turn to something serious," Papee said, "like tennis."

That evening Muller stopped by the Residence on his way to dinner and reported his discouraging conversation with Papee to Lester.

"Papee's driving to Gydina first thing in the morning to meet Beck. He expects to be back after lunch and will make an appointment to come see us."

"I'm afraid I don't expect much," Lester replied, "but let's wait and see."

***

Papee was true to his word and called the next afternoon, making a 4 PM appointment. He arrived punctually and Muller escorted him up the stairway to Lester's office. As Papee took his chair for the meeting, Muller noticed that he looked pale and tense, his hands jerking nervously.

"I am instructed to deliver a message," Papee began, clearing his throat and obviously uncomfortable. "I am instructed to advise you that the transcript of the secret Council meeting that you illegally and improperly shared with me a few days ago is invalid."

Muller looked at Papee incredulously. "What the Hell are you talking about, Papee," he sputtered, "I got it myself from the League record office and signed for it."

Papee began perspiring, lighting a cigarette awkwardly, his hand shaking as he lit it.

"Minister Beck has advised me that the document you showed me is erroneous and that a corrected transcript has been prepared by the Secretariat at his instructions, with the concurrence of the Rapporteur, Mr. Eden. The corrected version makes no mention of any threat by Poland to defend Danzig by force."

Muller managed to complete the translation for Lester before blurting out, "that bastard!"

Lester held up his hand.

"And what does this 'corrected version' say, Mr. Papee?" Lester inquired quietly, his eyes boring in on Papee.

Papee ground out his cigarette in the ash tray and shifted uneasily in his chair.

"I wasn't shown a copy, Commissioner. I was told by Minister Beck that documents reporting secret sessions of the Council must remain exclusively in the possession of the records section at the Palais."

Then looking down at his hands, obviously unwilling to meet Lester's penetrating gaze, he added, "But Minister Beck told me that the gist of the document was that it authorized him, as the Polish representative, to approach the German government and the President of the Danzig Senate and ask for their recommendations on steps that might be taken to reduce the risk of civil disorder."

Papee looked up and added. "I am instructed to make an appointment tomorrow with President Greiser and ask for his suggestions."

Papee, coughed nervously into his hand. Then he stood. "That is the message I am instructed to deliver," he said.

"It gives me no pleasure to deliver it. I know my way out."

Lester and Muller sat in silence. The sound of Papee's footfalls receded as he descended the stairway.

Finally, Lester spoke. "The ultimate betrayal."

Muller remained silent before nodding slowly and repeating Lester's term. "Betrayal is right, Commissioner. Eden's fingerprints are all over this."

Lester nodded. "The League's mandate over Danzig was threatening to become an obstacle to British appeasement policy and its quest for European peace. So it became another pawn that Eden and his allies could sacrifice in pursuit of their larger objective."

They sat another moment in silence taking in the magnitude of the message Papee had delivered.

Finally Lester sighed. "If Papee's going to see Greiser tomorrow, this business could blow up very soon. I need to move up the departure date for Elsie and the girls."

He stood, "Muller, you ought to make your plans to leave too."

But as Muller rose, he suddenly turned to Lester and said, "Commissioner, you bought a nice new Leica camera for your ski vacation last winter, am I right?"

Lester nodded,

"And it has film in it?"

"Yes, but..." He stopped. "No, Muller that wouldn't be the right thing to do."

Muller held up his hands. "Nothing you need to concern yourself with, Commissioner; I just want to take a few souvenir photos of our last days in Danzig."

He smiled disarmingly at Lester.

Lester hesitated, then, evidently making up his mind, smiled back. "Right. Of course. Let me get it for you."

***

Muller took the camera down to his office and locked the door from the inside. He rearranged the lamps so they brightly illuminated the center of his desk. Then he went to the safe, unlocked it and withdrew the transcript of the secret Council session. He laid the first page on the desk beneath the lights.

The Leica camera was one of the newest models, the DX5, which featured a small aperture on top to view the lenscape and lever on the side to adjust the focus. Lester began experimenting, seeing how close he could

434

get to capture the full page and still get a clear focus on the typescript. He carried several books from the bookcase and placed them on the desk where he could place his elbows to steady his hands and hopefully avoid movement that could blur the images.

He tried several dry runs, adjusting the lights and changing the height of the piles of books for his elbows to steady his grip. Finally, he thought he had it right. He turned the knob on the bottom of the camera and fed a new negative into the chamber, aimed, focused, and carefully pushed the shutter button. There were nine pages in total. Three of them he had to shoot twice, fearing he'd moved and blurred the image. But in thirty minutes he was done.

He returned the transcript to the safe and twirled the combination lock. He returned the books to their shelves and he moved the lights back to their accustomed locations. Then he opened his coat closet door, stepped inside, closed the door and, in the darkness, advanced the film knob until all of the film was successfully rolled into the metal container and safe from exposure. Opening the closet, he cracked open the camera and extracted the sealed container, putting it safely in his pants pocket. Then he went upstairs and left the camera on the stairs to the family living quarters on the third floor so Lester could put it away.

Exiting the residence by the door to the garden, Muller walked to the garage and pulled a bicycle off its storage hooks, checked to be sure the tires had air and pedaled out onto Silberhutte, right past the Residence, waving to the Gestapo guards, several of whom shouted at him, then animatedly gesturing at one another, pointing in several different directions in obvious confusion.

Muller laughed aloud. He was sure none of the agents they had stationed to follow him had a bicycle; on foot they couldn't keep up with him and trams were useless.

Screw you guys, he said to himself, pedaling quickly away.

It didn't take him long to get to Sternfeld's Department Store. He asked the doorman to look after his bike, then he walked to the stationary department and purchased a small box of folded note cards bearing engraved scenes of Danzig and accompanying envelopes. Walking to an unused counter, he opened the box and extracted a note, one showing the soaring tower of the Danzig Rathaus. Muller pulled out his fountain pen and scrawled a note that read 'Please guard this. If you do not hear from me or the Commissioner in 30 days, develop the film and make use of it to the extent you can'. He then placed the card in an envelope, carefully sealed it, and wrote on the front "Elizabeth Wiskemann. Confidential".

This was no time to communicate with Eirene, he thought to himself, but with only a small twinge he was glad to notice.

He discarded the unused stationary in a nearby receptacle and walked up a stairway to the glassware section where he selected two of the same wine glasses he'd purchased the last time he was there. He proceeded to the checkout counter and inquired about using ocean freight to ship his gift to London. This clerk was as helpful as the one he'd used earlier.

After the clerk folded a box into shape and put in the straw to cushion the glasses, Muller asked if he could get it gift wrapped.

"Certainly," the clerk said smiling. "Let me just go in the back to get some designs and you can choose the one you like best." She flashed an even brighter smile.

"Thank you," said Muller, and as the clerk went through the doorway to look for the giftwrapping, Muller put his sealed note in the bottom of the box, pulled the film container out of his pocket, put it in one of the wine glasses, then carefully rearranged the straw so neither could be seen.

When the clerk returned, Muller selected a wrapping with garish floral design, then waited patiently as the clerk carefully cut the paper, neatly sealing the fold, styling it with a bright red ribbon, then wrapped the carton again in brown shipping paper, secured it with packing tape and finally tied it up firmly with twine. Muller had filled out the address form with Elizabeth's name and the London address of *The Statesman*. He had inserted a phony return address and, after reflecting a moment, filled in the sender line with the name W.A Mozart.

After paying the clerk, who was by now clearly flirting with him, Muller inquired about where he might find the call box.

He dialed the headquarters of the Social Democratic Party and asked to speak to Ernst Brost.

After a moment, Brost came on the line. Assuming the phone was tapped, Muller did not identify himself and spoke brusquely.

"We need to meet. Urgently. The place where Kreutzer passed the message to Muller when he was hurt."

There was a pause.

"I know the place."

"9 PM tonight."

"Agreed."

***

Muller departed Sternfeld's by a different exit, leaving the bicycle behind.

He decided to make his way to the Shivet Pub by a series of crisscross tram rides, getting on and off quickly, going in different directions, then doubling back. By the time, he got to the bridge over the Mottlau near Laagergasse, he was sure he was not being tailed. It was still bright sunshine in the Danzig summer, so he had no shadows to duck into. But he remembered that this part of Danzig was more sparsely populated, and he was able work his way in the direction of the pub using short streets where he could see that there was no one behind him.

Getting to the pub, Muller hesitated a few moments, then entered and walked to the bar. No hint of recognition from the bartender. As his eyes became adjusted to the dim interior, he looked around the room and saw only a handful of patrons, none of whom were paying him any mind. He ordered sausage and a beer and carried them to a table in the back where he could watch both the entrance and the doorway leading back to the SDP meeting room where he'd met Kreutzer.

He ate the sausage hungrily, finished his beer and waited. Shortly before 9 PM, the doorway to the meeting room opened and two men emerged into the pub. Muller recognized them from the night with Kreutzer. Spying Muller in the back, they approached him.

"Please follow us," the older of the two said.

Muller followed them through the doorway.

The meeting room was not so brightly lit this time, but a shaft of sunlight angled in from a high window. Ernst Brost stood up from the folding chair he had been occupying and offered his hand with a smile.

"I assumed it had to be you Muller," he said. "Not many others know about the meeting you had with Kreutzer. I decided to bring him along tonight, for old time's sake."

Stephan Kreutzer rose from the chair beside Brost and shook hands with Muller.

"You look a lot better than the last time we met here," said Muller.

"Thank you, sir," Kreutzer replied. "The cuts are healed with only a few scars, but I haven't been able to get my tooth replaced." He pointed to the gap in his mouth.

Brost motioned for them to sit together on folding chairs facing one another.

"May I speak with the two of you alone?" Muller asked. Brost nodded and motioned for the other two men to return to the pub. He leaned back in the chair and looked at Muller, appraising him.

"If my memory is correct, Muller." he said, "every time we've met before has been at my initiative—when I've been seeking help of some kind from the Commissioner. The fact that you asked for this meeting—and the way you did it—suggest that things have changed."

He paused, "Perhaps for the worse. Maybe we're approaching the last act of the drama that we've all been involved in here."

"I'm afraid that's a pretty accurate assessment, Brost," Muller replied, nodding.

"I'm here on my own, incidentally. The Commissioner doesn't know that I'm here, let alone what I'm going to propose."

Muller paused, then took a deep breath. "To use your analogy, Brost, I want to stave off that last act. I have an idea about how to do that and I'm hoping that you'll agree. It's risky and it may backfire; but it's either that or, as you suggested, the curtain's about to fall on the League's mandate here."

"All right," Brost replied. "I'm listening."

"I'm sure that you know that the last Council meeting in Geneva was...how to describe it," Muller hesitated, "very unsatisfactory."

"*A near total loss*, I think you were going to say," Brost smiled. "We had observers present, so, yes we're very well informed. We know about the rumor that Goebbels wrote Greiser's hateful speech, that Greiser even thumbed his nose at the Council—cocked a snook, for goodness sake—and that the Council couldn't even muster a motion to censure him—not for his attacks here in Danzig, not for insulting everyone in sight in Geneva, not for anything.

"Yes," Brost nodded ruefully, "we know all about it. It was very disheartening news to be truthful."

"Then you also know that a secret session was convened at the end," Muller said.

Brost nodded. "But we don't know what happened there."

"I'm about to tell you," Muller replied, "and to suggest how you can use that information as a way to try and forestall that last act we want to avoid."

Brost leaned forward, his elbows on his knees. "You want the *Danziger Volkstimme* to publish secret information?"

"Yes," Muller replied, nodding. "Tomorrow morning, in fact."

He put his elbows on his knees too, leaning forward with his head close to Brost's, so he could speak in a low voice. "The information will be very embarrassing to the Polish Government in particular, but also to the Germans and, of course, to the Danzig government and your friends Forster and Greiser. I assume they'll try to confiscate the newspapers after you begin distributing them, but we can make certain that enough get passed around so the story will get out on the wires to the wider world. If it does, I'm counting on it to create enough consternation in European capitals–and at the League–to forestall abandonment of the mandate."

Muller paused, letting his words sink in.

"In addition to confiscating the papers, they'll padlock the newspaper office and probably arrest me," Brost said. He rubbed his hands together, his gaze lifting to the window, evaluating his options, then turned to face Muller.

"If the mandate goes down the drain, opposition parties like ours will be outlawed and our newspapers will be shut down. Hell, Greiser's already threatened to shut us down for the rest of the year, so there's not much added risk. And they can arrest me again anytime too. It's no fun, but I've been through that routine before. So," he said to Muller, "You'd better tell me the story."

Brost looked at his watch. "There's enough time to do an article tonight, but we'll need to work fast."

Turning to Kreutzer, he said, "Take notes, so we can write the story."

Muller proceeded to describe in detail the transcript of the secret Council meeting, paying particular attention to Polish Foreign Minister Beck's undertaking to threaten the use of military force in his negotiations with Germany and the Danzig government. Brost asked questions which Muller answered, with Kreutzer scribbling frantically in his notebook.

"The next day, the Commissioner and I met with Beck in his office," Muller continued, "and he told us he had issued instructions for plans to be drawn up by the Polish military for deployment into Danzig from Gydina."

Brost whistled briefly under his breath. "This is some story, Muller."

"There's more," Muller continued. "When nothing happened to restrain Greiser's behavior, the Commissioner called in Papee, the Polish Consul, to find out what was going on with Beck's negotiations in Berlin and here in Danzig. Papee knew nothing about any of it, especially about the threatened use of military force."

Here Muller paused, instinctively looking around him for eavesdroppers before turning back to Brost.

"I have a copy of the League secretariat's transcript of the secret meeting in my safe, so I went down and got it and showed it to Papee. He was astonished. The Commissioner snatched the document away and told me to put it back in the safe, But Papee had seen more than enough to know that we weren't exaggerating. The Commissioner then sent him off to find Beck and get an explanation about the negotiations he was supposedly conducting."

Brost looked grimly at Muller. "The negotiations never occurred?" he asked.

"Worse," Muller replied. "Papee saw Beck this morning and immediately came over to brief the Commissioner. He had been given explicit instruction on what to say, and looked as uncomfortable–and embarrassed–as I've ever seen any diplomat."

"What did he say?" asked Brost, clearly intrigued.

Muller smiled faintly. "Papee said he'd been instructed to tell the Commissioner that the transcript of the secret session of the Council that I had shown him was an error and that a new transcript had been prepared by the League's Secretariat instructing Beck to approach both the German government and the government here in Danzig for suggestions on how the tensions might be reduced. There is no mention whatever in this new document of Beck's threat to employ military force to protect the Free City."

"What?" exclaimed Brost. "They changed the document?"

Muller nodded. "Wiped clean. As directed by Beck–and by Eden, too. Papee said he's been instructed to approach Greiser tomorrow morning for his 'suggestions' on how to reduce tensions. At that point, all bets are off, so that's why I insisted on meeting tonight and why I hope you'll publish the story tomorrow morning."

Brost sat up in his chair, hands on his hips now, energized, his eyes blazing. "Why those bastards!" He stood up, squaring his shoulders. "This is a story that absolutely needs to be published and I'm only too happy to be the one to do it. Leave the rest to me Muller!"

He turned, taking Kreutzer by the arm. "Come on, Kreutzer, we've got work to do."

They exited the meeting room by different doors and Muller carefully made his way back to his boarding house in the gathering twilight that passed for night in Danzig in July. He was tired. He finished the last of the open bottle of wine, reviewing in his mind the conversation with Brost and the consequences he hoped it would set in train, then fell into a deep sleep.

CHAPTER 24

Summer, 1936

Muller awoke to a pounding on his door and shouted commands to get up. With a crash his door splintered and bright flashlights shone in his eyes. When the overhead light was turned on, he saw three uniformed Gestapo troopers standing in the room gesticulating and shouting at him to get up. Disoriented, Muller fumbled for a pair of trousers which he pulled on and he got one arm through a shirtsleeve before two troopers pulled his hands behind his back and snapped on very tight handcuffs which bit into his wrists. Shouting insults at him, they yanked him out the doorway, dragged him down the stairs, still shoeless, and heaved him into the back of a Black Maria van. His feet were shackled and his handcuffs were chained to a rack above a hard wooden seat forcing his body into a painful contortion. The door shut with a crash and Muller heard it lock.

The van began driving with the klaxon sounding the feared siren used by Gestapo vehicles. Miller's mind spun, trying to understand what was happening. He tried to shift his body to a more comfortable position, but the van bounced on the pavement and made sharp turns causing him to lose his balance and push painfully against his constraints. The van was pitch black and Muller had no sense of the direction he was being taken.

Suddenly the van braked to a stop. Muller could here snatches of conversation as the van was evidently being cleared through some kind of checkpoint. It accelerated briefly, then came to a stop again, and the rear doors were opened. Uniformed men unshackled him and hauled him into a courtyard under bright lights. They frog-marched him to a doorway, then up a flight of stairs to a black steel sliding door. They dragged him inside, sliding the door back into place, then forced him down several flights of steel steps that cut into his bare feet.

At a landing, they pushed him into a corridor with exposed bare lights hanging from the ceiling and barred cells on either side. They stopped before one of the cells and a guard inserted a large metal key, opening the cell door. One of the guards stood by the doorway and the other yanked Muller into the cell and removed his handcuffs.

Trying to make some sense of what was happening, Muller turned to the guards. "Why are you doing this? I'm an accredited diplomat."

"A diplomat are you?" said the nearest of the guards. "Well we have a special welcome for diplomats." He punched Muller hard in the stomach and, as he doubled over, brought his knee up to catch Muller full on the jaw, then planted a roundhouse punch on Muller's right cheek, driving him to his knees. A kick to the ribs sent him sprawling on the cold, hard cement floor.

"That's what we call our diplomatic reception," the guard said, locking the cell and walking away with his companion, the two of them laughing.

Muller lay in a semi-conscious daze. Finally, he was able to drag himself up on his hands and knees, and inch his way toward a slop bucket he spotted in the dim light from the bulb in the corridor. His stomach heaved and he retched, groaning with the pain in his ribs where he'd been kicked. Finally, he rolled on his back and lapsed into a semiconscious daze. He awoke later–he had no idea how much time had elapsed–to find himself shivering on the cold floor. Rousing himself slowly on all fours, he saw a cot of some kind on the far wall and forced himself to climb up on it, a hard board, covered by a thin, foul-smelling blanket which he tried to wrap around his shoulders. He cradled his head on an arm and lapsed into semi-consciousness again.

Suddenly, he heard a commotion on the stairs and saw another prisoner being dragged into his corridor. Muller was able to raise his head then push himself into a sitting position. The prisoner had his head down, but Muller could see blood dripping from his mouth. The guards hauled him upright, removed the cuffs and unceremoniously tossed him into the next cell.

The guards shouted obscenities at both of them, then climbed back up the stairs.

Muller looked at the new prisoner, who was beginning to move and finally forced himself into a sitting position facing Muller.

It was Brost.

"Brost," he hissed. "It's me, Muller."

To his surprise, Brost turned toward him and began chuckling. "Well, Muller," he said. "We meet again."

He paused, grimacing, then crawled to the cot and sat facing Muller. He had a split lip, a bloody nose and badly bruised cheeks. "I'm not surprised. They found your card in Kreutzer's pocket when they took us. So I figured they'd pay you a visit too. Sorry about that," he added.

"The plan got blown?" Muller asked.

"Someone at the printer squealed on us," Brost said nodding slowly. "We got the story written but we weren't half way through setting the type when they came for us. Nasty group.

"They roughed up poor Kreutzer a little bit, then found your card and threw him out on the street. They brought the owner of the print shop and me here, beat us up a little more, then let him go and told me I was going to enjoy their hospitality for a while longer. So here I am."

Then Brost pointed to the wall, cupping his ear with his hand and putting the other to his lip, signaling silence. Listening device, thought Muller. That's why their jailers had put them together. Muller nodded, hoping they hadn't already said too much.

"Let's try to get some sleep," he said, rolling onto his side and curling up.

Muller had spoken the words for the benefit of the listening device.

But sleep would not come. His mind was spinning. His plan to publicize the Council's betrayal had failed. Greiser's forces had certainly confiscated the story Kreutzer had written, so Greiser and Forster knew the whole plan. They had him here under lock and key; would they also arrest the Commissioner, he wondered? His disclosure of the information about the Council's secret session was in clear beach of his League of Nations duties. Would he be dismissed and stripped of his diplomatic immunity? That would leave him completely at Gresier's mercy. He shivered involuntarily.

He must finally have drifted off to sleep because he was awakened by the clanking of his cell door as it was flung open and a guard entered, dousing him with a pail of ice water.

"Aahhgg." Muller groaned as his body recoiled from the shock, every fiber protesting.

"Get up, diplomatic asshole," said the guard. "Someone's got plans for you this morning." He pulled Muller to his feet and roughly pinned his hands in back, snapping the handcuffs on his wrists.

Muller swayed and the guard grabbed him by one arm and yanked him out into corridor and up the steel stairway, the rough steps again cutting into Muller's bare feet.

To his surprise, they retraced their route from the night before and descended the exterior stairs to the courtyard where a Black Maria van awaited them, gleaming menacingly in the sunlight. Once again, Muller was flung into the back of the van, shackled and left in the pitch black as the doors were slammed shut.

Muller lost track of time and couldn't identify the direction they traveled, but only a short time later, the van stopped, the doors were opened and, after being unshackled, he found himself standing in front of his boardinghouse. One of the guards shoved him through the door and back up the stairs to his room, with the door still in splinters and his belongings scattered.

"Get dressed fast," barked the guard, removing the handcuffs. "I'm under orders to deliver you to the Commissioner's residence in fifteen minutes."

Well, Muller thought to himself, this is a new development. Certainly better than being dragged into some new jail and being beaten up, which was what he'd feared.

"I need to start in the lavatory," Muller said.

Inside he ran the water to get it hot and looked at himself in the mirror. The right side of his face was red and badly swollen, with the beginnings of a black eye. His face stung as he doused it in the hot water, washing off the dirt and, he noticed, bits of blood. He tried to shave, but found his hand shaking too badly and settled for toweling himself off.

After Muller dressed, the guard snapped the handcuffs back on then hurried him down the stairs and back into the van for the short drive to the residence. Muller scarcely had time to think about what was in store for him, but feeling a little better, washed and dressed and returning to familiar territory, he decided this was not time to be contrite or defensive. And he was angry; this was a time to brazen it out.

The guard opened the van door and led him up the staircase to the second floor where he knocked on the Commissioner's door. Greiser appeared in the doorway.

"I am delivering the prisoner," said the guard, coming to attention. "Heil Hitler."

"Heil Hitler," Greiser responded, then walked back into the Commissioner's office, leaving the door ajar for Muller to enter.

The scene that greeted him was hardly what he expected. Papee, the Polish Consul General was seated at one end of the long conference table, the Commissioner at the other. Along the near side ranged between them sat von Radowitz, the German Consul General, and Greiser, who was returning to his seat with a smirk on his face. Muller could sense an atmosphere of tension and hostility.

"Goddamit Greiser, get those handcuffs removed," Papee said sharply.

Greiser rose, slowly strolled to the doorway and summoned the guard to remove Muller's handcuffs, then laconically returned to his seat, still smirking, clearly relishing being able to humiliate Muller.

"Got to be careful with dangerous criminals," Greiser said.

Papee appeared to be in charge of this impromptu meeting.

"Muller," he said, "You are a subject of this meeting, but we also expect you to perform your translation duties. Are you prepared to do that?"

"Yes," Muller replied. "But I need large cup of black tea. I had a busy night."

Muller watched a tight smile appear on the Commissioner's face as he signaled for the tea to be brought.

Papee looked at Muller in irritation. "What you did last night was to commit a clear and deliberate breach of your duties as an employee of the League of Nations. Your misconduct affects vital interests of the nations represented around this table, other members of the League Council and the office of the High Commissioner, of which you are a part. This is a serious case of insubordination."

Muller translated for Lester, then shrugged.

"This was my first experience of dealing with deliberately falsified Council documents," he said. "I decided I needed to improvise in order to set the record straight."

Greiser's face turned bright red. "You little shit," he snarled and turned to the others. "That's exactly why we should arrest the two of them, Lester and Muller, right now. I'm going to declare them persona non grata, deport them on the next train and complete our takeover of Danzig. Why waste any more time?"

As Muller began translating for Lester, von Radowitz leaped out of his seat, grabbed Greiser by the necktie and shoved his chair over backwards, sending Greiser sprawling.

Von Radowitz stood over him, pointing his finger in Greiser's face, "Greiser, you are an incompetent fool. We are dealing here with a vital interest of the Fuehrer himself; I will not have you stupidly interfering with serious business. Now sit down and shut up." He returned to his seat and Greiser submissively picked himself up, and regained his seat, looking chastened.

The Commissioner spoke quietly and evenly from his seat at the other end of the long table.

"Let me be very clear about my position on this business," he said. "I did not instruct Muller to approach Ernst Brost last evening or to disclose to him the contents of the secret Council meeting. But I stand behind him and will defend his actions both here and in Geneva at the appropriate time.

"The recent behavior of your Minister Beck," he said, pointing at Papee, "and by the Council's Rapporteur, in falsifying the record of the meeting and altering the instructions approved by the Council by unanimous vote are completely unprecedented in my experience. I consider it both a betrayal and a breach of trust." Lester leaned forward, resting his elbows on the conference table. "And so I would not be unhappy to see this treacherous behavior plastered on the front pages of the world's newspapers. That was your motivation, Mr. Muller, am I right?"

Muller translated and nodded in confirmation. "Yes, Commissioner."

Lester turned to face Greiser. "If you follow through on your threat, Greiser I will convene the press upon my arrival back in Geneva and make a full public airing of this scandal. That is the message I attempted to convey early this morning to Consul General Papee in my limited French and why I told him to convene this meeting where Mr. Muller could be present both to translate and to participate."

"That is an accurate statement, Commissioner," Papee confirmed. "And I understood you to say as well that you had some ideas of how this issue might be resolved to general satisfaction. I conveyed this information to Consul General von Radowitz, who agreed participate and to bring Greiser along."

"I don't like the threat of revealing secret information that you've just made, Commissioner, he added. "So let's move on to the issue of how to resolve this matter."

Lester nodded. "All in good time," he said, pausing a moment before beginning to speak.

"I understand, Consul General Papee, why your government does not want the information about threatening force to defend the Free City then backing down and falsifying League records to be made public. It would hold your government up to ridicule."

Lester then turned to von Radowitz. "I understand also, Consul General von Radowitz, why Germany would not like it known publicly that the League Council was so convinced of Germany's complicity in a likely coup d'etat against Danzig that it called on a member nation–Poland, in this case–to threaten the use of military force against Germany. I understand that your Fuehrer," he said, looking at both von Radowitz and Greiser, "would find that accusation deeply and personally insulting."

Von Radowitz glared at Greiser as Muller translated.

"So I view the interests around this table–and frankly those of the British Foreign Office too–as wanting to bury the record surrounding the League's secret session, am I right?" Lester looked around the table.

"I would frame the matter differently, Commissioner," said Papee, "but proceed."

"Yes, proceed," von Radowitz echoed.

Lester nodded. "For my part, I want to avoid a situation where the Government of Danzig declares the League's High Commissioner and his staff persona non grata, deports us back to Geneva and uses that event as a pretext to nullify the League's mandate and take over the Free City."

Lester paused and looked around the conference table, giving his audience time to absorb his words. Then he continued. "I believe there is a way to accommodate both sets of interests."

"What do you have in mind?" Papee asked.

"I begin with the proposition that my mission here is finished," Lester replied.

"I cannot continue to serve as High Commissioner after having been betrayed by the leadership of the League Council. It is therefore my intention to depart Danzig and return to Geneva at an early date with a view to bringing my appointment to an end, either by resignation or through some other means."

Lester looked around the table again. "I'm confident that decision will be cordially received in some quarters here," he said. Gresier responded with a big smile, but kept silent.

"I am prepared to go quietly," Lester continued, "and remain silent on the subject to the Council's betrayal and falsification of documents. But there must be no coup d'etat," he said. "No takeover by the Senate or the NSDAP. The Danzig Constitution must remain as it is; the League's mandate must not be overthrown by force. That's the quid pro quo."

"I'm afraid there will not be much left of the League's mandate after I depart," Lester went on. But I insist that it remain in force. None of us can foresee the future; there may come a time when the affected parties will want to breathe new life into it."

With that, Lester spread his hands and looked around the table. "Those are my terms," he said. "If you agree, I'll instruct Mr. Muller to remove the transcript of the secret session from his safe, bring it up to the office here and we'll burn it. That will destroy the last shred of evidence of this sorry story."

There was silence as people weighed what Lester had said.

Finally, Papee and von Radowitz exchanged glances, nodding at one another. "I agree," they each said, and Greiser, without prompting, said, "I agree."

"In that case, Muller kindly go downstairs, remove the document from your safe and bring it up here to be destroyed."

Muller translated, but then said, "There is one more condition. Ernst Brost must be released from prison today."

Greiser reddened and opened his mouth to protest, but von Radowitz pointed a finger at him. "Shut up Greiser," he said impatiently. "Brost is only one of the lowlifes that you'll be able to deal with after the Commissioner leaves Danzig. Agree at once!"

Greiser heaved a big sigh and shrugged his shoulders. "Yes, I'll order his release—at least for now." He glared at Muller.

Muller stood and walked to the stairs which he descended slowly, feeling the pain in his injured ribcage. He opened the safe and removed the document, placing the pages at the precise point on his desk where he had photographed them a day earlier, then picked them up and shuffled them into order.

He smiled to himself as he did so. The Commissioner knew what he had done and hadn't breathed a word of it in the meeting. The photographic copy he'd sent to Elizabeth might yet prove a vital anchor to windward he thought, as he mounted the stairway to the big office with the secret document under his arm, ready to be burned.

Without ceremony, Papee took the pages from Muller and lit them afire with his lighter. As there was no fireplace, he attempted to burn them in the large ashtray on the conference table. But as the papers ignited, they fell onto the surface of the conference table, leaving large black scorch marks that polish would not remove.

***

As Muller replayed the scene in his mind several days later, on the long train ride back to Geneva, he thought about how the burning documents had scorched the surface of the conference table, leaving indelible scars. He concluded, ruefully, that those scars would serve as the only permanently surviving trace of a once robust League of Nations mandate to protect the Free City of Danzig.

The End.

EPILOGUE

At the League Council meeting in September, 1936, Sean Lester was appointed Deputy Secretary-General of the League of Nations. He thereupon formally resigned as High Commissioner in Danzig. News of his resignation set off jubilant celebrations in Danzig by the Senate and the NSDAP. By the middle of October, most opposition politicians who had not earlier fled, had been arrested and all opposition publications had been shut down. The Senate issued dozens of new directives imposing National Socialist doctrine. Among the changes was an amendment to the criminal code making it illegal for any citizen of Danzig to file a petition with the League of Nations without first obtaining the consent of the Danzig Senate.

***

In January 1937, Polish Foreign Minister Josef Beck negotiated arrangements with the German government to restrain the Danzig government from interfering with Polish citizens and Polish rights to the Free City under the Treaty of Versailles. It was tacitly understood that Poland would no longer support League protection for the Danzig Constitution or the German population in Danzig that opposed the NSDAP government. It was precisely the kind of agreement that Lester had warned Beck would prompt him to resign. Beck privately assured Casimir Papee, who remained Consul General in Danzig, that the arrangements reflected the new reality of a strong Germany and that Poland's paramount interests were no longer to protect the mandate of a weakened League, but instead to deepen Polish bilateral relations with Germany.

***

The League Council appointed Carl Burckhardt, a Swiss historian and diplomat, as High Commissioner to replace Sean Lester in February, 1937. Burckhardt was fluent in German and, while not a Nazi Party member, he was generally viewed as a Nazi sympathizer. The appointment was largely symbolic, as Burckhardt made clear that he did not interpret his responsibilities as extending to involvement in the internal affairs of the Danzig government. Upon his arrival in the Free City, Burckhardt called upon Albert Forster, the Nazi Gauleiter, and declared that he looked forward to working closely with Forster. Burckhardt said that he supported the view that the German population of Danzig "should choose the form of government deemed most appropriate to Germans" and that he had no intention of interfering with government actions.

***

While the League Council held periodic meetings thereafter purporting to deal with its mandate for Danzig, they came to be viewed as a cynical charade, contributing to the League's diminishing reputation and its descent into irrelevancy as tensions in Europe continued to escalate, finally erupting into war on September 1, 1939 when the German battleship *Schleswig Holstein* fired the first salvo in Danzig at precisely 4:47 AM.

***

On the first morning of war, Albert Forster did, in fact, order High Commissioner Burckhardt to leave the Free City within three hours.

***

In the summer of 1940, Sean Lester was appointed the last Secretary General of the League of Nations, which had effectively ceased to function after the outbreak of war. His appointment was part of a successful effort to foil a plot by Secretary General Avenol to convert the League into a Nazi appendage. Lester acted as caretaker for the League during the war until it turned over its assets and archives to the United Nations in 1946. Lester ordered the white marble League of Nations headquarters building, which had been constructed during the 1930's (and which Lester and Muller had remarked upon, gazing down from Beck's office in 1936), boarded up. It remained vacant until 1946, when it became the European Headquarters for the United Nations, a function it continues to occupy today.

**

During the war, Albert Forster and Arthur Greiser both played prominent roles in Nazi Germany's murderous extermination programs. Forster was named Gauleiter in Danzig-West Prussia and Greiser became Gaulieter in neighboring Warthegau. They both instituted racial laws that characterized Poles and Jews as sub-humans and installed brutal, systematic extermination regimes. Interestingly, their rivalry continued in these new roles, with Greiser accusing Forster of permitting some Poles to work as slave laborers instead of murdering them. Predictably, Hitler declined to intervene against Forster. In 1946, Forster was captured by the British and handed over to the Polish government. He was convicted of war crimes and crimes against humanity in 1948, and held in captivity, incommunicado, until he was hanged in February 1952. Arthur Gresier was captured by the Americans and also turned over to Polish authorities. He was promptly convicted of war crimes and crimes against humanity and on the morning of July 21, 1946 he was publicly hanged before a crowd estimated at close to 300,000.

***

Captured Polish fighters who survived the attack on the Post Office that began on September 1, 1939 were executed and buried secretly behind the abandoned Saspe cemetery, where Paul Muller stepped off the tram at the turn-out to see if he were being tailed on his trip to Oliwa to meet von Radowitz in 1935. Their remains were discovered in August 1991. The cemetery holds bodies of an estimated 14,000 Poles and other victims murdered at the infamous Stutthof Nazi concentration camp that was established within what had been the territory of the Free City of Danzig right after the outbreak of war. Initially intended to imprison Polish intellectuals it was greatly expanded and became a large forced labor and extermination camp. The US Holocaust museum estimates that, of roughly 110,000 inmates passing through Stutthof, 85,000 were killed or died of disease or exposure. After the war, the re-named Zaspa Cemetery was restored as a monument to the memory of the victims whose remains were buried there.

***

Allied bombing attacks upon Danzig began in July 1942 and continued with increasing ferocity during the war. The City came under artillery fire from advancing Soviet forces in early March 1945 and was subjected to a full scale Soviet assault later in the month. Soviet forces overran the City in a violent spasm of rape and pillage. The City was set afire and, by one estimate, 90 percent of the City's structures were destroyed. As the Red Army continued West toward Berlin, Polish militia and civilians swarmed into the city in its wake and deadly conflict ensued as the Poles killed and expelled Germans and other residents in a rage of mass-eviction, revenge and retaliation.

DANZIG

***

After the war, the territory of what had been the Free City was fully absorbed by the Polish government and the city became known by its Polish name, Gdansk. The shipyards and dockworkers of Gdansk became the foundation of the trade union movement known as Solidarity that was instrumental in toppling the Communist government in 1989. Today, Gdansk is an integral part of a free and prosperous Poland that is a member of both NATO and the European Union and is part of the Euro Zone. Many of the landmark buildings of the city have been restored, including—importantly for this story—the Commissioner's residence, whose stately, red brick Gothic architecture, tall windows, and dark slate roof remind us of the drama that unfolded within that precinct eighty years ago.

AUTHOR'S AFTERWORD

This is a work of fiction, but it incorporates a faithful account of the history of the tense years 1933 to 1936 which the story encompasses.

Sean Lester was in fact High Commissioner in Danzig during this period and the role he played in the unfolding drama is the centerpiece of the story. The real Sean Lester did not speak German and his French was mediocre. These linguistic shortcomings limited his effectiveness. He really needed a translator/interpreter to perform his job. So I created the fictitious Paul Muller, a tri-lingual Swiss secretary and translator for Lester, and inserted him in that fictional role as the main protagonist. Muller becomes the vehicle for telling the story and we see the drama unfold through his eyes.

The other characters featured in the book are also fictional, but many are modeled on actual figures in the history of the time. They appear as I imagine them to have been.

We have already read of the well-deserved post-war executions of the odious Albert Forster and Arthur Greiser. Their roles in the period covered by the book are faithfully described in the story. The public execution of Arthur Greiser can be viewed on You Tube by Googling Arthur Gresier.

The event related in the story of Arthur Greiser sticking out his tongue and 'cocking a snook' at the press in the 1936 Council meeting is historically accurate and was the subject of widespread public ridicule in the Western press.

British appeasement policy played a major role in undermining the League and it was a particular hindrance to Sean Lester in seeking to defend the constitution of the Free City against attacks by the NSDAP. So I

463

decided to begin the novel with a weekend party at fictional Berkshire Abbey and a group of characters engaging in spirited repartee that served to introduce both the fictional Paul Muller, and, more importantly, the reader, to this important subject.

The sympathy expressed by most of the characters at the party for Germany's complaints of mistreatment under the Versailles Treaty, was a widely shared opinion in Britain at the time. The League of Nations Union was in fact an influential British organization supporting the League of Nations. As Eirene and Gladys bragged in the story, it did permit active participation by women, and it was a strong voice favoring disarmament and accommodation with Germany. Though hard to believe at this distant remove, there was in fact a campaign to dissolve national air forces and confer a military air force monopoly upon the League of Nations. At the time of the weekend party in the story, where everyone extolled its virtues, it was a very fashionable cause.

The Peace Ballot was a major project of the League of Nations Union, as described in the story. The eleven million ballots cast and the results and consequences of the event, as related in the story, are accurate accounts.

Eirene Jones, to whom we were introduced at the weekend party and who became Paul Muller's lover, is a highly-fictionalized depiction of the lady of that name who was in fact the daughter of TJ Jones, the high-ranking civil servant and active member of the Cliveden Set that promoted appeasement during the period of the story (the historian Arnold Toynbee was also involved in the Cliveden Set and both he and TJ Jones paid private visits to Hitler, who enchanted them). The real Eirene was not involved with the League Nations Union. She was instead an active supporter of the Labour movement. She was elected to parliament, but not until 1947, and after retirement in 1970, she was given a life peerage as Baroness White. (She never married, perhaps pining, unknowingly, for Paul Muller.)

Anthony Eden, who played such a key role in supporting–but also undermining–Sean Lester's mission to Danzig, became one of Britain's most important leaders. He resigned as Foreign Secretary in February, 1938, breaking with the appeasement policy that he had done so much to encourage. He became Winston Churchill's Foreign Secretary during World War II and was among Churchill's closet advisors. He ultimately served as Prime Minister 1955–1957.

RCS Stevenson was staff secretary to Eden during the period covered by the book. He went on to a distinguished diplomatic career.

Elizabeth Wiskemann was a journalist and she did in fact report regularly about events in Danzig during the period of the book. She authored a book, entitled *The Europe I Saw*, published in 1968, which reported the story of her being arrested and interrogated by the Gestapo in Berlin in July 1936 after filing an article critical of Nazi interference in Danzig. She wrote that she had boarded the train connecting her to Zurich and was conferring with representatives of the British Legation when uniformed Gestapo officers entered her compartment and placed her under arrest. They removed her from the train and drove her to 'the feared Gestapo headquarters' at Prinz-Albrecht-Strasse. She was taken to a bare room in the basement where, under the glare of a single bright light bulb, she was subjected to questioning by two SS officers who demanded to know the sources for her article reporting German involvement in the anti-League campaign in Danzig. Wiskemann said she was terrified, but stood her ground as the interrogators threatened her and accused her of being in the pay of the High Commissioner. She experienced a rush of relief at finally being escorted back to the main floor and released after intervention by the British Legation representatives with whom she had been meeting at the time of the arrest. She wrote that her press credentials were confiscated and she was advised not to attempt to visit or transit German territory again.

Her book is also the source of the incident related in the story about a Nazi official snatching a cigarette from the mouth of a female traveler seated next to Paul Muller in the restaurant at the Freidrichstrasse Banhof in 1934. Wiskemann reported that happened to her in the dining car of a German train.

Her book does not include any mention of receiving a canister of undeveloped film in the summer of 1936 or a later message directing her on how to dispose of it.

Hermann Rauschning played the role attributed to him in the story, including his 1935 election-eve letter breaking with the Nazi Party, which Hitler never forgave. He fled to Poland in 1936, then later to Switzerland and France, ultimately emigrating to the US in 1941 and becoming a citizen in 1942.

The remarkable sweep of events that cascaded upon Europe during the fraught period of the mid-1930s is among the most compelling features of the novel. I endeavored not only to summon up the events themselves, but also to portray the impact they must have had upon the hot-house atmosphere that was the struggle for the Free City of Danzig. Germany's resignation from the League, Hitler's Night of the Long Knives ("murder week in the Reich"), German occupation of the Rhineland and its decision to re-arm—all these were dramatic episodes playing out on the world stage. But they had special resonance in Danzig. The same was true for the steady drumbeat of failure at the League of Nations, which undercut Lester's mission, not just in Geneva, but also in Danzig. Highlighting these events and focusing on their impact upon Sean Lester's (and Paul Muller's) lonely efforts in Danzig to sustain the League's mandate provided a vehicle for capturing both the epochal struggle at the highest levels of government and the dramatic impact of the events upon the individuals jockeying for position in Danzig–people whom we feel we've gotten to know in the story–trying to carry out their jobs in what was, by any standard, a diplomatic and political pressure cooker. Lester's mission failed of course; the League's mandate was abandoned and the NSDAP seized power, a result contributing to the spiral of events leading to the outbreak of World War II.

The downfall of the League's Danzig mandate was not quite as dramatic as portrayed in the fictionalized tale of the Council's betrayal of Lester and falsification of documents as related in the novel. But by the summer of 1936, the League effectively abandoned efforts to enforce the mandate. Returning to Danzig from the climactic June, 1936 Council meeting, Sean Lester, accompanied by Elsie, did in fact bravely walk from the Central Station to the Residence, not knowing if he would be attacked. He was not, but the Residence was immediately sealed off by police and Lester was effectively placed under house arrest. Lester's appointment as Deputy Secretary General of the League in September 1936 was a face-saving step taken by political leaders to camouflage what was in fact a humiliating retreat from any pretense of maintaining the League's mandate.

While endeavoring to capture an accurate historical account of the period covered in the novel, I took a major liberty with the facts of the outbreak of war. That famous first salvo, unleashed by the German battleship *Schleswig-Holstein* on September 1, 1939, was fired, not at the Post Office, as I relate, but instead at Polish fortifications at Westerplatte, situated directly across the Vistula River from the Post Office, sparking a battle in which Polish fighters, out-manned and out-gunned, nevertheless held out for nearly two weeks against the German assault. The site of this battle is now a Polish monument.

Immediately after the bombardment of Westerplatte by the *Schleswig Holstein* began, German soldiers mounted an attack on the Post Office and it too became a battlefield. I situated the first salvo as being fired at the Post Office in order to dramatize the death of the fictional Pyotr Starbusch, whom we met in the first pages of the novel and again at the eventful Franz Schiller picnic later in the story. I used that first salvo as a device to introduce the reader to the violent outbreak of the war that was to engulf unsuspecting Polish citizens like Pyotr, who was living a normal life, loving his wife and children, and then was suddenly obliterated. We can only imagine what hardships his family endured before very likely being killed as well.

One final observation: the incendiary rhetoric attributed to Nazi spokesmen in the story, with its racist, insulting, often bloodcurdling references, is an accurate rendering of the language used at the time, with only light editing. In today's digital age, we are often drowned in a cacophony of words, but nothing approaches the constant barrage of offensive verbiage common to that period.

ACKNOWLEDGMENTS

I especially want to acknowledge the assistance of Piotr Mazurek, President of the Free City of Danzig Museum, located in the shadow of the Green Gate in the Historic Center of present day Gdansk. Address: ul. Długi Targ 25/27, 80-830 Gdańsk. Piotr and his son Mateusz hosted my wife and me on a tour of the principal surviving landmarks of the Free City. The museum has an extensive collection of memorabilia which an aspiring author found fascinating and interested readers will enjoy. Early in my research for the novel, Piotr sent me copies of tram line routes and schedules and maps of the Free City and its environs at the time the story took place. They were instrumental in enabling me to describe events and situate them authentically for the reader. Mateusz provided contemporary photos of the epoch which capture the image of a city be-decked in Nazi plumage. I thank them both for their help and encouragement and thank the museum for granting permission to reproduce the photographs.

I am also indebted to Colin Wells of the United Nations archive in Geneva for providing valuable information on the League of Nations during the period of time covered by the book and for providing access to archived documents from the period.

There is a wealth of information available on the web concerning Danzig at the time of the story, including wonderful photos. See, Danzig-online and Free City of Danzig–Gdansk Sightseeing in Gdansk–In Your Pocket city guide–essential travel guides to cities in Poland.

Finding and reading Sean Lester's diary was the inspiration for this book. It can be found online at:

http://biblio-archive.unog.ch/detail.aspx?ID=32586

The incident related in the book concerning the request of The Shoe Club of America for Lester to send them one of his shoes to add to their collection of shoes worn by distinguished citizens is drawn directly from Lester's diary. Even an imaginative author can't make up that stuff.

The passions unleashed in the drama that was the Free City of Danzig continue to resonate even to the present time, including a fiery website that rails against alleged Polish genocide and demands that the UN restore the Free City of Danzig as an independent state. www.danzigfreestat.org

***

I would like to extend my gratitude to the many friends who provided support for this undertaking, reading early versions, giving helpful advice, making corrections and otherwise offering assistance, especially John and Carolyn Twiname, John Heanue, Collier Kirkham, Dod Fraser, Parker Lewellyn, Jackie Plumez, Anne Green, Bob Shearer, Carol Loomis, Christine Jones, Larry Freundlich, Michael and Joann Rooney, Helen and Michael Goeller, Joanna Walker, Sara and Adam Viener, Al Dungan and Tom Fleming.

My editors, Rhonda Dossett and Marian Borden, not only edited with great skill, they also suggested new initiatives that enhanced the manuscript.

PHOTOGRAPHS

It is unusual for a novel to include photographs. A novel, after all, is a work of fiction and photographs depict real, not fictional things.

But the Danzig of the 1930s, as captured in the novel, did in fact exist as a real city. Photographs of Danzig from that epoch survive and I decided to include a selection of them here for readers to peruse. I hope they provide you a window through which to peer back in time and convey a feel for the space that was the city during the period covered by the novel.

In the first photo, a detachment of Brown Shirt storm troopers is marching in formation, a profusion of Nazi banners proudly borne along. It is a scene–endlessly repeated–that manifested the look of Nazi power, uplifting and reinforcing to Party members, but unsettling–even intimidating, as was doubtless intended–to opponents.

The second photo captures the scope and scale of Nazi Party ornamentation, with huge banners adorning the entire façade of the West Prussian Bank Building.

Next are three photos of Danzig residential neighborhoods which appear calm and respectable, almost bucolic, with decorative ironwork, Dutch stoop entryways and leafy foliage–but all festooned with Nazi banners and flags. These scenes illustrate how intrusive and omnipresent the Nazi ideology had become.

A photo of Langgase, with St. Mary's Church in the background, conveys a similar impression of what it looked like going out to shop, amidst Nazi bunting.

The photo of the archway displaying Nazi swastikas juxtaposed with the Danzig Free City symbols is redolent of the atmosphere.

471

We are fortunate to be able to view photos of the institutions that played such pivotal role in the novel–and in the real life of the Free City. We see the Danzig Senate building and the Volkstag building–both of them vast, imposing structures built in the Baltic style. Seeing these photos, we can understand why they conveyed the sense of gravitas that Paul Muller experienced upon first viewing them in the novel. Both structures were destroyed during World War II and were not rebuilt.

Finally, this section concludes with photographs of the High Commissioner's residence as it appeared when it was occupied by Sean Lester in the 1930's and as it appears today, fully restored to its original splendor, where it serves as the city hall of the municipality of Gdansk.

Photos reproduced by permission of the Free City of Danzig Museum, Gdansk, Poland.

474

476

The Danzig Senate Building

The Volkstag Building

The High Commissioner's Residence circa 1933

The High Commissioner's Residence 2015

ABOUT THE AUTHOR

photo by Albert W. Dungan

William N. Walker brings to his new novel a lifetime of experience as a diplomat, government official and international businessman.

Mr. Walker was Ambassador and Chief Trade Negotiator for the United States in the Tokyo Round of Multilateral Trade negotiations conducted under the auspices of the General Agreement on Tariffs and Trade in Geneva. He lived in Geneva for more than two years as the senior diplomat in residence and brings first-hand diplomatic knowledge to telling the story of *Danzig*. While the GATT was hardly the League of Nations, international organizations now, as then, are unwieldy and susceptible to the kinds of infighting and manipulation that we witness in the book.

As a member of the Nixon Administration, Mr. Walker was also a close observer of the political intrigue that destroyed Nixon's presidency. He was general counsel of two government agencies and was among the principal architects of the US government's response to the Arab Oil Embargo. Later, he served as Director of the Presidential Personnel Office for President Ford. After leaving government, he became a partner in a large Wall Street law firm, running a successful international law practice. Later, he established a company, which he continues to operate, devoted to international business that has included transactions in Europe, the former Soviet Union, Turkey, Central Asia and the Middle East. He describes himself as a recovering attorney.

Like Paul Muller, Mr. Walker is an experienced base choir singer and he has performed most of the great works in the classical choral music repertoire, including those mentioned in the book. Again like Muller, Mr. Walker is also an accomplished athlete. He signed a professional baseball contract with the Baltimore Orioles upon graduating from college. (Dispatched to the minor leagues, it quickly became evident that he would never hit the slider and he was released.) In law school, he co-founded the Virginia Rugby Club (he was inducted into the Virginia Rugby Union Hall of Fame in 2013) and then, after having moved to Chicago, started what is now the famed Chicago Lion Rugby Football Club. He doesn't play much tennis any longer, but he is a keen golfer and member of Winged Foot Golf Club (where he and his partner won the overall championship of the club-wide member's tournament in 2013, a feat memorialized on a plaque in the Grill Room of that august institution).

Mr. Walker is a winner of the Distinguished Alumnus Award from Wesleyan University. He is the father of three grown children and lives with his wife in New York City and neighboring Westchester County.

Made in the USA
San Bernardino, CA
01 May 2020